# AMONG FRIENDS

# AMONG FRIENDS

## Alexandra Raife

# CORONET BOOKS
### Hodder & Stoughton

First published in Great Britain in 2001
by Hodder & Stoughton
A division of Hodder Headline
A Coronet paperback

1 3 5 7 9 10 8 6 4 2

ISBN 0 340 79292 2

Typeset by
Phoenix Typesetting, Ilkley, West Yorkshire
Printed and bound in Great Britain by
Mackays of Chatham plc, Chatham, Kent

Hodder & Stoughton
A division of Hodder Headline
338 Euston Road
London NW1 3BH

# Chapter One

Though it was empty once more, the big light room was no longer the unquestioned refuge of the past two years. The empty tumblers and sherry glasses, the plates which had held the smoked salmon sandwiches and the little biscuits covered with duck pâté, the chairs drawn towards the fire, changed it with a completeness that went far beyond their physical presence.

Almost in terror, Louise stood by the door as silence flowed back, the brief spurt of social effort over, the voices to which the room was unaccustomed gone, the dutiful well-meaning voices, untouched by emotion. If this room failed her then she had nothing, it seemed to her in that moment of emptiness and exhaustion. For after the first shock of Beatrice's death, going in to wake her on that morning which now seemed a year ago, and finding that without sound or protest she had slipped away, the need to act and cope and arrange had carried Louise along, holding panicky fears at bay. There had been no time to realise she was alone. Almost it had seemed Aunt Bea was still there, that strong calm presence at the centre of the secluded world she had created for herself, its interests intellectual, its smooth rhythm making each day the same.

Which was why the altered look of the room so shook Louise. The world, shut out for so long, had found its way in, bringing vividly back the loss which had first driven her here, sharpening the pain of her present loss.

Mechanically, for she too liked order, she fetched a tray and began to tidy up, but the disturbing presences still lingered, the shape in this chair flattened by the broad rump of the minister, the plate used with disparaging spareness by Phyllis, the dram glass filled again and again by Nevil. Nevil, Beatrice's nephew, who had been Louise's father-in-law; Nevil, the only blood relative in the room, yet how long was it since he and Phyllis had last been in the house?

A friend from Lady Margaret Hall days, Beatrice's doctor, the elderly neighbour who used to come and play chess with her for long silent hours, a fellow professor who had also retired to Stirling and who would call occasionally to bore her with diatribes about what university education was coming to . . . A handful of people, yet Beatrice had been a woman of wit and warmth.

How sad to realise this scatter of mundane objects represented the tally of the living souls who had felt the wish or obligation to say goodbye to her. Even at that, Beatrice would probably not have chosen to have any of them at the crematorium or here, but Louise was made of gentler, more conventional stuff, and minded that a woman of such qualities should be so little valued.

Pushing the heavy chairs back into their places, returning the room to its normal pattern, Louise saw what she had done. On one side of the fire stood the winged chair she herself always used, and opposite was the space for the wheelchair.

An empty space of carpet. The empty space she must face in her life. Beatrice would have mocked the triteness of that with her little huff of sardonic amusement, accompanied by the awkward jerk of her head and the wince that always followed, as though, still, she had not accepted the rigidity of her arthritic joints.

Yet she had been so well. In spite of the limitations of her crippled body, and the pain she never talked about, they had established a way of life which could have rolled on through the years, mutually supportive and with its own rewards, certainly with love and pleasure in each other's company. And above all, safe, shielded from anger and disillusionment. And shielded from larger things, from financial worry, from the necessity to earn a living or have anything to do with anyone who didn't fit into this rarefied world.

But five days ago, as she was sleeping, Beatrice's heart had stopped.

Louise sank onto her knees in front of her chair, her hands over her face, her back to the space beside the small table still crowded with books, papers, magnifying glass, paperknife, pens, spectacles holder . . .

*

She had come, stunned by the death of her husband and twin nine-year-old daughters, on a stormy day in late February two years ago, to this eccentric wedge of a house, and had never left it since. At the corner of an elegant Victorian terrace, it had once formed part of the last house before the curve, but had been sliced off from it a generation ago. It consisted of four storeys with one west-facing room on each; in the windowless V at the back, bathrooms and a modern kitchen had been built. The tall windows of the first-floor room opened onto an iron-railed balcony, below which was a paved courtyard, sheltered and sunny. The basement, once a kitchen, provided storage. A lift had been added to carry the wheel-chair from the drawing-room to Beatrice's bedroom above, and above that again was a low-ceilinged attic with gable windows looking out over the Gargunnock Hills. Louise had settled into it with numb gratitude.

It was some time though before anything could penetrate her ice-cold inertia, and beyond immediate physical care, which Louise gave with loving readiness, Beatrice had asked no more of her for many months, offering only the refuge of her house, and the comfort of being ready to listen if and when Louise wanted to talk.

An ordinary Sunday. Charlotte and Gemma making a united attack at breakfast about having a television in their room.

'Absolutely every single person at school has their own television.'

4

'Every single person.'

United like this, as they almost invariably were, Louise found them hard to resist, but they were also good-natured and reasonable, and the protest had petered out in resigned mutterings. They were old enough to recognise that their father's new enterprise of driftwood carving, begun after he had quarrelled with Grandpa and they had moved to this collection of workshops and antiques salerooms in an old steading yard near Coulter Moss, was not going to provide many luxuries.

It was while they were upstairs, getting ready to go out for the day, together, as a family, (delayed because Charlotte had changed her sweater while Gemma was in the loo, which meant Gemma, anxious and flurried, had to change too), that Owen had casually told Louise he had agreed to go shares in setting up a new kiln for the potter in the next unit, and intended to pot too.

Already on edge, not so much from refusing the children a television, which she didn't see as a serious deprivation for them no matter what their peer group had or did, but from the dragging daily awareness that their circumstances were growing ever more straitened and their future ever more uncertain, Louise had responded with uncharacteristic anger.

There had been no time to discuss it, no time to deal with her distress, as the children came rattling down the stairs pouring out familiar appeals.

'Why does Gemma always have to wear what I wear?'

'We were going to wear our sweaters with the little fringes and Charlotte went and changed.'

'Those fringes are stupid. I'm going to cut mine off.'

'Charlotte, you can't! Mum, tell her she can't!'

Gemma's orderly soul, so like her mother's, had been horrified.

'For goodness' sake, be quiet, both of you. Nobody's going to cut anything up. Go and get into the car – and take your boots with you, you know perfectly well you'll need them at Lennoxtown.'

They had gone, subdued by the sharp tone she so rarely used, and guilt about that, added to the shock of what Owen had just told her, had suddenly filled her with despair. The prospect of getting through a whole day with other people before they could discuss it had been unbearable, and she had said to Owen, 'Look, I don't think I can cope with the Tomlinsons. I feel so shaken by what you've just told me. I don't know where you think the money's going to come from—'

She had been unable to continue, faced yet again by the gulf between his feckless optimism and her concerns about what to put on the table, how to buy the children clothes, how to pay the rent.

'Come on, this isn't like you,' Owen had said with the facile breeziness with which he met every attempt to make him face realities. 'We can talk it over later if you want to, though I can't see there's much to discuss. But there's no point in spoiling the day for everyone. It's ages since we've been over to Lennoxtown, and the girls always enjoy a day there. Have you got everything?'

She had refused to go. For the first time in her married life she had opposed him. Even when the twins had run in again to plead with her she had refused to budge, longing only for them to drive off so that she could be alone to cry.

And so Owen had been angry, and when Charlotte and Gemma had wanted to go by their favourite route over the Campsie Fells he had been brusque with them.

'For God's sake, that'll take hours. We're late already.' And with only a token lift of his hand to Louise he had lurched off fast down the hard-frozen ruts of the track and headed onto the motorway.

And so she, with her even temper, her capacity for taking the heat out of quarrels, her willingness to support Owen in everything, even the break away from the future mapped out for him by his parents, had seen them off in weary anger, and less than an hour later the police car had come nosing up the lane.

The family had scarcely known what to do with her. Owen's family, that is, not her own. Her parents had been quite clear about what she should do. They had refrained from saying they had known all along that her marriage would end in disaster, even they were not that brutally insensitive, but they had taken it for granted that she would go back with them to Launceston, and had been baffled and offended when she refused. But even in her confusion of shock and grief, Louise had recognised that they saw the tragedy as an opportunity to draw her back into their orbit, and it had made her all the more ready to accept Owen's father's proposal.

Nevil Donaldson, though more shaken by the death of

his son and grand-daughters than he let anyone see, was still able to weigh the benefits of the solution he suggested. He and Phyllis would be seen to be looking after their son's widow, and Louise could look after his Aunt Beatrice, whose increasing immobility had recently led to a succession of problems over her care which he had been obliged to deal with.

Phyllis Donaldson had been as bitterly negative about the plan as she had been about the marriage in the first place. She regarded Louise as a girl without drive or ambition, as indeed she was, and therefore of no use to Owen, though without going so far as to admit that he would get nowhere without someone to push and bully him. In her eyes he had to be perfect, and so she had laid at Louise's door his decision to abandon his comfortable prospects in the family firm of solicitors, and become 'arty'.

In the distortions of a stupid and biased mind, exaggerated by grief, she had tried to comfort herself after her son's death by establishing several immovable tenets of faith: Louise had persuaded Owen to leave the flat adjoining his parents' house where they had lived when they were first married; Louise had squandered their money; Louise had refused to allow the twins to go to boarding school; and Louise had been selfish and irresponsible to let Owen go off on his own with the girls on that dreadful day. No proper, caring mother would have done such a thing. She should have been there, with her family, when . . . But there even Phyllis drew back.

So, almost without knowing how it happened, Louise

had found herself established in the tall narrow house, and gradually its quietness, its sense of reclusive security, had worked a kind of healing. Gradually the balance had swung from Beatrice comforting her, to Louise tending and caring for Beatrice. A pattern had emerged which suited them both. Beatrice continued to write erudite papers, mostly for her own pleasure, and to correspond with friends in the academic world on her chief interest, the eighteenth century, a period of order and clarity which Louise felt suited their composed and uneventful existence.

Louise typed up sheafs of notes, not without difficulty, in her great-aunt-by-marriage's scholarly hand, and familiarised herself with an obscure cross-reference system. She went almost daily to the library, and to shop for fresh ingredients to tempt the appetite of the older woman, who after losing so many battles with incompetent or indifferent carers had allowed herself to fall into slipshod habits over food.

Louise began to take an interest in the house, restoring the wood of its solid Victorian furniture to glowing richness, repairing needlework chairs, rescuing enormous curtains from the ravages of sun and time. It was more rewarding to do this for Aunt Beatrice than it had been doing the same sort of thing to fill the cold hours looking after one of the antique shops at Coulter Moss, in order to add a few pounds a week to the kitty. She planted the tubs in the little courtyard, cut back the ramping clematis and repainted the decorative ironwork of the balcony, finding a satisfaction in all this which she had not felt since they had left the bright little flat adjoining Owen's parents' house.

She and Beatrice read, played Scrabble, watched any and all 'information' programmes on television. Late into the night Beatrice listened to talking books or to music, while Louise got through the hours as best as she could, remembering, unable not to remember, yet in time remembering differently, bearably.

Owen's parents, usually separately, called for a while, then allowed the gaps between visits to lengthen. Phyllis always came prepared to be indignant about something and Beatrice readily provided her with grounds, having a poor opinion of her mentality and character and disapproving of anyone calling anywhere uninvited. Nevil came primarily to seek comfort from Louise's presence, but as time passed needed that less, withdrawing once more to a distant dutiful care for their welfare.

And so it could all have gone on; an undemanding way of life in a pleasant house, the world at arm's length, wounds hidden by scar tissue, hurting less. Till Beatrice died. Till her body slid silently away to be reduced to ashes, mixed, whatever they pretended, with the ashes of other unknown bodies burned that day. How little Beatrice would have cared about that, or what happened to them.

And people who never came here had come as of right, had eaten and drunk and selected those things to say which they deemed acceptable. Acceptable to whom? To Beatrice, who according to her own beliefs would not be listening? Or acceptable to each other? They had spoken in carefully adjusted voices. Had one after another disappeared to the loo because it was a stark and freezing day. Just like the day when . . .

And they had left behind the visible signs of their intrusion, breaking apart the safety of this place.

# Chapter Two

The agency was unexpected. Louise, looking for an office, searched twice along the road in the suburb of St Ninians before turning into the drive of a square stone house with bay windows and a well-used garden. Indeed, the sight of a swing suspended from a beech tree, and a ball kicked into the rough wintry grass under a holly hedge, almost made her turn back, so ingrained had the habit of shielding herself from reminders become. But she could no longer afford the indulgence.

She parked Aunt Bea's cumbersome Vauxhall beside an expensive-looking Volvo with mud splashes high on its sides, and her doubts grew. No plate by the door, no name above the bell to tell her she was in the right place. But she knew her doubts were compounded by a churning irrational fear. She wanted this to be the wrong place; she wanted to be let off. She wanted to rush back to the known safe haven where everything was within her capacity to handle. There had been enough time, however, since Beatrice had died, to see how dangerous the temptation was to stay for ever in that tiny corner, meeting no one, facing nothing. Without the need to care for Beatrice, the twenty-four-hour-a-day need, for latterly she had had to be helped with everything, there was no meaning to life, and no excuse for evasion.

How swift the swing had been from satisfying busyness to purposeless vacuum. The activities which had seemed necessary and worthwhile, cleaning and polishing, keeping the vases filled with fresh flowers, tending the plants, planning and cooking meals designed to sharpen a failing appetite, had become pointless, the hours they failed to occupy frighteningly long.

She pressed the bell with a quick nervous touch, as though still playing games with herself. If they don't hear I can go away. Searching for anything that would make decisions for her, she thought with shame, putting her finger on the button again with a more convincing firmness.

Dimly in the hall behind a second door she saw someone coming, and drew in a wavery breath. She was being carried along this route whether she liked it or not.

'Louise Donaldson? Hi, come in, I'm Cass Scott.' A very tall girl, perhaps further into her thirties than Louise, with short densely curly hair and a friendly smile that crinkled her eyes to blue slits. Her voice was not the Scottish voice which had arranged the interview. 'Come in. It's a horrible day, isn't it? It feels as though spring will never come. Warm in here though – do you want to dump your coat somewhere?'

Not an office, but a comfortable sitting-room, its usual clutter contained to leave a space where business could be done. Toys were parked under the table which held the television. A baby-walker was pushed askew into a corner, a mug with a spout, wooden building blocks and a grubby white rabbit on its tray. Louise took in no other details of the room, and was unaware of the quick searching look Cass gave her.

'Don't worry, they won't invade us, one's asleep upstairs and the other's in the park.' Cass spoke without any special emphasis. 'Would you like coffee? I've just had lunch with a friend but we talked so much that we ran out of time for coffee. Sit by the fire and get warm. I shan't be a moment.'

Cass was annoyed with herself as she went to the kitchen. She ran the main office of the employment agency in Perth, but either she or her assistant came to Stirling once a week, using as a sub-office the house belonging to another of her staff, one of the monitors established throughout Scotland as contacts and trouble-shooters for employers and employees. She was so used to coming here, often preferring the informal atmosphere Susie's sitting-room provided, that she had forgotten the obvious drawback in this particular case; signs of the children were everywhere. And Louise's completed application form had contained the proviso, 'Nowhere where there are children.'

The way her face had tightened at the sight of the toys had not only made Cass feel exasperated at her own care-lessness, but had increased her interest in that application.

Cass had several years' experience of recruitment, originally establishing a London-based company but expanding it to include Scotland two years ago, at the same time moving north to live. She was well aware that women of Louise's age, free and willing to go into other people's houses to cook and care for children, the ill or the old, frequently had some story behind them, a failed marriage perhaps, financial difficulties, no home. Her task, over and above the normal selection process, was to make sure that these problems were not the result of some flaw which would be carried into whatever job was undertaken, causing disruption in the very households which most needed help.

She came back with the coffee to find Louise huddled over the fire. Though she smiled at Cass over her shoulder and, Cass noted, already assessing, at once drew a low table within reach and made room on it for the tray, Cass had the impression that while she had been out of the room Louise had been refusing awareness of anything.

Chatting easily, her long legs in endless jeans (with, Louise in her turn noted, the tiniest hems possible coming unstitched at the heels) stretched out on the hearth, Cass explained about using Susie's house for the interview, told Louise about her own cottage up at Bridge of Riach, and talked a little about the background of the company.

'Originally we placed cooks, nannies, etc. for what were laughingly called "permanent" posts. Then we branched out into temp jobs, mainly filling gaps for hotels with short-term, next-day staff, no interviews, sight unseen. It's a system that suits travelling Australians and so on.

Recently, however, we've started to supply stopgaps on a different level, quality cooks — no, hang on a minute, this is just broad-brush,' as Louise opened her mouth in alarm, 'and carers for house-bound old people whose regular carers are on holiday, or for families while Mum's in hospital or whatever.'

Damn, I should have left that one for the time being, she thought, seeing Louise's look of distress deepen. Still, this was an interview; it was vital to learn as much as she could about any applicant since the jobs carried so much responsibility. 'I'm hoping to establish a small core of capable people who can respond to that type of need, preferably with a home base of their own, but who are reasonably free of commitments.'

This time she didn't add, 'especially in the school holidays,' but even so Louise rushed in. 'No, I'm sorry, I don't think it's going to be any use. I shouldn't have taken up your time. I'm sure I couldn't offer what you need—'

'Oh, I don't know.' Cass, who was more business-like than she looked, had drawn Louise's application form from her bag and, flipping back the top page, was already at the section she wanted. 'You seem to have some quite heavy guns. A home economics qualification —'

'It was the only thing I could—'

'— cooking for a nursery school, running your own household,' Cass read smoothly on, 'sole carer for elderly wheelchair-bound relative for two years. It's very much the sort of background we look for.'

She did not add that in other, less definable ways,

which did not appear on application forms and needed no questions to discover, Louise was more than acceptable. From the moment of seeing this small, neat girl, with her thick golden hair, nearly as short as Cass's own, in her dark-green car coat with silk scarf tucked into the upturned collar, hearing her quiet voice and meeting her shy smile, the 'yes' of gut reaction had been there.

And yet . . . 'no children'. The look of sadness in Louise's eyes when she wasn't smiling, her doubts about her own ability, and more than anything else an air of withholding herself, protecting herself almost, told Cass that there were dangers here too.

Women alone, women emerging from some tragedy, women whose lives had fallen apart, tended to seek, whether consciously or not, what they had lost – a family, a home, a man. In almost every case, they needed to be needed, but that need of theirs could seriously undermine their capacity to give a hundred per cent to any job they took on.

'I'm not really qualified at all,' Louise was insisting. 'The home economics certificate means very little. I did a year at a college when I was eighteen, the most obvious stuff imaginable, shiny folders full of pages with one pie chart and one sentence about nutrition. You could learn more from a wrapper in the supermarket. I'd hate you to think I knew all sorts of technical stuff.'

'What about the nursery school?'

'That was very basic too, I'm afraid, and on a small scale. Only a few of the children stayed for lunch. I was just helping the friend who ran it. I'd come up to Scotland to stay with her for a week or two, and she asked me to stay on.' How dazzling the realisation had been that she could do just that, defy her parents, earn her own living. 'Apart from that I've only ever cooked for – done home cooking. Looking after Aunt Beatrice, a great-aunt by marriage really, was something I slipped into because I was there, living in her house. I know nothing about real nursing.'

So she found it hard to speak of the husband she had lost. Already Cass knew she wanted to help this girl if she could. 'People who need actual nursing employ a nurse,' she said easily. 'You are qualified for caring in the best sense – you've done the job for two years.'

'But only – I mean, in other ways I'm terribly out of touch, I haven't been doing anything very demanding.' Louise found it impossible to put into words her fears that life, the real world, had moved on without her, her doubts of being able to establish a place in it again, alone. Lately she had sometimes felt as if she scarcely knew who she was any more.

'So you don't want a job?' Cass spoke teasingly, hoping to make Louise relax a little. To her dismay the small face opposite, its golden skin tones complemented by the richly coloured scarf, tightened in what looked like despair, eyes wide with misery.

'Oh, how awful of me!' In her consternation Cass pulled in her legs and tipped forward onto her knees, putting a hand on Louise's arm. She could feel its rigidity, rejecting contact, and withdrew her hand quickly. But she didn't move away.

'Look, I'm sorry. That wasn't a serious question. I wasn't winding up the interview.'

Louise nodded jerkily, engrossed in holding back tears, and Cass waited, still on her knees, looking into her face with sympathy and concern.

Louise was appalled by this violent need to weep, by the pain in her throat, the hot pressure behind her lids, the sensation that if she released control she would be lost in a storm of crying, wild and unreasonable, related to nothing.

'You can talk to me, you know,' Cass's voice came quietly. 'Even if you decide against the job, even if we never see each other again, you can still talk. I'm in no hurry and no one will come in. The house is ours.'

An image of the sleeping baby upstairs came to Louise, and fumblingly, hardly conscious of what she was doing, she reached out and felt Cass's long capable hand take hers.

'I'm sorry,' she managed to say again after a moment, 'but I really think I've wasted your time. I'm not sure I'm ready to take a job yet. I thought I was. I must actually, or – well, that's another problem. Heavens, though,' with a grasp at ordinariness, and a smile whose tremulousness made Cass feel close to tears herself, 'you're hardly likely to want to send a lunatic like me into some household in crisis.'

The very fact that Louise could see the problem confirmed Cass in the opinion she had formed. She could use this person; but was it too soon? What lay behind this tension and anxiety?

'I think we should talk,' she said, giving the words an unhurried judiciousness which, as she had intended, Louise found comforting.

'I'm not sure I'd know where to begin,' she said, but she settled back a little into her chair, and her smile was less strained.

'Tell me a bit about where you're living, and your day-to-day life. I've only got the bare bones here.'

It wasn't difficult to talk about Beatrice, or the empti-ness of the house. 'I find it hard to remember how we filled the time,' Louise confessed. 'We were always busy, but now, though I think I'm doing more or less what I did before, there seem twice as many hours in the day.'

Gently, casually almost, her questions pitched more at helping Louise to go on than eliciting information for her own purposes, Cass drew her out.

'Are you OK for cash?' she enquired after a while, not clear what Louise had been living on.

'Um. Not quite as well as I thought,' Louise admitted.

Aunt Bea had always said, 'Whatever I have will be yours. After all, I've no one else to leave it to,' and Louise, at first too numb to care, had soon grown used to a lifestyle where bills were paid without pain and an effort-less level of comfort maintained. She had assumed, though they had never discussed it, that Beatrice owned the house and also had capital which yielded a satisfactory level of interest. Certainly cash was never short in the Donaldson family – until Owen broke out of the mould and his father refused to help him – since as well as the legal firm they owned extensive property in the town. But three weeks or so after Beatrice died Nevil had called, having made a formal appointment to do so.

Beatrice, it appeared, had had a small amount of capital, which produced a small amount of interest and was now to be Louise's. She had lived as comfortably as she had because her nephew had made her a generous allowance. The house belonged to the family; to Nevil, in short. Louise was to have the car.

'I thought – I had understood – Beatrice always spoke of it as though the house was hers,' she had stammered in shock.

'Certainly, for her lifetime,' Nevil had agreed smoothly. 'That was always understood. Absolute security of tenure.' He had studied Louise with a calculating sharpness which did not accord with his unctuous tone, but which she, stunned, had not seen. 'Naturally we are happy for you to continue to live here . . . our son's widow and so forth . . . family property . . . grateful to you for looking after Beatrice when no one else was available . . .'

Or willing, Louise had amended afterwards, with a dreary bitterness, when the fresh shock had been assimilated and her brain was working again. Not even willing to visit Beatrice more than a few times a year, let alone look after her, help her to dress, take her to the loo, lift her from bed to chair, get up half a dozen times a night to try to ease her pain. Louise hoped, how passionately she hoped, that she had not revealed to Nevil her assumption that the house would be hers.

Some, not all of this, Cass gleaned, and sad tale though it was, much of it suited her requirements. Somewhere to live, freedom to take jobs wherever they cropped up, no ties, and limited means making some form of employment essential.

But the emotional baggage. There she had a definite responsibility, and unfeeling as it seemed to question Louise, Cass knew that for the sake of her clients she should find out more.

'Look,' she said, 'in spite of all you say about not being qualified, you seem ideal for our needs. You could do any of the jobs we offer standing on your head. But I do just have to ask, if you don't mind, concerning this stipulation about children. There may be some—'

'No,' Louise interrupted violently. Then, taking a swift grip on herself, 'Sorry, I'm usually rather a calm person. But no, children would be a problem. I can't talk about it but if it means you can't take me on, then that's all there is to be said.'

'It doesn't mean that at all. There are plenty of other jobs. But my worry is that no matter where I send you there may always be extended family, unforeseen visits and that sort of thing. I think if I could just understand a little more—'

Scrunching of gravel outside, the front door opening, then the inner door, feet running across the hall, a voice calling, 'No, you mustn't disturb Cass, she's busy. Don't go in.'

A child's voice protested, 'This is my best cone to show Cass.' The door knob turned, there was a brief scuffle, followed by a receding wail of, 'It was the best cone I ever had and now you've dropped it.'

Louise came to her feet, her face white.

Somewhere upstairs, with a reedy, just-awake girning, the baby began to cry.

# Chapter Three

The coffee bar was warm, subtly lit, with solid tables and bench seats covered in green leather-look. Its lights reflected back from copper fittings and shining surfaces; fat fruity scones and cream-filled cakes tempted from behind gleaming glass; the air was rich with the scents of fresh coffee and fresh baking.

Gradually Louise stopped huddling over her mug of black coffee, its in-curved earthenware sides inviting just such a tense clutch as hers. Cass saw her shoulders relax, could almost read the signals her brain was sending to her muscles: 'Don't be a fool, it was nothing. Nothing happened. It's over.'

Louise had been surprised to find Cass leaving when she did. She had supposed there would be other 'office' business to attend to, matters to discuss with Susie, and that her own interview, because it had turned out to be a non-starter, would vanish from their minds at once. She had hardly been aware of Cass pushing the folder into her

bag and swinging the bag over her shoulder, calling Susie
into the hall to say goodbye rather than going to find her,
following her to the door. She had supposed, as far as she
had been capable of giving it any thought, that she was
being seen off. She had barely said goodbye to Susie, her
whole being concentrated on getting away, back to her
own normality, the safe burrow which looked out only
one way.

But Cass had come out with her, onto the wet gravel,
into the dank afternoon, and had said gently, 'Louise, I
don't think you should go back alone. Shall I come home
with you? Would that help?'

'No, no.' Louise had shaken her bent head violently,
fumbling to find her keys, then had been appalled to hear
how her answer sounded, quite outside all normal courtesy
and friendliness. But she could not cope, in that moment,
with the thought of the challenges which had just been
presented to her and which she had failed to meet, being
renewed or even referred to in the only refuge she had.

'I'm sorry to be so rude. It's just——' But how could that
reluctance be explained to someone she had never seen
before today?

Cass had seemed nevertheless to understand. 'There are
plenty of nice places in the town centre where we could
talk,' she had said. 'Warm ones too,' with a shiver. 'Come
on, I'll follow you.'

She had made it so simple, removing the need to look
any further, and obediently Louise had set off for the big
carpark she used when her shopping was too heavy or
bulky to carry home.

'It's good of you to give me your time like this,' she said now, normal perspectives beginning to filter back. 'Especially,' managing a tight smile, 'as I seem bent on convincing you that I'm unemployable.'

'How long is it since your aunt died?'

Cass's directness was strangely steadying. She obviously believed they could now go to the nub of what needed to be said, but she also made Louise feel that her interest was more than professional. There was ease between them, immediate understanding; they talked the same language.

'A month.'

'Was it expected?'

'Not in the least. Well, I suppose yes, in the sense that she was eighty-one, but apart from the arthritis she was so well, her brain tremendously alert, her interest in her own field still keen. Or perhaps I was blinkered, seeing nothing.'

Cass waited a moment, watching the transparent thoughts; a realisation of a more serious blinkering. 'What happened?' she asked, wanting to keep the thoughts coming if she could.

'Heart. She just slipped away in her sleep. The bed wasn't even disturbed. It was the most marvellous way to go, of course, and the end of pain for her.'

'Did you have to deal with everything on your own?'

'Oh no, her nephew looked after most of it. My husband's father. My late husband's father.' The phrase sounded dated and awkward; she had always avoided it till now. But having used the words she found unexpectedly that she wanted to go on. 'My husband died two years ago. Was killed.'

Cass waited.

'Just over two years ago. In the car.'

Cass, aching for her, wanted to assure her it wasn't necessary to say more, but guessed it would probably help her more than anything to do so.

Around them humdrum comings and goings, voices and steps, clatter of crockery and trays, hissing of cappuccino machine, street noises muted beyond plate glass decorated with golden curls of elaborate lettering, formed a protective screen of indifferent normality.

'Do you mind my telling you this?' But Louise knew that she wanted to go on now, afraid that if she went home and found herself alone with her thoughts once more, having fallen at the first hurdle, she would be incapable of trying again. It was about more than getting a job. And however tenuous the link with this apparently casual but kind and perceptive stranger was, Louise had the feeling that she would never find a better person to confide in.

'Tell me anything you want to,' Cass said, making an effort to keep compassion out of her voice. She didn't think it would help at this moment.

Louise looked away across the busy tables, at people shrugging into coats, gathering up shopping bags, and saw nothing.

'I had two daughters,' she said. 'Twins of nine. They were in the car too.'

And I do not think, she registered with an almost

objective interest, that I have spoken the word 'daughter' since that day.

Louise drove along the well-known road to Bridge of Allan in a state of suspended awareness. The village was almost part of Stirling, and there was a sense of anticlimax mixed with her nervousness. She had geared herself up to face all kinds of challenges, and here she was driving, as it were, to the other end of town to look after one temporarily disabled old lady.

Methodically packing, refusing more apprehension or speculation, Louise had kept coming up against the sheer ordinariness of her preparations. She had only to turn the heating down, make sure the windows were closed. There were no animals to worry about. She didn't have to work out a route, check the car. She had only to pack what she would ordinarily wear. The solitary decision she had had to make was whether to tell Nevil and Phyllis where she was going. But that would have led to telling them what she planned to do in the long-term.

In the long-term. Anxiety had seized her again and she had turned her mind away from the alarming phrase, reminding herself that whatever she did it was of no interest to her parents-in-law. It was hard to imagine she ever entered their minds or conversation. What link was there now that Beatrice was dead? The widowed daughter-in-law, with no longer any role to fulfil in relation to son or grandchildren, superfluous. From their first meeting Owen's mother had resented Louise, moving swiftly from a jocular jealousy to open criticism. There had been no defence against it, for it had been concocted out of Phyllis's own spoiled pettiness. Until Louise had appeared on the scene Phyllis had had her well-trained husband, her adored only son, to herself, and had had her way in everything.

There might have been little contact with Nevil and Phyllis when Beatrice was alive, but there had nevertheless been an awareness of the family tie, Nevil the authority in the background, the ultimate bearer of responsibility. In the weeks since Beatrice's funeral Louise had continued to take this for granted. Little as she liked the Donaldsons, it was chilling to realise that, in their eyes, she was now a separate entity, nothing more than a reminder of grief they wanted to forget.

It had been bleak to finish her packing, make sure in her methodical way that bins were empty, no fruit left to rot in the bowl, no food in the fridge which would not survive her absence for nine days, then without a word to anyone, for there was no one to tell, go down and get into the car.

It was a small comfort, as she made the brief journey, to let her thoughts turn to Cass. Does there have to be somebody, she mocked herself, can't you just be you, on your own? But Cass's appearance in her life was too important at present for the mockery to sting.

After their conversation in the coffee bar, where they had talked for a long time – until, as Louise had been gratefully aware, Cass was sure she was ready to face being alone – there had been a second 'interview'. Cass had wanted to give Louise plenty of time to think things over, and be absolutely sure that she was ready to move out of her secure niche, and that, more importantly, she was ready to give others the care and attention which would be exacted.

On this occasion Cass had played devil's advocate, not mincing her words about the downside of the job, stressing the long hours, the lack of freedom and the demanding nature of many of the clients, elderly, ill and often lonely. There were the problems to consider of familiarising herself with new kitchens, new equipment like stair-lifts and bath-lifts; there was the impermanence of being part of a succession of households for brief periods, the isolation of being always the stranger.

Louise had understood what Cass was doing and had been grateful for it. She had gone over these aspects endlessly for herself, but to hear someone else spell them out brought them into sharper focus. Yet what, in truth, apart from the mechanics of different houses, was so different from her present existence, cut off from contact of any kind?

'I want to try,' she had said, and Cass, her serious business-like expression overtaken by her warm smile, had looked ready to hug her.

'Good for you!' she had exclaimed. 'I honestly think you need something like this, if you feel ready to tackle it. At worst, if you find it's too much to cope with at present, you can put the plan on hold, and we'll work out something for you later.'

This promise had meant more than she could have imagined to Louise, assuring her that contact with the outside world was accessible to her, and that whatever happened the daunting blankness of her lonely existence had been pierced.

One more thing Cass had felt obliged to warn her about. 'I can do my utmost to find you jobs where there are no children, but I can't ever promise that you won't encounter them at some point. Families are families. That's the one factor which makes me wonder if you should wait a little longer.'

'It's been a long time already,' was all Louise had been able to say. She was barely coming to terms with how long herself, for it seemed now that for the two years spent with Beatrice time had stood still as far as her acceptance of the twins' death was concerned. She felt as though she had been buried in ice, every function suspended, only now coming agonisingly back to life.

'It will be all right,' she had continued after a moment, realising Cass needed some reassurance. 'There are children everywhere, I see them when I go out, I hear them, see them on the television.' Though there were many programmes it tortured her even to catch a glimpse of by accident.

'But they are separate from you, you can shut them out,' Cass had said astutely. 'If they were in the same house, with names and personalities, it wouldn't be so easy. Could you cope with that?'

Louise had drawn a long uneven breath. 'I actually don't know.'

'But you still want me to find you a placement?'

'Yes.'

'Well done,' Cass had said quietly, and the words had brought a momentary threat of tears.

The job she had found was so tailor-made Louise had accused her of creating it specially.

'You won't think so when you meet Mrs Baines,' Cass had retorted. 'She has a very disagreeable temper indeed. The last temporary carer walked out after a couple of days.'

On her way to face the cantankerous Mrs Baines Louise added up with determined optimism the advantages of the post, large and small: the reassuring feel of a familiar landscape, even shops she knew, the knowledge that her bolthole was close by if she needed it. And what could be so difficult about looking after one elderly lady for such a short time? There was an unmarried son who had been living at home since his mother had been semi-immobilised by damaging her knee in a fall, but he was due to go off on a course of some kind. Still, if things went badly wrong Cass was at hand.

Louise knew she was being unadventurous, but she clutched at these comforting facts without shame as she cruised along a quiet road, found the right number and turned into a steep-tilted drive.

# Chapter Four

Heat. Dry, blanketing, inescapable heat, which made her skin feel tight-drawn and her eyes prickle, which exhausted her yet made it difficult to sleep at night. That was to be Louise's enduring memory of Drummond View. The heat reached out for her as she stood on the stone doorstep of the small traditional Scottish villa, flanked by stone urns each holding a miniature conifer, and the door opened onto a narrow hall carpeted in wild red and orange swirls.

Mrs Baines' son, Dale, a colourless wisp of a man in his forties, welcomed her with nervous fussiness, his uncertainty increasing visibly as he ushered her into the 'lounge' to meet his mother. Mrs Baines, recovering after her fall, could get about with the aid of a zimmer frame, but was not ready to admit it yet. Apart from the strapped-up knee, she suffered — or, Louise was to decide, did not suffer — from aches in her legs which defied diagnosis, migraines, indigestion, osteoporosis, heart flutters and breathlessness. Her temperature could soar on the slightest provocation past some safe cut-off point, bringing her out in a furious scarlet rash and a furious temper to match. After two or three of these unpleasant episodes it emerged that she was supposed to take anti-histamine pills but often 'forgot'. Louise thought it might help to turn down the heating.

Her welcome from Mrs Baines was very much of the 'Humph' and compressed-lips variety, delivered in a single glance away from the television screen. Dale suggested hurriedly that Louise might like to see her room. Louise thought, on the evidence so far, that she probably wouldn't.

Every original detail of the century-old house had, where possible, been stripped away or modernised – fire-places, floors, stairs, electrical fittings and of course plumbing. The door to the lounge was of dimpled glass, window frames were of PVC and offered only a mean slit to leave open at the top.

Dale hovered on the landing with a no-woman-is-at-risk-in-this-house virtuousness while Louise carried in her bag. Rosebuds and white candlewick; some 'dainty' smell whose source would have to be tracked down as soon as possible; and the feeling that the concentrated heat of the house had poured up the stairs and collected here. But the room was sparklingly clean and it would do.

Dale showed her round the kitchen, interpolating between every other sentence an apologetic, 'But I'm sure you know more about this than I do,' while his mother added strident information one step behind where they'd got to.

'You be sure to turn that off at night,' she bawled, as Dale was showing Louise the plant food she had to use for the grape ivy, five drops at a time. And, 'It needs a good slam,' when they had passed on from the vagaries of the fridge door and Louise was being instructed about the budgie's diet. She hated birds in cages; the idea of any winged creature confined to inches of space for the whole of its life could bring tears to her eyes. This particular budgie also made one hell of a racket.

Dale vanished as soon as he could, on tenterhooks about his journey to Glasgow. Louise speculated about what emergency kit he would carry in his elderly Ford. After the torrent of information she had been struggling to absorb there was suddenly a nasty blank when it dawned on her that that was all the briefing she would get, and that she was alone in this unappealing little house to care intimately for a highly unfriendly woman.

She was to come to the conclusion that most of Mrs Baines' complaints arose from boredom, which arose from the complete vacuity of her brain. She had never used it. Anything difficult, threatening or tedious her husband had looked after and now Dale did, though not, it seemed, to her satisfaction. She resented his having moved into his own house, and made no secret of her satisfaction that her accident had forced him to come home. She had wanted him to take long leave from his job at the bank and had been angry at the compromise of day-time care when he was at work. Louise wondered where he had found the strength to resist, but two days of Mrs Baines gave her a rough idea.

It was a strange time, a time of huge adjustments, with a sensation of taking huge steps, yet in other ways Louise felt she was merely marking time in an alien place, inhabited by a disagreeable woman whose querulous voice from morning till night objected, carped, criticised and demanded.

On the face of it, she was doing what she had been doing for the past two years — living an indoor life, on hand more or less continuously to look after a single female old enough to be her grandmother. But what a gulf between the arid wastes of time here — the endless television not even interrupted by meals or all the other indulgences of coffee and tea, biscuits, sweeties and snacks — and the even-paced calm of life with Beatrice, filled with pursuits which satisfied the mind, shared humour, shared interests, mutual consideration and respect.

Listening to the babble of a morning chat show as she prepared the unbelievably early lunch Mrs Baines liked (never had afternoons seemed so endless, with the washing up done by twelve-thirty), Louise would think with loving amusement of Beatrice. Beatrice and her mountains of papers, her pile of reference books sprouting markers, one pair of specs on the end of her nose, a second, forgotten, pushed into her rough white hair. Beatrice deep in the agricultural problems of post-Union Scotland, or running a pencil, mouth pursed in muted approval, down some paper she had produced years ago

*— Fletcher of Saltoun: an evaluation of the problems of the sorners and compulsory servitude*; or *The Scottish Society for Propagating Christian Knowledge — the Legacy of the Highland Missions*. Louise, potato and peeler suspended above the earthy water, would find herself longing with a wrenching nostalgia to be back in the high-ceilinged elegant room, the great windows open to the balcony, typing a rework of Aunt Bea's commentary on the 1748 act abolishing Heritable Jurisdictions.

If sometimes a tear slid out at the contrast with her present surroundings, Louise thought on the whole that was a good thing, a direct benefit of these days at Drummond View. If she had stayed shut in and safe, would she have wept? Would she have moved forward at all?

Cass phoned on the second evening, and hearing her voice brought a delightful feeling of contact with home, with sane normality.

'I thought we weren't allowed phone calls.'

'I'm your boss, idiot. How's it going, or can't you say at the moment?'

'Hang on. She wants to know who's phoning.'

Mrs Baines, red-faced, was demanding to be helped up. This was her house, her telephone, and the call could only be for her and from Dale, anxious to know how she was. If he tried to go on about his dratted course, though, she'd soon choke him off. A load of nonsense, that was. The Management of Executive Stress. What did they think they were on about?

Louise thought the lecturers should first deal with

Dale's level of domestic stress, after which the rest of the course probably wouldn't be necessary.

Mrs Baines shouted and rattled her zimmer frame, the television blared, the budgie responded with a combative outpouring, and Louise was half-deafened by the time she had got Mrs Baines back into her chair and returned to the phone, which squatted on a shiny table all its own with a book that said Telephone and had six numbers in it.

'God, rather you than me,' Cass commented.

'That's rich.'

'Is it bearable, though, really?'

'Oh, sure, once you know that everything you do is going to be wrong it's perfectly simple.'

Louise had cooked fish for lunch. Mrs Baines had spat out her first mouthful, saying angrily, 'This is off, this is.'

'I put some fennel in.' Louise had resisted adding placatingly, 'Just a touch.'

'Ruin of a nice bit of plaice,' and the plate had been pushed sourly away.

Moral: don't imagine you will please by trying to improve on what people normally have.

Cass was saying, 'I wish everyone was as pragmatic. But are *you* all right?'

'Roots aching a little perhaps.'

'Oh, you poor dear. I'm sorry it's horrid for you.'

Don't be kind. Please, please don't be kind.

Perhaps Cass understood that, for she went on, 'Anyway, it's a great relief to me that you can stick it out. I don't know where I'd have found a replacement, and with poor old Dale on the loose for once Mrs B really couldn't be abandoned.'

'Oh, I can stick it. It's not for very long.'

'Well, if you feel lonely or want a chat pick up the phone. And if you get any hassle, just remind her that the rules don't apply to phoning the agency. You've got my number at home if you need it, so — any time. Oh, by the way, do you want me to find you another job right away, or would you like a pause? Or a re-think?'

'Ah.' Flurry of temptation; vision of solitude, cool and welcoming, translating swiftly into bleak and empty. 'Yes, another job, please.'

'Sure? We can take our time over this, you know.'

'I'm sure.'

'Good. I'll be in touch soon then, and many thanks. You're doing brilliantly.'

Dale came back on Sunday afternoon, breaking into the omnibus edition of *EastEnders*, which his mother was unforgiving about in spite of having seen every episode already. He was jaunty, gorged on undigested gobbets of new wisdom, his management skills freshly furbished, his ego bolstered by the fulsome encouragement of his mentor, as improbable but dazzling as the rantings of a revivalist preacher. His mother soon knocked all that out of him.

'I got back on Friday evening, as a matter of fact,' he confessed defiantly to Louise, under cover of helping her to 'get the tea'. His ears were still pink from his mother's drubbing, and he picked with futile persistence at the corner of a pack of sliced ham which was not designed to peel back.

Louise took it from him, angry for a second that she had had two extra days here which she need not have endured. But this was a job; this was the way she was earning her living, how could a day more or less matter? And seeing the way Dale humbly rendered up the ham, observing the twist of his lips and the sag of his shoulders as his mother effortlessly re-assumed her mastery, Louise forgot to be indignant. How had he employed the stolen two days though? She entertained herself with lurid improbable visions.

As she drove home that evening Stirling had the appearance of a foreign country, though she had twice come into town to shop for Mrs Baines. But it was she who had become the foreigner, she realised, as she closed the garage, let herself in at the basement door and went up the stairs whose treads seemed oddly higher than she remembered. She felt a physical trepidation, her stomach quivering and her hands clammy, as she went into the drawing-room, and after only nine days at Drummond View her first reaction was disbelief that she could ever have existed in its frigid temperature. But of course she had turned the heating down. Hurrying, still in her coat, trying to ignore her feeling of strangeness, she adjusted the dial, switched on the convector heater they used as a booster on winter mornings, and put on the kettle to make more palatable tea than Mrs Baines' taste in teabags produced.

Going up to her room, still trying to shake off a feeling of disorientation, Louise knew that the protective casing which had enclosed her since Owen and the children had vanished on that appalling morning had splintered apart for good. Around her the silence of the house seemed weighty, as unmoving as the chilly air of the March dusk. The house seemed gaunt and shadowy, big and unwieldy. She felt panicked and alone. If her own room rejected her . . .

It didn't. The blow heater was soon blasting away, the lamps on, her bed, her books, her neat possessions welcoming her.

Gradually the rest of the house received her again, and her sense of strangeness dwindled and was forgotten, but just the same she knew she had some serious thinking to do. From the moment of meeting Cass she had allowed herself to be rolled along by events, but now, with the first job under her belt, it was time to make a more balanced evaluation of where she was heading.

She was sure it had been a good thing, however incongruous the setting, to move into different surroundings and face new demands. She had been in serious danger of burying her grief at Beatrice's death in the same way that she had dealt with the twins', turning her back on every reminder or potentially bruising contact.

She was clear that she must not slip back into cowardly solitude, but was the best answer to pass her days in other people's houses, at the mercy of their taste and standards, forever a transient? Then alarmed thoughts swarmed up, the thoughts that had driven her to look up Cass's agency in Yellow Pages in the first place – what else could she do? She had been married at twenty, had had the twins at twenty-one, knew nothing about anything beyond children and cooking and house-keeping – and typing informed views on the role of the Scots Greys in the armies of Marlborough, she reminded herself, with a small unsteady laugh.

Round the thoughts went again. Not every client, surely, could be a Mrs Baines? And she was lucky to have been offered employment with such amazing ease and speed. Then, for the first time for a long while, a tiny ripple stirred which she had almost forgotten – excitement. The new and the unknown were waiting for her. Where might she go, what new situations might she encounter, whom might she meet? Some of it might actually be fun. And if it wasn't, then she had this marvellous base to retreat to. She would be idiotic to give up now.

She slept well, waking to a bright blowy morning, wet stone and budding trees gleaming after overnight rain, a stir of spring in the air as she ran round to the corner bakery for fresh croissants.

As she was having breakfast a letter from Cass arrived, or more accurately, from the agency. Details of a job, somewhere north of Perth. Going through the form, by this time familiar, with its coded abbreviations for non-smoker, car-driver, etc, there were one of two slight jolts to ride over.

The first was realising that in future this was how communication would be made. Louise saw with embarrassment that she had been thinking of Cass as a friend, taking for granted her personal attention and, without any justification except her own need, rushing to hang upon that peg the telling and jokes it was fun to share. The form seemed for a moment a rebuff, but Louise was too sensible to let the feeling take hold. Cass was kind, fun to be with and they had established an easy rapport, but to her Louise could only be one of a host of employees. There would be no further meetings; there was no need for them. The interview stage was over.

Cass had, however, scribbled a note at the bottom of the last page. 'Think about this one, and give me a ring (office or home, whichever suits) as I'd like to talk it over. Only fairly quickly, for obvious reasons!'

For the second jolt was that the starting date for the job was four days away.

# Chapter Five

'What I wanted you to know first and foremost is, it's a household with children – no, hang on, Louise, let me finish. They won't be there, I can absolutely promise you that. The parents are divorced, and though the children live at Fallan with their father they spend part of each school holiday with their mother, and they won't be back till just before Easter. A cook had been booked – by another agency, nothing to do with me – to cover the whole month, but now she's got some domestic crisis and can only do Easter itself and the second half of the holidays.'

'Cass, really, I'm not sure about this,' Louise broke in. 'I don't want you to waste your time giving me the details if—' She felt literally breathless at the idea of this careless contact, of being surrounded by objects belonging to children, being in their home, but she knew her reaction was unreasonable and extreme.

'Let me tell you a bit more?' Cass cajoled.

'I know I must sound terribly negative, and I'm grateful

to you for finding me posts, so quickly too, but I just don't think I could—'

'Believe me, I do understand,' Cass assured her, 'but you can trust me. The children won't be there, you won't see them. Let me tell you the bare bones of the job before you make your mind up. Bare bones they are too, because none of the family will be there. Father works mostly abroad. All that's wanted is a couple of weeks of freezer-filling. Grub for the holidays, and slightly fancier stuff for guests over Easter. But that brings me to a couple of reservations on my part, which I want to make clear to you.'

Perceptive as she was, Cass hadn't realised how the fact that she might have problems herself would work in her favour with kind Louise.

'This is a new client,' Cass explained, 'and one I'd like to capture, since the request has come on recommendation from a source I value. But I haven't been able to check the place out because it's all happened so swiftly, and we're always up to our eyes at this time of year, supplying hotels and other seasonal employers. That's one problem, but apart from that I'm told the Erskines have had endless fights over staff with other agencies, and while that's a challenge it does raise question marks.'

'You'd had problems with Mrs Baines,' Louise remarked, and though she thought she was merely making an observation Cass caught a promising hint of involvement there.

'True enough,' she agreed, keeping her tone casual. 'Now, what else do we know — ? Oh, yes, there's someone *in situ* already—'

'Then can't she do the cooking?'

'I gather not.' Cass sounded amused about something. 'It's a biggish place so they have someone to run the house, and they bring in a cook for holidays, shooting parties and so on. No other living-in staff, daily cleaner and handyman/gardener couple who live out. So it would be just this girl and yourself, and some nice creative cooking at your own pace.'

'Don't try blandishments on me,' Louise warned, and Cass laughed. The tone of that was far removed from the tension and uncertainty Louise had revealed at her initial interview. But Cass didn't comment on it; Louise had a long way to travel yet.

'I think you could do the job,' she said instead.

She was keen to fill this vacancy, with its promise of a long-term account, but also it was harder than Louise could know to find suitable slots for her at this stage. Cass not only had the children ban to work round, but also Louise's lack of self-confidence and limited experience. There were a good many jobs where at present it would be impossible to send her.

Louise's reasons for agreeing to go were largely negative. She didn't want to fall at the second fence, losing ground already gained; she had no valid excuse for letting Cass down; she needed to occupy her days; and she could hardly ask for a less demanding post.

Braced by reaching a decision, pushing out of her mind worries about the size of the house, the level of cooking required, the 'other person', she was surprised to feel a lift of energy sweep her up. She checked through the kitchen cupboards with a view to being away intermittently for the foreseeable future, made a dentist's appointment, reminders about which she had been ignoring for weeks, and phoned Nevil. He was busy with a client, and his secretary said she would get him to call back. That, Louise knew from experience, could take hours, so she put the thought of talking to him on hold and with set face tackled something else she had been putting off – she had not been into Beatrice's room since the day of the cremation. Even if she still found it impossible to deal with the personal belongings waiting there untouched, she could make a start on less poignant tasks that must by now need attention. Dead flowers, abandoned plants – evidence of a neglect so contrary to Louise's nature that it made her realise for the first time how incapacitated she had been during those stunned weeks.

Pills, toilet things, spectacles, rarely used make-up, the heavy tortoiseshell combs Beatrice used to ram ineffectually into her untidy hair, it was possible after all to make a start with these. And once this step was taken Louise found she could go steadily on, packing up for disposal nightdresses, underwear, squashed-down slippers, rubbed velvet housecoat. But some of these objects were so familiar, so shaped to Aunt Bea's shape, so much part of life with her, that to see them shabby and discarded was desperately sad, and tears weren't far away as Louise went stubbornly on with this awful job. There was no one to comfort her, to assure that there was no urgency, that all this could be done gradually, when she was ready. And there was no one to do it for her.

There were many things she didn't know what to do with, lifting clothes from the great mahogany wardrobe and helplessly putting them back — suits and skirts years out of date, yet of tweed so robust they would last for ever; severe blouses of superb quality; silk dresses with draped bosoms and dipping hems; a fur coat with puffed shoulders which had died long before Louise was born; and a row of brown leather shoes, every pair stiffened with shoe-trees. Who could want such things? Yet what a sin to throw them away.

She was rescued from her sad dilemma by Nevil calling back to say that the first available moment he had free was tomorrow evening, but if a meeting then would be agreeable to her he would call on his way home from the office. He sounded edgy, and Louise wasn't sure if it was because she had phoned him at work or because, as he told her, he had tried to contact her several times during the past few days without success.

Louise didn't explain. But when Nevil rang off she didn't go back to Beatrice's room. She had hurt enough for one day. Going on with the job at some later time would not be so hard as making the start had been.

Relieved that a dialogue with Nevil had been postponed, she spent the evening writing to her parents, telling them as simply as possible what she planned to do. As long as she stayed in Scotland, resisting pressure to return to Cornwall and 'be properly looked after', they would disapprove of anything she did, but at least the duty of keeping them up to date was done.

Being by now in a sorting and clearing mood, she went on to turn out her desk, and the next day, which was sunny, was inspired to give the courtyard its spring tidying, preparing the tubs for planting and bringing out the garden seats from winter storage in the basement. What a sheltered corner this was, she thought as she pottered about, and how she liked the way the house tucked its rump into the high terrace and faced out onto light and space. Contained, easy to live in; she was so lucky.

En route to Perth two days later she felt very different, reluctant to go anywhere, oppressed by new fears. Ahead lay another unknown house, where apart from doing the job she had been sent to do she would be incidental to its way of life, sleeping in another unknown room which in so short a time she could never make her own. And behind her, more disturbing because they were less definable than this dread of venturing into a new place, were the seeds of doubt Nevil had sown.

Not that there had been any doubt about his frame of mind. He had come in with his quick fussy step, with the air of a man who has been short of time all day and still has tedious matters to attend to before he can relax for the evening. Louise was shaken, not for the first time, at the speed at which she had moved from being the daughter-in-law, grudgingly accepted (not a Scot for a start) because she was Owen's wife, and the mother of his children, to being someone whose only connection with the family was as a carer for Beatrice. And now Beatrice had gone. Had the chill of that been there before Nevil's startling speech or was it part of her reaction to it?

'No. No, thank you,' he had said, waving away her offer of whisky or sherry. 'I shall be very late getting home as it is. But I have been trying to speak to you, as I said, for some days.'

Louise had resisted apologising, and his look of impatience – or of something else which she couldn't quite pin down – had deepened.

'However, now that I am here . . .' He had glanced around him, at the high secretaire which still had no chair in front of it, at the glass-fronted bookcase between the windows and the shelved recesses on either side of the fireplace also full of books, two-deep on the lower shelves, and everywhere piled along the crammed rows. 'You will understand that many of these books are possibly quite valuable.'

Cautious lawyer-speak, when what he clearly meant was that they were very valuable indeed.

'They should be revalued for insurance?' Louise had suggested, following his glance round the room. How slack she had been, thinking of none of these things for herself. Perhaps Nevil was justified in being annoyed, even if technically her carelessness was no business of anyone but herself.

'Revalued for the purpose of selling them,' he had rapped out. 'And the paintings as well, though I cannot say the family were very generous in their allocation when Aunt Beatrice first moved in. There is nothing of any particular distinction here, though two or three may find moderate favour in today's market.'

'But I had thought—' Louise had begun, shocked into speech, but in the same instant she had realised how impossible it was to go on. Her expectation, Beatrice's promise, that everything would be left to her, had been so large and vague that suddenly she saw it as something which she should never have taken seriously. What right had she to any Donaldson possessions? It had been made clear enough she did not belong to the family. And this precious store of books, these beautiful bindings, these collectable Victorian water-colours, what possible right did she have to any such thing?

But what she had minded most, what had kept her awake for half the night, was her own cowardice. In that horrified instant she had relinquished any claim to such valuable items, but she had not had the courage to ask Nevil what the terms of Beatrice's will had been. There had been a dismissiveness in his manner, something furtive behind the business-like exchange, which made her feel uncertain and uneasy. She knew she should have asked him whether, as a legatee, she would be given a copy of the will. She had no idea what normally happened, but that would surely have been a reasonable supposition. However, intimidated by his brusqueness, his hurry, his annoyance that she would no longer be available whenever he needed to contact her, she had asked nothing.

This morning, too, she could have phoned any solicitor and asked that question about seeing the will, but she had found she wasn't ready to precipitate another clash with Nevil. Besides which, if she established that she should have seen it, where did she go from there?

Today was not the day to resolve such an issue. She had enough to contend with, prising herself once more out of her retreat, harder to do this time as she remembered certain disagreeable aspects of life *chez* Baines. But still the little niggle of dissatisfaction with herself remained.

Thank goodness she was meeting Cass in Perth.

'I should be able to dash out for a cup of coffee at least,' Cass had said. 'I'd like to see you on your way and wish you well.'

Even diving out for coffee was not easy at this hectic time, but she thought a little encouragement might do Louise good, and incidentally wanted to reassure herself that Louise could cope, for once the arrangement was made she had had her doubts about the advisability of sending this more or less untried person, with problems of her own, to a new and reputedly difficult client.

At least Fallan was within easy reach, which was the first thing she said to Louise as they settled into the French-run bistro round the corner from the South Street agency. 'In fact I'll be even closer to you from home than from the office, so give me a shout if things get tough and I'll come straight over.'

'I didn't realise that,' Louise said. 'I've checked out Fallan, but I don't exactly know where Bridge of Riach is, other than north of here.'

'It's at the top of Glen Maraich. I love living up there, but it can be a bit of a nightmare getting up and down in the winter.'

Louise wanted to discover more of Cass's life, to ask a dozen questions. A desire to consolidate a potential friendship, or to distance, with other thoughts, her trepidation about where this journey was taking her? Either way, there was no time for questions today.

'Anyway,' Cass was continuing, 'I shouldn't imagine there'll be any major problems.' This was not the moment to enlarge on Fallan's poor track record as far as employing cooks went, or the fact that she had not been able to inspect the house or Louise's accommodation. Though in spite of Louise's evident nervousness, Cass somehow didn't think such factors as a comfortless room would worry her unduly. In her quiet way she gave an impression of competence and self-discipline, which her gleaming hair and trim appearance and the unmistakable quality of what she wore reinforced.

For now, Cass could only make sure that Louise was clear about her route and how to find the house, promise that she would be in touch very soon, and send her on her way with good wishes and a hug.

# Chapter Six

Although the A9 wasn't particularly busy at this time of year Louise was sufficiently unused to driving these days to feel pressured by it, as though the traffic moved faster than she remembered and was somehow hostile to her. Once past Pitlochry it was a relief to turn off onto a quiet narrow road, though her increasing nervousness as her destination approached, in spite of Cass's reassurances and the simple nature of the job, made it seem to wind for ever. The road was mostly buried in dark stretches of conifer but occasionally emerged over rises which gave long views up the loch to big hills crowding to the west. But sight-seeing was not on Louise's mind today, and her mouth was dry, her hands clammy on the wheel, as she turned right at a no-through-road sign, and climbed away into Glen Fallan.

She knew her tension was the penalty for the years of sheltered isolation, and it only proved how vital it had been to break free of their hold. But it was clearly going to be a case of no pain, no gain, and as the road twisted on she grew calmer. It was the emptiness of the landscape which worked on her first, as the unfenced road looped rock outcrops, cushioned with heather and bilberry, and meandered over mini summits, their turf worn bare by the wheels of summer cars. These natural viewpoints overlooked sheep-dotted hollows where the March sunlight drew a glowing brown that was almost pink from flattened last-year's bracken, and struck crimson fire from the scarcely thickened buds of birches. On the left a busy burn, engorged with snow melt, broke in the cream foam of peat water over rocky lips, or slid dark and smooth through alder-hung pools. Louise had almost forgotten snow. It had become a white line enhancing faraway hills seen from windows, a news item when blizzards struck, a factor determining whether she took the car or walked when she went shopping. In the recent warm days winter had seemed remote, done with for another year. Now, the trees thinning, she saw that snow still clothed the stark peaks rising to the north which shut in the little glen.

It seemed to emphasise the divide she was crossing between the old life and the new. The nine days in Bridge of Allan were now like some muddled trial run, a blur of heat and sound from which few details stood out. This was another landscape altogether, and looking about her with keener attention Louise saw that it was magical, exciting, full of promise.

She also realised she hadn't met a single vehicle since she turned into this hidden-away glen. From time to time she would pass a cottage with weathered sheds, a patch of garden fenced against deer, a line of washing flapping behind, a glass porch stuck on in front, a muddy vehicle parked outside. One or two sported the embellishments which marked them as the homes of the affluent retired, their porches conservatories, their windows double-glazed, their gardens landscaped.

Where a straggle of houses with shop and pub and post office formed a small hamlet, a turreted white meringue of a castle swam into view and for a heart-stopping moment Louise thought it was Fallan. But according to Cass's directions she still had a couple of miles to go, and quelling her panic she drove on past high wrought-iron gates behind which a drive dark with new tarmac wound out of sight.

There could be little doubt when she reached her objective. Well-established trees, efficient fencing supplementing old stone dykes and a spread of buildings told her a big house was coming up, exactly where it ought to be. She checked momentarily at seeing the weather-worn words 'Nether Fallan' carved in the granite gateposts. No one had said anything about Nether. But 'by the bridge', Cass had said, and here the burn twisted away to the right, and the road, by now more like a private road than a public highway, crossed it to disappear over a steep brow. Besides, there was nowhere else. This was the end of enclosed ground, of trees, of human habitation. Beyond this point empty heather-clad slopes climbed to grey scree and those cold, high, white ridges.

The drive, a hundred yards or so long, had a wide border of lawn which had not yet received its first cut of spring. At regular intervals were rhododendron, laburnum, and other unknown bushes. Between them and a handsome double line of beeches and sycamores, Louise saw that the grass was dense with the spears of daffodil leaves. Through bare trunks to the right were glimpses of a well-laid-out garden. It all spoke of permanence, care, money, 'big house', yet the house which faced her had at first glance no such pretensions. It was white, like that absurd castle, but its walls were creeper-covered and it was comfortably tucked into its setting, a two-storied L shape, one arm facing west, the other overlooking the big garden. A round turret in the angle housed porch and front door.

A comfortable and reassuring house, Louise thought with relief, getting out of the car and uncramping limbs she had not realised had been so tense. A house well protected from the wild weather which must rage up here at times. Nothing hostile reached towards her.

Nothing welcoming either, she discovered, as she rang the bell and waited, making the small gestures of nervousness, tweaking at her scarf, pushing her bag further round on her hip, rethreading the strap through its loop, an unconscious action of orderliness.

Silence. No bark of dog, no approaching feet. She rang again and stepped back to glance along the line of deepset windows, up at the ones close under the eaves. Questions began to swam — the wrong time, the wrong day, the wrong house? Why had she ignored that puzzling 'Nether Fallan'? But there was no other house.

She looked around her uncertainly. To the left ran the stone wall of a barn, leafless roses trained along it. A gap between it and the house led to other buildings, and probably the back door. Should she have looked for the back door first? No, of course not, common sense protested. But to make someone hear? Well, if she was going to find someone in the house she could start here; she was about to live in it after all.

The door was open a few inches; Louise didn't think the day that warm. She pushed it back and found herself in a spacious hall with a long window lighting wide stairs. There was an impression of comfort, of old furniture at home where it stood, of worn but still beautiful rugs on stone flags. Sleepy stillness. Not a natural shouter, Louise did her best. Silence hung like a blanket.

Still with the sense of being in an enchanted place which had come upon her as she drove up the glen, she looked right along a narrow corridor, white-walled, carpeted in red, pictures hung along its length, a door at the end open onto a room which gave an impression of space and light. Its general air was one of settled and civilised comfort, but clearly no one was to be found in that direction.

A door on the left opened into a dining-room. Louise took in little beyond a beautiful and obviously early table which would seat at least sixteen. Under the turn of the stairs a door opened into a second corridor – and into a different house. Gone was the atmosphere of graceful comfort; the very air was altered, with a hungry bite to it, a hint of damp skirting-boards, mop buckets and sunless stone, of swill tubs and mice and mouldy bread and uncleaned larder shelves.

Nineteenth-century poverty, Aunt Beatrice's voice

summed up crisply, and Louise shivered as the baize-lined door swung to behind her with a dull thud. She called again, less certainly, the dank air draining substance from her voice, and still silence met her, almost tangibly resistant.

She turned, though hardly wanting to see more, into a gaunt kitchen, meagrely lit by two small windows set high in a wall all of three feet thick. Not a plant or single decorative object relieved its starkness; not a calendar brightened its dingy walls, patterned only by shadowy maps of damp and barely covered scars where the range of a former era had once stood. In its place, almost frivolous against the scale of its surroundings, its rings and top brown with burned food, stood a white-enamelled cooker, raised on a couple of bricks.

Damp-infiltrated and knife-scored Formica, littered with rubbish, curled up from the work surfaces which ran above cupboards along the walls. Louise was thankful to see that one set had been wrenched out and a dishwasher pushed into the gap. At midfloor stood a solid table, scrubbed, though clearly not recently, half a dozen chairs with rush seats and ladder backs round it. On it was spread the detritus of what looked like several meals.

Cold, repelled, and suddenly feeling desperately alone, not just in this moment but forever, in herself, in her life, Louise stood in the doorway and found she was trembling. Well, she needn't stay. There was nothing in the rules to say she had to stay anywhere as revolting as this. No wonder previous cooks had fled. It would be letting Cass down, but Cass was a professional, she must be used to such things, she would find someone else. Or whoever was coming at Easter would just have to cope without a freezerful of food prepared by someone else. This vengeful reaction towards a stranger would have shown anyone who knew Louise how seriously she had been rattled by this inhospitable scene.

The crash of a distant door and the sound of feet racing along the passage startled her, so completely had she accepted by now that no one was there.

'Sorry, sorry, sorry!' exclaimed a panting voice, and into the kitchen skidded a bundle of skinny limbs, to land with a crash against a cupboard and right itself with a feeling 'Ow!', a hand going up to straighten a large pair of spectacles and wipe back a spill of fine mousy hair. 'How awful of me, and I'd absolutely vowed to myself I'd be here when you arrived, but you know how it is, things just seem to crop up and before you know it . . .'

She picked a curly wood shaving from the sleeve of a sagging brown cardigan whose shoulder seams came to her elbows, and which she now huddled around her over a pale-blue top tight over pointed breasts and bony ribcage. 'I'm Abby.' And she blinked the softest, longest, furriest mouse-brown lashes Louise had ever seen, giving her a smile of such sweetness and warmth that indignation evaporated on the spot.

'It's quite all right. I'd only just arrived.'

'Oh, good. And you found your way in all right. Shall I put the kettle on for tea? Thirsty work.' She didn't say what the thirsty work had been.

Louise saw that it was quite in order for her to have

come in. Abby was not her hostess; they were there on equal footing, employees, staff, dwellers below stairs. Abby was accustomed to the comings and goings of cooks on temporary assignments, and her question about filling the kettle suggested that she already saw the kitchen as the new arrival's domain.

Louise watched her as she did so, leaving the green-mottled brass tap faintly hissing. She was tall, though not as tall as long-legged Cass, nor did she move with Cass's free stride. She was very young, twenty at the most, and painfully thin, her shoulders drooping, her spine a long curve as she waited, one bony hip thrust impossibly far out, for the kettle to boil, chattering happily. She only galvanised herself to gather up mugs, teabags and milk as the kettle began shrieking. She drew it aside, making a couple of attempts to pull off its whistle, flipping her fingers and swearing, and Louise saw that half the cap was missing.

'Oh, damn, all the mugs are in the dishwasher. They always are, aren't they?' Abby said cheerfully.

Very often, Louise conceded, but when it's crammed as full as that the contents are usually clean. She didn't think much loaded into it at present would be usable even when put through the cycle, and tried not to wonder how long it had been there.

Abby, still chatting, rinsed out a couple of mugs with cold water and her fingers. 'I'm so glad Hugh finally got in touch with a new agency. We have had some weirdos in the way of cooks during the last year or so, I can tell you. And they go squawking off at the least thing.'

What would Abby call the least thing, Louise queried mildly, seeing what she had thought was a leaf stalk sticking to the wall begin to inch its way upwards.

'Now which milk's this, I wonder?' Abby debated, sniffing. 'Seems OK.' She spoke as though she, like Louise, had just arrived. 'Anyway, no, I hate being on my own, which I all too frequently am, alas, and now you're here it means I can get the days off I've been promised since I don't know when. Oh, biscuit? Super-quality shortbread at present, bits of ginger stuck in it and a' thing, as they say. Old Maxine buys in posh goodies for *them*, stuck-up tart, but the moment her back's turned I hoover through the lot. Drives her mad. Every, every time.' She spoke in the careless clipped voice of the English upper middle class. She looked the part – long pale face, veil of colourless hair, stick-like wrists and long narrow feet in stained suede granny boots which seemed only tenuously connected to her thin legs.

She hooked a chair out with one of them, nearly tipped it over, checked it with the hand that was carrying her mug, slopped tea over her wrist and put the mug down with an exclamation of pain and a bang that sent more tea over the table. She pulled down her sleeve and held it against the ball of her thumb while she spread the spilled tea further with a casual swipe.

Louise was clutching at the wisps of information and references. 'Hold on, could you go back a bit?'

'Oh, sorry, sugar. Forgot to ask.' Abby leapt up, jarring the table and splashing tea out of both mugs this time.

'I don't take it, thanks. Please, please sit down,' Louise

begged, in spite of herself beginning to laugh. 'Can we fill in a few gaps? I don't know much about the set-up. Hugh is Mr Erskine. I can get that far.'

'Grumpy bastard,' said Abby, without malice, dredging up the teabag she had forgotten to remove, pressing it briefly against the side of her mug then arcing it in spattering flight towards the sink, which it failed to reach.

Louise disciplined herself not to go and pick it up.

'And he's away at present?' she asked, not prepared to go into the question of her employer's character.

Abby shrugged and took an enormous bite of rich shortbread. 'This isn't bad,' she said through the crumbs. 'You'd pay for the fancy tin, though, wouldn't you, all that dark blue and gold? Yeah, dear old Hughie's away, but he never says where or why or when. Hates being asked too. Likes to come and go as he pleases, which is why I'm supposed to be around even if the kids are away. God, it's boring sometimes.'

'And Maxine?'

'Secretary. Control freak. New millennium woman. Power dresser. Like the north face of something. Can't think why Hughie – oh, well.' The incredible lashes swept down, and a long dimple appearing in the thin cheek acknowledged bounds which could not be overstepped. With a gesture which was to become familiar to Louise, a signal that she had thought better of saying something outrageous, Abby pushed her glasses, ill-fitting and rickety to the last degree, back up her nose.

'Does Maxine come here?' There had been no mention of a secretary, high-powered or otherwise.

'Oh, God, never lets him move a muscle without her. Winds him up in the morning, wipes his — nose. She still has time to give me a hard time, though. Very keen about money, our Maxine is, I warn you, whether it's hers or not. Apart from that she plinks about on her computer, sends five million faxes and another million e-mails. Oh, and chooses the wine and tries to get the temp cooks to produce Thai food and does the flowers. Who needs flowers, honestly? She doesn't do much else, except buy way-out catwalk-type clothes for the children which they won't wear.'

Here Louise veered sharply away. 'What did you mean about having a few days off?' It had certainly not been mentioned in her briefing.

'Oh, a couple of days, that's all it would be, honestly!' Abby tried to sound offhand but the dimple gave her away. 'Just a tiny, mini, minuscule break before Easter, somewhere with shops and lights and life after dark. Do a little clubbing, get a little high, be where it's at.'

'But are you supposed to go?' Louise decided she'd rather not know what getting a little high meant. 'It isn't up to me to say, surely?'

'Oh, no, it's time due me. Well, I'm supposed to get everything ready for Easter, but there's nothing much to that, and Bella does the part that matters anyway.'

'Bella?'

'Wife of Lennie Soutar, the gardener. I look after the nursery wing, this part of the house, and she does the rest. Goes ballistic if I touch anything through there.' Louise thought she could see why. 'She comes dabbing round with a duster most days, to keep her hours up, and when there are guests she goes into orbit about things like emptying the Hoover bag and keeping one shoe brush for brown and one for black and not letting the boys ride their bikes down the red corridor. I suppose it keeps her happy, poor dear,' Abby wound up, licking her finger and sticking it in the sugar bowl. 'Life with Lennie can't be much of a thrill.'

'But what happens if you're away and Mr Erskine comes back?'

'You can call him Hugh, you know,' Abby said kindly, as though recognising with pity the hang-ups of a different generation. 'He won't be back.'

'I thought you said you never knew?'

The sidelong little grin again. 'Oh, well, this time I know for certain he won't be here till Easter.'

'Why don't I believe a word you say?' But Abby was impossible to dislike, in spite of the chasms of uncertainty she liked opening under other people's feet. A first feeling of tolerant acceptance of this place stirred unexpectedly in Louise.

'You agree then? I can go?' Abby asked. 'That's great, I owe you one. Listen, though,' with a glance at her wrist where no watch appeared, 'I ought to show you your room, it's getting late. I've made the bed,' she added over her shoulder as they went to the door, pleased with herself at having thought of it. 'And if you're worrying about supper there are masses of things in the freezer, well, one or two anyway, only I must scoot off, or I shan't get a lift and I get so tired of walking down that bloody road.'

'But where are you going?' Louise demanded, hurrying after her.

'Darts night,' Abby said succinctly. 'Come on.' She took a dark wooden stair at the end of the kitchen passage two at a time. 'Bathroom there. Make the most of it before the boys fill it with submarines and water guns and smelly socks. Now, this is you. Oh,' she swung round with her hand on the door knob, 'would you like to come to the darts night? It's a good laugh, usually. Come if you'd like to.'

Louise recognised the kindness which prompted the invitation, impossible as the suggestion was. Apart from pub lunches with Owen in the early days, before cash grew too limited for even such simple pleasures, she could hardly remember when she had last been in a bar.

'It's very nice of you to suggest it, but I won't, if you don't mind,' she said.

'That's OK,' Abby said easily. 'Sorry to dash off but there's a telly in our sitting-room and everything. Anyway, this is your room. Just rummage round for anything you need. See you tomorrow.'

'What time do we — ? Abby!'

But Abby was gone.

# Chapter Seven

As Abby, evidently ready to go out just as she was, racketed thunderously down the wooden stairs (the children would doubtless do that too) Louise stood for an irresolute moment at her bedroom door, scarcely daring to discover what accommodation had been provided for her. Then she was annoyed with herself; on the scale of things she was facing at present this was hardly important.

A glance told her that the room was far nicer than anything seen so far at this end of the house had led her to hope. She had been bracing herself for bare boards, iron bed, deal furniture and marble-topped washstand. On a breath of relief she stepped into a sloping-ceilinged room, shabby it was true, but friendly and welcoming. A kidney-shaped dressing-table with frilly skirt, the glass which covered it cracked across; a wooden-ended bed with a faded silk quilted cover to the floor; a low buttoned chair, its flounces sagging on the worn carpet where a small rose pattern was just discernible. But what pleased Louise most were the two steps leading up to a cushioned seat in the gable window, which looked across a big vegetable garden to the open hill.

It would more than do, though it occurred to Louise to wonder if she would have been quite so pleased with it if she had come up here directly from the hall. She hadn't brought her bag in yet. Going out into the corridor she opened the door which closed it off to the left. It led to a landing which included the turret over the porch, and held a chintz-covered sofa, piecrust table and glass-fronted china cabinets. She went down to the hall, wondering if using this staircase was 'allowed'. Doubtless the rules would be different everywhere, but that didn't worry her. She had always found rules easy to keep, ready to believe they were based on good sense.

She didn't explore, though she didn't suppose it would have mattered if she had. She confined herself to walking along 'the red corridor' and standing in the doorway of the room at the end. As she had guessed, it was a big drawing-room, with french windows opening onto a stone-paved terrace and, though dusk was beginning to gather now, hinting at a glorious view down the glen.

The hour would go forward in two days' time, and she felt a little rush of pleasure that the light evenings of spring were at hand and she was here in this lovely place. In this lovely house. Then she went through the swing door which cut it in half, and took the word back.

It was not a good evening. First, there was the bath-room. It had not occurred to her, though of course it should have done, that she would be using the same one as the children. Kicked into a corner, presumably by Abby, lay a jumble of brightly coloured plastic; on the tiles round the bath were rubbed transfers of Noddy and Paddington Bear, and the bath mat, rumpled and dirty, depicted Pingu and Pinga. There was more trace, however, of Abby, notably a mat of hairs in the plug-hole, grey with soap, and a phalanx of bottles and tubes and jars, half of them empty and all unstoppered, dribbling and oozing. Their combined smell, however, overlaid others less attractive, which Louise supposed was something.

There was a bad moment when she turned from washing her hands to pick up the wet rag of towel Abby had slung over the edge of the bath. She suddenly saw small firm bodies, heard high voices break into giggles as the elusive soap, bent on living a life of its own, escaped yet again, the laughter rising to a hysterical pitch at the bubbling rumbles of forbidden farts. She saw the gleam of light on satin-skinned arms coloured by the sun to the cut-off point of a T-shirt sleeve—

Don't, don't, don't. But as though pain itself drew her on, she found herself at each of the doors along the corridor in turn, pushing them open at arm's length with her fingertips, as though someone with a knife lurked behind them. Barren and tattered those rooms were, uncovered duvets rumpled on stripped beds, scuffed up rugs on lino floors, a curtain rail sagging, a piece of hardboard meant to stop draughts from a chimney fallen forward, its back dredged with soot. Louise wished she hadn't looked, angry with Abby, every instinct aching to put this careless neglect to rights.

In Abby's own tip, at the north end of the wing, the curtains were half closed, the light was on, the bed unmade, the wardrobe, empty except for a tangle of distressed shoes, with its doors hanging open, and every object Abby appeared to possess strewn across the floor. Likeable as Abby might be, what made her a suitable person to look after other people's houses and other people's children?

Sadness dragged at Louise as she unpacked and went down to see what was on offer in the way of food. 'Masses of things in the freezer,' Abby had said, but she had not said where the freezer was.

It was strange to be alone in the house. The emptiness of it stretching around her kept catching at Louise, making her listen, trying to translate into the commonplace the background sounds of new surroundings. Certainly the mammoth freezer which she found pounding away in a cavernous larder made enough noise. Small wonder, for when she opened the lid – the jagged edge of the broken handle catching the side of her hand – she saw it contained nothing beyond a few gaudy packets in its baskets.

On the kitchen table their mugs still stood, added to the residue of other meals. There was the crammed dishwasher. Neither presented a problem, but they did pose a question. To what degree, coming for a brief time into someone else's house, was it appropriate to interfere with its normal working? At Drummond View she had learned that trying to improve on what she found was not necessarily what was wanted. Yet here she was the cook; the kitchen would be her responsibility. She couldn't work in it till it was clean.

As she scoured sink and draining boards, depression seized her. Cleaning up other people's mess — was this to be her life? Creating order then going on her way, forgotten before she reached the gate.

This washing-up liquid, in its dribbled container, was just about done. Would there be more somewhere? Where did Abby note down things she was running out of? The need to ask things, be shown things, and not fumble around in the dark and cold like this, almost overwhelmed her, but she made herself go on, lighting the oven, putting in a vegetable lasagne to heat up — was Abby vegetarian, anorexic, bulimic? — while she finished tidying and began to explore cupboards to locate things and take stock. What she found was so bizarre she gave up. Tomorrow would be time enough to tackle this mad *mélange*.

Sitting alone in the stark room forking in mass-produced pasta without character or quality, she finally faced what was really upsetting her — the subtle background presences, the fear that at any second she might stumble against some agonising reminder . . .

She shouldn't have come here. She should have withstood Cass's persuasion. It was not enough that the children wouldn't appear during her stay; they were here already, everywhere. In future she must stick to households like Drummond View. Procreation looked the last thing on Dale's mind. The effort to lighten her mood failed, for apart from the feeling that emotions she couldn't deal with waited round every corner in this house, there had nagged all day at the back of her mind the vague worries Nevil's visit had raised. He had been so fidgety, so hurried and dismissive. Or was she exaggerating the impression because she was feeling lost and uncertain in a new place? Anyway, it would serve no purpose to go over it here; it must wait till she was home. Home, scents of wax polish and flowers, unhurried days, the quiet room open to the air and sun, Aunt Bea's rare throaty chuckle— Louise came sharply to her feet, and hurriedly tidied away her dull meal. Abby had said they had a sitting-room of their own, indeed the fact had appeared on the job details. She would find something undemanding to watch, and try to shed this bleak mood before going to bed.

The sitting-room had a red curtain nailed across its window in the absence of a rail. It had two armchairs covered in wrinkled throws. It had a television, a dolls' house with the fragments of its furniture in a wastepaper basket beside it, a couple of huge cushions on the floor, pulled together, a blackboard with a drawing she hoped she didn't understand, and the whole room was silted with lager cans, beer bottles, wine boxes, mugs, plates and glasses. In the dead fire and across the hearth, crisp bags, cigarette packets, cigarette ends and used tissues were scattered.

Tears, the tears that had lain in wait since the moment in the bathroom when those voices had echoed with such devastating clarity, rose up and engulfed her.

Louise laid breakfast for two, thinking as she did so that she was probably being silly. It was shortly after eight, which seemed a reasonable time to appear with no family to cook for, and she was eager to get to work, the thought of the chaotic store rooms and cupboards tormenting her.

Abby didn't appear. Louise wondered if she should wake her. Was that the first duty of a workmate? But what time were they supposed to start?

Nine o'clock. The kitchen looked a different place, though starker than ever. Nine-twenty. Surely Abby would be horrified if she was allowed to sleep much longer. Perhaps she had forgotten to set her alarm clock; perhaps it hadn't gone off. Though reluctant to interfere in someone else's life, Louise went upstairs.

Abby's room was empty. Louise's mind flew to accident or disaster, but that was not really her style, and in a moment she was reasoning that if anything had happened she would have been told. (Or would she? Did anyone know she was here? The thought was briefly disconcerting.) Abby had probably had a good evening at the pub and spent the night with a friend. Whatever time she showed up for work was her own business. If she took advantage of her boss's absence that was up to her.

Louise told herself to lighten up and returned to the cupboard she had discovered in a distant store room, its shelves a yard deep and the two highest ones, though they appeared full, inaccessible without a stepladder.

With a torch she found on the corridor windowsill she started at the bottom, and after a few moments of amazed exploration crawled out feeling like a speleologist who has uncovered unknown treasures. The several cubic feet of mousy-smelling space was full of what looked like unopened wedding presents, their cards curling with damp on the cobwebby flags.

The next two shelves formed a record of the ideas a series of cooks had had for enlivening the Erskine diet, the dates of their reigns tabled by terrifying sell-by dates. Tins of snails, birds'-nest soup, rum babas and lobster bisque were ranged with jars of ghostly vanilla pods, green fig preserve and a lump of furry candied angelica. Apparently the done thing was to scorn your predecessor's choice and stock up with your own. And no one, it seemed, was ever responsible for clearing out the unusable – or the frankly death-dealing. So what about the efficient Maxine and her passion for economy? A small fortune had been squandered here.

Louise was back at the kitchen table, having fetched pad and pen from her room after a vain hunt for either downstairs, beginning a list studded with question marks of what it was actually possible to eat, when Abby twined herself round the kitchen door with the ingratiating guilt of a spaniel who has just raided the larder.

'Hi, sorry I'm late, must have overslept or something—'

'Not in your own room, you didn't.' Louise didn't care where Abby had been, but wanted to make it clear she wasn't interested in subterfuge. To her surprise Abby blushed a deep pink, unpeeling herself from the door and coming to the table with hunched shoulders, wrapping her shapeless cardigan round her with her fists balled in its pockets, and sinking shakily into a chair.

'I know it was awful of me. I hate myself really. I always

promise myself it will never happen again but somehow it always—'

'Look, Abby,' Louise cut in, 'you don't have to tell me anything. I only meant that I'd gone up to wake you and found your room empty. It's nothing to do with me where you've been or what you've been doing.'

'I feel such a shit.'

'A hungover shit, I presume,' Louise remarked, getting up to put the kettle on, reflecting as she did so that as far as she could recall it was the first time in her life she had used the word.

She heard a splutter of laughter behind her, followed by a quiet but feeling 'Ouch.'

'You look so gentle and soft – well, not soft in the head, I don't mean, of course. But you're not really, are you? Anyway, I'm sorry I wasn't here to show you things.'

'What time are we meant to start?' Louise asked in a general tone, putting black coffee and the milk jug in front of Abby. The latter was ignored, no surprise.

'How do you mean?' Abby asked, after a first gasping gulp.

'Start work,' Louise said patiently.

'Well – I don't know.' Abby seemed baffled. 'I mean, there's no one here, is there?'

'But even so, surely we're supposed to put in a certain number of hours? We're being paid after all.'

'Oh, you don't have to worry about *that*. No one cares. And when the children are here it's a question of being around all day – and all night too,' Abby added in a sad private aside. 'So it sort of balances out.'

'I'm here on a different basis.' Louise had not meant to sound so sharp, but blurred as the morning workings of her brain were Abby didn't miss the altered tone.

'I say, did that get to you? Maxine did say you hated children, and warned me not to talk about them. Forgot, sorry. You know me.'

Hate children? The words struck Louise like a blow. That such a thing should be said of her; it was unbearable.

Abby peeled her hair away from her glasses and peered myopically into Louise's face. What she saw there brought her to her feet in concern. 'Oh, God, I've said something dreadful, haven't I? I knew I would. Please don't mind. I won't say another word, I promise.'

She put a tentative arm round Louise's rigid shoulders, then let it fall away, afraid that touch might be the wrong thing. She stooped to look into Louise's face, as guilty and anxious as a child herself.

And to that Louise could never fail to respond. 'It's all right,' she said in a stifled voice. 'But I like children, that's all. Do you understand?'

Abby didn't, but nodded eagerly. It was a bit early for all this stuff.

Boots sounded in the passage and with a fierce effort Louise brought her mind back to immediate reality.

'Who will this be?'

'Oh, only Lennie coming in for his morning tea. And Cameron usually turns up too.'

'Who's Cameron?'

'Keeper up at the big house.'

What big house? And why did he come here for his tea-break?

'They generally come in here, or use our sitting-room if the kitchen's busy.'

'And who makes their tea?' Louise enquired.

'Whoever's in here—' Abby caught the lift of an eyebrow. 'Well, I will, of course.'

Tea, toast, biscuits. Tea-break was evidently a settled ritual. The men were friendly enough, but their rallying of a new female on the scene, their assessing glances, a slyness in their laughter, showed that they had seen many cooks come and go in this kitchen, and on the whole despised the lot. Lennie, a dour man in his fifties, confined himself to jokes of the 'Ach, you'll no' be here five minutes' variety. Cameron, younger, with dark impudent eyes, displayed briefly for form's sake, then accepted that Louise wouldn't fall for it. Still, there was always Abby.

Both men treated her with genuine affection. They teased her, put her down, but Louise realised that they found in her something irresistibly hapless and vulnerable. Noting Cameron's eyes follow her gangling movements, relishing the glimpses he caught of her small breasts as the cardigan yawned open, she also saw that to them Abby was deliciously sexy – and available?

As tea-break meandered on with its uninspired repartee, its slightly fired-up mood because of the presence of a newcomer, Louise resolved that no long-drawn-out sessions like this would interfere with her cooking once she got to work. But how to get to work? Where to obtain the hundred things she would need, mostly basic items. There had been, for example, no more washing-up liquid to be found. The shop in the village — how on earth did it survive? — could presumably produce that, but what else would it offer? And after that where did one go? Where would a good butcher be found, decent cheese, fresh vegetables?

'Come on, Abby, we'd better get started.' It was a governessy note to introduce into the morning langour, but she had already set herself apart by asking Cameron not to smoke. Though he muttered he had complied, and she guessed the request was something he was used to from these daft lasses who came to cook. At least the need to smoke at last uprooted them, as without a word of thanks they scraped back their chairs and tramped out.

'I'd better have a quick shower,' Abby said, and slid out after them.

Clearing the table, wiping up the toast crumbs, finding it was well after eleven, Louise wondered how much, in two weeks, it would be possible to achieve.

# Chapter Eight

'You see, the trouble is, I love sex.'

Abby sounded apologetic and faintly despairing.

'That must be awful for you.'

For a second Abby took Louise's grave tone seriously and looked more gloomy than ever, then she took a quick look at her and giggled. 'It's lovely, actually.'

'So do you have a boyfriend?'

'Oh, no one special.' The airy, too swift reply, did not accord with the lift of a bony shoulder as she looked away again, changing the subject. 'It's really handy that you've got a car. I'm supposed to have the use of the jeep, but Lennie keeps the keys and he only lets me use it for shopping in Aberfyle.'

'Why is that?' Louise asked, her attention on negotiating a steep blind bend. She vaguely recalled that 'use of car' had been included in her information sheet from Cass, but judging by the way in which everything she touched at Fallan seemed to come apart in her hand she was happy to continue to drive the ponderous Vauxhall she had inherited from Beatrice.

'Oh, just because I had a little bump or two. Men get so worked up about that sort of thing.'

Louise thought it might be rewarding to see Lennie worked up about anything. 'What did you bump into? Another moving object? A sheep? A human being?'

'Once the end of the barn. And once,' the long dimple appearing, 'a rock. Only the rock, which you'd have thought big enough to stay put, rolled over, and I ended up in the burn. It took them all day to get the jeep out. They borrowed a winch from Gask, and Cameron had to come down to help, and the burn was really high and it poured the whole time. It was fun though.'

Louise could imagine Abby enjoying the chance to down domestic tools for such a fine piece of entertainment. 'This big house where Cameron works, where is that?'

'Just above us. Fallan.' Abby sounded surprised.

'I thought we were at Fallan.'

'Where we are was once the old farmhouse or something.' Abby always sounded vague when it came to facts.

'So why does Cameron have his elevenses in our kitchen?'

'He likes to.' What odd questions Louise asked.

'Ah. And what or where is Gask?'

'You must have seen that as you came up. You couldn't have missed it. That huge white castle. It was bought a couple of years ago by a Danish billionaire who makes some kind of cardboard box, can't remember what, though Geordie told me all about them and they've been madly successful. Worldwide,' Abby added, as though recalling the term would substantiate her story. 'You can build filing systems with them, archives, that was it. What are archives? They sound incredibly boring.'

'Who is Geordie?'

'Geordie?' Abby's voice went up and then became elaborately casual. 'He's no one in particular. Just one of the glen men. Thinks he's God's gift and all that. He works at the sawmill on Gask.'

And was someone in particular. But Louise asked no more.

They were on their way to stock up with elementary items at the village shop. There had been no need for Abby to come but as she evidently expected to, and was unlikely to do much that was useful if left behind, Louise hadn't argued. And any shreds of information which could be extracted from her were better than nothing, though her starting point seemed to be that everyone would naturally know more about everything than she did, and her notions of what a new arrival might need to know had not been honed by repetition.

The village was larger than Louise had realised, swollen by a spread of darkly creosoted holiday chalets shadowed by well-grown conifers, which successfully concealed them but created a gloomy environment that made her shudder. It seemed they were regularly used, however; some, privately owned, as weekend retreats. Their presence had kept the tiny store and post office open, supported as well by the work now available on Gask, where streams of money were being poured into fencing, repairing dry-stane dykes, tree-planting, experiments with rare breeds, the sawmill, cottages and other estate buildings. Though the children still had to go thirteen miles lower down the glen to school, though the church was abandoned and many houses long past repair, the injection of new wealth was enough to keep the small community alive.

Louise received no clear picture from Abby on the subject, but gradually pieced it together during her time at Fallan.

She learned more about Abby as they mucked out the staff sitting-room.

'It is a bit of a mess,' Abby conceded. 'I've been meaning to tidy it up for ages.'

'Good, then you won't mind getting stuck in now,' said Louise, flapping open a binbag with a resolution that made Abby cover her eyes. 'You must be used to this — new brooms of holiday cooks raising dust.'

'Yes, well, they often begin that way. Most of them sink to my level pretty soon, I'm thankful to say, but I knew the moment I saw you that you'd stick to it,' Abby said mournfully. 'You're so *neat*.' She used the word as though it represented some not altogether desirable ideal. 'And so clean-looking. You're older than most of the others, of course. Oh, not *old*, not nearly as old as Maxine for one, but you know, older than me.'

How old did she seem to Abby? How old did she seem to herself? An interesting question. Her youth, being young, seemed decades ago, a time small and bright and faraway down the reversed telescope of time and pain. She was thirty-two, but her contemporaries seemed girls to her, belonging to a different generation. And to Abby there probably seemed as well an almost parental level of disapproval, which went with boring habits like putting things away, ironing clothes, wanting to work whether anyone was there to see or not, and respecting other people's property and privacy.

Abby had offered to show Louise round the house; another handy delaying tactic. 'We can go anywhere we like. No one minds. Well, Bella gets a bit wound up sometimes. The boys go and jump on the beds after she's made them and – oops, sorry, forgot I shouldn't say that. Anyway, I'm meant to be looking after the house, so I can go anywhere I like, can't I?'

'And I'm meant to be cooking, so there's no reason for me to go anywhere but the kitchen.'

'No, but everyone likes a little snoop around, don't they?'

'No.'

Abby sighed. 'God, you're so unbelievably moral. No one's as scrupulous as that. Anyway, you ought to look around the house, then you'll know what sort of people you're cooking for.'

'Good try, Abby,' said Louise. 'However, if you don't mind I think I'll just stick to this wing.' There would be photographs, pictures, toys, the strew of possessions which would tell too much.

'Bor-ing,' Abby sang, tilting a lager bottle to see if it had anything in it and, finding it didn't, dropping it into her rubbish bag with a careless crash.

'I'd like to explore outside, though. Would that be all right?'

'Outside?' Abby paused to peer through the window as though she had never seen what lay beyond it before. 'You can go wherever you like, I suppose. They go on a bit about lambing but I don't think that's started yet.'

'I suppose if it had there would be lambs?' Louise suggested, and thought as Abby giggled that it wasn't hard to understand what men saw in her. For apart from the fragility of her skinny limbs, and the helpless look her short-sightedness lent to the big soft-lashed eyes, she had a natural sweetness of character which was very endearing.

'So are there any tracks, or places to walk to?'

Abby sat back on her heels and put her head on one side to ponder this.

'You can go on working while you're thinking about it, you know,' Louise pointed out.

'I don't know where you could walk to,' Abby said, not moving. 'There's nothing above here, really. Just horrible heather it's impossible to plough through, and streams you're up to your knees in before you've seen them, and scary bogs that are all round you suddenly and you think you're going to sink into them without trace and no one will ever find you.'

Louise laughed. 'How long have you been here?'

'Over a year. I must be mad.'

'So why do you stay?'

'Catch a rich bloke.'

'Here?'

'You should see some of the shooting guests. And the

way the cooks carry on with them, come to that. Dear Hughie himself would even do, old as he is, if he wasn't so cross all the time.'

'Come on, Abby, why do you really stay?'

'You never know, I might get lucky,' Abby protested, then gave in with a shrug. 'It's a job, I suppose.'

And there were always the charms of Geordie? But it must be a lonely existence in term-time, especially during the winter.

'Where's your home?' Louise asked.

At this ordinary enquiry, however, Abby's face became instantly closed and mutinous. 'Nowhere,' she said, trying to ram a fat wodge of tattered magazines into the mouth of an already bulging binbag.

'Abby, what do you mean?'

'I'm one of the homeless, didn't you know?'

'But don't you have any family?'

Abby grunted, having turned her attention to trying to shift one of the heavy armchairs, which had lost two of its castors and had one leg caught in a hole in the carpet.

'Lift it.' Louise went to help her.

'You see, that's what I mean,' Abby burst out, though Louise couldn't immediately see the connection. 'Everyone else always sees what to do, and I never do. I just crash about and fall over my feet and make a complete bollocks of everything.'

'What's the matter, Abby?' Louise asked gently, abandoning the chair – and what it had concealed – and giving Abby her full attention.

'Oh, I don't know.' Abby dragged back her hair and

twisted it into a rope. 'People like you make it worse, somehow. Oh, God, that's an awful thing to say, I didn't mean it like that. Only you're so sort of composed, so efficient without even trying. You've only got to raise a hand and it's like a magic wand bringing order.'

Louise thought her assault on the kitchen had involved a little more than waving a wand, but didn't say so. 'Let's leave this for a while and go and make tea,' (was she succumbing to Fallan ways herself?) 'and talk. It's not like you to be upset like this.' Even on so slight an acquaintance she was sure of that.

Abby's father, she learned, had spent his life working for the Foreign Office and was now an Ambassador. Abby had had a childhood of being shunted from one residence and one country and one school to another, privileged in material and cultural terms, but deprived of emotional stability, the security of a permanent base, and even a sense of family.

Louise didn't learn the whole story in this first outpouring, but in the course of other conversations discovered a sad picture of neglect and, by the sound of it, outrageous selfishness on the part of Abby's parents. There were three older sisters. 'All big achievers,' Abby said hopelessly, and could not guess the response this struck from Louise, who all her life had had her two brothers held up to her as examples of what she had so dismally failed to be, intelligent, academic, and ambitious.

'And lookers, every one,' Abby continued with a sigh. 'Not just attractive, either, they're quite bright. They learned languages properly, whereas I could gab a bit when

I was little but everything flew straight out of my head later. I was hopeless at school and everyone used to bang on about how I'd had all these advantages and should be doing brilliantly. And my sisters know about clothes and make-up and hair and all that stuff that my mother gets so excited about. And they can dance and ride and play golf – well, Blanche can, she's the one next youngest to me.'

What a daunting list, Louise thought, and what memories of long-ago struggles it brought back, but she didn't interrupt.

'Then they all *did* something with their lives. The eldest is a lawyer and says she'll be a judge in the end. I bet she will, too. The second one only got married, but she married a Danish count, so of course my mother was utterly thrilled and makes a big thing of it. And Blanche, who used to be quite good fun, looking after me when we were sent away to school and all that, she's the worst of all, because now she's going into the Foreign Office and Dad's over the moon, and all the maddening business about what I'm going to do with my life has started up again. As if they cared about me. They only want to be able to say, "And our youngest daughter is doing so well. She's a – something." If only they'd accept that I'm useless.'

Abby related this without a vestige of bitterness, which impressed and moved Louise.

'Is that why you're looking for a rich bloke?' she asked, to bring her back to happier thoughts.

'It would kill an awful lot of birds with one stone,'

Abby admitted, cheering up as Louise had hoped she would.

'I can sympathise about the brilliant sisters, you know,' she offered.

'Yeah?' Abby sounded doubtful.

'Only it's brothers in my case. Two. They make appalling amounts of money, have wives and houses my mother approves of, and – oh, well, they just do everything right.' She had come close to saying the simple words, 'and they've provided her with grandchildren,' but at the last instant they had refused to be uttered.

'I was meant to be a boy. They lost one at birth, that's why there's such a big gap between Blanche and me, and that's why they tried again. They certainly didn't want another girl, particularly so much younger than the others. But I can't see what your parents could mind about you, especially as they had two boys already. You could have any job you liked.' Abby could find a bright side when it was someone else who was miserable.

'That's nice of you, Abby, but I'm afraid I've never done much beyond keeping house and looking after an elderly aunt. This job is about my mark, I'm afraid.' Time to duck away from topics which might provoke dangerous questions. 'Now, it's about time we got back to work. And what about supper? Are you in tonight?'

'Oh, Louise, is it awful of me, but would you mind very much if I wasn't? I have to— I've got some stuff to sort out. Personal stuff.' The dimple was there, her eyes sliding away. 'I promise I'll be early tomorrow and we'll get masses done before my train. Only, I wondered, would you mind giving me a lift to Pitlochry? There are things you want to get anyway, aren't there?'

'You're going away tomorrow?' There were so many things Louise still hadn't found out. 'Oh, Abby, couldn't it be next week? I don't even know what I'm supposed to be cooking yet. I've got nowhere today.'

'But there's a party!' Abby wailed. 'I specially wanted to go to it, I haven't been to a party for ages. I know, I'll make lists for you.' She seized on this as sure to please someone as methodical as Louise.

Louise could hardly bear to contemplate what lists from Abby would be like. In any case, it was clear what was going to happen; it seemed futile to waste any more breath on discussion.

'By the way,' Abby stuck her head in at the kitchen door on her way out an hour later, 'I suppose you wouldn't think of lending me your car? No, I thought not,' as Louise opened her mouth in horror, and her laughter and the skittering of her uncoordinated feet vanished once again towards the back door.

# Chapter Nine

Abby wasn't quite as late the next morning, and came rattling down the stairs from her own room, but she was shivery and hollow-eyed and little use for anything, huddling at the table with her feet wound round her chair legs, folding her thin body round her coffee mug, for once silent. Louise, thinking she was probably wasting her time, made porridge, but Abby received it with amazed gratitude, visibly reviving as its satisfying warmth did its work.

'Um, that was good,' she exclaimed after her second plateful. Louise expected to see the replete curve of her stomach swell like a gorged puppy's. 'I wish I knew how to do old-fashioned cooking like that.'

'Add water, you mean?' Louise enquired.

'Is that what you do?' Abby was astonished.

'To the kind of oats I found in your cupboard, yes. You have to stir it as well, of course.'

'Ah, I knew there'd be a catch.'

Since there was only the morning left for them to work

together, Louise did her best to pin Abby down about a dozen things she needed to know, from what sort of things the family preferred to eat to the numbers of guests expected over Easter; from the names of suppliers to where sewing things, tools, freezer bags and marker pen might be found. Abby was little help, not only because she appeared to have had no sleep at all, but because she didn't know half the answers in the first place.

'The cooks do all that,' she would say. Or with a benevolent admiration which was no help to Louise, 'Goodness, you're keen, aren't you? No one bothers with that sort of thing as a rule.'

But who's in *charge*? Louise knew by this time there was no point in putting the question. She had assumed that the person there on a permanent basis to run the house would tell the short-term cook what was required and that, since this situation was repeated every school holiday, some sort of routine would kick in. But it was evident that Abby, under-confident and ready to be lazy at the slightest encouragement, regarded these visitants as awesome beings with skills too arcane to emulate. Each in turn had done her best, or worst, and sailed away, leaving her share of exotica on the store-room shelves.

A house like this couldn't run without some sort of management, Louise would find herself arguing, adding yet more items to a stupendous list and wondering if Abby had shown her all the available cubby holes, only to find, as in the case of the meat order, that she had not. Harassed by the yawning emptiness of the freezer, forgetting the reasonable idea that the Easter cook could do her share of filling it, Louise had totted up how much she would need to spend. The total appalled her.

'You just get it on account,' Abby said blithely, as though in this way it would cost nothing.

'I can't put charges like that on the account of someone I've never even met,' Louise protested.

'We all do. No one minds.'

'I thought Maxine minded?'

'Oh, not about real bills, she just goes on about not having invoices for things like — oh, I don't know,' casting round for an example, 'like buying the boys ice creams if we're out. Invoices for ice cream, I ask you. God, she's sad. She just likes to have something to whinge about as far as I can see. But no one could complain about the butcher, could they? I mean, what else can you do with meat but eat it?'

This was almost sensible, though it didn't allow for a level of waste which Louise hardly dared to contemplate when the Fallan kitchen was in full flow.

'Anyway, there's all that other horrible stuff, across in the garage.'

'What horrible stuff?' Louise paused with pen poised over the scribbled pages on the table.

'Dead birds. Chunks of creatures. I never look in there, it's too revolting.'

'Game?' For a girl of her upbringing Abby seemed curiously ignorant of such things. Had she really been shut away all the time in the modern equivalent of nursery and schoolroom as she liked to describe?

'I thought it was fuller than this,' Abby commented,

curving her long back over hoary bundles of uncouth shape. Perhaps it had been, Louise thought. It must be very tempting, standing out here, its contents accountable to no one. But, though it was a relief to see the extra supplies, ploughing through those icy packages — and more to the point trying to establish their age — meant another huge job and Louise's heart sank. A job she would do alone, presumably, for when would Abby reappear?

They left for Pitlochry immediately after lunch, so that Abby could introduce Louise in the shops which Fallan patronised. It had been Louise's idea.

'I can't just go into places where they've never seen me before and order pounds-worth of goods.'

'Of course you can. Just say it's for Fallan.'

Louise thought this, like the half-empty freezer outside, would bear investigation, but reminded herself that she couldn't interfere in areas which did not concern her. Nevertheless she had insisted on Abby accompanying her, ignoring her exaggerated sighs.

It was quite sad to put her on the train, with her plastic carrier luggage (one bag splitting), the immensely long woollen scarf which the moths had been at catching in the door, and as Louise went out to the car she knew that she was going to miss her.

There was a timeless sameness about the days while Abby was away. It was odd to be alone in someone else's house, a stranger's house. Sometimes it seemed to Louise that the silence created its own sounds, as pausing to listen intently one can hear the pulsing of one's blood. Running feet, slamming doors, calling voices, squabbles and laughter; fragmentary glimpses of faces round a table, presences on the stairs; and behind all this the image of the bleak warren of neglected rooms above.

Sometimes, preparing some expensive dish and going to look for a freezer-proof casserole for it among the china and glass stored in the tall cupboards of the pantry which divided kitchen from dining-room, she would feel real anger at the contrast between how Hugh Erskine lived and how he allowed his children to live. What sort of man was he, so obviously rich, so indifferent and so selfish? Ultimately it was down to him and no one else to get a grip of this disorganised household and make it work. From what she had learned he was a highly successful man, heading a vast organisation which operated mines of one kind or another throughout the world. Was it beyond him to find some effective way of running his family?

But it was nothing to do with her. That was the hardest thing to get used to. Since it went against her nature to accept dirt and chaos, she had launched without hesitation into the task of dealing with them, but in two weeks' time she would be gone, like the other cooks before her, and back would wash the easy squalor, the careless extravagance of those who didn't have to foot the bill. There would be no trace left of her. How absurd, then, to care about the mess, more especially to care about these children she would never see. For that was the root of it; she wanted to mend and fix, clean and alter, to establish warmth and colour and comfort for them.

These things were not wanted. That was what she had

to fix in her mind. People lived the way they chose to live. There was no yardstick of right or wrong.

By the evening of the first day alone, for as it was Sunday Lennie and Cameron had not appeared, and she had still not so much as glimpsed Bella, this looming of the house behind her thoughts had become intrusive, so that she caught herself listening too tensely, too aware of empty rooms and corridors and the unknown wing at the other end of the building.

As the hour had gone forward ('That's not fair! I shall *lose* an hour of my holiday!' Abby had cried when she had finally worked it out) the afternoon was longer, and as at this latitude at this time of year the light in any case increased each evening at almost visible speed, Louise decided it was time to do some exploring.

She had worked hard all day and felt happier. In fact, with the job fairly begun, she had swung from panicked conviction that she would never get through half of it, to wondering if it would take two weeks. In this satisfactory frame of mind it was a pleasure to put on the boots she hadn't taken out of the car till now, and head a little self-consciously for the hill gate at the back of the steading yard.

There is a special delight in the first long evening of spring, a quality in the light which seems subtly different from that of the previous evening, producing a surge of optimism and wellbeing. There was too, for Louise, an almost forgotten pleasure in walking like this straight out of a house into open landscape, and a landscape of such beauty. There were sheep away to her right – ewes shortly to have their lambs? She hesitated for a moment, but they were taking no notice of her, so she went on, keeping to the dry-stane dyke which, as she had seen from her window, climbed ruler-straight to the skyline.

Coming out onto a level stretch of heather she turned to lean against the dyke before looking for a way over it, and caught her breath at what she saw. With a few minutes of effort the glen had opened out below her. Beyond the dark blur of the trees at its mouth she caught the sheen of water, and above it, floating and insubstantial in the evening light, the dramatic cone of some high peak she couldn't name.

Exhilarated, wondering why she had left it so long to come out here, she turned to look towards the head of the glen, and was startled to see below her a large gaunt house. It could not have been in greater contrast to the white-harled, creeper-clad, sheltered house she had come from. Built uncompromisingly of granite, it faced out from the bare hill with a dour lack of adornment, its buildings separate from it, a grey huddle in the dip where the burn tipped down. Below them again Louise saw a big walled garden, and realised that two people were busy there. Though they were too far away to distinguish much about them, she became riveted by what they were doing.

A white-haired old man was halfway up a tree wielding a saw. Below him, face upturned in spite of the showers of twigs falling on it, a stout woman stood. As the man sawed and wrenched at each branch, and Louise caught the echoes of vigorous oaths even from where she was, he threw it down to the obedient figure below, who grabbed it and waddled off to stack it on a pile presumably intended for burning. For some reason, haste seemed of the essence, and since she wasn't keeping pace with him the old man in the tree began hurling branches at her, felling her at the third or fourth attempt.

With a gasp of protest, but amused in spite of herself, Louise watched as the woman struggled to her feet, another branch descending on her as she floundered. The sounds of wrath from the tree swelled.

Who on earth were they? The gardener and his wife? The owners of the house? It seemed a violent form of entertainment for a Sunday evening, whoever they were, and Louise watched for a few moments longer, half expecting she might have to go to the rescue of one or other, catching faint but peremptory orders and fainter cries of pain.

Turning away eventually, deciding it would be discreet not to cross the dyke on this occasion, Louise turned her back on the ridges to the north, cold against a cold sky, and walked down the gradual descent of turf below the heather. Peewits and oystercatchers called over the narrow strip of ploughed fields beside the road, and there was no one to tell her they had just returned to their summer haunts.

As she walked, feeling a bite in the air which said winter hadn't entirely gone, her mind turned back to the busy pair in the garden. At first she was amused, then without warning she was seized by a piercing loneliness. There would never be time, in these short-lived jobs, to make contact with people, to penetrate even slightly into the life of a place. The long-drawn-out calls of the birds, the toneless light on the hills, the shadows gathering in the gut of the glen, seemed now unbearably melancholy, even the sprinkling of lights offering no comfort, and she was glad to hurry down a muddy track which brought her out onto the road.

She tried to comfort herself by having for supper one of the trawler pies she had made that afternoon, enjoying its rich sauce and golden-brown top, and following it with blueberry tart and cream, for the garage freezer had yielded up more than game. Then there would have been nothing for it but to read or accept whatever ITV offered, since it was the only channel which didn't produce a double image, if she had not been rescued by a phone call from Cass.

'How are you getting on? Is it all frightful?'

The breezy tone put everything into perspective. The sort of 'frightful' Cass meant could be happily joked about, though Louise was interested to realise, thinking it over afterwards by the sitting-room fire, that she had not wanted to be too swingeingly critical. Protective of Abby? Yes, that was part of it, but she also knew that the things she minded about here were too nebulous, too deeply felt, to be put into words even to someone as kind and sympathetic as Cass. They were part not only of being here, but of a painful emergence from the dark places where she had been hiding for too long.

On Monday morning, cooking absorbedly, she was surprised nearly out of her wits by a hoarse whisper behind her.

'My man said he doubted you'd get this place sorted, and I'm thinking he was right.'

'My God,' Louise exclaimed, getting her breath back and putting the newly sharpened knife she'd been trimming meat with at a safe distance, though it was a bit late now. 'I didn't hear you come in.'

So this was the dusting Bella, a shrunken little woman with madly permed hair, wearing scarlet jersey trousers with a stitched seam down the front, and a quilted jacket with kapok straggling out of its rents.

'I'm Louise. And you are – Bella? Mrs Soutar?'

The woman nodded, compressing her lips, then volunteered, 'I don't wear my teeth in the forenoon.'

This Louise correctly took as notice that there would be no conversation.

'Would you like some tea?' she asked, deeply uncertain of the etiquette but wishing to be friendly. She was rewarded by an offended shake of the head. Bella then pointedly selected various cloths from the newly washed contents of the duster drawer, gave Louise a challenging look and scuffed away as soundlessly as she had come.

Oh, lord, I've washed her dusters, Louise exclaimed to herself with delighted horror. Outrageous, unthinkable! But though she giggled, she still thought it would have been nice to have had someone to chat to. Lennie and Cameron would presumably be in soon, however, and she supposed today she would have to make the tea. Perhaps Bella would appear with them, and had merely been affronted at tea being offered at the wrong time. But she remained absent; the dusters were never seen again.

Alone with the men, who behaved quite normally without Abby present, Louise took the chance to say there were one or two things which needed mending, but before she could ask Lennie to look at them he rapped out, 'You're no' touching ma tools and that's flat.'

Louise sighed inwardly at the laborious route that had to be followed to get the simplest thing done. Lennie was the handyman, as far as she knew. However when he had agreed to have a look, 'just a look, mind,' after a little hackle-smoothing on Louise's part, and had even let her accompany him to his workshop to locate a fitting she couldn't describe, she fully understood his reaction. In gleaming order ranged his tools; every nut, bolt, screw, hook, nail and staple was in its appointed box. Coils of wire, lengths of flex and pieces of leather, twine and cable, beading and copper sheeting were carefully hoarded. So one corner of Fallan was efficient, Louise thought, warming to the dour elderly man and sympathising with his contempt for the flighty birds of passage he was obliged to watch squandering and laying waste.

All the same, there was no getting close to him, and if Bella came and went in the days that followed Louise never saw her. Used as she believed she had become, in the weeks after Aunt Bea's death, to being alone, it was less easy to accept now that her life had been jolted out of its familiar pattern. She had prepared herself for new contacts, new experiences, and although she had plenty to do she was conscious of the slow crawl of time in those solitary days, when her chief pleasure was gradually lengthening walks in a landscape that filled her with increasing delight.

It was a lovely surprise when, days before she had expected her, Abby, looking amazingly fit and rested, came sidling and grinning round the kitchen door.

'Abby! How marvellous to see you!'

Abby looked pleased at this welcome. 'Wow, you've been busy,' she said, looking around her. 'Any grub going at the minute? I'm starving.'

As Louise began making bacon rolls she asked, 'How did you get here? I could have fetched you.'

'Got a lift with the plumber. On his way to the big house.'

'I've seen that now. It looks terribly grim. Oh, and there were two elderly people in the garden one evening, pruning a tree and fighting. I wondered who—'

'Yes, potty old pair,' Abby agreed, 'but listen, wait till you hear what I did in Edinburgh . . .'

# Chapter Ten

Although Abby did her best to paint a lurid picture of her activities, it seemed to Louise that she had had a remarkably wholesome time in Edinburgh. She had stayed with a school chum whose father lectured at Heriot Watt, and rather than a wild defiant fling there was an impression of a decorous visit to a civilised household, the theatre and a family dinner party accounting for two evenings. It was evident that Abby had had more sleep than she managed at Fallan, and the highlight of the brief holiday, rather than diving into the realms of *Trainspotting*, had been ransacking the charity shops for sixties gear. Abby had solved the problem of carrying the loot home by ditching everything she had taken with her, except for her scarf, which she said she slept in (when alone, presumably) and couldn't live without.

It was fun to have her back, though her function at Fallan still remained something of a mystery, and she did little beyond recover from one evening in the village pub in time to take herself off for the next. Louise gathered at any rate that they began in the pub, though she was learning they could end up anywhere.

'I wish I was more faithful,' Abby would moan, hooped over the table at lunch-time, never having made it to breakfast. 'I do mean to be, I make an absolutely iron resolution every time I go out, but people are so *nice* to me. I wish they wouldn't be. Geordie gets so wild, and now he says he's forgiven me for the very last time.'

'But if you're so fond of Geordie why don't you stick to him? It sounds as though he's been willing to put up with a lot from you.'

'Oh, he has, he's wonderful, but then you see, it's so difficult, with Easter coming up.'

'What does Easter have to do with it?' Because Abby would have to stay in in the evening? It was hard to imagine.

'All the gorgeous rich blokes. I told you. I mustn't neglect my life's ambition, I have this duty to check out the scene. Just think, my parents would approve of me at last, remember who I am even. My sisters would speak to me again, mixed blessing as that would be, and I'd never have to wash a dish or make a bed again—'

'You seem to have that part sussed out already.'

'Louise, how can you be so cruel? I know I cleared the table yesterday – or was it the day before?'

'You can't catch men just by planning it.' And Louise wondered, with affectionate compassion, what rich young man would spare a second look for this coltish scarecrow, sexy, generous and sweet-natured as she might be. A good wash might help.

Louise enjoyed the next few days. Even though she was usually alone in the evenings, Abby's return changed the mood of the house, silencing its disquieting echoes. A pleasant feeling of familiarity was by now overtaking its strangeness, based partly on having got through to the bottom layer of domestic muddle and knowing what stores were on hand, where everything was kept, and that nothing capable of endangering life remained. Even Abby, prodigal as she was with her employer's resources, had been awed at what had gone into the bin.

'Wasn't some of that quite posh stuff?'

'Yes, and very little of it belonged in the last decade,' Louise had retorted, and Abby had grinned and asked no more.

Though Bella remained elusive, toothless and therefore incommunicado, Cameron and even Lennie had thawed and were ready to accept Louise as more than yet another feckless and faceless passer-by.

'Aye, you've done a good job here,' they would say, reaching for another chocolate brownie.

There was more time to enjoy her surroundings and, sure now that she would be able to fulfil her commitment, Louise forgot about ordering her days by the clock. She liked being able to seize a gap between showers on a rainy day to go and walk without feeling guilty, or to make marmalade all one evening because bags of Seville oranges were taking up space in the outside freezer. There were days off too. She had almost forgotten about those.

'You must take your proper time off,' Abby urged. 'You're not doing anyone a favour if you don't. No one cares, anyway.' A favourite theme song, though Louise couldn't entirely believe it.

Her contract stipulated two free days a week in assignments which didn't involve caring, and feeling more carefree than she had for a long time she seized the chance to make expeditions round the big lochs reaching westward, and up into quiet glens. Although here everything was at least three weeks behind Stirling, every day there were new signs of spring, and responding with pleasure to the wide and empty beauty of this landscape she would feel excitement stir at the prospect of discovering other unknown places, meeting unknown people. But there would also be the wrench of leaving places she liked, for already she knew it would be hard to say goodbye to Abby and Fallan.

It was this thought that persuaded her to give in to pressure from Abby to go down to the pub with her, though she did enquire, 'Does the fact that it's pouring have anything to do with the pressing nature of the invitation? I thought you were being suspiciously helpful.'

Abby was making the coffee as her contribution to a supper of salmon fish-cakes (which she had first childishly turned up her nose at, then devoured with uninhibited greed once she had tried them), followed by baked apples oozing sultanas, cinnamon and golden swirls of syrupy juice through slathers of cream.

'I thought you might enjoy it.' Abby did her best to sound affronted, but her dimple betrayed her. 'Bella won't let Lennie out again this week, and Cameron's after some bird over in Glen Ellig, daft git.'

'I'd like to come,' Louise said, and Abby, turning in astonishment, spread a gritty swathe of coffee grounds over worktop, draining board and floor.

Louise did wonder what had possessed her as she negotiated the gleaming switchbacks above the roaring burn, wipers on fast – and she also wondered if they would ever get back as water washed over the road in a couple of places. But she was agreeably surprised to find, when she raced through the rain and into the bar on Abby's heels, that the awkwardness she had expected to feel didn't trouble her. It was not merely that the scene itself was unthreatening, though heads turned and eyes took her in with unabashed scrutiny, but that without noticing, without trying, she seemed to have achieved some new level of confidence. Whatever these people thought about her didn't matter; she didn't have to win their respect or convince them of her worth. She could be herself. For the first time she was accountable to no one. This thought, and the novelty of doing something so outside the pattern of her normal life, was oddly fortifying.

She scarcely knew what to order though. About to say, 'Whatever Abby's having,' she hastily changed her mind when she found it was beer.

Though the introductions mostly passed her by, she was sure the name Geordie had not figured in them, but apart from that minor disappointment she let herself go with the flow. When it occurred to her after some time that it must be her round, she handed a twenty-pound note to a man across the table and he obligingly went off and spent it for her. That solved that problem.

She was briefly chatted up — she supposed it could be called that — by a couple of the younger men, both heavy on arrogance and light on conversation. They put out an undisguised message that these were routine approaches with one end in view, and they soon gave up. After a peaceful interlude of simply being present, the half-comprehended gossip and jokes lapping round her, she found the man who had bought her round beside her, a solid quiet man, perhaps in his late forties, with a clean-shaven, strong-jawed face and humorous deep-set eyes. He told her that his name was Fraser Kerr and that he ran the sawmill on Gask.

'Doesn't Geordie work there?' she asked.

'Geordie Macduff? He does.'

'Is he here tonight?'

Fraser nodded towards the bar. 'Aye, daft lad, he's over there, wearing his heart on his sleeve for the corbies to peck at.'

Louise, savouring the phrase but finding it sad (the throat-catching white wine was having its effect), saw a thickset, sandy-haired young man, his square, candid face too openly revealing his misery as he hungrily watched Abby at the centre of the noisy group.

'Ach, there's no talking sense to him. He's his own worst enemy,' Fraser said, but his voice was tolerant.

'I think Abby's fond of him,' Louise hazarded.

Fraser gave a resigned chuck of his head. 'I'd agree with you there. But she'll mebbe need someone to give her a good skelping before she comes round to seeing it.'

He stayed at Louise's side all evening, a lift of his chin to the barman producing drinks when he wanted them. He talked quietly to Louise when the spirit moved him, between bouts of the kind of music she normally avoided, and she found to her surprise that she was content. Fraser told her he had lived in the glen all his life with one brief exile in Aberfyle which he had hated.

'I'm not one for the towns,' he said, and Louise thought of the tiny place and relished the words.

'No doubt you'll be fleeing away like all the rest?' he enquired as drinking-up time finally expired. 'What is it about yon place that drives you lasses away?'

'I like being at Fallan.' Louise found she had scarcely known how true that was till she said it. 'But I'm only filling in for the cook who's due at Easter.'

'And you'll not be back?'

'No, I won't be back.' The words made her feel un-expectedly forlorn, a reaction she put down to having drunk far more than she was used to.

'Aye, well, more's the pity. They're sadly needing someone like yourself to take the place in hand. Not like that flighty wee besom,' he added, fixing Abby, at last in a huddle with the long-suffering Geordie, with a sardonic eye. 'There's the little lads running wild, up to all sorts, and as for Emily, I'd not like to be in her father's shoes for the next few years. He'll not have his troubles far to seek with that one.'

He spoke with genuine concern, and for a moment Louise was tempted to ask more about the Erskines and their strange, untenanted, unloved home, but the old fears flurried up and she said nothing.

'I'll mebbe see you again before you go,' Fraser said, giving her a direct look under the glare of the outside light as everyone spilled out into the rain, turning up collars, making a run for vans and jeeps and pick-ups.

'I'd like that,' Louise said, and meant it.

Driving home alone which, in view of the oblivious clinch Abby and Geordie had got into, was no surprise, she tried to analyse her pleasure in the evening. More than pleasure, there was a sense of quiet achievement. She had done what other people did – gone to a pub, breathed in the odours of whisky, damp tweed, woodsmoke, crisps, cigarette smoke, men, wet boots, wool and lavatory freshener; she had sat on a seat covered in maroon plastic, her ears assailed by the sounds of nailed boots, scraping chairs, roars of laughter, arguments, the screech of unoiled hinges, the plunk of darts and blasts of music; and she had talked, liking the bulk and maleness of him, to a kindly stranger who had made it plain that he enjoyed her company.

It had a significance for her she knew no one would understand. Doors opening. Her mind moved forward. The uncertainty Nevil had aroused about what would be done with Beatrice's belongings would have to be faced without delay. As soon as she got home she would not only talk to Nevil again, on her terms this time, but also, since he as a beneficiary was not handling the will, she would make an appointment with the solicitor who was. To cope with the nomadic existence which seemed to be taking shape, her background situation must be clearly defined.

'Oh, my God, no, I'm out of here!'

Abby swung from the kitchen window, caught a wire rack of scones with her cuff, scattered them far and wide but didn't halt. 'Sorry, but if I get caught I'll never get away. Freedom's over. Pretend I was out, do whatever you think for dinner.' And pausing only to kick off the down-at-heel pumps she slopped round in indoors, she fled noiselessly down the kitchen corridor.

'But who — what — ? Abby, come back!'

Panic jolting her, Louise went to the window. The wall was so thick she could only see the tail-end of what looked like a very smart car indeed, which had whispered unheard up the drive and was now at the front door.

The children? Her heart slamming, Louise turned with the undirected movements of panic, almost ready to follow Abby, then with a fierce effort summoned control. If the worst had happened then it had happened. She was leaving in the morning; she could bear anything, surely, for one night. Then other questions flocked up — should someone go to the door to welcome the arrivals? Abby's role, surely, not the cook's? Yet it seemed cold and unnatural to stay in the kitchen. Who had brought the children? Their mother? Friends? Whoever they were, they should be welcomed. Irresolute, furious with Abby for abandoning her, Louise released a long 'O-o-o-oh!' of exasperation.

A decisive step sounded in the corridor and a man

appeared in the doorway. Though of medium height and build, his personality made such an impact that most people thought of Hugh Erskine as a bigger man. His thick darkish hair was already grey at the temples, though Louise thought he couldn't be more than forty, and a pair of intolerant eyes examined her under lowering brows, presumably not impressed to find her standing doing nothing in the middle of his kitchen.

'And you are——?'

Not a warm greeting.

'Your cook, I imagine,' Louise said, in a tone deliberately more courteous than his. 'Louise Donaldson.'

'Ah.'

Cooks in this house, as Louise was getting tired of finding, did not rate.

'And Abby has fled the camp?'

Not a man who would miss much. His whole appearance spelled competence, success, power. He was wearing a grey suit which fitted with the smooth carelessness of superb quality, and in spite of having, Louise supposed, just flown in from somewhere, his shirt still looked immaculate. Even after so short a time in the glen she was struck by the incongruity of what he was wearing, though she decided in the same moment that he was a man who would make his own rules in this as in everything else.

She didn't answer his question about Abby, and he gave her a shrewd look as he enquired, 'I take it you will be able to manage dinner for one, even at this short notice?'

Not a man who would apologise for demanding dinner with no warning in his own house. If he had said 'produce', rather than 'manage', would he have sounded less challenging, Louise wondered? But stronger than dislike of his tone, more important than the swift mental check on the options for feeding him, she was conscious of a weakening relief. He had not brought the children; behind him the house waited undisturbed. However brusque and unfriendly he was, he would spend his evening at the other end of it, and tomorrow she would drive away.

Having reassured herself of this, her irrepressible instinct to look after people immediately got in the way. Was his room ready, should she light the fire in the drawing-room, was there a drinks tray or cupboard furnished with all he would need? She squashed down these questions, though it went against the grain to do so. Presumably the house was geared to his unannounced arrival. That was where Bella came in.

'What time do you like to have dinner?' Louise asked, and meeting his cold stare knew he understood the message she was sending him by refusing to be ruffled.

'Would eight give you enough time?' Not patronising now.

'Quite enough, thank you.'

'Good.' He turned on his heel and was gone.

# Chapter Eleven

Abby was down before Louise in the morning, her hair, which looked like silk after being washed and like dirty string two days later, still wet, her shirt clean but unironed. She was three-quarters awake, busy and penitent.

'Sorry about sliding off like that last night. I hope everything was OK?'

'You'd better ask your boss,' Louise said, looking with interest into a pan of hot water where Abby was attempting to unlock some kippers from their frozen embrace, and deciding it was nothing to do with her.

'I meant to leave you a note to say not to worry about doing breakfast, only I forgot,' Abby told her, evidently believing this would please. 'After all, you've finished working here really, haven't you, so you needn't have bothered to get up at all.'

'What a good thing I'm not keen about having a long lie,' Louise commented. She had grown used to dragging herself out early, knowing that Beatrice woke at excruciating times and found the wait for morning to arrive the worst part of the whole twenty-four hours. Then it had become a habit. Besides, it had not occurred to Louise that Abby would think of appearing.

'These are getting kind of blurred and pale,' Abby said, peering anxiously at the kippers. 'Do you think they'll be all right?'

'No,' said Louise, without moving.

'Oh, don't be mean!' Instant wail. 'You know I don't know about things like kippers. I just thought it would be sort of – well, you know, making an effort.'

'A propitiatory gesture?' To her, Louise wondered, or to the master of the house, whose arrival had startlingly altered its atmosphere of marking time.

'Probably. Whatever it means. Oh, God, look, now they're falling apart.'

'Make pâté of them,' suggested Louise, going to lift the pan off the heat.

'What an appalling idea,' Abby said, taking it from her and dumping the contents, without draining off the liquid, into the pedal bin.

'That's nice,' Louise said equably, as steam curled from under its lid.

'Oh, fu-footle, phooey and fudge! And just look at the time. I'll never be ready. Please, please be a gem and a star and a darling and help me. Whatever else can I give him?'

'Bacon and eggs?'

'Brilliant idea.' Off charged Abby, while Louise, laughing, switched on the grill and reached for the percolator.

'Hell, I should have put the warming cupboard on in the dining-room ages ago. The best way is to bung everything into that and clear off, then you don't have to speak to him. He's not a happy man in the mornings; well, not at any time, to be honest, but mornings are the worst. Oh, and the hotplate, I shall never be ready—'

'The warming cupboard?'

'The bottom bit of that trolley in the pantry. You wheel it in by his place and leave it. He doesn't like us galloping in and out.'

Louise could imagine it. But it would have been nice to have known about the practice last night. There had been many frustrating questions as she had prepared dinner, not least what sort of food Hugh Erskine liked. Then, should she call him when everything was ready or did he just come in; should she serve him; how did she guess when he had finished one course and was ready for the next; should she have done something about wine? Exasperation with Abby had filled her, and it had produced an uncharacteristic reaction. Was it part of her new mood of liberation and independence? She had decided Hugh Erskine could appear when it suited him.

It had been agreed that dinner would be ready at eight, so no reminder should be necessary. She would put the first course on the table and vanish while he ate it. A vision of herself standing meekly against the wall, hands folded across her stomach, while her employer ate his way through three silent course, had made her laugh and scattered her worries. She would guess about the timing of the next course and that would have to do.

What had become clear as the meal progressed was that whatever she did, short of tipping something into his lap, Hugh Erskine would barely notice. He was used to paying people to put food in front of him. Apart from saying he wouldn't bother with coffee, which she had already made, he hardly addressed a word to her, and in the end she had found that rather soothing, reducing the entire exchange to the practical and impersonal. After all, why should he make the effort to speak to her, a stranger he would never see again?

It made her all the more thankful to be leaving, though. Just by being here this man created a charged atmosphere, through which threaded a vague expectancy of uncomfortable things waiting to happen.

With Abby on hand to serve breakfast, even if Louise had taken over the cooking, there seemed no fear of seeing him again, and she felt distinctly uncooperative when Abby said she was wanted in the office.

'Whatever for?' she demanded indignantly, and realised she sounded just like Abby herself.

'To be paid?' Abby suggested, amused. 'Or have you been slaving and sweating all this time out of the kindness of your heart?'

'The agency posted a cheque after my last job.'

'Yes, well, there's not much point in old Hugh sending them a cheque and them sending you a cheque when you're here and he can give it to you, is there?'

'How did you become so rational all of a sudden?' Louise grumbled, but she could see there was no escape.

The office, the second door along the red corridor,

startled and repelled her. It was a high-tech modern power-base, with nothing but the view of garden and glen from its window to suggest that it belonged in this old house so full of character and, in this wing at least, of charm. A Maxine grotto, Louise decided, glad that at least she didn't have to meet her.

Hugh Erskine also surprised her. As she entered he rose from behind a desk as big as a bed, and came round it to greet her. The cheque he handed her was in an envelope, stiff, white and square.

'I wanted to thank you for all you've done here,' he said without preamble. 'You must have worked very hard indeed to reduce not only the kitchen but all the store rooms and larders to such order in so short a time, and I'm grateful to you.'

Perhaps I never got round to doing any cooking, Louise was tempted to say flippantly, caught off balance by this speech, but in the same moment the conviction came that he would know exactly how much food was now in the freezers and on his shelves.

He was wearing this morning a check shirt, a heavy green sweater with elbow patches, and moleskin breeches. She was illogically pleased, for someone invariably trim herself, to note that the latter had clearly seen much hard wear. He also had the look of a busy man who has already got through a good deal of business since getting out of bed, and she had a vision of him striding about house and garden, steading yard and buildings, brisk and alert, inspecting and checking with an unforgiving eye. It was not an attractive image, particularly as her own efforts had come under scrutiny. Yet he sounded genuinely grateful for what she had done, and in spite of herself Louise warmed to that.

'I gather from your details that you only agreed to be here until the holiday cook arrived,' Hugh was saying. 'Is there any possibility that you could be persuaded to change your mind and stay longer?'

'But the new cook is due this afternoon,' Louise said, taken aback. Of all the negative reactions which flew up at his proposal, this was the simplest to voice.

'We could probably dispense with her, if you would agree to stay.'

Dispense with her? What a heartless phrase.

'But she's probably already started out—'

'Does that mean you would consider staying? The fact that she's on her way doesn't mean we can't send her home again.'

*We?* Don't include me in such behaviour.

'That's awful!' Louise protested. 'It's unethical and unfair, a truly dreadful way to treat someone.'

'This particular someone has already let us down, if you recall.'

'Let you down? You make it sound deliberate. Didn't she have some family crisis which meant she couldn't come on the agreed date?'

'She didn't do what she was engaged to do,' Hugh said impatiently, turning away. 'Though I suppose I can be grateful to her in that you came in her place. However, if you don't agree to my proposal—'

Smooth dismissal, leaving so many hot retorts on

Louise's lips that, finding herself out in the corridor without quite knowing how she got there, she was almost provoked enough to turn round and go in again.

'Goodness, you're looking pink,' Abby observed as she came crossly into the kitchen and dropped into a chair. 'Old Hughie been lashing out the charisma?'

'He actually suggested dumping the new cook, at no notice at all, if I would stay on.' Apart from her anger, so rare for her, the thought of what else that would have meant had shaken Louise deeply.

Abby whistled. 'That's quite a compliment, coming from him.'

'You're as unscrupulous as he is! What about this poor girl and her job?'

'Oh, well, she's probably ghastly,' Abby said. 'OK, OK, I do see what you mean. Only I wish you'd stay. I hate the thought of you leaving. Why do you have to be so conscientious and *good* all the time?' She looked so dejected that Louise's wrath evaporated.

'Oh, darling Abby, I shall miss you too, you can't think how much.'

'Honestly?'

'Of course honestly. And I want you to write and let me know how you are. Not too much unexpurgated detail, just the respectable parts.'

'Of course I will. Well, when I can find a pen that works. You know what this place is like.'

They laughed, but up in the room she had grown so fond of, packing the last of her belongings, the words came back to Louise and she considered them with a rueful honesty. In cold truth she had achieved nothing here beyond filling a few cubic feet with offerings which in a couple of weeks' time would have been consumed. She felt sad for a moment, needing to hold onto some kind of permanence, hating being uprooted, dogged by a sense of unfinished business. She wished she had done more while she was here, been more receptive, got to know people better, reached beneath the skin of the place.

She was still thinking of this as she went out with Abby to the car.

'I'm glad you made me go down to the pub with you,' she said. 'Otherwise I really would have felt I'd lived on the surface of things while I was here. I suppose the neighbours are too used to all the comings and goings to take any notice of them, but it would have been nice if they'd been friendly.'

'What neighbours?' Abby looked puzzled.

'Abby, I know you don't walk an inch that you don't have to, and look neither to right nor left in your pursuit of men and alcohol, but even you must remember there's another inhabited house just up the hill.'

'Well, they're not exactly neighbours, are they?'

'What would you call them then?'

'Family. That's the big house, our big house. It belongs to Hugh's father.'

'The children's grandfather?' It struck Louise even as she spoke that the way she phrased the question was telling, revealing where, always, the focus of her thoughts lay.

'Yep, and his dotty old second wife, Gloria. Picked her up in a brothel, or something.'

'Abby!'

''Strue. Everybody knows. Hugh can't stand her, and the children aren't supposed to go near her, and nor is anyone else from here, come to that. So his father, who's got an even worse temper than he has, won't speak to him, and so it goes on.'

'But how sad and horrible. And why didn't you tell me it was the grandparents who lived there?'

'Didn't I?' Abby couldn't see that it mattered.

'But I asked you, after that evening when I first went out walking. I said I'd seen an old couple in the garden.'

'Well, I thought you knew who they were.'

'How could I know?' But the familiar feeling of struggling through a quicksand, which attempting to establish facts with Abby could produce, made Louise abandon the point in despair.

'Anyway, too late to get in a tizz about it now,' Abby pointed out cheerfully, and Louise was laughing as she gave her a last hug, wanting to say all the looking-after things which Abby drew from one. Make sure you eat properly, make sure you get enough sleep, don't stand out here in that thin shirt . . .

Was this jumble of feelings — a sharper sense of uprooting than there had any right to be after so short a time, the satisfaction of having achieved what she came here to do, mingled with a sense of incompleteness — to be repeated as each future job ended? Could she stand the emotional wear and tear?

Winding down the narrow road, the far view of the loch opening before her, passing through the village with a wave at one or two faces she knew, glancing across at the sheds and logpiles of the sawmill, what engaged her attention was this surprising new information. It seemed to add yet another touch to the desolate mood of Fallan; feuds, strife, family members so near and yet cut off from each other, the children deprived of one more 'normal' relationship.

She found, however, turning east along the busier loch road, that hard as it was to shake off these images, she was glad she had come, and after an interval in the comfort of home she knew she would be ready to set forth again wherever Cass elected to send her.

One more thing occurred that day which rattled her. On opening the cheque from Hugh Erskine she found he had bumped up the figure due by an arresting amount. Her first reaction was to send the cheque back, but he had included a note: 'Please accept this in thanks for all you have done. I am much indebted to you,' and she knew the demands of good manners would make such a satisfying gesture impossible.

# Chapter Twelve

When the phone rang Louise was so confident it would be Cass with her new assignment that she went to answer it with eager pleasure. Nevil's thin voice was a shock, bringing back guilt that as yet she had done nothing about establishing her precise legal position.

'How fortunate to find you there,' Nevil said with the cold sarcasm he used when someone was inconveniencing him, 'as it is now a matter of some urgency to arrange for the contents of the house to be valued.'

'The paintings and the books?' Louise felt hustled and threatened at once. 'Any time would be con—'

'Everything must be valued,' Nevil interrupted impatiently. 'Surely you had understood that. Shall we say this Thursday? You will be available then?'

'Of course.' Everything? Why must everything be valued? Was it all to be taken away? Louise felt panic rise. Nevil must be in some way manipulating the law; he couldn't do this. Clutching at common sense she sought some form of protest which at the same time would not make it seem that she had expected too much. I had understood Beatrice was to leave me all she owned . . . I had believed I would receive . . . There was no way of putting it which did not sound grasping, or worse, accusing. But she was this man's son's widow. Did not that constitute a claim? The very word was anathema. She knew she would ask for nothing, query nothing. Then a vision of the house, stripped and gutted, rose before her, bringing a sensation of rootlessness and exposure so unnerving that she could barely take in what Nevil was saying.

He had now adopted a tone of fulsome reassurance which she supposed he must employ to clients after dealing them some mortal blow. It rang exceedingly hollow to her.

'Naturally we have no intention of making changes for the time being. Although the house would produce a very considerable rent, we recognise that it is your home and that you have nowhere else to go.'

Beatrice had trusted to her wishes being understood and carried out by this man. What had she truly intended? Louise knew she would never ask.

'Then of course you have the capital sum my aunt left to you,' Nevil pursued. 'A generous legacy, if appropriately invested.' Granted, Beatrice had had the right to do as she liked with her money, but he would see to it that no other family interests were jeopardised.

How skilfully it had been done, Louise thought, turning shakily from the phone. First administer the shock of making her realise everything could be taken away, then apply the salve of assuring her nothing would change, so that she would be grateful to him. Yet around her the house already felt different, her tenure there frighteningly under threat.

She forced the thought away. In real terms nothing had altered. And she had her own strengths to call upon now, new resources in place. For a start she would ring Cass and find out if there was a job in prospect.

'Hi, nice to hear from you. I was going to phone this evening, as it happens.' Cass's friendly voice brought normality rushing back, chasing away the shadowy fears. 'A job's come up which I think would suit you. Wait a sec, I've got the info here somewhere. Yes, up near Banchory, one elderly man living alone, muscular wasting disease, carer has to go into hospital for a minor op—'

'Not actual nursing?' Louise asked quickly.

'Let's see.' Pages flicked over. 'Nurse calls in, regular visits to day-care centre. Just lifting, bathing and dressing. Could you deal with all that?'

'I think so.' There was huge relief in having the next post in sight, knowing she was needed somewhere.

'Contact's the sister, head of the local primary school, lives nearby. Short notice again, though, I'm afraid. Are you free to go at the end of the week?'

'No problem.' After Thursday.

'Am I glad I found you! Oh, and by the way, I've had a glowing report from Fallan. First coping with the dire Mrs Baines and now taming the hard-to-please Erskines. Good for you.'

'It wasn't too difficult,' Louise pointed out, though warmed by this praise. 'No one was there.'

'Well, the place itself sounded challenge enough to me. Anyway, they definitely want to use us again, so thanks for that.'

Cass's encouragement was just what Louise had needed after the exchange with Nevil, which had left her feeling her entire world could be swept away at his whim. Nothing had changed, she assured herself once more; nevertheless, open hostility leaves its mark.

Though set in rolling farmlands, Tipperhill was one of the most characterless villages Louise had ever seen. There seemed no explanation for its uniform ugliness, except perhaps that in the case of the newer houses — dark-grey harling, dark-brown paint — the local builder had followed his own fancy. The place straggled along an exposed stretch of road facing bleak uplands whose only feature was the fortress-like outcrop of Clach-na-Ben, and seemed to have little reason for existing.

Terence Smollett's house, with the bare look lent by metal window frames and a roof with no eaves, rose from a lumpy lawn where a few daffodils brightened the straggly snowberry which edged it. Inside was a barrenness of cut moquette and spider plants. The television was on.

Miss Smollett was there to greet Louise, an overpowering woman of slithery bulk, faintly perspiring and faintly out of breath. The latter did not prevent her from expressing firm views on every subject, though in time Louise learned they were based on nothing more than opposing whatever anyone else said. Her powers of reasoning were so limited that it was appalling to think of her having anything to do with the minds of the young.

It was not the best place to be when Louise was feeling so insecure. Though she told herself that Baines-type jobs must alternate with more attractive ones, a fear grew as the days passed that perhaps they were the norm, and the beauty of a place like Fallan, the fun of meeting someone like Abby, would not often come her way. She would have been comforted to hear a conversation between Cass and Lindsay, her assistant, as they wrestled with the jigsaw of next month's staffing.

'We must do our best to find something decent for Louise,' Cass said. 'It hurts me to waste a first-class person like her on dull jobs.'

'Most of the good ones are with families,' Lindsay pointed out. 'Louise has boxed herself in with this hang-up about children. She doesn't give us much choice.'

'Give her time. If we can lead her along gently for a while, giving her confidence a chance to grow, that will solve itself, I'm certain. Meanwhile I'm afraid she'll end up with people like the Smolletts who do sound pretty deadly. I'll ring this evening and cheer her up.'

'Can't Nina call and see if she's all right?'

Nina was one of the part-time staff employed by the agency, who worked from home to liaise with clients and staff and deal with minor local difficulties.

'Nina has no one to look after the children. She has to

take them with her,' Cass reminded her, and Lindsay raised her eyebrows significantly but said no more.

Terence Smollett was over six feet tall and had once been a heavy man. Now the skin hung from his frame and he weighed less than seven stone. Offered no encouragement, helpless under his sister's bullying, he had given up on life, and his days were spent in front of the television in deep passivity. Apart from the absence of any sign of interests or occupation in the house, Louise was repelled by its starkness in other respects. Mustard and beige predominated, geometric wallpapers made darker by brown varnished woodwork. Everything was skimpy and mean. On her cheap divan bed the sheets would barely tuck in, the pillow was foam, and the feathers of the thin eiderdown, beige with tired roses, had gone into lumps. The bathroom smelled of old face-flannels.

Louise tried to establish a rapport with Terence, but the habit of indifference was too deep. She cast around for ways to stimulate him and took trouble with his meals, only to have his sister, who found time to appear far too often, cry scathingly. 'Oh, he won't touch *that*!' or, even more infuriatingly to careful Louise, 'There's no need to go buying that sort of rubbish. It's our money you're throwing around, remember.'

Suggestions about playing cards or board games, getting talking books or finding something he could do with his hands were shrugged off by Terence or decried by Miss Smollett. That doubt again – helping or interfering? Since Louise was here for so short a time any suggestion looked like the latter, yet it was hard to do nothing.

The visiting nurse was sympathetic but not hopeful. 'It's what he needs, of course, encouragement and stimulus, but I don't think you'll get very far. The normal carer spends half her time down the village blethering in somebody's kitchen. It's not for me to say anything. His sister must know what goes on.'

At the day centre, to which Terence was taken twice a week, he sat out the time as he sat out his days at home, as, Louise saw, with a lump in her throat as she watched him, he would sit out his life. She couldn't help him, couldn't alter his condition by one iota.

The experience made a deep impression on her and she even wondered, as she drove home after two endless weeks, whether she could go on with this job. Perhaps the therapy of new scenes and experiences had already done its work. Perhaps she was more suited to the familiar and safe? There must be local jobs which would be less harrowing. But when she reached home two communications among the bills and junk mail swung her back to optimism, one a fat letter from Abby, fat not because it contained much news but because her writing took up so much space.

'Lost the add. at your job, sorry, so I'll send this to Stirling,' it began, and that took up half a page of misappropriated Fallan writing paper. Laughing but blinking away a tear, for her time at the Smolletts' had left emotions very near the surface, Louise sat down on the stairs to read it. Its mixture of immature babble about

Geordie and actionable comments on Maxine and the new cook, which tailed off as the green biro ran out and were forgotten when the letter resumed in blue felt pen (even fewer words per page), brought Abby so close that Louise felt a sharp nostalgia grip her. Fallan, common sense warned, had gained in attraction by comparison with the sterility of Tipperhill, but how good it would be to turn once more into that narrow glen with its air of secret beauty, and be welcomed by Abby with the generous affection which spilled out of this letter.

'Lennie and Cameron were asking after you,' Abby wrote. 'Sick of old dig bics, I expect. And Fraser wanted to know how you were getting on, I think you made a hit there. We had a wild time when the boys—' (words scribbled out) 'Oops, forgot!! I'm doing my best with the rich blokes, I'll keep you posted . . .'

She ended with 'I miss you!' heavily underlined. Louise knew she was clutching at the frailest straws of contact but the thought that anyone remembered her in a friendly spirit meant a lot just now. Looking through the sparse pages she was reminded of details which had at last fallen into place. Cameron had his tea-break at Fallan because, though technically employed at 'the big house', it was one unit. And 'Nether Fallan' finally made sense. It was all vividly close for a moment.

Then Louise turned to Cass's card. 'Up north for a few days. I'll phone when I get back. But for now, to reward you for sticking out grim Tipperhill, I think I have something *very nice* in store for you!'

Abby and Cass. People who belonged in her own

world. Louise gathered up the rest of the mail and her bags and went upstairs feeling brave again. Even when, sifting through the business envelopes after tea, she found a letter from Nevil detailing arrangements for the removal of 'items of value' from the house, the comfort of those contacts could not be undermined. It seemed that, each time she needed help, the next stepping-stone was in place.

'What a marvellous house!' Cass came into the big room with an eager step, her face bright with interest. Though taller than Abby, she carried her height so differently. Where Abby hung her head, veiling her face in her lank hair, shoulders drooping, Cass moved with an energetic stride and an air of happiness hard to resist.

'It was,' Louise said, intending a light rejoinder, but to her dismay her voice failed on the words.

'Louise, what's wrong?' Cass turned in concern.

Louise, fighting tears, made a brusque gesture round the ransacked room, unable to speak.

When Cass had phoned to say she was in Stirling and asked if she could call, Louise's immediate instinct had been to refuse. To let anyone come here after what had just happened, seeing this devastation, had seemed unthinkable. And there had been a flurry of panic at the thought of the two parts of her life, the old and the new, colliding. Then she had swept resistance and panic aside. This was what her home consisted of now and, of all people, Cass would make no judgements. And what else was she, Louise, attempting to do but shape one coherent life for herself?

Now, fortitude threatened by the concern in Cass's voice, that reasonableness was hard to hold onto.

'What's happened? Tell me.' Cass's voice was gentle, but her arm firm round Louise's shoulders.

'It's just that,' Louise drew an unsteady breath, 'this room didn't look like this a few hours ago.'

Cass looked about her, frowning, and saw the pale rectangles on the walls, the empty shelves of a massive bookcase. 'What's happened?' she demanded again, more sharply. Had Louise been obliged to sell things?

'Look, I'm sorry,' Louise said, 'you don't want to hear about this. You're here on business. I mustn't waste your time.'

'If it was strictly business I'd have phoned or sent you a form,' Cass pointed out. 'I came because I wanted to see you. Because I thought it would be nice for us to get to know each other better.'

Cass would never know how much that meant, coming at this moment.

'I'm not good value today,' Louise warned, but to Cass's relief her voice sounded lighter. Something very odd had obviously been going on; Louise had looked terrible when she arrived.

'Let's have tea and the story,' she suggested.

This morning the paintings, the Rockingham dinner service which Louise had never seen used, the books and ornaments, Beatrice's tall secretaire and several smaller pieces of furniture had been taken away. The property of 'the family'. But surely, Louise had thought in despair, watching the swift expert packing, the extensive scholarly library could only have been amassed by Bea herself? And of what possible value to any other Donaldson could her papers be, her commentary on the social effects of the abolition of the run-rig system, or a dissertation on the impact of Scottish-American trade on the industrialisation of Clydeside?

Louise released some of these wild, distressed questions to a quietly listening Cass. 'I feel like Ana de Mendoza when Philip of Spain made her imprisonment gradually more and more horrible,' she said, at last able to laugh a little. 'As if at any moment the bell will ring and someone will appear to whisk away the carpets and the curtains. Oh, I know I'm lucky. I can go on living here which is the important thing, but it was awful to see strangers tramping about helping themselves.'

'Ana de Mendoza? *That Lady?*' Cass pursued the point deliberately, hearing Louise's voice rise again at the memory. 'Didn't Philip wall her up in the end?'

'Yes, inch by inch he curtailed her freedom. In that respect I suppose the opposite is happening to me. Great spaces are appearing!'

Cass, registering with interest how protective Louise could make her feel, longed to question her, to establish what right the family had to remove these objects, and to find out whether Louise had taken legal advice. She guessed, rightly, that such an approach would be unthinkable to her, so instead offered the only practical comfort at her command.

'It must be desperately sad to have your aunt's things taken away like this,' she said. 'I can imagine how strange the house must feel. Would it help to go away on the job I mentioned? You might enjoy it, even though it happens to be another elderly brother-sister duo.'

As she had hoped, this drew a reaction. 'Cass, not more Smolletts? You wouldn't do that to me?'

'Quite, quite different from the Smolletts, I promise you. I know the people rather well.'

'All right, tell me, then,' Louise said in an exaggeratedly guarded tone.

'Down in Dumfriesshire, gorgeous house, every comfort. All you have to do is look after one healthy male living alone, no entertaining. He's an actor, or perhaps ex-actor, Aidan Shaw. Never heard of him? Well, he's a dear – the only trouble is he might try to grope you.'

'Livelier than poor old Terence at any rate.'

Cass laughed. Louise was going to be good value when she had put these sad times behind her.

'Not a serious or dangerous groper, he just likes females and enjoys life. He's idle and spoiled but very generous. We always supply a temp when his housekeeper is off on the amazing number of holidays he gives her, and it's a popular job.'

Louise was too new an employee to ask why in that case it was being offered to her, and Cass didn't mention the protests she had had to beat down from Lindsay. Cass was strongly drawn to Louise, horrified by the tragedy which had shattered her life. She guessed that Louise had never fully faced her loss, and could see how tempting it must have been to bury it under the demands immediately to hand, hiding away in a comfortable seclusion which kept her out of touch with the real world. For the time being, Cass felt, Louise needed all the help she could get.

'So where does the sister come in?' Louise was asking.

'She lives close by.' Cass seemed amused at some thought of her own.

'Not meddling day and night like Miss Smollett?'

'Aidan's sister is not a Miss Smollett,' Cass said definitely.

'Perhaps I can face it then. But you know,' Louise became serious again, 'even at the Smolletts', in spite of counting the days till the job was over, there was a tug at leaving, a feeling of something left unfinished.'

As there had been at Fallan. Would its memory always be tinged with the feeling that she had dodged, been a coward?

'I know,' Cass said. 'You have to learn to leave it behind though. It's part of short-term jobs. Other people's kitchen cupboards, other people's lives. A bit like nurses, the closest possible physical intimacy, then nothing.'

'It takes a little getting used to.'

Cass looked at her consideringly. Louise was going to be, already was, valuable just because she had this strong caring streak, but it brought a price with it.

'Would you consider, later, when you're more used to the system, taking on longer assignments? They might suit you better.'

'Not yet,' Louise said instantly, her eyes sweeping the big room, however bare and unfamiliar it now looked, with anxious need.

'Don't worry, we can work it out at any pace that suits

you,' Cass assured her. 'That's the beauty of it. Life is bounded by the next job, and you can't worry about the ones after it because they're unknown quantities. Now listen, are you sure you're OK, because I really ought to be going.'

'I'm fine, truly. But, Cass, you'll never know how much it's helped to have you here today.'

'Don't ever be lonely,' Cass said, gripping her arms for a moment and looking into her eyes. 'I mean it.'

Louise knew, as she closed the courtyard gate, that from regarding Cass as an employer, an arbiter in the background of her life, to be depended upon and trusted certainly but still somewhat remote, she had today become very much more. The thought gave Louise courage as she turned to face the denuded house.

# Chapter Thirteen

Kinnafoot House opened its tall wrought-iron gates and its friendly arms to welcome Louise. A first considerate touch had been that she should arrive on Tuesday to avoid the bank holiday traffic. With this kindness in her mind, the sun brightening all the way, and Cass's promises and assurances in her ears, it was a journey made in a mood of optimism. Though she was not quite ready to admit as much, it had been a relief to run down the basement stairs this morning and lock the door behind her. She had spent some time in the past few days bringing books down from her room and shifting furniture around, but nothing could fill the new emptiness of the big drawing-room, and in her heart she knew that Aunt Bea had slipped away for good. So it was with rising anticipation that she drove through the handsome gates and took the curve of the gravel circle round an emerald lawn, to pull up at the steps of a stone house of perfect proportions and an air of serene well-being.

The door stood open. Louise rang the bell and unleashed a volley of barks, overtaken by a huge voice roaring for silence. The crash of feet, as heavy and un-deviating as those of a squad on the march, could be heard approaching, but even before their owner was visible the great voice was calling, 'Is that Louise? Where are you? Don't hide out there, let's be having you!'

Having me? So soon? What would Cass say?

The doorway was filled with a giant of a man in a red shirt and heavy-duty olive cords, his smile flashing through a curly beard which, like the thick hair that flowed to meet it, was still more black than grey. Cass had been right, Louise recognised the face: Greek fisher-man, leader of a Mongol horde, Yukon fur trader, hulking support for better-known actors playing escaping POWs or commandos blowing something up — easy to picture him in these roles but had she ever known his name?

He held out a hand like a ham and Louise's disappeared into it, but his grip, which she had braced herself to find crushing, was surprisingly gentle. She could feel his kind-ness in it.

'Come in, come in!' Aidan Shaw surveyed Louise, in pink cotton trousers with a small floral top, the sun on her golden hair, with open pleasure. The pair of black Labradors grinned and wagged, jostling around them, not so much pleased to see a stranger as ready to enjoy any diversion that came their way.

'So you found us?' Aidan boomed, then gave a bark of laughter. 'Damn silly question. God knows why we ask it.

Now, the important thing –' waving her ahead of him into a square hall lit by an elegant cupola, '– is that you are to make yourself totally at home. The house is yours. Go anywhere you like, read the books, drink the booze, help yourself to anything you fancy. All right? And the next thing is, let's have tea. I'm starving. Only you're going to have to make it. I've never found the kitchen yet and don't intend to start looking for it now.'

It was an all-encompassing welcome, and Louise, dwarfed by Aidan's size and thundered over by his powerful voice, felt slightly breathless. But the way to deal with him seemed to be to go at his speed.

'Right,' she said. 'As I can't expect directions I shall go in search of it at once.'

Aidan's laugh, which was of the slow, hah-hah-hah variety, filled the hall. 'That's what I like to hear. This is where I shall be.' He headed with his earth-shaking stride towards a door on the left, but turned with a wink to indicate another door below the exquisitely turned curve of the stair.

'I think I'd worked that out, thanks,' Louise said cheerfully, already on her way, and heard the rumble of his laughter as the door swished to behind her.

The kitchen, like its owner, took her breath away. Large, light, splendidly equipped, its colours were the yellow of wild iris and a deep strong blue. It was immaculately kept and full of beautiful things — old-fashioned brass scales, a row of magnificent ashets, giant blue cast-iron casseroles she longed to fill — and on the table lay a tea-tray already prepared. By whom? It meant no hapless floundering around to find things, whoever it had been. No one, Louise guessed, touched, would ever be made to feel so little at home in this house.

'Now, when you've seen your room and settled in, wander round to your heart's content,' Aidan ordered, after posting a large tea down his gullet in the sunny drawing-room. 'Have a prowl round the house and then explore outside if you feel like it. We've waited long enough for a day as nice as this. Never been a colder April.' As Louise was to learn, he spoke in vigorous positives about everything.

'What about cooking dinner?' she asked, already at home with him.

'Oh, that would be too unkind on your first evening. No, no, all kinds of things come in packets these days, I'm led to believe. And we have a microwave oven. Can you operate one of those? A mystery to me, of course. If it proves too difficult we shall take ourselves off to the village, where there is an excellent hostelry – why am I talking like this? We'll have dinner at the pub.'

'I can probably fathom the microwave.'

'Oh, how I admire such verve and initiative.'

Louise laughed, fond of him already, enjoying the way he used his deep resonant voice, the way he set himself up, his larger-than-life warmth.

Her room was a pretty guest room at the front of the house with its own bathroom, full of expensive bath preparations, scented soap and huge fluffy towels.

'It's lovely. Thank you.' Louise's voice was unsteady as unsavoury Smollett memories swarmed back.

One of those enormous hands descended on her shoulder and gripped for a moment.

'No reason why you shouldn't be comfortable.' And away Aidan strode, demanding of the dogs at the top of his voice what they thought they were doing coming upstairs. Louise could hear them flying for their lives. Presumably they understood the game.

Was that grasp on her shoulder the run-up to a grope? Never. She was ashamed even to have asked the question. She looked around the comfortable room and felt her soul expand in gratitude.

Too shy to explore the house as instructed, Louise, after the pleasure of unpacking completely in order to take possession of her room, found her way out by a garden door. Though in front of the house there was little but curves of lawn and drive, so that the eye would not be distracted from the graceful façade of the building, at the back a beautifully kept garden descended in slow steps to a big orchard. From lawns set with beds bright with spring flowers and flowering bushes, she went down to a half-moon of granite slabs on a lower lawn dotted with larger trees, and through an arch into a walled garden. Laid out in a design as perfect as the repeated pattern of a kaleidoscope, its paths edged with trimmed box, it was a satisfying sight – not least because of the produce a cook could expect from it. Greenhouses ran along the wall to the left, beyond which appeared the roofs of other buildings.

Beginning to feel almost drugged by sun and silence and beauty, her nostrils filled with the sweetness of the appleringie she had rubbed between her fingers, Louise went on through a second arch to the orchard. Seeing the gleam of a river beyond the trees she was about to go down to it when she paused in doubt.

Half-hidden by the white blossom of a huge gean tree stood a gypsy caravan. That was the description that sprang to mind, for there was an impression of a huddle of objects forming an encampment, clothes on a washing line barely moving in the light air, and smoke going up, pale against the fresh green of the larches behind it.

About to draw back with the feeling left over from childhood that the dwellers in the van would be unfriendly, even if she didn't believe any more that they would be dangerous, and in any case not wishing to intrude, Louise checked again. There was something odd about this van.

It was nothing like the traditional caravan or its modern equivalent. It was more like a small furniture van, long past its youth, yet in its side was a window with curtains, and from its roof protruded the chimney that was producing that blue spire of lazy smoke. As Louise puzzled over the strange vehicle a woman came round the end of it and began to take the washing from the line. She was slim and straight-backed, wearing a flowing purplish skirt to her ankles, and her dark hair was tied back.

Louise stepped hastily into the archway, feeling ashamed of having watched even for those brief moments. This was someone's home. How typical of Aidan, she guessed, to give people permission to camp here.

'Gypsy woman?' Aidan's delighted bellow of laughter

brought the dogs to their feet and turned heads in the hotel bar, though to judge from the tolerant smiles its customers were well used to him. He had decided after several large gins that Louise should do no work this evening, and in spite of her protests that she had everything ready and dinner wouldn't take ten minutes he had swept her off with him. They had walked here through the village and since Aidan talked to everyone he met they had arrived as the kitchen was packing up, which Louise gathered from their reception was not unusual.

'Gypsy woman! That, I would have you know, is my sister Erica.'

Flustered, Louise reviewed her glimpse of the dark-haired woman in this new context. 'But, I thought – she looked – I mean, that van looked pretty gypsyish to me. What was she doing there?'

'She lives there. We'll go and say hello to her on the way home. She'll enjoy meeting you.'

'Isn't it rather late for calling on people?' Louise suggested, as Aidan tore himself away from his cronies a couple of hours later, showing no signs of an astonishing intake of gin, wine and brandy.

'Late? Erica never sleeps. She'll be delighted.'

But when he had led Louise into the orchard through a gate from the lane, and they were at the foot of the wooden steps, his confidence deserted him. After a trumpeting call to his sister which made the dogs bark hysterically and would have woken the most obdurate sleeper, he said, 'I won't come in with you. Old Eric has such a poor opinion of me that in her presence I bumble,

I fluff my lines, I wonder if I've scrubbed my knees. Until breakfast . . .' and with surprising smartness for a man of his build he removed himself from the scene as the top half of the van door opened.

'I'm terribly sorry,' Louise faltered, looking after Aidan with a strong desire to abandon good manners and follow him, and deciding that his breakfast would be accompanied by a few pithy observations.

'Not at all,' said a courteous voice above her, a voice whose musical depth struck Louise even in that embarrassed moment. 'Come in.'

The lower half of the door was pushed open and a rectangle of lamplight fell on the steps. At least, Louise thought, calming down, the windows had been lit as she and Aidan had approached across the dewy grass. But reason and normality were scattered once again as she stepped up into the van. Already glutted with new scenes and impressions, faces and names, for Aidan had introduced her to at least twenty people in the course of the evening, what her eyes fell on now made her feel as though she had stepped through a wardrobe.

The van, which from the outside didn't look big, contained a four-poster bed with curtains of ruby velvet, a small oak sideboard and a wood-burning stove, and was as richly draped and warmly lit as a fortune-teller's booth. Louise gasped aloud, and heard her hostess chuckle.

'Impossible not to,' the warm voice said, amused. 'When you've recovered sit here and have some coffee. I had just made a fresh pot – how very lucky.'

With a thin dark-skinned face, older than the upright

figure Louise had seen this afternoon might have indicated, hooded dark eyes and an expressive mouth ready to
curl in contempt or laughter, Erica Shaw was as colourful
as her setting. Her clothes were layered, eccentric, of worn
but beautiful fabrics.

'Are you sure it's all right to descend on you at this time
of night?' Louise asked.

'Did Aidan's flight unsettle you?' Erica took a tin from
the dresser cupboard. 'Oatcakes, cheese, or has my brother
stuffed you full? He overdoes everything. But his exit had
nothing to do with the hour. I frighten him.'

'He said something of the sort,' Louise admitted,
relaxing and letting the colour and warmth of this extraordinary place lap her round. She supposed she would be
able to get into the house, and she supposed she would
discover what to give Aidan for breakfast, where and at
what time. That could take care of itself. It was an abandonment to the moment rare for her, and she found it
delicious. So was the coffee, hot and strong. And so was
Erica's readiness to welcome her and to talk all night if
that was what they felt inclined to do. For, as with Cass,
Louise felt an unquestioning ease with her, a certainty of
communication and trust.

They talked for hours that first evening, comfortable
among the cushions of a padded seat at the foot of the
bed. Erica, as she explained, had constructed the latter *in
situ* herself. It was made of plastic, from moulds she had
taken from Elizabethan bed-posts. The dresser front was
real, the rest, shallow in depth to fit into the van, was a
mock-up. The flap which concealed the storage space, or

extra bunk, above the cab, was an old monk's bench. The pot-bellied stove, however, was exactly what it seemed, and on it Erica made coffee in a brown enamel jug.

In this first meeting they put in place only the framework of their personal histories, the conversation being less an exchange of information than the flow of one topic into another, learning each others minds if not, at this stage, each other's lives.

Erica had been a paediatrician, practising in Manchester. Retiring eight years ago, she had divested herself of a house and a lifetime's possessions, converted this van and lived in it ever since. 'Here and in a few other chosen spots,' she said.

'It's actually mobile? You can drive it?'

'Oh, certainly. That was the object. Though I confess I can't bring myself to use caravan sites. I have friends who let me park in odd corners — and plug myself in, for, as you may not realise, I do have electricity. They also let me use their bathrooms, a luxury I cling to.'

'And here? Do you use the house?'

'I never go near it. Aidan exasperates me too much with his worship of the twin gods of Gargantua and Mammon.'

Louise, putting aside the cavil that Beatrice might have disallowed Gargantua as a god, decided that not only did brother and sister share the marvellous quality of their speaking voices, but a certain extravagant turn of phrase. Crisper, perhaps, in Erica's case.

'Aidan inherited the house and a quite indecent amount of money from an aunt, threw up his career, third-rate as it unquestionably was, and has slopped around here ever since. The only acting he does now is to play himself, a part circumscribed by the limitations of his character. No, I don't use the house, but tomorrow I shall reveal to you how thoroughly I cheat.'

She walked with Louise up the long garden, in a May night which had never grown properly dark.

'Are you sure I haven't kept you up?' Louise asked. It had been hard to tear herself away.

'Kept me up? I don't much follow patterns,' Erica said, glancing at the sky which looked paler by the minute as their eyes adjusted. 'I shall walk a little now.'

I shall walk a little now. Louise repeated the phrase as she hurried into bed, her conditioned mind guilty to see that it was after two, beset in spite of herself with worries about tomorrow. There was a new kind of freedom, she suspected, to be learned here, and she savoured the thought, glancing round the room with pleasure before switching off the painted porcelain lamp with its ivory silk shade.

# Chapter Fourteen

'I believe I saw a Chinaman in your garden this morning,' Louise said composedly. A Chinese male in blue denims, working in a *jardin potager* laid out in Italianate geometric design. Why should anything at Kinnafoot surprise her after last night?

It was ten o'clock, the day was glorious, and the dining-room filled with that special mood of wellbeing which having a large, late, leisurely breakfast in a sunny room produces. Louise had woken far later than usual and had bundled out of bed in horror, but the silence of the house, the yawning, stretching welcome of the dogs from their bean-bags in the kitchen corridor, had reassured her that it wouldn't matter. She had had everything prepared and ready to cook the moment Aidan appeared, and had still had time to take the dogs out and drink in great draughts of scented air herself.

'Ah, yes, Wacker. Did you talk to him?' Aidan asked. 'No? Pity. Lovely chap. Not that he ever says much. Hails

from Liverpool. Mrs Wacker cleans. Dear little soul she
is too.' Had she set out yesterday's tea-tray? 'She and Alice
don't see eye to eye, of course. No one does with Alice, or
should that be the other way round?'

'Alice?'

'Housekeeper. Inherited her with the house. She's
about seventy-five but terrified of retiring. Says she's sure
she'll drop dead if she stops working, but the fact of the
matter is that she only has some dismal niece to live with
so I keep her on. Can't let her do too much, though, which
is why I do most of my entertaining at the pub. Sad, I
enjoy having people about. A waste of the house too.'

He sounded so wistful, as he moved on from kippers
to bacon and kidneys, fried bread and scrambled eggs, that
Louise began to turn an idea over. If Mrs Wacker – could
that possibly be her name? – did the cleaning, there
couldn't be a lot for the cook to do. Well, Cass had said
as much; it was held to be one of the attractions of the
post, though idleness never greatly appealed to Louise.
However, if breakfast routinely finished at eleven, there
wouldn't be vast spaces of day to fill.

It seemed unfair to be paid for being here, she decided,
walking to the village an hour later with a shopping basket
over her arm – a splendid, traditional basket, as all the
objects for both use and ornament in the house seemed to
be splendid and pleasing. Pathetic fallacy in full swing, she
warned herself, pausing to lean over the parapet of the
bridge to watch the river slide below, amber as a collie's
eyes in the sunlight.

But shopping at an unhurried pace, welcomed with a

friendliness she guessed would be accorded to anyone connected with Aidan, nothing could lessen the contentment which filled her. After her round-the-clock responsibility for Terence it was agreeable for once to fritter away time. Aidan had gone off somewhere for lunch, as he had told her he often did, and beyond cooking dinner for them both there was nothing in the world she had to do.

At the house Mrs Wacker, a round smiling young woman with harsh blue-black hair who turned out to be called Rosalie, had come in to 'do' Aidan's room, and Louise's too.

'Not much sense me comin' in any earlier, is there?' she said in a strong Merseyside accent, which it took a minute or two to relate to her appearance. 'Seein' as he's never up till midday. I stopped that when we first come 'ere. And never picks nothink up, just leaves it where it falls, you never saw nothink like it.'

Louise, fascinated by her, sinking willingly deeper and deeper into fantasy, tried to keep her talking, but Rosalie, like her husband, preferred to work and forged away before Louise had had anything like enough of her, her blue-jeaned bottom bobbing, her coarse hair flapping.

Louise made lunch for herself of the lemon chicken she had taken out of the freezer for last night's dinner, and a salad lent interest by the herbs Wacker — who didn't appear to have any other name — brought in for her. She allowed herself a glass of wine from the box on the larder shelf (a row of five more stood beside it for everyday consumption), chose a book from the library – oh, darling Bea, where are you? – and carried the tray out to a seat in one of the leafy enclaves of the top lawn. The birds were silent, village noises thin and unreal with distance and heat, and apart from the bees the only other sound was the voice of the river as it gurgled over miniature weirs of tumbled stones.

Nothing could be this perfect. But it was. There was no reason not to accept the moment. A sense of assuagement spread through Louise. Tomorrow it might rain, Aidan might pounce (but annoyed with herself for the cheap thought she at once rejected it), some unforeseen disaster might strike. But for now, she could soak up the sun, indulge in somnolent peace, and it felt good. *She* felt good, good about herself. She was coping. Presently, when the inclination took her, she would stir herself and see if Erica was around, awake, and prepared to reveal more of the secrets of her strange lifestyle.

Erica, still in her purple skirt, with the addition of scarred yellow wellingtons and work gloves, was clearing a corner of the orchard where elder and hogweed were out of hand and nettles a foot high among last year's pale stalks.

'How very nice to see you,' she said as Louise came down the slope.

'You look busy. I don't want to interrupt.'

'Don't be daft.' Erica pulled up her skirt and stepped with clowning strides out of the nettle patch. 'It took me five years to learn to slow down after I retired. I've mastered the trick now. I only undertake any job on the clear understanding – with myself, I mean – that I have the rest of my life to do it in.'

Once again the magic worked, as Louise felt herself drawn into the special peace Erica created, the product of good sense and a well-honed sense of proportion. Another kind of luxury, Louise was beginning to see.

'I could help,' she offered. 'I like doing things.'

'You have such a clean look about you,' Erica said regretfully. 'Those light colours. And sandals.'

'I brought boots.'

'Well, maybe later, if the spirit moves us. Thank you for offering. But meanwhile let us sit under the gean tree and look at the sky through that breath-taking tower of blossom, a magical sight which will soon be gone, and talk about ourselves.'

As before, conversation flowed. Louise still found it hard to embark on a direct narration of the tragedy that had overtaken her life, but on the other hand she felt no constraint. It was easy to draw close to memories and then let them recede once more to the dark place in her mind where they lived, without feeling the need to justify or explain. While Erica in her turn, for the first time in years, found herself talking about the frustrations of her working life, the sense which in the end had nearly overcome her of the mountain of suffering, bureaucracy and human cruelty that she, that no one, could ever move. It was not her custom to spend time talking to her brother's temporary cooks, in general a vapid and unrewarding section of humanity, and as she and Louise talked part of her mind examined with interest the empathy which had sprung up between them, in spite of the differences of age and personality.

The note from Cass had woken her curiosity first. 'I'm sending Aidan someone very special this time. Do try to get to know her a little if you can. Not exactly a lame duck, but definitely wounded.'

Then Louise had stood at the foot of the van steps, with that anxious child's face under the bright hair, basely deserted by Aidan (to whom Cass had *not* written, fearing he would be as over-protective as a Newfoundland dog who refuses to believe the person splashing in the water can swim) and Erica had felt a rare and immediate attraction stir.

It was late afternoon before they moved.

'I promised I'd show you how I cheat,' Erica said. 'Come along.'

'Do you really regard it as cheating?' Louise asked. 'Had you set out to do something specific?'

'Perhaps. Establishing values and refining them, a source of satisfaction which too many people overlook. I don't feel guilty about the refinements, that was a little mild self-mockery. They are part of me.'

Beyond the garden wall lay the farmyard. The Wackers lived in the former farmhouse — restored with mouth-watering care, Louise observed, momentarily envious — and the buildings had mostly been taken over by Erica. In two she had installed a bathroom and a small laundry, and in others she stored logs and kindling, onions, potatoes and garlic, dried herbs, apple rings and fungi, hazel and beech nuts and pine kernels. She had installed a deep-freeze, and kept her books in a set of heavy glass-fronted bookcases purloined from the house.

'Have to be mouse-proof,' she said. 'And if possible keep out the damp. I benefit from the boiler Aidan runs for heating the greenhouses. Greenhouses plural, for one person. *Such* extravagance.' That disdainful '*Such* extravagance' summed up the gulf between Aidan's view of how to enjoy life and his sister's.

Erica also brewed wine, showing off her workman-like apparatus and the long row of demijohns with pride. Louise thought of Aidan's row of cardboard boxes and was amused at the pair of them. It seemed a pity they couldn't be more friendly. Yet there was no real acrimony in their sparring; it was more like a nursery habit too enjoyable to abandon.

'So you see, I have provided myself with the comforts of home,' Erica said, closing the store room door. 'All very conventional really.'

'Not exactly,' Louise protested laughing, as they went back between the apple trees to the van.

'No.' Erica paused to look at it, an expression that was almost tender appearing for a second in her mocking face. 'The great and glorious difference is the freedom. I committed myself to a career which meant staying in one place. I love to up sticks from time to time. You can't think how good it is to drive out of the gate with my home on my back.'

Seeing Aidan's car as she went up to the house, Louise wondered if she should have been on hand to give him tea, but rolling snores from the library told her that even if he had wanted it when he came in the thought wasn't troubling him now. She would make dinner extra nice. But she knew the impulse went deeper than a guilty conscience about not giving him tea. This man poured out goodness in every direction, as far as she could see, and she wanted to pamper him a little in his turn.

'Would Alice be mortally offended to find you'd been doing some entertaining in her absence?' Louise enquired casually, when a replete Aidan, raising paeans of praise to the devilled whitebait, the escalope of pork, the brandied peaches and the snipe, had in spite of protests filled her wine glass yet again. Even he had accepted by now that he could not persuade her to port, liqueurs, brandy or malt whisky.

'Alice can be offended about anything,' he rumbled, scarcely taking in what Louise was saying. Then, waking up, 'What do you mean, entertaining?'

'Or would Mrs Wacker object to her gleaming rooms taking a mauling?'

'Be thrilled, I should think. Give her something to do that actually needed doing. But what are we talking about here?'

'Lunch in the sun? Drinks party? Dinner? Depends what you'd like.'

'Louise, my darling, darling girl! Do you mean it, would you really do it? A temporary cook who actually seeks to be busy! I must telephone Cass at once, she should hear about this. But first I must—'

He surged to his feet and snatched Louise up out of

her chair and into a whirling hug. He didn't give her time to put down her glass, and her wine splashed up in little waves. It was like being briefly glued to a tree-trunk, but not disagreeable.

The pent-up instincts of a prodigal host were joyously given rein during the rest of Louise's stay. Aidan was a man who liked to carve huge hams and roasts, slice great pies, pile plates, fill glasses. He was aching to fling open his doors and share the beauty of his house with his friends, sit laughing and gossiping for hours in the garden till the sun went down, then move indoors to a fire of birch logs, soft lights and deep chairs, letting the mood carry them through half the night – till dawn if Aidan had his way. Sometimes tears literally stood in his eyes as he thanked Louise for making all this possible, and allowing him to return the hospitality his friends were always offering him.

'Of course Alice couldn't possibly do it,' he would remind himself fairly, prowling along a laden buffet table, feasting his eyes on the joys to come. 'This is just a one-off anyway. Couldn't go on like this all the time.' But Louise could see he yearned to do just that – and surmised that his friends wouldn't object either.

She had been afraid, once she had put plans for the first lunch party in motion, of the age range the friends might span. But Aidan, a bachelor of sixty with a spinster sister even older, did not know many young couples or young families, and Louise's fears died as the eager response to invitations produced almost exclusively people of his own generation.

She enjoyed meeting them but, in contradictory fashion, as soon as she felt safe from having to deal with private traumas, she began to wonder if it was good enough to go on meeting only one section of the population. Good enough? What did she mean by that? Was she being brave enough; was that what she was asking? She didn't know, and didn't want to dig too deep for an answer, but there persisted an uncomfortable awareness that the course she had chosen was not a natural one.

Erica might have told her this unease was a symptom of recovery. For Erica knew a great deal about Louise by now. They talked at every opportunity, sitting by the fire Erica used to build outside, ladling out poacher's stew from her black round pot (Wacker much approved of her inroads among the rabbits) while the soft curtains of the dark closed round them; or clearing the orchard – unless Erica was in full swing with her chain-saw; or working in her part of the kitchen garden, though here Wacker, in despair at her tolerant views, frequently weeded surreptitiously. They walked too, often at times which seemed strange to Louise, through the shallow valley rich with the growth of early summer, or on hills gentler and greener than the steep screes and heather-clad slopes enclosing Glen Fallan.

'Am I becoming a substitute Aunt Bea?' Erica asked one day as they came down the field behind the house after one of these walks, for which she had roused Louise at dawn. Since Aidan liked to sit up till the small hours it had been an effort to turn out, but Louise was glad she had, in an early morning of thin cool air and knife-sharp shadows, of vibrant birdsong and that mood of entering a secret world which doesn't belong to man at all.

Taken aback by the bluntness of the question, she floundered. 'Do you think I'm — ? I hadn't thought of it, but I suppose — is it so obvious?'

Erica, a few paces below her, paused with her foot up the slope, her head tipped enquiringly.

'That makes you feel defensive. Why?'

'Because — well, because—' Louise found she had to take a careful look at why. 'I suppose it implies some deficiency in me, and seems an imposition on you. As though I am making an assumption that you are willing to fulfil some need in me.'

'Do you regard me in the same light as Beatrice?'

'I don't quite know.' Louise stared out across the green mass of forest which spread to the south.

Erica waited, without hurry.

'Not consciously,' Louise said at last. 'You are very different.' The thoughts dropped like pebbles. 'But yes, someone older than myself, intelligent and informed, whom I respect. Wise, I could say. And yes, which I suppose is more important than anything else, someone who has established her own way of life and shaken off subjection to other people's views.'

Louise came out of her concentration on these thoughts to find Erica's expression alert, unsmiling but satisfied.

'Yes,' was all she said.

'But do you mind?'

The smile came now, the twisted sardonic smile which Erica didn't allow herself very often.

'Delighted,' she said. 'Flattered, moreover.' And she turned and went down the hill.

Louise, smiling too, followed her.

Aidan insisted that on Louise's last evening he and she should dine tête-à-tête. 'No slaving, no hurrying about, no looking after people. Except me, of course.'

Louise was happy to agree. She had enjoyed the party cooking, surprised and pleased to be given unstinting support by Wacker and Rosalie, who seemed to feel they gained status from Kinnafoot offering hospitality. She had enjoyed the compliments, the giving of pleasure, the kindness of guests, many of whom drew her aside to thank her for what she was doing for Aidan. But for the last evening — and she could hardly bear to accept that it had arrived so soon — it would be nicest of all to have a quiet time alone with him.

# Chapter Fifteen

Quiet evening or not, it began in festive mood. Louise had decided, as a surprise for Aidan and to create a feeling of occasion — and since the weather for the first time had turned grey and bleak — that they would dine at a small table drawn up to the fire in the library, the cosiest of the spacious Kinnafoot rooms.

She did pause to wonder whether this would send signals she didn't intend, but Cass's warnings about Aidan were hard to take seriously by this stage. As far as Louise had observed, his behaviour was nothing more than the normal responses of a flamboyant, big-hearted man whose emotions ran very near the surface. There had been nothing beyond affectionate pats, a few rib-cracking hugs, and extravagant compliments which were more likely to be about her food than about her. Little to fear there, and once again Louise felt ashamed of the moment's doubt. How hurt Aidan would be if he knew of it. Her cheeks were pink as she hurried on with her preparations.

But when she came down after her bath, wearing a favourite dress of soft hyacinth blue, she found that Aidan too had been making plans. He had already discovered the plot in the library, having gone in, as he often did, to smack his lips over the dining-room table and count the knives and forks to see if he was getting a savoury or not, or to sharpen the carving knife in sensual anticipation. He had been thunderstruck to find the table bare, and had come charging out again with a baffled roar, to be headed towards the library by Mrs Wacker, who didn't want anything smashed while her mad employer hunted for his dinner.

For Mrs Wacker, and Wacker himself, felicitously shedding the role of gardener and transforming himself into a silent-footed, punctilious butler of his own invention, had, as Aidan's own surprise for Louise, been pressed to serve dinner and wash up, and she was forbidden the kitchen for the evening.

More than this, beside her chair in the drawing-room, where Wacker brought her wine (from a bottle and from the cellar), lay a small velvet tray with a cellophane lid, containing an orchid. It was so much a gesture of Aidan's generation, with its message of the trouble he had taken — for it had had to be planned and organised — and of a wish to give something exotic and precious, that tears sprang to Louise's eyes.

'I have never, ever been given one before,' she said, enchanted by its elaborate and amazing beauty. She laid it against her shoulder, and Aidan, seizing the chance of laughter, protested in outrage, 'What are you doing, my delectable innocent? Other way up. My God, the youth of today. Here, let me.'

Louise, relinquishing the delicate bloom, which seemed almost as live to the touch as a creature, stood before him like a child, and noted without surprise that the huge hands were light and deft.

'There now.' He bent his big shaggy head and smacked a resounding kiss on her cheek. 'You look as delicious as a little scone, warm from the oven.'

I think I'm safe enough, Louise decided, laughing at the comparison, but suspecting he had chosen it with a design at once perceptive and reassuring.

Wacker came in, enjoying himself tremendously, his nails sore with cleaning, bearing hot cheese straws which Louise recognised, and giving no hint of the violent altercation that had just blown up in the kitchen about who was to remain behind the scenes.

As with Erica, there was never any shortage of things to talk about. Aidan had a fund of anecdotes – Louise had never heard him repeat one – some unforgivably vainglorious, others told against himself with identical gusto and frankness, still others full of intriguing gossip about well-known figures. Laughter was the key to them all, and Aidan's appetite for it, his massive good looks, his happy mood, darkening from time to time with extravagant despair as he remembered that tomorrow Louise must go, made a combination hard to resist.

Indeed there was no reason to resist it. Louise felt that the friendships which had been formed in this place would not vanish. Aidan, of course, had the future mapped out beyond argument.

'Cass will send you back here on every possible occasion. Alice shall have as many holidays as she can bear. Better than that, I shall do up the farmworker's cottage down the lane and put her into it. I've been meaning to tidy it up for quite some time.'

'It doesn't have a roof,' Louise said, biting into the burning-hot devils on horseback she had last seen pale and wan on a plate in the fridge and thinking what a marvellous creature Mrs Wacker was.

'A roof, a roof! How can you be so small-minded?'

'I don't know if I will be sent back here, you know,' Louise warned him.

'Of course you will. I shall see to it.'

'It will have to fit in with everything else.'

'What everything else? I shall pay a vast retainer for you, have you permanently poised to come the moment I lift my finger.'

But later, when they had moved to the drawing-room so that Wacker could clear away, and the house was empty and quiet around them, Aidan expressed his feelings more simply, and more poignantly.

'I can be myself with you,' he said, his craggy features, sad for once, limned dramatically by the glow of the fire. 'I can rant and roar and stamp, give you a hug when the urge possesses me, and you never flinch. Darling girl, how I've loved having you in the house, slipping about so neat and clean and busy. I've loved the way you put heart and soul into what you do, and I don't need to tell you how wonderful it's been to be able to throw all the parties, have people here. But there's more to it than that. Can I talk about it?'

'Of course.' Louise found this quiet tone from him incredibly moving, and her own voice was very gentle.

Aidan shifted his big frame restlessly, taking the poker to rearrange a couple of logs with his surprising delicacy of touch, stirring them into flame.

'Loving and being loved.' He sat forward on his chair, the poker idle in his hands, a line of firelight running up its shining steel length. He flipped it up and down for a moment, making it look as light as a knitting needle, then laid it carefully beside the tongs. 'I've missed the boat in that department, it seems.'

Louise was very still. She knew this had nothing to do with her; something important was coming, something hidden deep beneath Aidan's exuberant excesses of speech and manner, which he needed to express but which it would hurt him to express.

'The buffoon,' he said with a sigh, leaning back in his chair, his voice a deep rumble she could scarcely catch. 'It's an easy role to play when you've got size twelve feet, hands like sides of beef, and a laugh like a barrel rolling down a cellar chute. Then you become the part and the part becomes you, and nobody can tell the difference. Girls, women, can't tell the difference. Oh, I expect I was clumsy, did everything wrong. For a while I even wondered if I should go after the boys. Pretty much of a last resort,' he added, with a laugh Louise didn't altogether like. 'No, in the end I never went down that road. But Christ—!'

He pushed himself up out of his chair with a suddenness that made her jump. '*Christ!*' He walked with his crashing stride to the window, the dogs following him, and stood there for a moment with his hands locked behind his back and his head up. 'What I've missed out on. What – I – have – missed – out – on.' The great voice had dropped, tolling out the words, and on an instinct of compassion Louise went to stand beside him, slipping her hand into his, leaning her head lightly against his arm. He bent his big head towards hers, and they stood like this for some moments, very still, the greyness of the May night throwing the big trees of the lower lawn into black silhouette.

'I'm not sure that having someone like you here isn't rather bad for me,' Aidan said after a while, and the effortful lightness of his tone was even more painful to hear than the bitter outburst of questioning and loss had been. 'A glimpse of something so easy, so full of moment-by-moment pleasure. There's always an image, I suppose, in everyone's mind. That impossible she. I feel as though I've gone on expecting, looking and hoping, without noticing the years piling up. Sixty years old, for God's sake, and still with that feeling that one day, somewhere . . . No wonder Erica gets so impatient with me. She says I've never grown up and I daresay she's right.'

'There could be someone still.' The sheer waste of all this affection and loving-kindness took Louise by the throat. Yet what could she say that would not be patronising and insensitive?

Aidan gave the hand he was holding a little shake, and smiled down at her. 'What a true delight you've been.'

'But Aidan, it hasn't been one-sided. You can't guess how much being here has meant to me – and helped me.'

'Yes?' He looked at her searchingly, wanting to believe it.

'Of course it has. I've been shutting myself away from things, from people. Here there has been such warmth and colour and giving, and it all stems from you.'

He accepted this in silence, but Louise was aware of his pleasure. He turned to face her, and taking her shoulders held her at arm's length away from him.

'Little Louise, do you know what I should like more than anything in the world?'

A crucial moment. That was how Louise saw it in retrospect, but at the time, in all honesty, had there been any feeling of decision? Had there not, more accurately, been a trusting wish to fulfil if she could whatever that longing might be, without fear that he would ask the impossible? But the moment was so fleeting, so uncomplicated when it came, that she answered without hesitation, 'Tell me.'

'I want to gather you up in my arms and carry you to the sofa and sit there with you in my lap.'

Louise smiled at him, slipping her arms inside his to put her hands on his shoulders, massive and solid as a beam of wood.

'Oh, Louise.' Aidan's face crumpled and broke, but he at once regained control, and with a return to his usual extravagance of gesture scooped her up, giving her a small toss into the air like a child, and carried her across the room with the dogs leaping round them. Flumping down with her in a swirling movement, he tucked her against him with a natural and tender ease which returned their mood to quietness, and for a while they were simply there together, close and silent.

In the warm cave of his arms, her cheek against the solidity of his chest, lulled by the strong beat of his heart, Louise felt a sense of timelessness steal over her. There were no questions to ask, no apprehensions to quell. Afterwards, she was to check on this; had she really felt no doubts? Had she gone into his arms without the slightest query in her mind? Had she, therefore, been prepared for this to be the prelude to something else? But no, sure instinct had told her this was the prelude to nothing. This was what this man needed, closeness, touch, a woman's body content and relaxed in his arms.

'Louise, I cannot tell you . . .' he said at last, huskily, and putting up her hand she found his cheek wet with tears.

'Oh, darling Aidan, don't, I can't bear it.'

'No, don't be upset,' he said, holding her palm there for an instant. 'Tears are part of good emotions as well as sad ones. Let them be.'

'This means a lot to me too, you know,' she whispered. 'It's so long since—'

'Don't talk about it if it hurts you,' he interrupted hurriedly, dreading pain for her as he would have hated to see her bleeding from the merest scratch. 'I know you've had terrible grief to—'

'I wasn't going to say "since Owen died",' Louise stopped him gently. 'I've already managed to say that, to Cass and to Erica. No, I was going to say, "since I've had any loving physical contact with a man". This is so good, you simply can't imagine.'

'So we keep telling each other,' he said, with a return to lightness. Then a moment later he asked, anxious again, 'You're sure I'm not gross?'

'Shall we say enormously attractive?' Louise suggested, and laughing again, securely comfortable, bonded by a shared need to give, and a shared capacity to receive, they settled down to talk the hours away.

Erica, against all expectation, came to see Louise off, shaking her head and tightening her lips as Aidan frankly blubbed, but nevertheless folding her into a firm embrace of her own.

'Oh, now another one in tears,' she exclaimed disgustedly, as Louise stepped back sniffing. 'You'll be here again, you silly child. Hasn't it occurred yet to my ridiculous brother that you don't have to cook to come and stay with us, and you don't have to persuade Cass Scott to send you either?'

'My God,' roared Aidan, clapping his hand to his head, 'why didn't I think of it for myself? Erica, that rapier-keen mind of yours has more uses than stripping the skin off me. Louise, did you hear her? I'll be in touch, I'll write, I'll phone—'

Erica, seeing her into the car, had one more thing to say. 'You're doing well. Keep in mind the valuable Scots saying, "It's the ganging foot aye gets." You've begun to gang, and you'll find it brings its own rewards.'

Louise, looking back past the little figure of a snowman, knitted for her as a leaving present by Mrs Wacker and for the time being jigging in the rear window, saw Aidan, tears still on his face, violently waving an enormous red-spotted handkerchief, while Erica, drawing her various garments round her thin body in a gesture of irritated contempt, stalked off towards the orchard.

Louise had to pull up, once she was out of sight behind the high wall, to dry her own eyes, but she knew she would find the enduring response to that memory of the two of them would be laughter, not tears.

The certainty braced her as her mind went forward to the moment of walking into the newly reduced and echoing emptiness of home.

# Chapter Sixteen

Leaving Kinnafoot, though sad, was not the wrench it had been to leave Fallan. Analysing this as she opened windows and brought the empty house to life again, Louise decided it was sad in the best sort of way, like the end of a perfect holiday, tearing oneself away from a place and people one hates to part from, but always having known it was an interlude. And in this case, tucking away the certainty of return, knowing something rich and good had come into her life which mattered to her and which had not been there before.

She was adjusting to this piecemeal way of living, ready to accept the upswings and the downs, beginning to like the sense of the unknown lying ahead and the widening of her horizons, both geographical and emotional.

There was the usual fat packet from Abby waiting, this time written on pages torn from the scribble pad Louise herself had left in the kitchen for the shopping list. Abby was not happy. She had stepped out of line once too often and Geordie was sticking to his word and refusing to have anything more to do with her, reinforcing the message by appearing at the pub with a girl from Aberfyle.

Abby used up two pages in saying how little she cared about this. 'I don't know why I ever looked at him anyway, he's so incredibly mean, always grabbing over-time or working on his boring old van, and then when he's there he'll hardly buy a drink or anything.' But the guest who had chatted her up at Easter had vanished, it seemed. 'Aren't they all bastards really? All that talk about taking me out to his apartment in New York, and how he'd introduce me to the power-boat crowd —' somewhere other than New York, Louise assumed '— and what a fantastic time we'd have . . .' Oh, Abby, dear credulous Abby, always yearning for such improb-able adventures. 'Only now he never writes or anything, and I daren't ask Hugh where he is and when I tried to phone him in New York I got some completely un-known person and Maxine went mad about the phone bill. I didn't know she'd be able to tell, and I'd hardly talked for any time anyway, why should she go ballistic, she doesn't pay. I think I'll just chuck it all up, it's horrible here anyway, there's no one to talk to and nothing decent ever happens. Only I don't know where I'd go, I couldn't stand another job like this. I've just heard my father's retiring, well, I knew he was, but they're going to live in the Bahamas, isn't that typical? I'd always thought it would be handy once they were back to have a place to keep things and get my washing done, some posh house in Berkshire or somewhere with loads of you-know-who dropping in, fascinated by ex-Ambassador's delightful youngest daughter. Well, I'd have loathed it really, I suppose. Maybe I'll clear off to India or somewhere . . .'

Louise could see her at the kitchen table, hair over her face, pushing up her glasses every other second, with that look of writhing round a chair rather than sitting on it which only Abby could achieve. It was surprising that she had gone on writing. Louise had imagined she might rise to one letter, in the first flush of their meeting and getting on so well together, but had thought the impulse would swiftly peter out as most of Abby's good resolutions did. Perhaps, as she herself had candidly said, it was because Louise was older than most of the temps who appeared at Fallan. Perhaps, and Louise made herself put this into words, Abby had found in her some maternal quality which drew her, and filled some lack in her lonely life. This decision of her parents to live permanently abroad had obviously disappointed her, and Louise could guess how, in spite of her assertions that she couldn't stand her family, she had been building cosy images of a new home and a new beginning.

What could she do to help? Louise pondered the question as she made supper. Would it appeal to Abby to spend a couple of days here? It was always time off which highlighted one's loneliness, as she had found out for herself. Not that much of it had come her way so far. In spite of the undemanding tempo at Kinnafoot, no days had been entirely free as they were officially supposed to

be, and she laughed as she thought how horrified Aidan
would have been if she had reminded him of it.

She was still smiling when the phone rang. It was Aidan
himself. She could imagine him in his huge chair, huge
drink beside him, huge feet stretched out – and was nearly
blown away by his huge voice. Had her journey home been
all right? Oh, darling Aidan, yes, all two hours of it. Was
everything all right in the house? Did she know where
she was going next? She must let him know the instant she
did; he didn't like not knowing where she was. And he
hoped she wasn't too tired – late to bed last night and all
that?

She knew what he was asking, circuitously and
nervously. 'Not too tired,' she said. 'Though I shan't be
keeping Kinnafoot hours here, that's for sure. But Aidan,
don't worry. It was lovely. I'm not looking back in the cold
light of day and thinking anything different. It was special
and good.'

'Oh, Christ, Louise—' Aidan expelled a breath of relief
which she could almost feel. 'I was petrified that you'd –
that it would seem—'

'Don't think about it again,' she ordered him.

'Oh, I'll think about it.' His great laugh volleyed round
the room as Louise held the receiver a foot from her ear
and winced.

Cass was the next to phone. 'Hi, can't chat, I've got
people for dinner. Noisy mob, you can probably hear
them. Sorry I haven't been in touch before, but I've had a
brilliant idea. I have to check out a new client at Yetts o'
Muckhart tomorrow and I was thinking, there's a very

good restaurant outside Rumbling Bridge, so how do you feel about lunch? Yes? Great, I'd hoped you'd come, there's lots to catch up on. One-ish? See you there.'

Louise, cheered by these contacts, longed to have someone to share her mood with, feeling she had dropped too sharply from the life and warmth of Kinnafoot and finding it hard to attune to the silence and the slow march of time in the empty house. Then she checked. This was part of the pattern. She was alone, but that was good too. Everything in her life was there to enjoy. Here, at home, she could luxuriate in the freedom to do as she pleased, watch any old rubbish on television, an unheard-of indulgence in Aunt Bea's day, go early to bed, read some old friend, and sleep for as long as she liked with no Erica to throw stones at her window in the soulless dawn. Tomorrow there would be the ordinary light-hearted pleasure of having lunch with a friend.

'I'm ravenous, that dismal woman didn't offer me so much as a biscuit. I'm not sending anybody there! Watch out, by the way, they go for the garlic with a heavy hand here. I'm going to have a pile of pasta. How about you?'

Louise thought not pasta. After the indulgences of Kinnafoot the waistband of her skirt was alarmingly tight. Unlike leggy Cass, who burned off everything she ate with her whirling energy, Louise had a tendency to roundness she didn't like. She turned to the salads.

'So Kinnafoot was an improvement on life *chez* Smollett?' Cass asked, raising her glass to Louise with teasing amusement.

'Oh, Cass, what a marvellous place. I can't thank you enough for sending me there. I loved them both, and the house, the garden, the Wackers, everything.'

'And they loved you.'

'You've heard from them?'

'I had Aidan on the phone when you were barely out of the gates.'

'Not sobbing, by any chance?'

'Sobbing, gulping, beating his breast. I fear for Alice's life, or at the very least her job.'

'Oh, he'll never get rid of Alice.' But Louise felt the glow of being wanted, unreservedly, and the smile she flashed at Cass showed how much it meant to her.

'No, he's far too soft-hearted to sack Alice,' Cass agreed. 'Silly old lump.'

'How well do you know them?' Louise wasn't sure whether her faint resistance to Cass's words was because they were too strong or because they were too affectionate. So she felt possessive about Kinnafoot? Life was moving along.

'They were among my first clients once I'd started up the Scottish end of the agency. You can't help getting fond of Aidan. Erica is more reserved, reclusive really.' Nostalgic images rushed back for Louise – the circle of firelight holding back the summer dark, the voluptuous colours of the little van, the hours of slashing and grubbing in the orchard, the sun coming up over the green hills, the hours of flowing talk. She said nothing, treasuring these things.

'The only thing is, Aidan sounded so overcome with

despair that I was afraid you might have had trouble beating him off. Did he behave himself?'

'Oh, Cass, he's just lonely. He has all this affection to pour out and nowhere for it to go, except on the dogs and Alice and the Wackers. Erica snubs him without mercy — though he's so used to it I think he'd actually miss it if she was ever kind to him.'

Cass smiled at the earnest tone. 'I'm glad I sent you there. Oh, and by the way, I have to tell you you have put up a record.'

'What, not being jumped by Aidan?'

'Every single person you have worked for has asked to have you back,' Cass announced. 'How about that?'

'Every one?' Louise was startled. Since she had felt herself in an alien climate with Mrs Baines and the Smolletts she had not imagined that they would take to her. And in her only encounter with Hugh Erskine she had been outspokenly critical in a way which could still horrify her slightly. 'That can't be true.'

'It certainly is.' Cass dived into her pasta, enjoying the effect of her announcement.

'But I didn't do anything out of the ordinary—'

'What you have to realise,' Cass interrupted firmly, 'is the abysmal level at which a lot of temps operate. I can interview and select and monitor, and I do have some good people, but it requires a high degree of self-motivation to do your best when no one's looking, when whatever you achieve can be wiped out the moment you've left, and when you know you'll probably never see the client again anyway. Also there's the personality factor.

You genuinely care, and people sense that. You're considerate about fitting into their households, and that sort of sensitivity can only come naturally.'

'But Mrs Baines?'

'Well, in her sniffy way. Best of a bad bunch type of thing. But Hugh Erskine has been on the phone more than once, or his PA has. Oh, don't worry, I know you don't want to go back, but it's nice to know they want you, and will use the agency from now on. And I had a call not from Miss Smollett, but from Terence himself, probably secretly—'

'Terence?' The memory of his arid existence tugged at Louise. 'Well, if he really wanted me back I suppose I could—' she began, deciding this was not the moment to examine the mixed responses which Cass's reference to Fallan had produced.

'I wouldn't ask. The trouble is,' Cass sighed, 'they have no idea how ghastly they are. However, if you *will* make yourself so valuable then I shall just have to look after you, shan't I? Which brings me to—'

She let the sentence hang, and Louise looked up quickly. 'What?' Could it get addictive; this buzz of slightly scary anticipation, this sense of the world out there, waiting? 'Cass, tell me.'

'How keen are you on driving?'

'Not terribly.' Where on earth did Cass propose to send her? 'I'm getting back into practice though. But it would be in Scotland, wouldn't it? I don't think I could cope with somewhere like London.'

'It wouldn't be London.'

'Come on, then, don't torment me. Where?'

'Not to a specific place. This is rather an odd one, but I think you could handle it.'

Louise waited, refusing to ask any more questions, and Cass laughed, then, in the way that was becoming familiar, launched into a swift summary.

'Sad, really. Etta Crawford, seventy-eight, has cancer, been given about six months. Wants to go on a circuit of old friends, old haunts. She has a sort of companion, called Violet, frightfully bossy but marshmallow inside and pretty useless, who's about the same age as Etta and can't face the driving. Fair enough, I suppose. Anyway, they want a chauffeur, navigator, courier, or whatever you like to call it, to haul them about for two or three weeks. And certified saint, I should think. A pilgrimage centred on Devon and Cornwall, though there may be one or two stops on the way. Mostly down in the south-west, at any rate. What do you think?'

'It's different.'

Cornwall, home, her parents. Louise felt jolted, suddenly confronted by uncomfortable issues she had believed safely tucked out of sight; but she did her best to concentrate on the demands such a journey would make.

'I'm not sure I'd do that sort of thing very well.'

'To be honest,' Cass retorted, 'I can't think of anyone who would do it better. I don't know who else I could send. It's outside our usual run of jobs, and for obvious reasons I have to assign someone who won't chuck the whole thing in the middle. I couldn't have those two adrift at the other end of the country, God knows what would become of them.'

'It sounds quite an undertaking.' Louise could feel resistance building. She would be far from her refuge; she had not driven on the busy roads of the south for so long; how would she cope with being shut up in a car with two nervous old ladies for three weeks? And come to that, what car would she be driving? But she knew these questions were not the important ones.

'Poor Etta wants to go so badly,' Cass said. 'I don't think she realises how tiring it will be. She'll need a lot of looking after and Violet will be far too busy concentrating on herself to be much use. In fact, Etta would probably enjoy the trip more if she left Violet behind, but there's no hope of that. She's afraid of trying some chauffeur service –' had Cass seen the suggestion rising to Louise's lips? '– but she'd feel safe with you.'

'Cass, don't work on me!' Louise protested, knowing her own fatal readiness to respond to such appeals. 'Give me a moment to think.'

'There's something else, isn't there?' Cass's eyes examined her. 'Tell me.'

'It's nothing to do with the job.'

'Tell me anyway.'

Louise hesitated, feeling that the old disharmony had no place in the life she was building, then swinging to the opposite view that because she was creating a new and independent existence this was precisely the time to meet her parents as her present self.

'Hey,' Cass said softly. 'It's me.'

Yes, it was Cass, who had never failed to understand yet. They talked for a long time, and when they went out to their cars Louise, as they had both known she would, had agreed to take Etta on her journey into the past.

# Chapter Seventeen

By the time summer was in full swing Louise felt rooted and settled, a strange description for her gad-about existence, but true just the same. It was working; working in practical and financial terms, and also answering needs in her that she had scarcely known existed, or had buried when she had buried the three people who had given her life meaning.

The trip with Etta and Violet had been the tragicomedy Cass had predicted – a great deal of exasperation, as they bickered and fussed and changed their minds, alternating with moments of real poignancy as Louise located some imperfectly remembered but loved spot and watched Etta revel in the pleasure of rediscovery. Some of the places were changed beyond recognition, and that was distressing for her. Some of the plans were too ambitious, and once or twice Louise had wondered whether she would get her charges safely home again. In times of crisis Violet had been, also as Cass had predicted, quite useless, complaining about the heat or her shoes or the morning tea being cold, while Etta, pale and silent, never complaining about anything, looked as though she had reached her last breath.

Some of the friends they visited were more doddery than they were, and one bad-tempered old man drove them off the premises waving his stick, denying all knowledge of Etta. This understandably upset her and that night, unable to sleep, she had confided to Louise – Violet was snoring like an eighteen-stone beer drinker next door – that once at a dance her hair slide had fallen out, and the young man he had been had picked it up and put it in his pocket *and kept it.*

'I always wished it hadn't been such an ordinary one,' she added sadly. The drama of the day had not shaken a belief in the significance of this action which she had cherished for more than sixty years.

She had been adamant that Louise should have a day off to see her family, though Violet had snorted, 'And what's to become of us, I should like to know?'

Had the meeting served any purpose? Certainly it had been strained and many old points of contention had surfaced once more, apparently as fresh today as they had been when Louise first left for Scotland, intending to stay for two weeks, and did not return. The problem for her parents seemed to be that there was nothing in her life they could define or categorise, and Louise thought ironically that her situation wasn't so far from Abby's. The need for an acceptable label. The discovery that now, as well as her marriage having 'gone wrong' as they had always said it would, she was doing some kind of domestic work deeply offended them. Why couldn't she be more like the boys?

The damning plaint, which had threaded Louise's childhood, was not voiced but it was still implied, and back had poured the misery of the child who, however hard she tries, can never fulfil the ambitions of those she loves and longs to know she is loved by.

Yet Louise was glad she had seen them. At least she had established the fact that at thirty-two she was not going to come back and be the biddable daughter at home, hunting for a second husband who would conform to her parents' values and wipe out the memory of the disastrous first one who had expected her to live in a hovel . . . And so on, as before. More importantly, forced to examine the way she was living in the light of their prejudices, she had been satisfied with what she found.

After this journey, when a grateful but exhausted Etta was back in her little house in Auchterarder and Violet, safe from alarming challenges, had reasserted control, Louise, bemused by incessant squabbling, her shoulders aching from three weeks of driving and lugging suitcases, would have welcomed a break. But an elderly widow with angina was lined up for her, and knowing how hard it was for Cass to match her requirements, and grateful for work, Louise felt she must accept.

It was a dull but blessedly restful post near Livingston, with a fat schnauzer to walk, mainly round a housing estate, uneventful days of few demands and minimal cooking, and a lot of reading in a barren plot of garden never free of the background hum of the M8.

The garden was also loud with the voices of children from neighbouring gardens, the house glutted with photographs of grandchildren, though Mrs Kenneth's married son lived in Denmark. Her unmarried daughter, who normally looked after her, was visiting him. Mrs Kenneth never attempted to show Louise these photographs, and did her best to bite back references to the grandchildren, but Louise, beginning to feel as guilty as a recovering patient who is letting the cosseting go on when it's not necessary any more, discovered that a long-overdue healing process had begun. There were still the inescapable pangs – the sound of a child's laugh climbing into squeals of delight; seeing a small girl rush across the park to grab a vacant swing, the almost uncontrollable urge to call, 'Be careful', as the empty seat swung; a blonde head bobbing at a mother's elbow – these would always catch at her. There was nowhere in the world where she could be protected from the pain they brought. But the day-to-day sounds of children's voices, the bicycles on the pavement, the ball coming over the fence, they could be accepted, were part of the ordinary fabric of life. And the photographs – gappy teeth and shining hair; kilts and white stockings and black strap shoes; skinny bodies through sunlight on splashed water in a paddling pool – when she made herself look at them as she dusted she found that after all they were harmless two-dimensional images with no relevance for her.

Back in Stirling, lulled by the sense of having reached level going, with nothing ahead that seemed likely to alarm, she decided she should tackle some much needed spring-cleaning. The mood of peaceful optimism was cracked apart by a double hammer blow. Phyllis, not Nevil, called to say Louise would be required to vacate the house within the month. And Cass phoned to ask if she would go back to Fallan.

Seeing Phyllis alone brought back a rush of uneasy memories for Louise. During the early years of her marriage, when she and Owen had lived in the annexe to the substantial Donaldson villa, Phyllis had displayed all the possessiveness of a neurotic mother and a spoiled woman for her only son, and Louise had been too young and too malleable to resist her. Now Phyllis, sure of her ground, assumed a patronising affability as she greeted Louise, asked how she was without pausing for an answer, and said tea would be nice, but not outside because of her fine skin, so much more delicate than other people's. But beneath the surface friendliness there was the hint of something more urgent, as though she had waited a long time for some treat to arrive which was now at hand.

She sipped her tea in tiny pecks, her close-set eyes under a lightly permed flop of fair hair, whose whiteness she still concealed, fixed on Louise with a strange intentness. Though Louise did not understand the look, it made her deeply uncomfortable. Afterwards she knew it had stemmed from a sense of triumph as focused, as oblivious to everything around it, as lust.

'Now that you've got over everything –' Phyllis cut across what Louise was saying and, setting her cup down with a click, hitched her bottom to the edge of her chair as though getting down to the real business of her visit '– Nevil felt it was time to have a little talk.'

Have I got over everything? When was that established? And why did the invocation of Nevil, combined with the words 'a little talk', sound so ominous? Louise knew these questions were a smokescreen between her and something she was going to dislike very much indeed, as Phyllis, knees primly clamped and angled sideways, eyes still with that strange glitter, patches of colour in her cheeks, allowed herself the indulgence for which she had come.

'We both feel we've looked after you very well, exceptionally well in fact, and given you as much time as anyone could reasonably want. Six months – well, it will be six months – is a considerable period, as you will appreciate, for us to sacrifice . . . I mean, when you think what a house like this, in a prime site, could realise, and of course it's far too big for one female living alone. Then you are hardly ever here, so it seems rather much to expect us to go on being so generous . . .'

This stream of barbs, so rapidly delivered that they seemed to escape Louise's clutch as they flew past, scarcely made sense at first, could not make sense until the one appalling fact fell into place. She was being asked to leave her home. And she had nowhere else in the world to go. In wild panic she came to her feet, staring at Phyllis in disbelief. Phyllis didn't move; didn't say, 'I'm sorry to have to break this to you,' or, 'I know this must come as a shock.' Instead she leaned back, relaxing sensuously, a sated expression on her face as though savouring a victory long anticipated.

That almost preening movement cut through Louise's panic. In it she read the culmination of years of dislike, the jealousy that had eaten into Phyllis from the moment she realised that her son was putting another woman in her place, and the grief over his loss which had twisted into irrational hatred. Shivering, Louise in that instant relinquished everything this neurotic and vengeful woman wished to take from her. It could go, all of it; it didn't matter. She had been here on sufferance all along.

'We shall let it furnished, of course, now that the valuable pieces are safe,' Phyllis was saying, looking around her. 'I believe you brought a few things of your own with you, didn't you?'

There had been very little to bring, but by this time Phyllis would not remember why.

'I shall leave everything.' Louise heard her own voice, rapping out the words in a way quite alien to her, before she was aware of having reached any such decision, but as she spoke she found herself fiercely certain that this was right. In such a clean sweep, what point was there in salvaging a bed, a bookcase? They would be mere encumbrances. The word opened up a yawning emptiness, but before it could terrify her she was aware almost of eagerness to meet the challenge.

'What date did you have in mind?' she asked, her voice not as firm as she would have liked when she actually brought out the words, but calm enough to cloud the satisfied gleam in Phyllis's eyes with uncertainty, and that had to be something.

'Well, Nevil thought the end of the month.'

Yes, drag in Nevil as hatchet-man now that you've enjoyed your moment of triumph. The end of the month. This month? July? *Christ in his heaven*, she heard Aidan roar, and was briefly comforted.

'Naturally, a few days here or there won't matter. You and I realise that,' Phyllis was saying chattily, allowing herself a specious matiness now that the enemy was routed. 'But you know how the legal mind works, everything cut and dried.' She gave a trill of laughter, and in it Louise heard a genuine lightness of heart to have enjoyed her afternoon so much. 'I expect you'll find somewhere to rent quite easily. After all, you don't need very much, and you have the lump sum Beatrice left you. You might prefer to be near your own family.'

Odd that she had seen them recently, Louise thought, and odd that they and Phyllis, for their different reasons, agreed on the desirability of this.

'Anyway,' said Phyllis briskly, getting up and brushing the front of her skirt with firm strokes, 'we can finalise the date when you've made your plans. And I'm sure you won't mind showing people round. Oh dear, it's going to be very inconvenient if you're away. You'll have to leave a key at the office.'

Cass phoned twenty minutes later, catching Louise in a state of trembling reaction as the reality sank in. Louise responded so automatically, however, that Cass had no suspicion anything was wrong and, in a hurry as usual, plunged at once into what she had to say.

'Look, I know I promised I wouldn't do this, and if it has to be no I shall quite understand, but I'm at my wits' end and thought it was at least worth asking. Would you think of going to Fallan again, just for a short time, before the holidays as you did before? Could you bear it? The thing is, Hugh Erskine is having some sort of business meeting there and wants it all to be perfect, and he won't have the person I've allocated to him at any price. She was there over the May holiday and though I knew he hadn't been impressed I didn't realise he'd refuse to have her back. She knows the house, so for a short job it looked the obvious answer. But he wants you, and he's used to getting his way. Could you think about it? Louise?'

'Sorry, hang on a sec,' Louise mumbled, the shaking almost out of control as this request came at a moment when she could barely bring her mind to focus upon it. She pressed the receiver against her chest, tilting her head back and closing her eyes. Taking deep breaths which seemed to make her feel more dizzy than ever, she could faintly hear Cass's questioning voice.

Lifting the receiver to her ear again as though it was weighted with lead, she said, 'Cass. Sorry.'

'What is it? Are you ill? What's the matter?'

'Are you speaking from the Perth office?'

'Yes, I am, but—'

'Could you stay till I can get there? Would you mind? Would it mess up your evening too much?'

Cass swiftly reviewed her plans – dentist in fifteen

minutes, then she had intended, after doing some shopping, to go home via Stanley, where she had to collect a damaged table which Rick, her husband, was going to restore. She could fit in the dentist before Louise arrived; the rest would have to wait. 'Come,' she said.

She had thought they might go to a quiet nearby bar, but one look at Louise made her dismiss the idea. She shouldn't have let her drive, she realised in concern. The composed, trim little person she was used to looked pale and dazed, and though with her short hair and simply cut clothes she could never look dishevelled, there was an air of being scrambled together about her appearance which was worrying.

Cass's assistant Lindsay, who lived above the office, signalled that her sitting-room was available if needed, but Cass, suspecting that whatever had upset Louise might take time to sort out, and unwilling to confine Lindsay and her husband to their kitchen for an unknown period, shook her head. The office included a comfortable interviewing corner; that would do. Lindsay, not given to wasting words, nodded and disappeared upstairs, to return with coffee, sherry and biscuits.

Cass put a hand on her arm in thanks, and they both glanced at Louise, who seemed aware of nothing. Lindsay locked the door so that her husband, seeing lights on, wouldn't be tempted to come in this way, and vanished.

Without consulting Louise, Cass poured out a mug of coffee, noting that Lindsay, bless her, had made it bracingly strong. She poured half a mug for herself, not sure how well she would cope after two injections.

'Drink this.'

Louise shook her head numbly.

'I don't care whether you want it or not. It's not up for discussion. Drink it.'

Louise took the mug and wrapped her hands round it, that tell-tale gesture of seeking comfort.

There was little other comfort she could be given, Cass reflected grimly, when the facts were finally extracted and they were talking more freely.

'There'll be no difficulty finding you jobs,' she said. 'That you can be sure of. And if you need to store things we have loads of room in Rick's workshop. There are lots of places to rent and if you do decide to go on working for the agency something small would do for the time being, wouldn't it?'

'I shan't have much stuff. I was thinking about it as I drove up. It seems silly to rent somewhere I wouldn't be using ninety per cent of the time. I wondered if I could B and B or something like that in between jobs.'

Why did the very term have such a desolate ring?

'Oh, surely you could do better than that,' Cass said, hiding her dismay. 'Are you very hard up?'

'Not really.' With what Cass paid her, plus car and other expenses, and what Beatrice had left her, renting somewhere to live or even getting a mortgage would not be a problem. What had hit her – so disturbingly that she couldn't talk about it yet – was that she had no idea where she wanted to be. Stirling? Why? What had she to do with Stirling, any more than any other place? Then where? The feeling of rootlessness, which seemed to have rushed up on her from nowhere, had been frightening.

'There could be longer-term jobs, if that would help,' Cass suggested. The option had not been attractive before, but things were different now.

Louise clutched at the idea. 'Why didn't I think of that? My brain's not working properly. I couldn't do it till everything's sorted out, but — wait a minute, you phoned me earlier, what was that about? Oh—'

'Forget about it. It doesn't matter.' Cass knew the Erskine job was not ideal and had no intention of adding to Louise's problems in any way.

'Fallan,' said Louise, and Cass had the impression that her thoughts had been carried far away. 'That might fit. Didn't you say it was a short job? Then I could have the rest of the month to pack up and find some sort of base. I need to do something, I can't hang around waiting for the axe to fall.'

'Fallan may not be a good solution just now,' Cass reminded her awkwardly.

Louise looked at her as though such doubts belonged to a different person, a different time.

'It will be all right,' was all she said, but she spoke in a tone of such conviction that, in spite of the wrought-up emotions of the moment, Cass believed it would be.

# Chapter Eighteen

Would the magic be there still? Louise felt almost more nervous turning up into Glen Fallan today than she had felt the first time, four months ago. There was a deep, almost aching fear, which she tried to ignore, that if this place failed to come up to her memories of it, then she would be truly adrift. It made no sense, but her hands were clammy, her heart hurrying, as she took the first curves up from the thronged road beside the loch.

This road was busier too. Although it was marked as unsuitable for coaches, and the glen led nowhere and offered no tourist 'attractions', people were lured into it for that very reason, and she passed a car or two in most of the places where it was possible to park.

At first she minded their presence, not prepared for it – her mind too full of larger worries at present to leave room for anything so normal – but as she wound up the glen she found that it adapted acceptably to summer mode. How could a few cars, a few people peacefully enjoying themselves, detract from the grandeur of the great ridges ranging ahead, or alter the feeling, as the road twisted deeper into the hills, of entering a secret and special world?

Going through the village she was suddenly aware that she was no longer looking at the scene from the outside; even if only for a minute span of time, she was part of it. Names came back, names she had never thought of in the harried days of packing and preparation. Was Geordie in or out of favour? Would she see quiet kindly Fraser while she was here? Was Cameron still cadging fly cuppies? And Abby would be there, scatty, maddening Abby, who was nearly as rootless as Louise was herself. Anticipation at the thought of seeing her again — if she had remembered to be in — filled Louise as she left the village and took the unfenced road through the more open landscape of the upper glen.

Only as she reached the bridge and the gates of Fallan did she remember with a jolt of apprehension that things would be different this time. It would not be Abby and herself muddling about in ill-lit store rooms and draughty corridors of stone. The house would be alive and inhabited; Hugh Erskine would be there with his business associates; Maxine would be in charge.

But even that thought could not spoil the pleasure of seeing again, as she went up the drive flanked with trees in summer foliage, the low, white house with the sun on its face, the barn wall beside it half-smothered in roses, the steep green fields climbing away to the moor. Its quality of established rightness in its setting woke the remembered response; this was a lovely place and she was glad to be back.

A sleek car, not the Daimler, was askew outside the door, and Louise did not stop there as she used to, but continued through the gap between house and barn, pulling up by the door to the kitchen corridor. Before her seat-belt was free the door burst open and Abby came leaping out.

'You can't think how I've been looking forward to having you back!' she exclaimed, dragging Louise out eagerly. 'I was terrified the Maxi-Monster would find some way of cancelling you. She was getting sniffy because Hugh was so determined to get hold of you again. Can't stand him singing someone else's praises, that's her problem. Is this all you've brought with you? God, it's for such a short time, I can't bear it.'

'Don't start wailing about it when I've just come,' Louise protested, hugging her. 'How are you, Abby?'

'Oh, I can't tell you. Fed up, lonely, reformed — read boring — and had it up to here with this place.'

'That good?'

But though they laughed Louise felt a stir of worry, noting that Abby, in spite of the 'reformed' part, which presumably meant more early nights then usual, looked exhausted, her eyes tired behind the slipping spectacles, her shoulders sagging forlornly. It wasn't the moment to pursue it.

'Am I in the same room?'

'Yes, and you should just see it,' Abby cried, perking up. 'I've done it *beautifully* for you. Come on.'

Contrasting emotions jostled Louise as Abby, talking over her shoulder and tripping over her feet, went ahead up the narrow stairs. Memories which now seemed far away – her dread about what she had embarked upon, the wintry cold of sunless corners, the sense of being flung into a place of disorder and confusion where there was nowhere to turn for help – mingled with an eagerness to see Fallan in summer mood, to be out in the garden, away up the hill. And deeper still was a recognition that she herself had come a long way since the doubts and nervousness of her first visit. Then, going along the nursery corridor, past the doors she did not look at, the rooms she did not wish to see even in her mind, she found that that element had not changed, the threat of pain lying in wait, too real and close.

'Look!' boasted Abby. 'I even remembered flowers.'

The quilt was crooked, the hem of one curtain sagged below the sill, gossamer furred with dust swayed lightly from the lampshade, but the dressing-table top and mirror were shining, the worn carpet had been hoovered, the air was scented by the roses Abby had shoved haphazard into a jug, and the window was open to the hill.

The misery that had dogged Louise since Phyllis's bombshell, the anxious totting up of resources, the zigzagging from one unappealing plan to another, and the sense of rejection which she could not banish, unreasonable as it was, fell away.

'Oh, Abby, it looks lovely. Thank you for taking so much trouble.'

'It's not bad, is it?' Abby looked round proudly.

'Bathroom's not quite up to this, I have to say. Ran out of time. You don't want to bother about unpacking, do you? Let's go and have tea.'

'And you can tell me about these people who are coming.'

'Oh, the *conference*,' Abby said, a wealth of scorn in her voice. 'Sorry, can't help you there. Maxine's department. God, she's a pain. They're not coming till tomorrow though, so we can have a good goss and then go down to the pub tonight. What do you say?'

'I say I'll find out what I'm supposed to be doing from someone a bit more reliable than you.'

'OK, be like that.' Abby didn't sound put out. 'I don't think there's all that much in the freezers, by the way,' she said as they went downstairs. It wasn't her job to see that there was, but it did strike her dimly that it wasn't fair for Louise to have to start from scratch all over again, when other cooks in the interval had cruised along on what she had produced.

'There's a surprise,' Louise said, but she had been prepared for it. She had also braced herself to find the tide of feckless squalor had swept back and looked round the tidy kitchen with startled eyes, catching as she turned a beam of gleeful satisfaction on Abby's face.

'You didn't expect that, did you?' Abby gloated. 'Cupboards and everything, look.'

'You did it?'

'Don't sound so disbelieving. I did. Well,' abandoning her injured tone with a giggle, 'only because Hugh made such a big deal about it. He hauled me in the day you left and bent my ear. Said now that you'd got everything in order it was to stay that way, and as I was the person here all the time it was down to me to see that it did, and if the temps arrived and found a midden they'd leave a midden behind. Something like that, anyway. I definitely remember midden. All very heavy.'

It seemed to Louise that Abby remembered what had been said with remarkable accuracy. Hugh had evidently made an impression.

'You've done brilliantly.' Louise couldn't help feeling pleased that her own efforts had not been wasted. Or was it that, in her relief to be away from Stirling and its problems for a few days, and back in this perfect glen, she was ready to be pleased at anything?

'Didn't rise to baking, though,' Abby said, shy at the unaccustomed praise, tipping a heap of Nutri-Grain bars onto the table, dropping a couple on the floor, picking out a blueberry one, peeling off its wrapper and biting off a third of it. Louise put the kettle on.

They had barely had time to exchange basic news when Maxine arrived. Sharp rap of high heels, sharp push at the door, sharp glance raking the room, Louise and the tea on the table, disapproval in place before she could have registered anything. She had pale hair as sleeked to her head as if she had just come up from a dive, and a sinewy leanness that was nothing like Abby's skinny immaturity. Thirty-five, perhaps older, with a strong jaw, an intolerant mouth, and pale eyes more green than blue. She wore navy; then and always, Maxine wore navy.

'Ms Donaldson?' How odd to hear someone say Ms, Louise thought. It didn't sound very friendly.

'Louise,' she said, rising to offer her hand.

Maxine seemed not to see it, her cold eye falling on the tattered wrappers in front of Abby. 'Maxine Trenchard,' she said, as though they had now arrived at what mattered.

'Would you like tea?' Louise asked. As she turned, assuming acceptance, to reach for a mug, she caught the wide-eyed surprise in Abby's face, exactly like that of a child confronted with some alarming breach of routine.

'No.' Maxine, frowning, made a dismissive gesture with her hand. Purple-red nails. 'Thank you.' Very much an afterthought. 'Could you spare a few moments?' She turned and clipped back to the door.

Now? Louise looked with raised eyebrows at the steam rising from her tea, and at Abby. Well, cooks came and went at Fallan; no one was going to waste time asking if she'd had a good journey here. She remembered Aidan, and the welcome he and the silly dogs had given her.

'Miserable old bat,' Abby mouthed, jerking her head towards the door. No busy feet had tapped away.

Maxine, waiting two yards along the corridor, gestured to Louise to close the kitchen door. Louise, feeling an unfamiliar resistance, did so quietly.

'Now, as you know,' Maxine began crisply, 'we are holding a very important business conference here, starting the day after tomorrow.'

And we're going to discuss it in the kitchen corridor? Louise looked at her in disbelief. What had been wrong with talking it over at the kitchen table with Abby or, if that was unthinkable, sitting comfortably in the office? She could have taken her tea, which was becoming more desirable in direct relation to Maxine's inconsiderate rudeness, with her.

'If we go into the matter of menus and timetable first thing in the morning,' Maxine pursued, with the single-minded concentration on her own concerns which would become familiar, 'that should give you ample time to shop and prepare.'

'I don't know about ample,' Louise remarked, with no particular emphasis.

Maxine checked, her brows coming down, as though this threatened a lack of cooperation which must be eradicated before it took hold. 'We're talking about six people here, not sixty. Hugh seemed to think you would be competent to handle that.'

'I've just arrived,' Louise observed mildly. 'I haven't so much as looked in the freezers yet — though I presume the main food ordering has been done and all the basics are in stock?' She didn't presume any such thing. Tomorrow was going to be a busy day.

'Certainly. Abby was told to organise that,' Maxine said, passing swiftly on. Louise didn't believe her. 'However, you'll have time to check your stores before our meeting, and we can base our planning on that.'

Good thinking, Maxine.

'For the moment, what I wished to say —' hurrying a little, so that Louise knew whatever was coming didn't suit this forceful woman, who seemed to carry anger with her from sheer habit '— there will be just the two of us for dinner tonight, Hugh and I, that is, so he asked me to suggest that you join us. There won't be any opportunity to do so after this evening, naturally.' She sounded happier about this part of the speech.

How unsure of herself Maxine must be, Louise reflected, in spite of her air of authority, to feel she had to spell out the message in this way.

'How kind of Hugh.' Louise thought of him as Mr Erskine, but it seemed a good moment to adopt the prevailing fashion. 'But what about Abby?'

'Yes, well—' Maxine cast a glance at the closed kitchen door and lowered her voice. 'Your status and Abby's are rather different.'

'Are they? How?'

Maxine looked as though she wasn't used to being challenged, however calmly. She evaded the point, her eyes hostile. 'Anyway, that's what Hugh asked me to say. Dinner at eight. Whatever it suits you to give us.'

Technically, Louise recalled, giving no hint of the anger she felt on Abby's behalf, she was not employed here until tomorrow morning. Maxine must know that.

'Eight o'clock,' she said, as though considering it, and turned back to the kitchen leaving Maxine frowning and uncertain. Not doubting that dinner would appear, her imagination didn't carry her so far, but conscious that

Louise had not grasped the true position here. That must be put right at the first opportunity.

Hugh sent Maxine to ask Louise to join them for a drink before dinner. Having tried to brush the idea aside, 'I should think she'll be too busy cooking, won't she?' and got nowhere, Maxine had been tempted to hang around in the corridor and go back saying Louise had refused, but she had worked for Hugh Erskine for long enough to know she couldn't risk it.

Louise, however, solved the problem by saying she couldn't leave her Hollandaise, and Maxine wasted no time in trying to overrule her. When at ten past eight Louise heard their voices in the dining-room she carried in the lettuce soup – she had thought wistfully, as she cut the bolted heads, of Wacker's lovingly tended rows – and found them looking at the two places she had laid.

'Louise, how nice to see you back,' Hugh Erskine greeted her with what sounded like real warmth. As she had been in the bath at the time, Louise was not aware that he had come to the kitchen to welcome her when he got home, taking Abby, flicking in mixed disgust and envy through a *Tatler* she had filched from Maxine's room, considerably by surprise. 'But I think there's some misunderstanding. You're having dinner too, aren't you? Don't we need another place – ?'

'How kind,' Louise said, as though she had never heard of the idea before. 'But I'm afraid I've already had dinner, with Abby. She would have been on her own otherwise. Everything's ready in the hot cupboard – I hope the

Hollandaise survives — and the percolator is ready to be switched on.' This she addressed to Maxine, making clear the assumption that it would be her job, then adding, 'I'll see you tomorrow, then — when I start work,' with a courteous smile she took her departure.

'But that wasn't—' Hugh began, with a sharp glance at Maxine, then, disdaining to waste words on what could not be altered, said crisply, 'In that case, I suggest we begin.'

Louise was already through the swing door. What a pleasure Maxine's expression had been.

# Chapter Nineteen

Louise was feeling very contented. Lennie had just stuck his head round the kitchen door to say in welcome, 'I seed yon old Vauxhall was back, time you got yourself a decent car,' and even Bella, who had already been at work for an hour in the downstairs rooms, had greeted her with resigned acceptance, as though to say that if they had to have someone to cook it might as well be Louise.

In spite of Abby's panics on their way to the village last night, Geordie had not shown up at the pub with his girlfriend, who was the daughter of the Gask gamekeeper and worked as a dental nurse in Aberfyle.

'She's so clean all the time,' Abby had complained, 'sort of glistening and hygienic. I don't see how Geordie can stand it, but she won't let go of him now, I know it. It'll be the altar or nothing, and serve him right.'

She had consoled herself with a shifty character who had come to the glen as one of a tree-planting squad and never gone away, but it had not escaped Louise that she watched the door all evening.

Louise herself had been surprised not only at how many faces were familiar, but at how welcoming everyone was. Fraser had been there, his leathery face creasing in a slow smile, and she had been happy to sit with him in a quiet corner, sometimes talking, sometimes facing silently across the room in the glen fashion, letting the hours slip undemandingly by.

She had also taken the chance to phone Cass, with a feeling that telephoning from Fallan might no longer be entirely private.

'How's the dread Maxine?' Cass had asked at once.

'Dreader than you could believe.'

'Honestly? Want me to come and sort her out? I've never officially inspected the place yet. After feedback from you and the others, and with Hugh Erskine away so much, that fell through the cracks somehow. But if anyone tries to give you a hard time, I'll be there!'

'You sound in good form, have you been drinking?'

'I have. My sister's staying, and she's always a bad influence. But listen, are you truly OK?'

'I'm looking forward to the challenge. It's going to be a busy few days. And it's good to be back in the glen, I'd forgotten how beautiful it is.'

'Which reminds me. How are you getting on with flat hunting? Any news on that?'

'Um, considering a couple of possibilities, but I haven't felt drawn to anything yet. I'll have to decide, though, as soon as I get home.' The harried feeling of time running out swept scarily back.

'Well, don't commit yourself to anything you're not keen about. We've got a spare room here, and once Roey's gone it's yours as long as you need it.'

Overwhelmed, Louise stammered, 'Cass, that's — it's terribly kind of you to suggest it, but I couldn't invade your house like that. What about your poor husband, for one thing — ?'

Cass laughed. 'It was Rick's idea. Actually, he had an even better one, which I can't go into over the phone. You'd have to see for yourself. So why don't you come and stay for a day or two after you leave Fallan? We'd love to have you, and it might help to talk over options.'

What a difference it made, Louise thought, whisking through preparations for dining-room breakfast, to have that next step, however tiny, safely in place. And what was Rick Scott's mysterious idea? She hadn't been able to persuade Cass to give her a hint of it, but merely learning that someone who didn't even know her was taking an interest in her welfare felt good. She knew she could go to Kinnafoot, if there was a gap between leaving the Stirling house and moving somewhere else, but she hadn't had the courage yet to tell Aidan what had happened. She was afraid that the indignation he would unleash on her behalf, the avalanche of impractical solutions he would pour out, might make her feel too sorry for herself. Perhaps the wisest course would be to write to Erica and let her deal with the first outpouring of wrath.

The door from the pantry swooshed open and blown

in on the draught came a very bad-tempered Maxine, her make-up doing little for her crumpled morning face.

'Breakfast is supposed to be at eight-thirty,' she snapped. 'Where's the coffee?'

'Good morning, Maxine. The coffee is there, ready to go in.' Louise nodded over her shoulder at the percolator, being engaged at that moment in turning a poached egg into a neat tadpole shape with a spiral tail. Abby – whose feet she had heard rattling down the wooden stairs, but who curiously enough had not appeared – was as fascinated as the twins had always been by this trick, and begged for her eggs to be done this way whenever she could face them. It was a delicate skill, the water had to be moving and no more, and Louise, believing the matter of the coffee dealt with and hearing the door swing, kept her attention on the job in hand. With the first egg safely drained and keeping warm, she slid in the second.

'I want the coffee brought in now!' The furious demand as the door opened again made Louise jump fatally – the egg white exploded in a little cloud which turned to stringy trails in the water.

'Good heavens, Maxine,' she protested, pulling the pan off the heat. 'What's the matter with you? The coffee pot's there, right under your nose.' She spoke in the easy tone one would use to a friend or colleague.

'I am not here to serve at table,' Maxine hissed.

'Well, I'm not sure that I am either,' Louise countered reasonably, starting to fish out the remains of the disintegrated egg with a slotted spoon, then realising she was going to have to start again with fresh water.

'Are you refusing to take that coffee into the dining-room?'

This seemed to be leaping into confrontation on an un-necessary scale. Louise looked at Maxine's tense face with raised brows, drawing back her own head in a little gesture of, Hold hard, where is this going?

'I'm busy at the moment, as you can see,' she said. 'Is it a problem for you to carry a coffee pot into another room?'

'It should have been there, ready. I shouldn't have had to come in search of it. And when I ask you to do something, I expect you to do it, without argument. I am in charge here, as you apparently fail to realise . . .'

'Goodness, you do have a problem.' Louise turned up the heat under her pan.

'Would you refuse to take that coffee in for Mr Erskine?' Hadn't he been Hugh last night?

'I don't think that's quite the same thing.' Louise still spoke easily, hearing a note in Maxine's voice which warned that she was fencing herself into a corner she would find it difficult to get out of.

'It's exactly the same thing!'

'No, it's not,' said a new voice behind her. 'And I think I've heard enough of this mindless squabbling. Bring in the damned coffee, Maxine.'

Louise curled her spoon with infinite care round egg number three. The door swung and fell silent. When she looked round the percolator had gone.

After a count of ten Abby stuck her head round the door from the corridor and whispered ecstatically, 'Yeah, go for it!'

'Where were you, may I ask?'

'Listening at the foot of the stairs. With one foot on the bottom step ready to run for all I was worth.'

'Thanks. Nice to know I had support on hand.'

'You didn't need me, you had old Hughie. Wow, didn't he bite? Tell you what, though,' Abby added a moment or two later through a mouthful of egg and toast, 'I wouldn't like to be you come menu-planning time.'

'I expect I'll be able to stand it.' Slightly to her surprise, Louise was certain that she could. She had never been any good at quarrelling, but in the last few months she seemed to have developed a dislike of being trampled on. She hadn't let Phyllis bully her and felt no qualms about facing up to Maxine.

Sitting in the office half an hour later, pen poised over her notepad, Louise observed with interest the devices employed by an angry Maxine to claw back the ascendancy so obviously important to her. She was sitting behind Hugh's desk, half turned away in a swivel chair, giving terse instructions to someone clearly not in a position to tell her to get lost, and at the same time scrolling up fearsome-looking diagrams on the computer screen. She could not — could she? — have orchestrated it, but on cue the fax machine began to disgorge itself of a lengthy message, and she was able to slap down the phone and turn with an exasperated sigh to deal with this new demand on her valuable time.

Louise, whose time looked likely to be even more valuable today than Maxine's, waited with a calm she was gratified to find she didn't have to work at. Act out the power-play, Maxine, but sooner or later you're going to have to come down to talking x pounds of sausages.

When they did get to work certain facts became apparent. Louise had turned into an enemy to be crushed. Maxine knew a great deal about current food fads in expensive eating places. Maxine knew nothing about cooking, and had surprisingly little idea of what might be available at short notice locally.

'Shall we forget about mascarpone, Thai fishcakes, kumquats and guacamole dips?' Louise suggested after a while. 'There's a fifteen-pound salmon in the freezer, some nice-looking teal and a haunch of roe. There are vegetables in the garden and I can get local cheeses in Aberfyle. Wouldn't the guests like the Scottish-produce touch?'

'I shouldn't think so for a moment,' Maxine said with scorn. 'That sort of thing is completely out. It would be an insult to offer them anything so boring.'

'And they arrive tomorrow?'

'Yes. I have a schedule here of the meetings, times of meals, and when we shall want coffee served in the library, which will be our main conference room. It's essential that this programme is scrupulously adhered to. Any delays will waste the time of some very high-powered people, and of course reflect on the image we wish to create.'

Louise didn't think from what she had seen of Hugh Erskine that his careless natural authority would be much impaired by the coffee and biscuits arriving late, but she nodded earnestly, intrigued to see how far Maxine would go.

'So what's the form for getting hold of this non-Scottish food in twenty-four hours?' she asked. 'Do you have it expressed from Harrods or flown up?'

Maxine gave her a suspicious look, but evidently concluded a mere cook couldn't be winding her up. 'That falls within your area of responsibility, naturally.'

Naturally. Louise decided this nonsense had gone on long enough. Saying briskly, 'Then I shall shop today, plan accordingly, and make sure all meals are on time,' she was on her feet and on her way before Maxine realised what was happening.

She did her best to regain control by repeating as Louise reached the door, 'Everything is to be of the highest quality. That must be clearly understood,' but Louise only smiled at her.

'You didn't tell me Maxine was so silly,' she remarked to Abby, sitting at the kitchen table to make rapid lists of her own.

'Silly?' Abby looked blank, and Louise laughed.

It was fun to be part of something, one of a busy group each with a contribution to make, fun to feel the deserted house she had first known wake and stretch itself in the sun, and it was a pleasure to produce food which was openly enjoyed.

The four guests, whom Maxine insisted on calling the delegates, were duly delivered by chauffeurs, or in one case by private helicopter which landed in the field known as the lambing park. They brought with them an aura of pressure, of having no time for distracting trivia, of having even more vital concerns to hurry on to after this. Though Maxine chose to make the whole affair as arcane as possible, Louise gathered that part of their business was to discuss the mining of gold in Sutherland, successfully undertaken in the 1860s and believed by many to be viable again on a commercial scale.

Louise didn't much care what they discussed. She had plenty to do with shopping, cooking three elaborate meals a day for six, baking bread and coffee-break goodies, incidentally feeding herself and Abby, and at the same time picking her way through the Fallan domestic minefield of equipment put away broken, the dishwasher refusing to rinse and the fridge filming in ice anything put into the salad compartment.

Abby worked heroically, though she broke quite a lot, her aim when pouring out tea and coffee could be erratic, and she had a nervous tendency to shoot biscuits into laps as she handed them round.

Lennie took an unexpected interest in what was going on, and brought in such quantities of unscheduled offerings from the garden, carried away by finding someone who would use them, that one evening Louise felt obliged to make a vegetable coulibiac to get rid of them. It was enthusiastically received.

Cameron, though very much the scoffing spectator and often seriously in the way, also made a contribution. Happening to be in the kitchen when a drama broke out about Abby having left the warm trolley switched on overnight with the cream jug sitting on it, he had vanished to return in short order with a fresh pint.

'Goodness, that was quick,' Louise exclaimed, assuming he'd been to the village. 'Let me pay you.'

'I'm no' needing paid,' he said and, with sidelong grin at Abby, slid off.

Abby giggled. 'Pinched it from the big house.'

'Abby, surely not?' Louise was horrified.

'It's all in the family, isn't it?' Abby said, unmoved. It was no time to debate the moral issue, but it reminded Louise that there was still much that was obscure to her about relationships among the Erskines.

Bella was magnificent. Silent, almost shrewish in her dedication, she brought the house to gleaming order every morning before anyone appeared, and had to be prevented from slipping back during meals to tidy up the library with the same ferocity of purpose.

The 'conference room' was in fact used less and less. As the sun shone and jackets were shed and ties removed, as reluctance grew to move indoors after breaks, which took place when they naturally occurred and became perceptibly longer, the terrace became the focal point of the gathering. Maxine did her best to reverse the trend, on the pretext that most of the material she had prepared required the use of her beloved hardware, but she was fighting a losing battle.

Her veneer of efficiency began to lift and peel as the sun poured down and people sprawled in long chairs, forsaking coffee for Pimms and frankly gossiping. The mining engineer from New South Wales appeared in shorts. Abby liked that. Breakfast began later and lasted longer. On the second day Louise served lunch in the garden. At dinner pudding, a flaming *glace en surprise* greeted with an uninhibited cheer, didn't go in till after eleven. One afternoon the Canadian summoned his chauffeur, holed up Louise knew not where, but certainly not in the Fallan pub, and took his Japanese colleague off to play golf.

The frowning, driven, self-important men to whom Abby and Louise had at first been faceless figures, paid to do a service job, now helped to clear the dinner table and stayed chatting in the kitchen while the dishwasher slurped and gushed, checked and died, and was coaxed on again. The Australian had to be dissuaded from dismantling it there and then. Hugh, looking relaxed and younger than Louise had thought him, jacket off, thick hair furrowed where he had run his fingers through it, went to fetch the Drambuie and they sat on till the small hours. Off-stage Maxine, stotting about preparing for tomorrow's session in martyred fury, looked forward to informing the agency without delay that Louise was not a suitable person to have in the house. Perhaps she foresaw that it would be Louise, not she, whom Hugh would thank for making the conference a success.

Louise and Abby – Hugh had not missed the point she had made about Abby the night she came, Louise noted with satisfaction – were borne into the drawing-room after dinner on the last evening, no excuses accepted, and there made much of. Louise enjoyed the party for an hour or so but, tired by now, slipped away as soon as a chance presented itself. Hugh quietly followed her.

'I won't keep you,' he said, catching her up in the hall.

'I know you must be exhausted. But I just wanted to thank you for all you've done. You probably weren't aware, and indeed why should you be, but there were a lot of major international interests involved here—' Seeing a courteously blank look spread over her face he laughed and began again. 'I've been trying to get this little lot together for ages. We can phone and e-mail and have virtual meetings till we're blue in the face, but this is what moves the mountains – being able to talk in an atmosphere where we can relax and be ourselves. All right, they liked the place and the weather was kind, but what made it work was that you not only gave them superb food but made them feel at home. I can't thank you enough.'

He wanted to say how much her personality, her gentleness and warmth, the impression she gave of wanting to look after people, had set the mood for the gathering. Her appearance was part of it too, the look he summed up to himself as her gingham-apron look, amused to think how outrageous a phrase that would be considered. However this, the most important part of his pleasure in what she had done, could not be expressed.

'I'm delighted it went so well,' Louise said, smiling. There could be no doubt that it had. Whatever the international repercussions, a handful of people had enjoyed themselves at Fallan. 'It's always a pleasure,' she added, laughing a little, 'to cook for people who do one's food so much justice.'

'Lord, they got through a lot, didn't they?' Hugh laughed too. 'I don't know how you kept up with them. But that brings me to something else I wanted to say, and then I really will let you go. Would you come back before the grouse shooting to put some supplies in the freezer again? You cook exactly the kind of food I like, and few cooks we've had have met your standards. No —' he went on quickly as Louise's smile was replaced by an anxiety which it disturbed him to see '— I understand that you don't want to be here when the children are home. I accept that. But as at Easter, the boys will go straight from school to their mother's, and Emily is to stay with her god-mother. No one else would be here, just you and Abby.'

Astute man. How affable he could be when he wanted something, his habitual impatience in abeyance. A man used, as Cass had said, to getting his own way. For a moment Louise's mind flew frantically round the matters still to be resolved in her own life, then steadied. There was nothing to alarm her here. And it would be another small slice of time accounted for. But what swayed her was the glow of achievement Hugh's thanks had brought, the friendly atmosphere of the last few days (Maxine notwith-standing) and the sense of inclusion she had liked so much. What reason did she have for refusing?

'I'll square it with the agency,' Hugh said, reading her decision in her face. 'Yes? Good, I'm delighted. We're lucky to have found you. Now off you go, get some sleep. We'll all have turned back into megalomaniac robots in a few hours and I can only apologise for the time at which we've asked for breakfast.'

'Dark suits. Blind eyes,' Louise remarked, turning to the stairs. 'Thank you for being so kind.'

Dark suits; blind eyes. Hugh's face was sombre as he

went back to the drawing-room. He knew Louise would not have said such a thing if she had not been very tired, but the words touched a nerve.

And it was high time Abby was chased off to bed, her own if possible.

# Chapter Twenty

Leaving Fallan was very different this time. Abby, only waiting for Louise to drive away before getting her head down for the afternoon, was less dejected, and solemnly promised to see that the repair jobs Louise had spent most of the morning organising were carried out. There was the comfortable knowledge of returning soon, to do a job she knew was well within her scope. There had been no opportunity on this visit to walk or enjoy the glen, or to find out more about the rift which kept the two Erskine households so rigidly apart (or to pay back the cream), so it was pleasant to look forward to at least the first of these in a couple of weeks' time.

What changes might have come about in her own circumstances by then? Louise's stomach gave a lurch at the prospect, very close now, of being so ruthlessly uprooted. But for a day or two longer she could keep at bay the realisation that she still had nowhere to go. Cass had been insistent that Louise should stay with her on her way home, even if only for a night. It seemed silly, she had urged, to drive down to Stirling then back almost as far north as Fallan again. All Louise had to do was come over the pass from the west, and she was there. It made sense, Louise conceded, approaching the crown of the pass now. Then she wondered if she was just being cowardly, grasping at any chance to put off dreaded decisions.

Cars were parked near the summit, where the road ran through a gut of rock, dark with moisture, for a light mizzle of rain had ended the spell of fine weather which had added lustre to Maxine's 'conference'. Once through this rocky notch the road fell sharply away and Louise could only snatch glimpses of the scene opening before her as she followed its tight bends, busy with traffic. The hamlet below, Bridge of Riach, was a mere cluster of dwellings by-passed by a new stretch of road.

There was no difficulty in finding the house, perched on a shelf of hillside on the far side of the glen. And Cass was there, leaping long-legged down the garden steps as the car rounded the bend in the track. She gave Louise a warm hug of welcome.

'I wasn't sure I'd persuaded you. I wouldn't have been a bit surprised if you'd phoned to say you'd gone straight down to Stirling. Come on, come in, and tell me what on earth's been going on at Fallan.'

'At Fallan? What do you mean? Don't tell me Hugh Erskine has phoned already?' Louise followed her up the steps, threading a way between sprawling lady's mantle, with the feeling she had begun to like of being swept up by Cass's cheerful energy.

'He certainly has.' Cass sounded amused as she led the way into a room running the width of the cottage, at one end of which a fire was burning. 'It's so gloomy today after all the gorgeous weather we've had that I thought a fire would be nice to have tea by. Shall we do that right away and you can see your room later?'

'That would be good.' Louise smiled, remembering Aidan making the same suggestion out of frank greed. She looked appreciatively round the room, simply furnished at first glance, but revealing many beauties on closer examination. It was a smaller house than she had expected; was there really room for her?

'So did Hugh book me to go back? Is that all right with you? You hadn't set up anything else for me?'

'No, I thought I'd wait till your plans were clearer. However, this business of Fallan—' Cass paused on her way to the kitchen, shaking her head dubiously. 'I can't say it sounds exactly straightforward to me.'

'What do you mean?' Louise followed her. 'What are you talking about? Is there a problem?'

'A conflict of ideas, perhaps.' Cass looked entertained about something as she reached long arms to unhook cups, switch on the kettle and get out the milk. 'You see, when Mr Erskine phoned I'd already had a somewhat different call from Maxine. Rick Scott,' she broke off in wrath, 'don't tell me you've polished off that entire cake! Oh, well, have to be ginger biscuits. No, we're in luck, he missed the flapjacks.'

'Cass, what do you mean about Maxine?'

'Well, according to her, Hugh Erskine won't have you back at Fallan at any price. Not up to the mark. They may have to reconsider using the agency. Serious stuff, Louise, I'm disappointed in you.' She didn't look disappointed, she looked as though she thought it a huge joke, but Louise was too perturbed to register that as she pursued Cass back to the long room, carrying the flapjack tin which had been thrust into her hands.

'But then if Hugh — ?' she asked in bewilderment.

'Ah, yes, Hugh. He phoned a little later, quite independently. Odd, I thought communication was all in successful business dealings. Are you comfortable there? Would you like to be nearer the fire?'

'Cass!'

'Actually it was quite funny,' Cass said, relenting, picking up the teapot but forgetting to pour. 'He raved on about how much your input had contributed to the general success of whatever it was that had been going on, got quite carried away about it, in fact, then began discussing dates for your next stint. At that point I thought it only fair to let him know that his secretary had not only sacked you, but had threatened to sack me into the bargain. The conversation became quite rewarding after that,' she wound up with a grin, offering the milk.

'You told him . . .' The full beauty of it was dawning on Louise.

'Mm,' Cass said with her mouth full. 'Maxine has never struck me as a very attractive person somehow.'

'Wow,' said Louise with slow relish, as Abby might

have done. Then, 'God, I hope she's not there the next time I am, she'll eat me alive!'

They were still gossiping by the fire when Rick came in, a huge slow-moving man, bigger even than Aidan, his powerful body heavy with muscles developed by physical work. He had none of Aidan's flamboyant cordiality, but in the clasp of his big hand, its palm smooth as leather, in his quiet smile of welcome, Louise was instantly aware of a perception and kindness which even Aidan could not match. His presence didn't break the peaceful mood. There was no feeling that she and Cass shouldn't have sat talking for so long, that the day ought to move on to the next stage. Rick simply stretched out in a chair and merged into the scene. In due course tea became drinks, and eventually their minds turned lazily to thoughts of dinner.

'I didn't feel brave enough to plan anything clever with Louise here,' Cass admitted.

'So what did you plan that wasn't clever?'

'I didn't get that far.'

'My best pasta again, is that what you're saying?'

'Oh, what an *excellent* idea.'

'I could cook,' Louise volunteered.

'Even better idea.'

But it seemed, when Louise had been taken up to a charming bedroom with a sloping ceiling and a dormer window looking down a glen already nearly dark, and had decided she was enjoying herself too much to take time off for a bath, that the accepted thing to do about dinner was to make it together. Time was clearly irrelevant to her hosts. What was important was pursuing the topic of the moment, abandoning whatever was on hand while some vital point was thrashed out, and keeping glasses filled while dinner rolled gently towards completion and the air was rich with the aroma of herbs and spices.

As they lingered at the table Louise knew that much of her delight in the mood of the evening stemmed from the evident happiness of these two people. She saw how Rick was focused on Cass, amused by her, watching her with pleasure. As they had circled in the movements of long practice preparing dinner he had touched her often, scooping her against him occasionally like an affable grizzly. And with him there Louise had noted that Cass, looking tall no longer beside his burly height, became less brisk, her voice and her manner softer. After the question-marks that lurked at Fallan, the lack of cohesion and awareness of strife, this atmosphere of accord was as soothing as an opiate.

The conversation turned to Fallan, since the Maxine joke was too good not to share, and Louise, normally not a big talker, found there was plenty to tell, sure of amusement shared.

'It seems a weird set-up to me,' Rick commented, after listening for a while and making his own assessment of Louise, whose story had touched his kind heart. 'Does Erskine use his house as a hotel? It sounds like it.'

'That's exactly how it feels,' Louise agreed. 'There's no family core to the house, no atmosphere of being a home, though it could be lovely, and the setting is magical.'

'And then this odd business of being on the doorstep of the big house,' Cass said frowning, 'but with no contact between them. Who runs the estate? Does Hugh Erskine have land or does it belong to his father?'

These questions had floated past Louise. She didn't have the faintest idea of how that worked, except that there seemed to be no outside staff but Lennie.

'It does sound peculiar,' Cass persisted, 'that you have never even met the old couple.'

'And that no one ever talks about them,' Louise agreed. 'The situation seems to be taken for granted by everyone. Perhaps they're cold fish, like Hugh Erskine. That's the impression he gives, anyway – that he's not interested in relationships, or can't cope with them.' Yet there had been moments when he had seemed more human. Fleeting images returned – his grin as he came into the kitchen the evening of that late-night session, hefting the Drambuie bottle in one hand and a clutch of glasses in the other; or laughing over his shoulder at some joke as he stood at the dining-room sideboard carving duck golden-glazed with chopped orange; looking into her face with what had seemed genuine gratitude as he thanked her for what she had done.

Going wearily to bed at last, tiredness – and far more wine than she had realised she'd drunk – catching up with her so suddenly that she could hardly drag herself up the stairs, it occurred to Louise that she still hadn't heard about Rick's idea. It was too late to worry about it now, but she was sure that whatever he had thought of would be helpful and generous.

Before sleep came rolling over her, she was aware, for the first time since Owen had died, that she wanted someone there to cuddle up to. It was no more than that, an impulse born of the friendly mood of the evening, but it brought a quite new pang of loneliness.

Cass was not due at the office next day. 'When I moved up here the idea was that Lindsay would run that side of the business and I'd do the driving round, meeting clients and so on, but leaving myself plenty of time to spend at home. It didn't work out like that, of course, partly because the agency took off in a way we hadn't expected, but mainly because I like working.'

'And Rick doesn't mind you being so busy?'

'Rick has a marvellous capacity for taking people exactly as they are.' Cass's face and voice became gentler as she spoke, in a way Louise was sure she was not conscious of, and the little flicker of loss that had woken last night returned. Louise had made her marriage work by putting her needs second to Owen's, recognising early on that this was the only way it would work. Later, she had made the twins the focus of her life . . . Her face tightened, her mind swung violently away. But she had made herself add the thought; she had got that far.

'Anyway,' Cass was saying, 'Rick's expecting us, so if you've had enough breakfast let's get going.'

'Expecting us? Are we going to look at his workshop? Good, I'd been hoping to see it.' Louise had heard last night about Rick's barn, where he restored and sometimes made furniture.

'It's raining but not much. Want to walk or drive down? It's only at the bottom of the track.'

'Oh, walk. It's more mist than rain, isn't it?'

'Right. We'll bung this lot in the dishwasher and be off.'

The barn was reached by an underpass below the new road. It lay in a curve of the river, screened by a belt of birch and hazel which also muted the sound of the traffic. A solid rectangle of stone, with skylights let into its slate roof, it stood close to the water, a group of rowans, their berries already taking on the first flush of autumn colour, beside it, and a serviceable-looking van beside them.

'What a marvellous place to work,' Louise said as they went across the rough grass, thick with wild flowers, to the big open doors. Rick was busy cutting fabric to cover a chair pale in new canvas.

'So you've come to see what you think,' he said, smiling at Louise as they came in.

'I haven't said anything yet,' Cass told him. 'I was letting first impressions sink in.'

'Ah.' Rick waited, with his air of having all the time in the world at his disposal.

'Said anything about what?' Louise asked, glancing around her. Surely not about something for her flat when she moved? It was the only thing she could think of.

'Come and see,' Cass said. 'You can have a prowl round this lot afterwards if you want to.'

Puzzled but amenable, Louise followed her through a door in a partition which cut off the end of the building. It led into a narrow corridor, where a door to the right opened onto a small bedroom with double bed, built-in cupboards and dressing-table against the gable wall, and a window knocked through to look out to the river.

'And here—' On the other side Cass showed her a bathroom with shower unit, and a tiny kitchen.

Louise, her heart beginning to bump, stared at her.

Cass put a swift hand on her arm. 'Rick lived here before we were married. We often use it as an overflow for guests – or we come down here ourselves and let the guests stay in the house. It's not needed at present, not for the rest of the summer. I know it's a bit of a contrast with your lovely house, but it might do as a stopgap. Oh, Louise, don't, please don't – Rick—'

For Louise, thunderstruck by the generosity of this offer, was shaken to find tears spilling down her face, as though they were tears for all sorts of other things which had been waiting for this moment to be released. It was Rick's arm which came round her, Rick's barrel chest into which without hesitation she turned her drenched face, and Rick's voice which reverberated through his denim shirt, saying, 'Come on, love, it's all right . . .'

Walking up the track again, red-eyed, excited, dazed with gratitude, Louise hardly listened to Cass.

'If you prefer to be in the house the room is yours. You mustn't think we're hoofing you out. And if you sleep in the barn you must use the house for meals and company, that's always the arrangement. In any case Rick will be down there with his tools screaming and whining, and he uses the space above the ceiling to store wood so he'd be crashing about over your head . . .'

It wasn't the impression of Rick's working style which Louise had gained.

'It's perfect,' she said huskily. 'I can't begin to tell you—'

But Cass stopped her. 'Look, before you decide, there's something I must tell you.'

'Yes?' Louise waited, with a tension that showed her how passionately she wanted to seize this solution, how deeply she had dreaded the bleak unknown.

'It's just that — well, we've got a lot of friends who come and go, mainly from there,' Cass paused to point up the glen to a house set high against the ridges and shoulders which closed it in, 'and from another house you can't see from here. They are all related and they're a big clan and — I think you should know —' she was finding this difficult '— there are a lot of children, new babies but also older children, and they come and go pretty freely. I couldn't promise that you wouldn't see them.'

Louise stood, indifferent to the rain, looking up towards that big building beside what looked like a ruined castle, but seeing neither of them.

'It has to be part of life,' she said after a moment, and Cass waited, moved by the look on her face. 'It's right.' Louise turned, her chin coming up in a gesture Cass hadn't seen before. 'I've hidden away for too long. It was wrong and unnatural. Children are everywhere. I don't think I could face looking after them, it would hurt too much still, but meeting them, in the ordinary course of life — Cass, of course I must and can.'

Cass hesitated, dreading what she had to say now.

'Look,' she brought out at last, 'you must know this. In one family there are twin girls.'

Louise's face set in a mask of pain which made Cass wish she had never embarked on this well-meant plan.

'How old?'

'They're nearly ten.'

Soft as the rain was, no more than misting their hair and shoulders, always, when Cass remembered the scene, their frozen stillness on the track and Louise's face, she believed that in the stretching silence she had heard it fall.

'Oh, Louise, I'm so sorry, come here . . .'

But Louise only leaned her forehead briefly against Cass's arm, then said steadily, 'It will be all right. I can't talk about it just for the moment, but it will be all right.'

She gave a nod to affirm this, looking into Cass's eyes, then turned to head up the track. As they went on without speaking Cass ached for her, for her courage and for her unimaginable grief. She was only glad that, in however small a way, she and Rick were able to offer help.

# Chapter Twenty-One

Louise had not envisaged that leaving the Stirling house behind would bring a sense of release. While from habit her mind had continued to regard it as home, she discovered that her feelings had moved on. As the objects which had given it its character had been stripped away it had become a bleak place, increasingly indifferent to her presence, its associations with Nevil, Phyllis and the Donaldson clan ranged behind them overtaking the memories of her ordered life with Beatrice. It had become linked in her mind with conflict, greed, and a growing feeling of beleaguerment.

She knew, good sense told her so, that living in someone's barn which was also a workshop was the merest interim solution, but it had all been beguilingly easy. There had been no reason to wait. Rick had come in his van, big enough to hold all Louise wanted to take with her, had carried her belongings down for her, packed them in and driven off. That was that. Anything she couldn't find space for in her new room was stored on the other side of the wall, where she could see for herself it was in no one's way.

She had felt nothing but relief as she had run down the basement stairs for the last time and locked the door behind her. It was as though Aunt Bea had vanished from the house when calculating eyes were laid upon her treasures, and indifferent hands had carried them away. She was not there to say goodbye to.

It was a moment of pure satisfaction to hand the keys to Nevil, not forewarning him by making an appointment but slipping in between clients. Two minutes were more than enough for what she had to do. The realisation that she need never speak to him again, never be at the mercy of his grudging spirit or Phyllis's jealous spite, produced a euphoria she couldn't remember experiencing before, and once in the car she had to sit for some moments to subdue her elation before driving away.

Where before a pall of uncertainty and emptiness had hung before her, that emptiness now appeared enticing, full of possibilities, and driving up to Bridge of Riach she realised, with a sense of shock, that what she was looking at was freedom. When had she last felt like this? Had she ever felt like this? Even when she had escaped from home to come to Scotland at nineteen, the grip of her parents on her life had still been firm, and though she had defied them by staying, and then by marrying Owen, she had felt guilt at that defiance and been troubled by their disapproval. She had still been caught in the net of inadequacy, of failing to live up to expectations, which they had woven round her.

Now, with an abruptness she couldn't fully take in, her life was in her own hands, and there was no sense of loneliness. Cass and Rick, with whom she felt happy and at ease, were there, and behind them other friendly figures who had entered her world this summer, behind them again the figures who would take shape as she went to new places and undertook new jobs.

In this mood of optimism and confidence, she had phoned Aidan and survived the blast of his rage at what had been done to her, his vows to right her wrongs, his absurd plans for her future. He had made her promise to come and stay at the first opportunity, and she meant to go. It would be wonderful to be back at Kinnafoot, particularly in this new mood of liberation. She literally felt she had no problems. What had they been, those mountainous fears? All she had to do was earn her living. And find somewhere to live? There were a million places where a female on her own could live. Even the absence of possessions was a bonus.

She thought of the room in the barn, going in past the battered furniture, past the workbench and the lathe, and the simplicity of it lifted her spirits another notch. Had she been influenced to accept it so readily because she admired the way Erica lived in her converted lorry? Perhaps; another thread weaving in. She thought Erica would approve of her new surroundings. She thought of the cottage up the track, Cass with her quick generosity, Rick with his more understated but equally perceptive sympathy, and she found herself dazed by gratitude and expectancy.

This mood was still with her when a few days later she crossed the pass to head westward for Glen Fallan. Ahead lay nothing but good things. She had her own little slot to fit into there; the dishwasher might even be working.

'She will be arriving in Pitlochry in the late afternoon and must be met. No, I don't know the time of the train, but I should have thought it not beyond the bounds of simple initiative for you to find that out. This whole thing is too infuriating, the child is completely out of hand. You are who? The cook? Well, where is the nannie, reluctant as I am to apply the word to such a feckless creature. Nannies were nannies in my day. So, I leave the matter with you. If her father isn't there to deal with the problem and allows his children to run wild over the countryside, and Leo refuses to have anything to do with his own grandchildren, I suggest you stop arguing and making difficulties and fetch the wretched child.'

Louise, winded by this attack, let her jaw drop at the receiver before she put it down. To be confronted by such aggression from a stranger was not pleasant and Louise's cheeks were pink. In one acid speech four people had been disposed of — five if she counted herself.

Then the practical implications swarmed up. Emily, not due home for another three days, was on her way to Pitlochry. The thought stampeded Louise into irrational rejection. This was nothing to do with her; she must get away. She had already packed, she was supposed to leave today, her job was over. But the reason she hadn't driven away two hours ago, the reason she had answered the phone at all to be met by that vicious onslaught, was that Abby was stuck on Mull. Her Edinburgh friends had a cottage there, and had invited Abby to join them for a couple of days. As it coincided with Louise being at Fallan, Abby had wheedled and begged and lied her head off about holidays due to her, and of course Louise had let her go. This morning she had phoned with a long tale about the car battery being flat, which Louise suspected Abby had had more to do with than she was admitting, about being as far from Tobermory as it was possible to get, and how there was no way she could get back till Monday, and would Louise please, please, please stay and bail her out.

'Nothing's happening here. Is there any need for me to stay?' Louise had asked.

At this Abby had become more incoherent than ever, and Louise gathered from her ravings that not only had she long ago used up all her holiday allowance, but that Hugh had said he intended to be back before the children arrived and might turn up at any moment.

Louise, knowing there was no urgency about leaving, except that she had been looking forward to returning to her new quarters, which had turned out to be more enjoyable even than she had expected – that went for the social life of Bridge of Riach too, into which she had been hospitably drawn – had sighed and accepted the inevitable. Hugh Erskine was not the man to be tolerant about the absence when required of his housekeeper, who in the normal course of events spent a lot of time doing very little at his expense. Anxiety about the children's arrival, now so close, had stirred and been suppressed. Abby would be back well before they got here.

Now here was Emily, actually on her way, and Louise's mind darted up blind alley after blind alley as the options for dealing with this were ruled out one by one. Lennie could go. No, Lennie had taken the pick-up to Aberfyle for a service. Leave a message at the garage, get him to go on to Pitlochry. But the garage said they were to leave the pick-up out and the keys on the wheel, and they didn't know when Lennie would be back for it. Bella — Bella didn't drive. Get hold of Cameron. She wouldn't know where to start looking, and in any case Cameron wasn't at her disposal. Then the obvious — book a taxi. It was a long way, but Hugh could afford such solutions.

Another check. The taxi might bring Emily home but she couldn't come back to an empty house. Bella then, she could do that much surely. But going along the kitchen passage Louise remembered that Bella had gone with Lennie for a days' shopping.

With a sob of frustration very far from her usual calm, Louise turned and put her fists against the wall, her forehead against its cold stone. She must calm down; this whirling anger would solve nothing. Then the answer came, the obvious, simple answer. Emily's grandparents could look after her, and Louise could drive away, back to her own life, as she was entitled to do.

Her blind dread wiping everything else from her mind, she went out of the back door and across the steading yard and took the path over the ridge which led to the buildings below the big house. She ran up the slope, her whole being concentrated on freeing herself from this intolerable imposition. She had hoped she might see Cameron, but no one was about. Passing the buildings she crossed the wind-scoured space to the house, seeing with relief that a light was on near the back door. She banged on it with an uninhibited vigour which would have surprised anyone who knew her well.

The door was opened by a woman who, in other circumstances, Louise would have been amused to see, so completely was she the cosy cook of children's fiction. She had a round face, with fat blobs of chin and cheeks like the sections of cottage loaves; her eyes, bright and friendly, disappeared behind pouches of flesh when she smiled; her hair was of a yellow so metallic it looked green; her sleeves were rolled up, she had flour on her arms, and her flowery pinny bound in a bosom so shelf-like that even in this fraught moment Louise wondered if she wore some kind of mono-bra. The same distracted part of her brain thought, This is my opposite number, and was briefly entertained.

'Is Mrs Erskine in?' she asked, remembering that in any references to the war between the two establishments it was always Leo Erskine's name that came up. 'I must see her. It's very urgent.'

'Lumme, what's up? That's me, for what it's worth. You'd best come in.'

Her accent was pure East End and, as she led Louise into the kitchen and crossed at once to shut the door to the rest of the house, her movement was so much that of the furtive employee hiding something from the boss, that for a second Louise's brain refused to take in what she had said. It also floundered at the sight of racks and racks of golden *vol au vent* cases and the baking smells which wafted deliciously in the draught as the door shut. How many people were being fed here?

'Mrs Erskine?'

'You're from down the road, aren't you? I've seen you about, knew I recognised the face. But what are you doing here, duck? Get us all into trouble, you will.' And again she glanced towards the inner door.

Louise had no time for any of that. Relief to have found someone to rescue her from the crisis into which she had been thrust overrode everything. 'It's Emily. She's arriving at Pitlochry station this afternoon and has to be fetched.'

The round face goggled at her. 'You come up here to tell me that? You flipped your lid or what?'

'But there's no one to meet her. Abby's away, and Lennie and Bella are in Aberfyle. I have to leave, I was supposed to leave this morning, and there'll be no one to look after her once she's here, so I thought—'

'Sorry, love, can't help you. You must know that. Me? Blimey, I'm the last person . . .' She chucked her head in a gesture of wry disbelief, then looked more closely at Louise. 'I really am sorry, love. I'd help you if I could, but it would be more than my life's worth. Anyhow, if you ask me, that little madam Emily knows full well how to take care of herself.'

'But she can't just be left there. And I have to go home, I was supposed to go this morning.'

'So you keep saying, but I'm telling you, there's nothing

I can do about it. I mean, I've nothing against the kids, poor little sods I reckon, but me go and fetch one of them from the station? You've got to be joking, he'd kill me.'

A noise of hammering followed by a crash and what sounded like violent oaths from somewhere in the depths of the house galvanised her into action. 'You'll have to go, duck. Sorry and all that, but you'll just have to sort it out as best you can.'

With a surprisingly firm grip her pudgy hand seized Louise by the shoulder and propelled her towards the door. 'Beats me you ever thought of coming here . . .'

Louise found herself on the doorstep. She was still gathering her wits when the door opened again and Mrs Erskine's face appeared in the crack. 'Go round the back of the shed, there's a dear. I'll never hear the last of it if he knows I've been talking to you.'

Obeying the urgency in her voice, in ten seconds Louise was out of sight behind a handsome stone building which she would hardly have called a shed. There she paused to pull herself together. For a second she was tempted to refuse to have anything to do with the mysteries and hints. She wanted to go back, thump on the door again and demand that someone assume responsibility. Mrs Erskine had not been hostile, indeed she had seemed ready to be friendly.

But she didn't go back. There was only one answer. The person whose responsibility this was, Emily's father, could do nothing even if she contacted him.

Numb as an automaton, she found out the time of the train, worked out that if she was to be in time to meet it she should leave at once, took out food for dinner – a bad moment as she wondered what Emily might like – and set off down the glen, doing her best to contain her bitter anger at what was being asked of her.

All the way resentment churned. Why should Abby, Lennie, Bella and above all Hugh Erskine not be there when they were needed? Why should that useless grandmother pretend she wanted to help while pushing Louise bodily out of the door? It was bizarre. They were all unnatural, inhuman, and she had had enough of them.

Some of her anger expended itself on the crawling traffic, at its peak now August had arrived. Even on the road along the loch there were few places where it was possible to overtake, and each time her intention was thwarted by a caravan or a beer lorry or, for an infuriating mile or so, an oblivious swarm of cyclists. She would be late, and that went against the grain for Louise at any time, but now, with a child waiting . . .

Abruptly her self-absorbed anger was thrown into shamed relief. She saw that, ever since looking into their rooms on her first day at Fallan, she had allowed these Erskine children to be symbols, images created from her own inability to deal with what had happened to her. They had become, in the background of her mind, a source of pain, to be avoided at all costs. They had had no life of their own, no personalities, barely names and ages. Everyone had been warned not to talk about them and had scrupulously observed the embargo. How kind that was; how astonishing, she saw now, that so much care should have been taken on her behalf.

Now, ahead of her, waited a child. A child who appeared to have run away from her godmother's house. Louise had not paused to take in that aspect. What had happened to make Emily fly for home? And who could blame her, if that tart tongue was what she was flying from?

The train was already on its way north as Louise reached the town, and she felt guilty because she knew her own hysterical behaviour had made her late, not the busy road. With a picture in her mind of a forlorn little person on the platform, and deep in her subconscious giving it fair hair and a golden skin like her own, she almost missed the darting figure heading for the gate into the hotel gardens. But though she had done her best to avoid seeing the photographs of the children in the house, the pastels of them at a younger age which hung on either side of the drawing-room fireplace, she had absorbed their details in spite of herself, and knew at once who that thin scowling face belonged to, stud in nostril, dark hair lank around it.

# Chapter Twenty-Two

'Emily!'

The darting figure wheeled and paused, the scowl deepening.

Louise walked towards her. 'You're Emily Erskine, aren't you?'

'No.' As rude a response as she could make it.

'I'm Louise. I've come to meet you.'

'What makes you think I'm going to believe that?'

'I'm working at Fallan.'

'Oh, a cook.' The disdainful tone reminded Louise of Emily's father, perhaps unfairly.

'Exactly. Abby is away for a day or two so—'

'Abby's an idiot.' Emily stared across the hotel garden as though ready to be on her way again, swinging an expensive but empty-looking leather bag so that it grazed the pavement.

Louise surveyed her. There seemed little to do with all this hostility and anger except convey it home. 'Come on.'

She turned to the car, not looking to see if Emily followed. She had no idea what she would do if Emily refused. However, it was a long way to Fallan; common sense would hopefully prevail.

It did. Emily dumped herself in the passenger seat and slid down so that her chin was on her chest.

'Don't forget your seat-belt.' Louise was already reversing out, but Emily made no move to obey. Louise pulled up and waited.

In a moment or two Emily, with her father's impatience, demanded crossly, 'What's going on?'

'Seat-belt.'

'I never put one on, they're boring.'

'Then out you get.' Louise didn't raise her voice or turn her head, but contemplated the taxi-stand ahead with calm interest.

'Oh, my God,' Emily groaned, heaving sharply at the strap so that it locked, yanking again in exasperation, pretending she couldn't find where to snap it in, muttering things under her breath which Louise made a point of not hearing. As she drove on, without comment, it occurred to her that exchanges between this farouche child and her godmother must be worth hearing.

'What were you going to the hotel for?' she asked, as she waited for a gap in the traffic threading along the main street. Larger questions, about Emily's flight, could be dealt with by those responsible for her. Louise was merely interested in what her objective had been when she first saw her hurrying across the parking area.

Emily shrugged but decided to answer. 'Short cut to

the shops.' Pause. 'There's always something you can nick as you go through.'

Gauntlet number two, Louise thought, nudging into the flow of cars.

'Were you going to phone home?'

A shoulder was lifted in an exaggerated shrug, head turned away at right angles. 'Honor was supposed to do that. Tell one of the plebs to pick me up.' Careful, Emily. 'Onner bike, I say.' Well-worn, perhaps, but quite good.

'And Honor is – ?'

'Don't you know anything? She's my horrible god-mother, and I was supposed to stay with her, but I got totally pissed off like I always do. She's always dragging in these losers from next door. Veggies. Greens. Forever wanting to save something. God, what for? My little play-mates, she calls them.'

'Playmates? Your godmother honestly calls them that?'

'Oh, well.' Back-tracking in slight surprise to find this had struck a sympathetic chord. 'Anyway, I decided to blow, not that home's much better.'

'Did you tell anyone you were leaving?' Louise's interest was more in the grim godmother's reaction than in what Emily had done.

'Left her a note.' Emily sniffed and rubbed the back of her hand across her nose, angrily, as though it had no right to annoy her. 'And now you're going to say, "And what did you put, Emily?"' She mimicked a patronising adult voice with savage exactness.

That's how we do sound, Louise acknowledged. What

had happened in this child's life to produce such savagery? Yet child was not the word. Louise had braced herself to meet a small girl, as biddable and good-natured as the twins had been, needing care and comfort. But Emily, though at thirteen not an adult, was certainly not a child; she was an individual, a fiercely independent entity. Even in this short space of time she had become herself, distinct from any previous images Louise had had of her, and that self was fascinating, and stimulating. She was also a sad spectacle, hunched and defensive, solitary and angry.

'I'll tell you what I put,' she said aggressively after a moment. 'I put, "Have stolen money from your handbag for train. Tell Abby to come and get me."'

'That was pretty clear.' Louise caught the movement as Emily's head came round, and felt her piercing scrutiny.

Emily tried again. 'I have to steal to support my habit.'

'Ah.'

'I do.' For the first time she sounded like a child, querulous and insistent. Then the adult veneer was back. 'Anyway, she's a frigging old bitch.' The words were carefully mumbled, as her objurgations to the seat-belt had been mumbled, and Louise was glad that an awareness of limits still obtained. It was a starting point.

A starting point for what? It was a minute or two before she caught herself up. This drive to Fallan was not the start of anything. She was filling a gap no one else had been available or willing to fill. As soon as Abby came back she would be gone and, now that what she had been promised would never happen had happened, that was the last she would see of Fallan.

She pushed this away. 'What school do you go to?' she asked Emily, thinking it would be more peaceful to turn to mundane topics.

Emily, however, fixed Louise with a stare of scorn so burning that Louise didn't need to turn her head to feel it. All right, they wouldn't talk about school. But had the question been so out of the way? Children did spend three-quarters of their life there. Conversation lapsed as they rolled along the loch road, where tradesmen's vans rattling homewards were giving hesitant tourist cars nasty frights.

Only after they had passed through the village did Emily ask, 'Where *is* Abby then?'

'On Mull, with a broken-down car and a missed ferry.'

'Oh, nice one!' For the first time Emily's sullen face broke into a grin of wicked delight. 'Yeah, I definitely like that.' She slid further down into the seat, her thin legs stretched out, her arms wrapped round her chest in a hug of pleasure.

Louise, smiling in response to that grin, was reminded of Hugh when his meeting was going well and everything was being done as he wanted it. She looked forward to a few words with him, should the chance arise.

'Presumably you abandoned your luggage,' she said, as Emily got out of the car at the front steps.

'Presumably I did!' Emily shouted back over her shoulder, charging into the house.

And presumably she had other clothes at home, Louise

thought peacefully, going round to lift from the back the bag she had put into it this morning. How nice, really, that she didn't have to worry about the question.

She was pushing open the door to the kitchen wing when she heard steps behind her and saw Emily sidling out of the red corridor, brushing her shoulder against the wall, rubbing at her nose again.

'Where have you been?' Louise asked the question more in surprise than anything, having assumed that Emily had gone up to her room. But she had a perfect right to go anywhere, and however sly she might look Louise wished she could bite back the words.

Emily didn't seem to object to them. 'Checking the office desk,' she said airily. 'Always worth a look, you never know what messages might have come in for Hughie, or Maxine, come to that. Nothing riveting today though.'

Louise squashed down the impulse to reprove, casting her mind back to the days of Mrs Baines. Her role in people's houses wasn't to alter their way of living. But someone had a job on their hands with Emily.

'What time do you like to have supper?' she asked, concentrating on what was her business.

Shrug. 'What's for supper anyway?'

'Pizza.'

'I hate pizza.'

Automatic, probably untrue. 'Then you can find whatever you like for yourself.' And cook it.

Emily sent her one of her smouldering glances, thrown,

Louise was almost sure, by the equable tone with which
her best efforts were received.

'You're paid to feed me.'

Louise smiled. 'Shall we say seven, then?'

Emily hesitated for a second. 'I'm going out,' she said.

'Fine.'

She saw real anger in Emily's eyes this time.

'You're paid to look after me as well.'

She sounded like Maxine. In fact, Louise reflected, she
had an unfortunate collection of role models all round.

'I don't think so,' Louise said quietly, pursuing her way
to the kitchen. It was against all her instincts to let Emily
go, but there couldn't be much serious danger to be found
on a summer's evening in this quiet place, and she had no
intention of fighting empty defiance.

As Louise went up to her room to unpack the things
she would need overnight, and to have a bath before
dinner, she heard an unholy row break out downstairs.
Opening the door to the landing, she concluded that
Emily had turned on television, radio, stereo and every
noise-making machine she could find to its full volume,
still hoping to provoke direct confrontation. Louise
wished she had gone out and thrown herself in the path
of abduction, rape and violence instead.

When she went down to the kitchen she found Abby
herself could hardly have done better in the way of mess.
The fridge door was open, a trail of Fruit and Fibre lay
across a pool of milk on the table, orange peel lent colour.
Had those pips been spat out? A tin of apricots contained

its fruit but not its juice. A slab of catering chocolate lay in fragments; brown shreds on the back of a chair showed where Emily had whacked it into pieces. The wrappings of both pizzas Louise had left out had been torn open, and their cheese surfaces raked back – by Emily's fingernails?

Suddenly Louise felt desperately sad. From the first moment Emily had faced her with the alternatives of do battle or go under, and she had not been prepared to go under. But did it have to be like this? What was burning the child up? Take your choice, Louise thought grimly, beginning to clear away the debris, and don't overlook genetic inheritance while you're at it.

It was not the best moment, from Hugh's point of view, for him to have phoned.

'Emily's here,' Louise informed him before he could say anything.

'So I gather. Honor Franklin phoned in a great state of displeasure. What on earth has been going on?'

'You'd better let Emily tell you that,' Louise retorted crisply, not liking his tone.

'But apart from that, what are you doing there? Weren't you supposed to leave today?'

'I was.'

'Honor told me she'd spoken to the cook. I thought she was confused, though she did make some scathing comments about Abby's irresponsibility which weren't reassuring. What's been happening?'

'What's been happening is that no one is interested in

the slightest degree about what your children are doing or where they——'

'Louise, that's a bit extreme,' he interrupted, angry at once, but Louise cut in in her turn.

'I had no alternative but to go to Pitlochry to meet Emily, since there was no one else to do it, but I should be grateful if someone who is responsible for her could come back so that I can carry on with my own life.'

She was aware of her voice rising and knew she had been more rattled by Emily than she had realised. She stopped abruptly.

Perhaps Hugh guessed something of that, for he controlled his own anger to say more calmly, 'I'm sorry you've had to do this. I'm not clear yet how it came about but I appreciate that it was something you had especially asked not to——'

'That's just the point!' Louise's normal composure had deserted her. The injustice of this episode, confused by a discovery she hadn't had time to examine yet, that in the event her fears of meeting the Erskine children had vanished when confronted by the reality of Emily, rose up in a wave of distress. 'I couldn't even get hold of you. What if there had been a fire, or——?'

'Louise.' Hugh's voice was very quiet now. 'Hold on. Where is Abby?'

'She got stuck – somewhere.' Belatedly she remembered that Abby shouldn't have gone away in the first place. 'She couldn't get back. It wasn't her fault. She'll be back tomorrow.'

Hugh, abandoning this as patently unsatisfactory, though it would have to be gone into at a later date, said decisively, 'Right. Never mind about that. I'm booked on the overnight flight and I'll be back during the morning. Can you assure me that you, or someone, will be there to look after Emily till I arrive?'

'Of course.' Upset though she was, Louise could not conceive of giving any other answer.

She missed the trace of irony in Hugh's voice as he said, 'I'm grateful. I'll be there as soon as I can.'

Hadn't he wanted to speak to Emily? Louise felt indignant as she heard the phone click. Of course he hadn't, he wasn't that kind of father. Would Emily have wanted to talk to him? This was an area Louise did not wish to get into.

Oh, bother them all. She turned her attention to cooking something for supper that had not been tampered with by anyone. She had just finished when Emily insinuated herself round the kitchen door in exactly Abby's manner, unpeeling herself when it was deemed safe to come in. Really, it was a toss-up which of them was the greater child, Louise thought.

'Don't make a mess in here again,' she said with authority, and Emily, taken by surprise at her tone, said, 'OK,' before she realised she was doing it.

Rallying, she went to rifle the biscuit tins and, having picked out the chocolate wafers, came to sit on the table with her feet on a chair. 'Cameron said you went up to the big house,' she said, biting the end off a biscuit and examining its layers with disapprobation. 'Got slung out on your ear by old Gloryhole.'

Louise raised an eyebrow. From what safe cranny had Cameron been watching? She could have done with him.

'You were mad, going up there,' Emily stated, stripping chocolate with her front teeth. 'Good job Leo didn't catch you.' Didn't she realise how much she gave away by this truculent use of Christian names? 'So what did you say to Gloria?'

'To your grandmother?' It was not a reproof; no passing reproof from a stranger would benefit Emily. It was strictly need to know; that fat, not unfriendly female surrounded by her mounds of baking didn't fit any picture Louise had formed of the Erskine family.

'She's not my grandmother!' Emily's rejection of the word was instant. 'She's nothing to do with us.'

'Isn't she married to your grandfather?'

'Oh, well, that. Yes, I suppose so.' About to wipe chocolaty fingers down the front of her T-shirt, Emily caught Louise's eye and licked them instead. 'Actually, she's not bad, old Gloryhole. That's what the men call her. They say she's a tart Leo picked up, but that isn't right. She was a taxi-driver, in London. Took him to some club, his club, I suppose. He's always talking about his club. Or he used to, we never see him now.'

'But why? What happened?'

'Hugh can't stand Gloria, he and Leo had a big fight. We're supposed to keep away, but sometimes I sneak up. Gloria's OK. Makes good cakes. I think she'd be quite nice to us if she was allowed. She's not my grandmother, though.'

I'm not sure I want to find out any more, Louise thought, pressing the lid down on the biscuit tin after Emily had helped herself to another handful and sloped off. Most of their misery was self-inflicted, as far as she could see.

# Chapter Twenty-Three

It felt odd and rather unsatisfactory to wake at Fallan and know that, without any real work to do, she must hang about till Hugh or Abby appeared. Abby she could scarcely expect for hours; goodness only knew how long it would take her to get back from Mull. More time than it would take Hugh to get from New York. The thought momentarily amused Louise, then the restless, cornered feeling returned, and she knew it was chiefly to do with uncertainty about how best to look after Emily. Her own instincts, she had been forced to recognise last night, fell on the side of cosseting and smothering. It had been hard not to fuss about where Emily was, what she was doing and whether she had a 'proper' supper.

Then there had been the question of her room. Louise could not imagine, although the children were due home in a day or two, that Abby would have progressed as far as getting ready for them. But would a bustle about making up a bed for someone capable of doing it for herself be regarded as intrusion, none of Louise's business, and a superfluous refinement in the first place? But in the end the thought of Emily curling up on a bare mattress with an uncovered duvet seemed so bleak that she had made up her mind. Emily had been watching a video in the library – Louise had had to stifle the urge to make sure it was a 'suitable' one, reminding herself that if Abby had been in charge, as Emily's father was content to leave her, there was unlikely to have been supervision of any kind – so she had gone upstairs and, without touching anything else, made the bed in Emily's little slice of a room.

Although she knew she was confining herself to this one act as much for her own sake as from a wish to respect Emily's privacy, not looking around her, trying to think of nothing but what she was doing, she had been instantly at the mercy of reminders, exactly as she had dreaded when she had stipulated that no households where she worked should include children. In spite of the time that had gone by, in spite of the strengths she believed she had acquired this summer, the memories were inescapable and ravaging . . .

The warm nursery of the early years decorated with soft cloud-scapes and pastel colours, the flowery curtains, the rank of stuffed toys, and in the cupboard the rows of delicious little dresses, half of them never worn more than once, an indulgence for her far more than for the twins. Then the chillier room at Coulter Moss, but there had still been the pretty curtains, the trinkets, the pinks and blues, the frilly pelmets and valances, everything feminine and delicate, and always, always, exactly the same for them both. She had once bought the same duvet covers in different colours but the twins had hated it, had been actually miserable about it. She remembered the tedious business of trying to find two more of each, but the colour range had been changed, the design was different, and nothing would do for Gemma and Charlotte but the absolutely identical. In the end, driven by poverty, she had taken the covers apart, stitching them together again with one side one colour and one the other, and the twins had been satisfied.

Shaking a pillow into its case last night for Emily, Louise had paused, arrested by the memory. Had she really gone to such lengths? Was that valid; should she have allowed Gemma and Charlotte to carry their insistence to such a point? She had believed it right to try to understand the bond between them, and not distress them by contesting it, but had she been helping them in the long-term by doing so?

For a second it had seemed to Louise, standing there oblivious of the messy, uncared-for room with its long-ago emulsioned walls, its stained rug and chipped furniture with drawers sagging open, that she could act differently in the future, that assessing how she had dealt with such situations meant she was being given another chance. And all over again, shatteringly, she had had to face the fact that if she had failed the twins in anything, then that must stand for ever.

She had thrown the pillow onto the bed and fled to her room, whirling in to stand leaning against the door, slammed behind her on the sort of tearing loss she hadn't felt for months. There was no refuge for her in this room, or in the house around her. Emily, somewhere downstairs, had seemed scarcely to exist.

Later she had heard Emily come up to her room, and had been appalled to think she could have stayed up here, indifferent to what a lonely child was doing with her time, or when she came to bed. But still she had made no move, sitting on the steps to her window, her back against the wall getting colder and colder, the calling of the owls through the summer darkness unbearably melancholy.

She had gone to bed at last but, chilled through and through, and tortured by images of a piercing vividness, had been unable to sleep. Deciding to make a hot drink – also remembering with guilt that she had done nothing about turning off the lights or locking the doors – she had dragged herself out just after one.

Emily's light had still been on. Could she not sleep either? What miseries were churning in her head? Louise had realised she didn't know yet if anything specific had driven Emily from her godmother's. How unfeeling not to have given her the chance, at least, to have talked about it if she wanted to. The door hadn't been properly closed. Gently Louise had pushed it inwards, not going in.

The overhead light and the reading lamp had both been on. Dead centre of the bed, strands of dark hair straggled from a tight ball of duvet, into which the pillow also seemed to have disappeared. A book had fallen onto a plate on which a soup spoon lay across the uncooked base of the despised pizza. But I put them in the bin, was Louise's first horrified reaction. In their packets, she had reminded herself hastily. But still . . .

She had picked up the book and wiped tomato sauce from its jacket – then was halted by seeing what it was. Half-unconsciously she had expected something like *The Name of the Beast* or *The Bondage of Love*, but here in all its innocence was an old favourite of her own, for Scotland had always held romance for her. *Orders to Poach*, the plan of the Stewarts' country coloured in with crayon, the photographs of real children against scenes of Highland lochs and hills bringing back a remembered sense of immediacy and adventure. She turned to the fly-leaf. Hugh Montgomerie Erskine; a neat hand with strong capitals.

Louise had stood looking down at the sleeping bundle of Emily, the book pressed against her breast, her face tight with compassion. She had felt she could hardly bear the racked emotions of the day, hers and this mutinous, embattled, unforgivably solitary child's. She had looked again at the arrogant signature in the battered book, and felt rage swell up at the man who had succeeded the boy. This lay at his door.

She was still angry with him as she lay now, sounding out the stillness of the house. Emily somehow did not have the look of a person who would leap out of bed with the dawn – or of a person who would be much interested in breakfast. Nevertheless Louise thought she would have some herself, and then find something useful to do until Hugh arrived and she was free to go.

Emily slouched into the kitchen half an hour later, a washed-out black sweatshirt which Louise was certain she'd seen Abby wearing slipping off one skinny shoulder, her face clamped in frowsty ill-humour and a generally unwashed air about her. She homed in with evident longing on the crisp bacon Louise was taking from under the grill, standing beside the cooker rubbing her face with her sleeve dragged over her hand as though some form of consciousness was stirring.

'Want some?'

'Slices off a pig? Yeah, why not? That pig only lived to feed me, you have to remember that.'

'Eggs? And no thank you, I don't have to be told where they come from.'

Surprisingly, Emily giggled, looking quite human. She yanked open a drawer, fished loudly for a knife and fork, and slung them almost cheerfully on the table. 'Any Marmite?' she asked, beginning a trawl of the cupboards that threatened to leave mayhem in its wake.

'Sit down and I'll get it for you. Would you like orange juice, toast?'

Only as she found the Marmite and put it on the table did Louise question her automatic response. It seemed to her fitting that a child should sit at a table and be looked after. But was that doing Emily the greatest service in the end? The thought was not so much important in itself — nothing she did here, as she kept reminding herself, could affect Emily's life one way or the other – but it seemed significant in relation to Louise's own outlook that she had asked the question.

'So what time is Hughie going to turn up?' Emily demanded, spreading Marmite on her egg, and Louise did not miss the black scowl that went with the name.

'Some time this morning, he said.'

''Orrible Honor's been bending his ear, I suppose,' Emily said morosely. 'He needn't come back if Abby's coming. He needn't come back till the boys are here, same as he always does.'

With the feeling of having strayed into an unmarked mine zone, Louise said carefully, 'They'll be here in a day or two, won't they?'

'How should I know?' Emily muttered.

'Doesn't your mother tell you?'

'My mother?' The first mine had exploded. 'What do you mean, my mother?' Emily stood up, scraping her chair violently back, her face furious. 'How dare you talk about her? You're a stranger, you only work for us, it's none of your business.'

'Emily, I'm sorry.' Louise went quickly round the table, putting out a hand towards her but withdrawing it as Emily jerked back her elbow with a warning gesture. 'Emily, I didn't mean to upset you. It's true, I don't know anything about your family, and I don't mean to ask about it. I just assumed that if the boys were with your mother you would know—'

'You're stupid! You're nearly as stupid as Abby,' Emily

shouted. The only hopeful point was that she hadn't stormed out. 'How can the boys be with my mother, why should they be, they are with *their* mother, sweet adorable Angie. *My* mother doesn't like children, didn't you know that? She doesn't like children and she didn't want me, and she's a bitch. Everyone says so, you needn't look so shocked.'

'Emily, sit down again. Come on, I didn't mean to upset you and I'm truly sorry that I have. I didn't know any of this, and I shouldn't have talked about it at all. Please, sit down . . .'

Gently she drew Emily into her chair again and sat beside her, close, yearning to comfort her but not daring to touch those taut shoulders in the hideous adult garment that made her look all the more defenceless.

'I didn't know you and the boys had different mothers,' she said, instinct telling her that Emily, whether she knew it or not, needed the release of passionate words. If in her anger they were an attack on Louise, then so be it; it didn't matter.

'Everyone knows that,' Emily said, pushing her plate away with the back of her wrists, once more wrapped in black sleeve; a gesture of anger that had nowhere to go.

'How old are the boys?'

'They're kids. Nine and eight.'

'I don't even know their names.' And Emily, my love, this may be helpful therapy for you, but I promise you I could do without it.

'Roddie and Matt.'

'Where does their mother live?'

'Near Dalwhinnie. She's married to someone called Freddie. We've always known him. He's OK.'

The first scraps of unsolicited information. Louise waited quietly.

'They always ask me to go too. I can go there any time I like, so don't think I can't. I just get sick of the boys sometimes, they're such infants. And Honor makes a big thing about me going to stay once every holidays. She was a friend of Grannie's and she's indecently rich and she's supposed to be going to leave me all her dosh. I couldn't give a stuff, really.' Not for the first time Louise felt mildly curious about Emily's school. 'Only the pickings are quite good when I'm there. In Edinburgh, that is. She leaves wads of notes in her desk and everywhere. New. Imagine anyone thinking it mattered whether money was new or not. Thinks she might get AIDS off someone's old tenners, can you believe that? Still, it's a change from here, you could go mad with boredom in this place and no one would ever notice.'

Yet she had fled here; because she had nowhere else to go. 'It must be better when the house is busy,' Louise hazarded. 'Do you ever have friends to stay in the holidays?'

A shrug, a snort of contempt. 'Hugh's friends, more like. And Maxine pretends it's her house, ponces about saying "we" all the time. The cooks are the worst, being sweet to the kiddies because they want to get off with Dad, then when that doesn't work buzzing off to the village to chase the blokes there. They're horrible, I hate them all.'

Before Louise could find some way to slip past this

gauche speech without embarrassment, she saw Emily realise what she had said, and would have done anything to save her the moment of mumbling, 'Sorry,' a tide of red spreading up to her ears.

'It's all right. I understand it must be grim for you,' Louise began, but the damage had been done.

'I've got to go and see someone.'

Emily spun off her chair away from Louise, and was gone. A couple of minutes later Louise saw her pedalling furiously down the drive.

With a feeling of something unfinished she watched her go. Any connection with this unhappy family would be over in a matter of hours, but those few moments when Emily had talked, of her own free will, making some things clear but hinting at so much more turmoil and hidden pain, had made a deep impression, and it was hard to accept that that was all the communication there was ever going to be.

Except for a few comments she intended to make to Emily's father.

The phone rang in the passage outside, and she could hardly bring her mind to bear on where she was or who it might be. Then out of the surface distress of her mind she decided it would be Hugh himself, crying off. Something more important than his daughter's welfare would have detained him; of course he knew he could rely on Louise to stay and hold the fort.

It was disorientating to hear Abby's breathless voice, once again pouring out explanations and apologies. They had set out in plenty of time, really they had, but it was miles to Tobermory and the car still wasn't quite right, and it had taken them much longer than they expected, and she was abjectly, desperately sorry, and she knew Louise would never forgive her, but they had missed the ferry again.

# Chapter Twenty-Four

This time Louise did not miss the Daimler sweeping quietly up to the door. She had been waiting for the last hour on the landing sofa, quite unable to settle to anything, or deal with the jangled emotions the events of the last twenty-four hours had released from their normal safe compartments. Her bag was ready in the car for a second time. She couldn't wait to go. The barn by the river, even Rick's comfortable presence beyond the partition as he worked, beckoned her with its calm, its distance from this morass of hurt and indifference.

Hearing the car, for her nerves were stretched and her senses acutely alive with apprehension and determination, she sprang to the window. The movement caught Hugh's eye as he got out and he gave her a quick nod, his face unsmiling, before vanishing below her into the house. He was alone, and though in her present mood Louise would have said what she wished to say whether Maxine was there or not, she was glad for Emily's sake. She turned to go down, having somehow envisaged any confrontation taking place in Hugh's office, and found him coming up the stairs towards her, quietly but moving swiftly with that concentrated energy of his.

'What in God's name is going on? Where's Emily?' he demanded. It was an aggressive opening.

'She's gone to the village.' Louise spoke calmly, instinctively resisting his tone, her eyes challenging him to find fault with this ordinary fact, and she saw his effort to crush down automatic disapproval, as though accepting he had no right to object.

'And Abby?'

'She'll be back tomorrow.'

'You said that yesterday. Where the hell is she?'

Louise, hearing his voice sharpen again, understood the temptation to make Abby the focus of the annoyance and frustration boiling in him.

'She went to Mull for a couple of days and she's had trouble getting back.'

'For a couple of days? She had no right to go at all. She's overstepped the limits this time. I can't have someone so unreliable in charge of—'

'I said she could go.'

Hugh checked and his eyes narrowed, his face becoming hard and angular.

'You said – ?' He let the words hang, icy, sarcastic. And by what right . . . ?

'I was here. And in the event, I have covered for her adequately. Nothing has gone wrong, except—' To her disbelief Louise's voice shook on the word. She had wanted to say so much and now, at the outset, her emotions were betraying her, emotions more powerful than even she had recognised.

'Except — ?' Hugh repeated, and she was too full of consternation at her own weakness to see that his angry gaze had altered; he was watching her intently, as though what she was going to say would be crucial to him.

'Oh, I know you won't listen,' she cried, feeling defeated before she began, overwhelmed by the complexity of the problems besetting this sad household, the lack of loving concern she had found here.

'Try me.' The clipped words were cold; it is never conciliatory to be told one won't listen before a word has been said. But Hugh held in his anger. He wanted to hear this.

Louise gazed at him, her usually gentle eyes a sapphire blaze, and even in the tension of the moment Hugh tucked the memory away. 'Don't you have any idea how wretched Emily is?' she burst out. 'Don't you care?'

The muscles jumped along Hugh's ridged jaw as he stared at her, and she could almost feel the force of his resentment. But he kept his voice quiet. 'I'd like you to tell me about it.'

'You should know!'

'Undoubtedly I should. However, I am a failure as a father, therefore I should be grateful if you would sit down here for a few minutes — or perhaps it will take longer than that to list my sins of omission — and give me the benefit of your findings.'

The lightly mocking tone, which he had summoned at

some expense to subdue the bitterness that filled him, almost destroyed any hope of a useful exchange there and then. He saw as much in the colour which rose in Louise's cheeks, and laid a quick hand on her arm.

'Believe me, I am in earnest about this. I'm merely attempting to avoid explosions of wrath which wouldn't do anyone any good. Please,' he added quietly, and was relieved to see Louise relax slightly. He gestured towards the sofa she had just left and, though she was biting her lip in a way he thought unpromising, she sat down, on the edge of the seat and not looking at him.

Hugh settled in the sofa corner, turned towards her, his elbow on its back, a pose designed to take the heat out of things, refusing confrontation. 'Go on,' he said.

Louise twisted her fingers together, her head bent. There was no point in saying anything. She would only make this arrogant self-assured man even more angry and resentful. How would that serve Emily? Furthermore it was none of her business. That was the essential factor to remember in all these jobs; nothing about these people's lives was anything to do with her.

'Go on,' Hugh repeated, still quietly.

The memory came back of that humped shape last night under the duvet in the comfortless room – and beside it the book that had belonged to this man, probably when he was younger than Emily. Louise swung round to face him and in the abrupt movement he read, correctly, not aggression but a deep concern, and he was conscious of a lift of gratitude for her courage.

'Look, I know there are all sorts of ramifications I'm

not aware of,' Louise plunged, speaking quickly, 'and none of this has anything to do with me, but what I've seen is a child who seems totally alone, rebelling against everything, uncared-for, unloved –' she saw his swift movement, as swiftly checked, but swept on; this wasn't about him '– a child already in her teens, and teenagers are virtually adults these days, who is frighteningly adrift. She's lying, stealing, joking about her drugs habit, she feels excluded from her brothers' relationship with their mother, she's bitter about her own mother – and I don't believe she even washes,' Louise wound up, trying to return to some level of ordinariness as Hugh had done a moment earlier.

He hid his shock. 'You seem to have covered a remarkable amount of ground in a very short time,' he remarked without emphasis. 'Emily is not normally given to confidences.'

'I know. That's at the root of it. Who can she talk to? Abby? Dear as Abby is, do you feel she's the best role model, or capable of realistic discipline? Of the two I'd hardly like to say which is the more mature.'

'I'd probably agree with you there, but I keep Abby on because she's the only person with whom Emily seems to have formed an attachment of any kind. At root, there's no harm in Abby, feckless delinquent though she is, and it seemed important that there was one familiar face at home to set against the changing procession of cooks.'

'But why does the familiar face have to belong to an employee? Isn't that the real question?'

It was, and when had anyone last had the guts to put it to him? Even Honor walked carefully here. Hugh stared at Louise in silence, his face unreadable, and hoped he was hiding the defensiveness the question had whipped up.

Louise, however, now that she had started, was so caught up in what she was saying and so truly disturbed by what she had discovered of Emily's situation, that she met his eyes directly, wanting an answer.

'Louise, you know what my life consists of,' Hugh said after a moment, his tone roughly dismissive, rubbing a hand down his face. Coming east, half the night was lost and, seasoned trans-Atlantic traveller though he was, he hadn't managed on this occasion to sleep at all.

'I don't know much about it,' Louise said, 'but does it have to be like that? Couldn't you be away less? Couldn't you change the way you live if other things mattered more?'

For one moment Hugh hesitated on the brink of accepting this, of saying, 'Yes, the way I run my life is madness, tell me what I can do about it.' He felt a violent need, absolutely foreign to him, to reach out for her, drop his head on her shoulder, and pour out to her his sense of entrapment in an existence which had taken him over, feeding on its own success to such an extent that he sometimes felt it consumed him. He longed to release a muddled load of anguish – awareness of the gulf that widened year by year between himself and his children, guilt that he never did anything about it, compounded by the conviction that he wouldn't know how to mend matters if he tried, and behind all this the huge irredeemable failures of the past.

But such an unburdening was impossible for a man of his type. Even as the temptation came, pride rejected it.

He was accustomed to dealing with his life alone, and a horror at the idea of making himself vulnerable to anyone swept through him, making him shiver. Though Louise drew him with her gentleness and composure, though the image of her often came into his mind, the shining hair and golden skin, the clear colours she wore, the neatness and air of probity which so oddly appealed, he barely knew her. They had never talked, and he had no illusions about her opinion of him. Consciously choosing anger and defensiveness he said shortly, 'You're right, you know nothing of my life. You also know nothing of the various issues concerning my family which you have so confidently touched upon. I make the best possible arrangements for Emily and the boys, and I'm afraid you must be satisfied with that.' He stood up with a brisk movement, topic closed.

'But how can they be the best arrangements?' Louise had thought they were about to talk; he couldn't leave the matter there. 'I mean, I don't know anything about the boys, but now that you know how miserable Emily is, now that you know she's smoking, stealing — she told me herself that was how she got the money for her fare home yesterday — you can't just say you've made arrangements and they have to stand! And the reference to drugs — I treated it as a joke and I'm pretty sure it was one, but aren't you going to find out?'

'What I do or do not do about Emily is my affair,' he reminded her. He had given his answer, he was not used to his decisions being questioned, and above all he was not used to being put in the wrong.

'What about her school?' Louise asked. 'From the language Emily uses, if nothing else, it sounds as though some checking out might be valid.'

'She goes to the best school in Scotland,' Hugh rapped out, and knowing he was saying the most expensive school in Scotland, groaned inwardly at his own crassness.

'The best school for her?' Louise had stood up too, and in spite of his open anger she continued to face up to him with a resolution he could only admire. What had turned the amenable girl he had so much enjoyed having in his house into this fierce battler? Concern for Emily? What had lain beneath her original reluctance to be here when the children were home? What secrets were hidden behind the ordered and contained façade?

But she had no excuse to push him like this. 'Yes, good for Emily,' he rapped out. 'And you are, if you will allow me to say so, involving yourself in matters which at no stretch of the imagination are your concern.'

'They became my concern when I met Emily.'

'There you are wrong. I appreciate your having looked after her, but by your own admission Abby was missing because you let her take days off to which she wasn't entitled, and so created this entire situation. If you had not, Emily's godmother would have phoned, found Abby here, and Abby would have gone to the station. In other words, the normal arrangements I have in place for the care of my children would have operated. I think there's no more to be said.'

Louise stared at him, disbelief and frustration nearly choking her. On this single logistical point he hung his whole argument, ignoring the fact that his daughter was rushing headlong towards disaster. This was who he was; this was how they lived. Louise compressed her lips on protests that would do no good, and turned away, feeling suddenly exhausted.

She did not guess the feelings her acceptance of defeat woke in Hugh. He hated to see her look of disappointed resignation, and in a different way he felt disappointed too, obscurely let down. Had he expected her to give him such a trouncing that she would force him to action? Had he wanted her to find some way out for him? In spite of his warning that there was no more to be said, he knew that he didn't want the discussion to be closed.

'It's good of you to stay till Abby gets back,' he said, as she turned to go downstairs. Whatever had delayed Abby might work to his advantage after all.

Louise looked at him blankly. 'Stay till Abby gets back?'

'Yes. You did say you'd do that, didn't you?'

'To look after Emily, so that Emily wouldn't be left alone. But you're here now.' She sounded so surprised that Hugh felt his cheeks redden.

'But you'll — well, you'll look after us both now, won't you?' His tone sounded unintentionally jocular and he winced to hear it.

'Look after you? Cook for you, do you mean?' Was the concept of having some servant on hand so ingrained that he couldn't imagine fending for himself and one teenager for the space of twenty-four hours?

'Well, yes, I suppose I mean that.' He meant much more; he wanted her there; he wanted, if possible, to return to the subject of the children, of Emily in particular. And, with shame, he admitted to himself that he wasn't sure he could deal with being alone with Emily. He couldn't remember when he ever had been. What on earth should he say to her?

'I'm sorry.' He would never have imagined Louise capable of such cold finality. 'My job here ended yesterday. There's plenty of food cooked and ready to be eaten. I think you'll manage. Excuse me.'

He moved, without any conscious intention of doing so, to bar her way. 'I'd be very grateful if you would stay till tomorrow. I should like you to be here.' He could hardly find the words to formulate a request that had nothing to do with a business arrangement.

'I'm sorry.' Louise looked as though she was hardly aware of what he was saying. Her whole being was set on getting away from him, being free to review and then if possible put out of her mind the attitudes he had revealed.

'But I haven't paid you. If you'd like to come down to the office . . .' Pathetic straw to clutch at, but he couldn't think of anything else. He had a sudden uncomfortable vision of Maxine's mocking eyes.

'Thank you. Please send the cheque to the agency. Oh, and please – don't blame Abby. As you say, it was my fault for letting her go.'

Hugh wanted to protest, absurdly, that it wasn't, that Abby, as permanent housekeeper, was supposed to be in charge, that he had been out of order to accuse Louise of anything. But Louise was past him, running down the stairs, crossing the hall to the front door. Was she going now, right away? Surely she couldn't be. Her luggage – but yes, the door closed, and turning back to the window he watched her go to her car. Would she look up? No.

He stood at the window for some time after she had driven away, with the chill feeling that he had taken another irreversible step into a way of living that was turning very sour indeed.

After a while he shook himself and looked around him. What was he doing here? In his whole life he didn't think he had ever used this landing as anything but a route to somewhere else; he was certain he had never before today sat on its sofa. His brain felt unable to do more than wearily pick at such trivia. He desperately needed sleep. But first he should find Emily. He didn't have the faintest idea where to start looking for her and, realising this, desolation filled him, an awareness of his own inadequacy which he foresaw would grow as his children presented him with fresh challenges. He was racked by the feeling that he had thrown away a chance which had been offered to him too suddenly, taking him unawares. His throat ached and his eyes stung.

# Chapter Twenty-Five

Back at Bridge of Riach Louise luxuriated in a sense of holiday, pushing disquieting thoughts of Fallan to the back of her mind. She could do nothing about them; they would have to fade away as other events overtook them. At present it was fun to share in the life of the glen as August rushed on towards the Twelfth, and every guest-house, cottage and B and B was full to bursting. As Cass had warned her, the Scotts saw a lot of their friends, and Cass herself was at home more than usual, for by this stage of the season, barring disasters, jobs were filled and staff in place and she could relax.

The Munros and the Mackenzies, who owned the estates which marched at the head of the glen, formed the main element in the group of friends. They were a spreading clan, and between the two households the children ranged from a sixteen-year-old girl to a baby born this summer. Bracing herself to encounter them Louise discovered, with surprise then thankfulness, that her fears were outworn. As with Emily, the children became individuals in their own right, and even when she finally met the Mackenzie twins, though she avoided having much to do with them directly and the memories could not be subdued, there was no pain she couldn't deal with. It was as though in being touched by Emily's plight, in, even so briefly, looking after her, the panicky dread had been exorcised. Or was it merely that time had passed, so that though random reminders would always bring a stab of loss, such feelings no longer came between her and ordinary chance contacts?

Certainly Sasha and Sybilla Mackenzie, a pair of dark-haired, scruffy tearaways, absorbed in hardy outdoor pursuits, were as unlike Gemma and Charlotte as they could possibly be – except for their good humour. They had a capacity for irrepressible laughter which was sharply evocative, but though it could bring tears to her eyes how could she truly mind such an engaging quality?

The meeting with Emily had been a watershed. Timing had been important, but the protectiveness Emily had reawoken in her, arousing in its turn the readiness to do battle on her behalf which had taken Hugh Erskine by surprise, had scattered the fears which had dogged her for so long.

Idling blissfully, enjoying her retreat in the barn, enjoying the company of Cass and Rick and the new acquaintances she was making, helping Cass throw a lunch party on a day of torrential rain which ended up with lightly clad guests digging out a car which had gone off the mud-slicked track, and exploring the glen which was almost as beautiful as Glen Fallan, though without its enchanted hidden-away air, it was hard to stir herself to think of the next job.

'Don't worry about it,' Cass told her. 'Relax and enjoy yourself. You've earned it.'

Louise wasn't sure that was true, but the prospect was tempting. 'No posts that urgently need filling?'

'While I let you loll about here? Dream on. No, seriously, take a break while you can. What with no-shows and walk-outs and other delights of the business I'll need you soon enough. But are you all right for cash?'

'You know I am, thanks to you.' Louise had met with firm resistance when she had tried to pay rent for the barn, and was barely allowed to contribute to the housekeeping. With the rates Cass paid, and everything found when away on a job — and usually nowhere to spend money and little time off to do so — she had nothing to worry about. Though the barn was a stopgap there was a comfortable feeling of other options waiting in the wings. Rick's suggestion that she might rent somewhere in the glen for the winter had been backed up by friends who owned cottages used for summer letting.

Louise knew, however, that her feeling of security (and of satisfaction at her decision to relinquish anything Beatrice might have intended her to have) was not only about income exceeding expenditure or having a roof; it lay too in the reassurance of being drawn into a large circle where people were always ready to help each other. She felt safe, and deeply grateful to Cass.

The protected feeling extended beyond Bridge of

Riach. Aidan was clamouring for the promised visit to Kinnafoot.

'But what about Alice?' Louise asked with well-simulated doubt.

'Alice? Alice?' Aidan boomed, as though he had never heard of her. 'I shall deal with Alice.'

'I thought she couldn't be upset or put upon? I thought she couldn't be asked to look after guests?'

'My precious Louise, do not trifle with me. I miss you, I need you, I yearn for the balm of your company, the sight of your smile. My sister lacerates me with her tongue, Wacker is refusing to speak to me because I sprayed one of his cherished bushes with something lethal, my friends grow old and die—'

'Well, stop bawling and roaring and tell me when you want me to come.'

Alice surprised everyone by taking to Louise from the first moment, infallibly detecting a sympathetic ear and a soft heart, and thereafter it was difficult to escape her.

'I thought she was supposed to resent me,' Louise remarked to Mrs Wacker, who had given her a beaming welcome.

'Yeah but, you're not here' (what Mrs Wacker said was 'yernorreer') 'as the competition, are you? And you listen to all that stuff about her niece. Rather you than me, does me 'ead in, that does.' And as she whisked away to polish something she called back enigmatically, 'Don't leave anything on your plate though.'

Louise came to understand all too well what she

meant. Whatever Alice started with she boiled it grey. It was only remarkable that she found the time to do so. She trotted in pursuit of Louise from morning till night with a dedication a new puppy couldn't have equalled, pinning her down at the kitchen table with a bony grip on her arm, embarking on long diatribes about the dip in the mattress she was expected to sleep on at her niece's house, describing (several times) what she could, or couldn't, hear before and after she had her ears dewaxed, and relating with little snuffling sobs how when she stayed with her niece and left her sponge-bag in the bathroom it was always put back in her room, and how unwanted that made her feel. Another theme was that she longed to give up work but Aidan would be lost without her. She dodged past Mrs Wacker to put gaudy bunches of flowers squeezed into tiny vases in Louise's room, and developed a habit of waiting at the swing door to leap out on her every time she crossed the hall.

'I thought *you* were the leaper,' Louise complained to Aidan, having been forced to use some diplomacy to prevent Alice from following her into the library.

'Happy to oblige at any time,' Aidan assured her with a leer which sent her out of reach behind the sofa. But it was the merest joke. She had half wondered whether by going back she would give him misleading signals; as soon as she was with him again the doubt had vanished. True, he would reach a hand for hers as they walked, would draw her into the circle of his arm when they sat talking, but she knew this was the limit of his needs. He loved touch and warmth, and was delighted to have her back.

Erica, too, had been openly pleased to see her, and as before Louise found it easy to talk to her, for hours and hours, about anything and everything.

'You've made great strides,' Erica observed one day, as they were digging up Pink Fir Apples to go with a casserole of pigeons she had shot, already gently bubbling over the fire in front of the van. 'You have the look of a person who has stepped into the light.'

The phrase struck Louise, and she stopped work to consider it, gazing across the garden, blind to its marshalled and fecund beauty. 'It isn't that I believe there'll be no pain any more,' she said after a moment. 'I'm not afraid of it. It doesn't keep me apart.'

'This child Emily. You'll leave the matter there?'

Louise looked at her, startled. Erica had not lost her habit of conducting conversations with an unsheathed blade in her hand.

'I don't see what else I can do.'

'Humph.'

'Erica, she has a home and a family. I'll never see her again. I can't do anything to help. I did try to talk to her father but he doesn't believe anything is wrong.'

'Well, maybe the help you feel you can't give her will benefit someone else,' Erica said dismissively, refraining from adding, now that you've woken up.

Louise minded the inference that she had given up on something that mattered, but said nothing. Bending to put potatoes in the old riddle she missed Erica's sardonic look of comprehension.

*

Louise was mowing the cottage lawn, deep in the abstraction of performing a mindless action while letting the mind drift around other thoughts. Rick had had a chair ready for friends in Braemar, and Cass had gone with him to deliver it. They had invited Louise to go too, but apart from the fact that the van was not very comfortable for three, she guessed they would be glad of time together on their own. Also it was good to have the chance to do something to help which clearly needed doing. First a spell of rain and then a spate of entertaining and being entertained had left the grass almost too long for the Flymo on high cut. She didn't hear the car coming up the lane.

Hugh Erskine, who among his faults did not number lack of courage, was conscious of a novel confusion of feelings as he nosed the Daimler up the track, and he deliberately focused his mind on wondering if it would have been wiser to walk up. Not that he pampered his vehicles, he expected them to do their job, but that ridge in the middle of the lane was dangerously high.

This briefly kept his mind from the doubts which had been building as he came over the pass. He was catching at straws, he knew, pinning his hopes on the sympathy and good nature of a stranger, someone moreover with whom he had parted on less than amicable terms. But of the options open to him, this solution seemed to hold the only gleam of hope. He knew he had pinned his faith to it more or less by default, but still he pursued it, not willing to relinquish hope till he was forced to.

The Daimler turned a bend and he saw the parking

space, the bank sprawling with flowers. The whine of the mower replaced the sound of his engine. She was there. He found his mouth dry as he went up the almost-buried steps, and that rattled him. Then he was faced with the problem of letting her know he was there without startling her. She'd be startled anyway, he reminded himself, without the danger of chopping off her toes thrown in. She was moving away from him, restricted to a slow pace by grass which looked as though it had never been rolled in its life. When she got to the line of rowans and hazels on the far side she would turn, see him and jump out of her skin. Then the engine died as she paused to throw aside stones pushed up by the moles.

It seemed a lucky omen, though even as the thought occurred to Hugh his habitual cynicism made him mock his own absurdity. But he didn't waste the moment.

'Louise,' he called, going quickly towards her, the scent of the mown grass rising around him, to be remembered afterwards with acute clarity.

Louise swung round, jolted to find anyone there at all, but even more incredulous that the voice could be the one she had thought it was. Hugh Erskine, here? And she spoke the words that sprang instantly to her mind, 'Has something happened to Emily?'

'Oh, Louise.' The involuntary question, catching him unawares, moved Hugh more than he could have imagined possible. It told him so much, but it compounded his guilt, pointing up his failure, not of care, but of caring action. 'Emily's fine.' His voice was disconcertingly husky and he made a conscious effort to speak briskly. 'At least, nothing has happened to her.'

Louise, realising how odd her question must have sounded, said quickly, 'No, of course, that was silly of me. But I was — it was rather a shock to see you here. Oh,' she blushed in fresh embarrassment. 'I'm sorry, I'm being ridiculous. You've come to see Cass, of course. She's away, I'm afraid, and I'm not sure when she'll be back. She and Rick are delivering furniture, but as it's to friends they may stay and—'

'I didn't come to see Cass. I came to see you.'

'Me?' She gripped the handle of the mower, and Hugh thought he'd rather her hands weren't quite so close to the starter switch. 'But why me?'

'Could we talk? Could you leave the mowing?'

'Of course.' Flustered, Louise let go of the handle but didn't lock it in position. It fell flat on the grass and she stared at it as though a solution was beyond her.

'Is there somewhere we could sit?' Hugh suggested. A seat against the house wall made the question superfluous, but it had the intended effect of making Louise pull herself together.

'Oh, yes — please.' She gestured to the seat, realised it was strewn with gardening gloves, extension lead and spare mower blades, the edging tool propped against it, and went hastily to move everything. 'Would you like tea?' She sounded flurried, finding his presence here so in-explicable that the ordinary rituals of hospitality seemed hard to summon. 'I know Cass—'

'Tea would be very welcome, thank you,' Hugh cut in

firmly, not liking to see her at a loss. It was not the image of her that he cherished. 'Can I help you?' Not a domesticated man, he never went near a kitchen if he could help it, but he was afraid his presence was so unwelcome that Louise might actually be tempted to slip away.

'Oh, no, please sit down, I shan't be a moment.' She sounded more definite this time. She needed a few minutes alone to adjust to his appearance here. Why had he come? Although she had done her best to forget it, her mind had played back far too often the angry exchanges of that confrontation on the day she left Fallan, and she knew she had attempted to meddle in matters which had nothing at all to do with her. Hugh had understandably enough not appreciated her comments. Had he come to raise a few more objections to what she had said? She could think of no other reason for his coming to Bridge of Riach.

The reason seemed obvious enough to Hugh, however. As soon as tea was in the cups and cake on the plates he said, 'You know why I'm here, don't you?'

'No, I don't,' Louise said helplessly, but laughing in spite of herself at this opening. 'I don't know how you found me here, or why you should want to.'

'It was simple enough to find you.'

'You spoke to Cass?'

Now Hugh looked slightly guilty. 'As a matter of fact, I didn't. I spoke to her husband.'

'To Rick? But do you know him?' This was getting more baffling by the minute.

'No, I don't, but he told me you would be here this afternoon and said I could come over to see you.'

'But why didn't he say anything to me?' Louise's voice was blank.

Hugh stood up with an exasperated movement and Louise found herself looking at him against the sun, unable to read his expression. 'Louise.' His tone was brusque. 'Will you come back to Fallan?'

She put up a hand to shield her eyes, her mind full of bewildered questions. Why hadn't he asked through Cass? Had Cass known he was coming to say this, yet had given her no warning? But above all, why did he want her back after her attack over Emily had made him so angry?

'Oh, God, that's not how I meant to start,' Hugh groaned, angry with himself, dropping down beside her again. 'I meant to talk it through, find out how you felt about——' He broke off as though he no longer had the resolve to tackle the question, staring away down the windings of the glen, which from this high perch could be traced for miles.

Though he was not attempting to use it in his favour, that defeated look stood him in better stead with Louise than any persuasive approach could have done.

'But don't you have someone just now, to cook, I mean?' she asked hesitantly. 'Cass hasn't mentioned any problems.'

Hugh ran a hand harshly back through his heavy hair. 'That's the point, there isn't really any problem one could define. Look,' he turned to her abruptly, feeling that before mundane details were discussed the decks should be cleared, 'first of all, I'd like to apologise for the way I behaved the morning you left Fallan. I know you were trying to help and were genuinely concerned about Emily, and I know everything you said was to the point. I deserved it all, only I wasn't ready to admit it. I've let the situation slip out of my grasp and, to be honest, I don't know what the hell to do about it.'

'I don't see how I can help,' Louise began anxiously, her heart beginning to make itself felt, hurrying and bumping, as though something was approaching here which was going to matter very much.

# Chapter Twenty-Six

'I'm here because I feel that you, of all the people sent to us in the last six years, brought something to the house it desperately needed.' Hugh shook his head with a brief warning smile as Louise opened her mouth, and she said nothing, realising he was not finding this easy.

'I appreciate that you've no reason to want to come to Fallan ever again,' he went on quickly, 'and that the agency must have a dozen jobs where you would probably be happier, but I thought – I hoped—' He stopped, rubbing splayed fingertips across his forehead, eyes closed.

'Go on,' Louise said quietly. She found him an abrasive man, sweeping in his judgements, determined to pursue his own interests at the expense of everyone around him, but she couldn't deny him the courtesy of at least listening to what he wanted to say.

'I feel if you could just give us a breathing space, give me a breathing space, I could try to work out some satisfactory long-term solution. You have a capacity for creating normality and wellbeing around you which is hard to define, but for a brief time you made Fallan feel like a home again. Now we're back to . . .' He shook his head, his face set in familiar lines of exasperation. 'This girl we've got at present, Davina or some God-awful name, is a first-class cook, and I've no doubt she will produce impeccable food for the shooting guests, as she's paid to do, but she works to rule, refuses to let the children near the kitchen, is unkind to poor old Abby.' Louise glanced at him with quick interest but didn't interrupt. 'Furthermore, she vanishes from the scene at every opportunity. Of course she's entitled to go where she likes in her own time, but it's a negative approach which affects everyone. That's the nub of it, I suppose; you pay, someone does the job by the book, and it doesn't work. You can interview, pay over the odds, but it takes a special person to have the self-motivation to make something of a set-up like Fallan. Or to work for a bastard like me,' he added after a pause, in a constrained voice, and in that moment Louise knew he had really come to talk and was seeking, even if he didn't recognise it, a release from problems that went far deeper than finding a suitable person to run his kitchen.

If he thought it would help to put cards on the table, she would do the same.

'No, you're not easy to work for,' she agreed, thinking this so self-evident that it would be best to get it out of the way. She had no idea of the dunt which the words, spoken with such candid objectivity, dealt Hugh. A vision of his own inadequacy rose before him, and he despaired of ever being able to reverse the long list of failures, those he had rushed into and those he had not been able to prevent.

'There's nothing wrong with the job itself.' The reasonable comment, so mundane compared to the guilt assailing him, forced a grunt of laughter from Hugh.

'Everyone else seems to find a great deal wrong with it,' he pointed out, adjusting to this level with ironic resignation. So much for baring one's soul.

'That's a pity. It's a lovely house in wonderful surroundings. The cook's room is nice too.' Hugh tried to work out which it was. How fortunate that it was acceptable. He rarely went into the other part of the house now, but recalling its down-at-heel shabbiness he felt an unaccustomed shame.

'The cooker's small, though,' Louise added fairly.

Hugh relaxed, amused. Did it matter what they talked about? He was here, in this pretty, unkempt garden with its lovely views, and he hadn't been sent packing yet.

'Oddly enough no less than three of the guests at my recent meeting commented on the cooker,' he said gravely. 'They couldn't think how you'd managed to produce such quantities of good food on it. However,' he turned to her with a new determination, unable to keep for long from the objective important to him, 'enough of trivia.'

Trivia. How other people lived. Disillusionment stirred in Louise, but Hugh's next words were positive enough.

'I want you to come back for several reasons,' he told her. 'You cook marvellous food, that goes without saying, you have the obvious virtues of cleanliness, sobriety, punctuality at one end of the day and a willingness to stay late at the other, you get on with everyone, and you look after sweet scatty Abby. But, more important than any of that –' Hugh paused to look into her face, all lightness gone from his own, leaving it taut and watchful '– Emily took to you. Yes, she did, even in so short a time. We – she – talked about you.'

He supposed other fathers set out with the intention of having an open and frank discussion with their teenage offspring, pleased with themselves for noticing the children were growing up and that the time had come for a new kind of dialogue, only to be treated with the same disdainful silence, the yawn barely suppressed, the blank expression just the right side of insolence.

But, the embarrassing performance over, Emily had offered one comment before she had slouched away. 'This new cook's horrible. The boys can't stand her. I bet they'd like that other one you had, the one you let go.' Blame firmly allocated.

Louise was looking at him in surprise. It seemed improbable that in one day and with minimal communication Emily would have a view one way or the other.

'What did she say?' she asked, frowning. Their contact had seemed almost wholly negative.

Hugh was about to repeat Emily's comment, but realised in time that it would sweep them forward to a point he wished to approach in his own way.

'Look, so far I've only talked about the situation from our angle,' he said instead, making an effort to iron from his voice his usual message that he intended to have his own way regardless. 'But I haven't forgotten your side of things, and more particularly I haven't forgotten your reservations about being in a post where there are children. I don't want to ask about anything you're not happy to talk about, but it did seem to me, when Emily appeared so unexpectedly and you were faced with looking after her, that you handled the situation very well.'

Louise's head was down, but when Hugh paused, bending to look into her face to make sure it was all right to continue, she gave a small nod, and he went on carefully, 'Your problem didn't seem to lie in coping with Emily, but in what you saw as my shortcomings over the issue. No,' as Louise made a small movement, 'I'm not going back over that ground, but what I should like to know is this – was I wrong in thinking you were drawn to Emily? To Emily herself, as opposed to disapproving of the way I look after her?'

A memory of scornful dark eyes and down-turned mouth came back to Louise, then another replaced it – the hostile face breaking up in a smile.

'No, you were right.' Louise's voice was stifled. She felt as though all she had learned and achieved this summer was being put to the test. Could she, calmly and simply, tell this man whom she scarcely knew what had built those reservations in her? There was no need to, but she felt she owed it to him, in response to his own honesty; and it would be another step along the route.

'I had children – once,' she said abruptly, then found she could say no more, the words sticking in her throat like stones.

Hugh floundered, horrified to have questioned her about it. 'I had wondered,' he said after a moment, his voice awkward. 'I'm sorry.' He wanted to put his hand on hers, which were hooked into each other with painful tightness, but didn't think his touch would be welcome or helpful. 'I shouldn't have asked.'

'I think I'd like to tell you,' Louise said, groping for the impulse behind the words but unable to pin it down. 'If you don't mind.'

I want you to tell me, but I'm not sure I shall be able to bear it, he thought, shaken by compassion. 'Don't tell me anything that will hurt too much.' How banal the words were. What could she say that would not hurt?

'I had twin girls. They were killed in a car crash. When they were nine.'

'Louise.' He could hardly shape the sound for the hard lump in his throat. He slid one palm under her rigidly locked hands and closed the other over them, and was glad when she leaned almost imperceptibly towards him in mute acceptance. 'How long ago did it happen?'

'Two and a half years. I should have got over it by now, I know. It's silly to——'

'Don't say such a thing!'

'I just felt, with the jobs, you know, that looking after children would be too difficult. It's not that I don't like children, but for a long time I shut myself away from them altogether. I'm getting over that now. Emily helped.' She looked up at him, wanting to be sure he understood this, and he saw the tears on her lashes and realised his own eyes were wet.

'Emily did?' he repeated, clutching at any words to carry them forward.

'By being herself.' Louise managed a trembly smile. 'And by being nothing like my daughters.'

'I think I can imagine that.' Making an effort in his turn Hugh smiled back, and she thought how alive his face was when a smile banished his habitual reserve.

'Can I ask – what happened to your husband?'

'He was killed in the same crash.'

The answer startled Hugh. Because she had not hinted at it when she spoke of the twins he had not imagined she had lost her husband in the same tragedy. Her tone struck him as odd, but Louise missed his puzzled frown.

She was probing cautiously for pain which had not come, and the discovery filled her with weak relief.

'I do see, now that you've told me this,' Hugh was saying, 'that of course I can't ask you to come back to us. I should have guessed there was some reason of the sort and I'm only sorry that events forced you into meeting Emily. It must have been very painful for you.'

Unthinkable to ask her to take on the little boys too. Emptiness filled him. He had pushed for this dream, pushed to the extent of manipulating Rick Scott into agreeing that he could come here today and talk to Louise alone. But all along it had been no more than a fantasy, a clutching at a solution, any solution, which would shield him from facing up to his problems.

'I'm sorry I've brought back sad thoughts,' he said. 'It was unforgivably selfish of me. I believed I'd seen an answer to our situation, and as usual I went all out for it.

I felt if we could get through these holidays it would give me time to work out something more adequate.'

Louise nodded. He obviously meant to stick to the same general arrangement. Nothing would change in his own life and it had been absurd to think it could.

'It's nice of you,' she remarked unexpectedly, 'to keep Abby on.'

'I suppose I've been reluctant to let the one person the children relate to, however scatty she may be, slip through my fingers. It does mean that, in spite of the chaos they live in, there's always someone there they can be sure of – and it also meant I didn't have to spend time addressing the problem. The rest I dumped in the lap of an agency – though I must say your friend Mrs Scott – Cass – has supplied better staff than any we've had before.'

But none of them had much liked Fallan, or had wanted to go back – or been invited back.

'Have you ever thought of getting rid of Maxine?'

Hugh, though winded, followed the train of thought. 'From time to time,' he admitted with a rueful grin.

'Then why don't you?' Louise enquired. 'She squabbles with everyone, doesn't she?'

'She does.'

'There must be other efficient PAs around.'

'Not all with a first in engineering, though. Yes, Maxine is a highly qualified lady. She is also a ferocious worker. If I dispensed with her I'd probably have to employ two people in her place. She has every detail of my highly complex interests at her fingertips.'

'She's a bit grumpy, though.' The nursery phrase, so

nicely offered, set Maxine's skills against a different scale of values, and Hugh laughed in spite of himself.

'She is, as you say, a bit grumpy.'

'Did you want me to cook just for the rest of the holidays?'

The business-like tone took Hugh by surprise. 'Do you mean — ?'

'You have someone doing the job already though, we mustn't forget. That would have to be—'

'Davina can go somewhere else,' Hugh leapt in, then caught himself up. Ruthlessness didn't cut any ice with Louise, as he had discovered in their first encounter; and this wasn't his decision to make.

'It would be up to Cass,' Louise said. 'Does she know you're not happy with the present cook?'

'We've been in touch about it. Davina has too — when she found there was no hairdresser in the village.'

'You made that up.'

This might actually happen, Hugh thought dizzily. She's ready to consider it. She's laughing at me, where five minutes ago she was telling me in that desolate voice I could hardly bear how she had lost her two small girls. And she sees herself as cowardly.

He had the perception, however, to realise that someone like Louise would find it hard to resist the appeal he had just made, and though he risked everything he so much wanted, he made himself say, 'I don't want to pressure you into anything you're not ready for. The Erskine family is in a mess, but that's my problem, not yours. We've been in it for some time, and nothing very much worse is going to happen in the next couple of months. Why not think things over when I've gone, and talk to Cass, who's bound to have her own ideas about what she wants to do with her staff. Apart from the children, though Abby is supposed to take care of their clothes and rooms, there will be guests coming and going throughout the summer. I shan't be there a great deal myself.' He was watching her face as he said this and, looking for relief, found it. 'Only one thing I must add — Roddie and Matt are not in the least like Emily. They are a cheerful pair, who take life very much as it comes.'

And they were growing, he knew, independent of him, in the way children left too much to their own devices do, out of self-preservation. They tolerated him good-naturedly, but there was always the faint impression that they were waiting for him to go so that real life could continue. But he needed them, he thought with sudden passion; it was too soon for them to leave him.

'There is one thing I should like to ask,' Louise was saying. 'Or perhaps not ask, state.'

'Go ahead.' Hugh pushed the troubling thoughts back into the twilight zone where he kept them, and let a pleasant curiosity take their place. Even so, he was not prepared for what came.

'I understand you and your father are estranged,' Louise said, looking nervous but determined. 'So I feel I should make it clear that if I did come back I shouldn't want to be involved in any quarrels.'

'That's none of your damned——' Hugh began angrily, then compressing his mouth bit back the rest.

How swiftly he could be deflected from conciliation.

'I know it isn't my business,' Louise agreed, 'but I'd find it uncomfortable to take sides, if the situation arose. Mrs Erskine seemed a kind person—'

'When have you ever met Gloria?' Hugh's anger poured back, and this time he didn't attempt to check it.

Louise stood her ground. 'I went up to the big house to see if anyone could collect Emily from Pitlochry. I talked to Mrs Erskine briefly, and though she said she couldn't help she was perfectly friendly.'

Hugh's face was shut. 'There's no contact between the two houses. That works best, and it's the way I prefer things to be.'

'That's up to you, naturally, but I don't think you can expect it to extend to your employees.'

'If you'll forgive me,' (Louise particularly disliked specious courtesy delivered with a sneer) 'there are a great many things involved here which you know nothing whatsoever about.'

Louise supposed there must be; but that didn't affect her position. She said nothing.

'I couldn't have you encouraging the children to go there,' Hugh insisted, needing a response.

'I wouldn't do such a thing. I simply wouldn't want to feel, if, for example, I met Mrs Erskine by chance, that I couldn't speak to her because of some fight that has nothing to do with me. That's all.'

'Are you making it a condition?' Even as he asked this Hugh wondered how long it was since anyone in his personal life had challenged him in such a way.

Louise thought about it. 'Yes, I suppose I am. It's something that would matter to me.'

Driving home, Hugh found himself reluctantly smiling as he played this back in his mind. It might not precisely suit him, but he could only admire such calm conviction on a moral point. It augured well, he thought, for Louise's influence on his wayward family, if Cass agreed to re-arrange her scheduling to suit his needs. He intended to lean on Cass very heavily indeed.

# Chapter Twenty-Seven

'Are you really sure you're happy about this?'

Cass, wanting to talk without interruptions, had proposed a walk along the hill. She and Rick had had dinner in Braemar last night, as Louise had expected, and by the time they got home she had already been down at the barn. She had told them at breakfast about Hugh's visit.

'Though I don't think the news will come as much of a surprise to you?' she had suggested to Rick.

'He sounded pretty keen to talk to you,' Rick had said, spreading marmalade on his fifth slice of toast.

'You could have warned me.'

'I could.'

'Rick, you knew Hugh Erskine was coming here?' Cass had demanded. 'How did you know Louise would want to talk to him? He can be very difficult to deal with. You could have given her the choice, or at least warned her.'

'I felt sorry for him,' Rick had said, in the calm way which made arguing with him feel like pushing a tank up a sand dune, and he had bitten off half the slice of toast in a placid but final manner.

Now Cass and Louise were strolling along the grassy track above the dyke which divided the steep fields from the hill, where bell heather, in rich bloom after the warm weather of early summer, filled the eye with colour.

'I don't want you to be bludgeoned into anything you don't want to do,' Cass repeated, hardly knowing how to approach the core of the subject. Although she knew that Rick, not a man to be pushed around by anyone, would have had his own reasons for letting this most difficult of her clients appear here, and although she respected his judgement, she looked forward to a few private words with him later. Louise was a special case, and in spite of her growing confidence as she successfully tackled each new challenge, Cass still felt protective towards her.

'I think it will be all right.' Louise had had time to think the matter over and though during the night deep-buried resistance had more than once panicked her awake out of confused dreams, she had found her resolution still firm this morning.

'But you did say — you were so adamant about no children.' Cass spoke hesitantly, but knew the question could not be ignored. 'There's no need for you to face that if you don't want to. There are plenty of other jobs, as you know by now. I'm well aware that Hugh Erskine can apply heavy pressure when he wants something —' he had been doing so for the past ten days but she had said nothing of it to Louise, sure the children embargo was solid and seeing no reason to distress her by even considering his proposal '— but this has to be your decision, what *you* want.'

'Cass, you are good,' Louise exclaimed gratefully, stopping and turning to face her. 'I couldn't have been better looked after during these past few months. But I feel I can do this. I know there will be times when — well, never mind about that. I just think I've reached the stage when I should face up to reality. I could go on for ever as I am now, always half-fearful, always on the sidelines of normal life, or I can take one step and move forward, freeing myself of the hang-ups for good. I'm beginning to feel ashamed of being cosseted, which has to be a good sign,' she wound up, with the smile she could always summon and which was one of the things Cass most liked about her.

'I think you're incredibly brave.' Cass's voice was gruff. 'But I still say,' she went on, pulling herself together, 'that that man shoving his way in here was a bit much. You're under no obligation to do what he wants, and if you do feel ready to face a family with children it doesn't have to be the Erskines. You could let things take their course, then if some job crops up that you think would suit you we could go into the whole thing properly.'

'But these children need someone. Emily does anyway.' Louise turned away to look down to the river, flanked by barley fields where ripening gold flowed in soft patterns through the green, but what she saw was a pair of contemptuous eyes in a peaky defiant face.

'But don't you see, that's exactly what's worrying me?' Cass said, putting a hand on Louise's arm to make her look at her. 'You have this built-in response mechanism to other people's need, and they trade on it. People like Hugh Erskine do anyway, and I don't think you should put yourself through the mill to suit him. His children are his problem. If he's made a ham-fisted job of looking after them it's up to him to sort it out, not you.'

'I think he's trying to,' Louise pointed out fairly. 'Anyway, as I see it, they're the ones who need help.'

Cass sighed. 'You're your own worst enemy. You really want me to organise this?'

'Not if you feel you should keep on the person you already have there, or if she wants to stay.'

'One of my very best cooks, and still the man isn't satisfied,' Cass grumbled. 'Oh, don't worry, Davina will be only too happy to go. She says the set-up is ghastly and Abby drives her round the bend. Also, as it happens, I'd been faced with sending a pretty pedestrian cook to a shooting lodge where the standards are high and where she'd have had a tough time, so I'd be glad to do some swapping around. That's never a problem. And I suppose the Erskine man has got a point. You're the only cook I've sent to Fallan so far who's been prepared to put up with the place and been in demand to go back as well. Even at that, we've improved on the previous agency's record!'

The car was pulled, not very competently, into one of the unofficial passing-places where vehicles squeezed past each other on the single-track road above the village. The tall green bracken, overhung by weeping birch, was almost in at the window, and the air was full of the sound of the little tumbling falls which made this stretch of the burn so attractive. Louise saw and heard none of it, oblivious to curious eyes as cars edged past. She sat huddled and defeated, her face wet with tears.

She had let Cass make all the plans, had been happy to be able to leave anything she wouldn't need in the barn, had made the rounds to say goodbye to the people who had been so kind to her while she had been in Bridge of Riach, and last night she had taken Cass and Rick to dinner at the Cluny Arms in Kirkton, a couple of miles down the glen. She had looked ahead to being at Fallan, had, she believed, made herself imagine what it would be like with the children there, and though she knew there would be pain to deal with she had thought she was prepared for it.

Now, as though those thoughts had no more than touched the surface of her mind, simplistic and imprecise, the reality of what she was about to do had suddenly hit her. She had driven through the village, glad to be back, and taken the last stretch of road without apprehension, her mind turning forward to what she would be expected to do about dinner.

Who would be there? Hugh and Maxine? Guests? What time did the children have supper and where did they eat it? The kitchen seemed the obvious place, but clearly during Davina's reign that had not been allowed. What could she give them . . . ?

And in that instant a composite image had risen up, searing and inescapable — a child kneeling on a chair, leaning forwards with forearms on the table while obeying orders to unfold its legs and 'sit properly'; her own hand holding a plate of sausages and baked beans out of the way while the unravelling took place. What child? Boy or girl? There was no definable image. There had not needed to be. Rending grief had rushed upon her, and the tears, absolutely unforeseen, had spilled out.

They were slackening now, but still she sat holding herself together, as if grief could at any moment spring again and seize her. How could she ever, for a single instant, have supposed she could do this? She must go back. Cass had insisted that the room in the barn was hers; had made her promise to use it for days off whenever she wanted to. Cass would understand that she had made a terrible mistake, and would find someone else to go to Fallan. That was what Cass did – she filled gaps, met emergencies, supplied staff at short notice. It would be inconvenient, but it could be done.

Louise reached to switch on the ignition, trying to work out where she could turn, then found she was trembling too violently to drive. She had suffered nothing like this physical reaction since the weeks immediately after the twins' death, and her mind struggled to find a reason for it. But as calmness gradually returned she knew the reason wasn't far to seek. In all that time this was the first attempt to face direct contact with children.

Then shame came to her rescue. Two and a half years. That, surely, was enough time to have held herself safe from anything which might reopen wounds. How much longer did she need? And if the step had to be taken then best to take it here, where she already felt at home, where she would have Abby's company, and where the need was real and obvious. How could she turn back now? And if she did, when could she expect this step ever to be easier?

On a more practical level, she was in people's way. She started the car and drove on feeling shaky, but clear in her mind that she had no alternative. She turned into the drive so slowly that the car nearly stalled, then as she juddered into movement again she saw a kite caught in one of the big trees backing the strip of lawn. A first visible sign. She set her jaw and kept going. That was what lay ahead — toys and possessions, calling voices and scudding feet, fights and laughter and bumps and bruises, likes and dislikes — and resentment, the sibling closing of ranks? But where she had feared for a moment that the glimpse of the kite might bring tears again, it steadied her. It was tangible, where the image that had so shaken her had been in her mind. The tangible could be faced.

No cars at the door. As she switched off the engine she heard a faint banging, and saw Abby waving at the kitchen window. She disappeared and before Louise could start up the steps she was coming down them in uncoordinated leaps, her face bright with pleasure.

'I never, ever thought this would happen. Thank God you've come to rescue me. You can't imagine how appalling Davina was, the very worst person we've ever had here. You'll never guess what she did in the bathroom—'

'Darling Abby.' Louise hugged her, with only time to register how thin she was, surely thinner than she remembered, before Abby was wriggling away to continue indignantly, 'It's not as though it was her bathroom, it's supposed to be for every— I say,' she broke off, suddenly noticing Louise's eyes, 'are you OK?'

'I'm fine.' Louise thought that after all she might be. Seeing Abby was always a delight.

'Oh, good,' said Abby, and returned to what she was really interested in. 'She got a binbag and put *everything* in it, my shampoo and mousse and body lotion and everything, and all the boys' things, some of their absolutely favourite toys, and she must have done it deliberately on bin day because when we found out the whole lot had gone and—'

'Well, so has Davina,' Louise comforted her, remembering how tempted she had been to do something similar herself, though not with the toys. 'I'll take my things upstairs and then shall we have tea?' She felt badly in need of its reviving warmth, but it didn't occur to Abby to go and put the kettle on. Instead she tagged after Louise, not carrying anything, still chattering.

As Louise opened the door into the nursery corridor she checked; through one of the open doors came sounds of thumps and scuffling and high-pitched giggling.

'They're always fighting,' Abby said. 'Come and say hello.' She had done her best, not always successfully, to avoid referring to the children in Louise's presence. Now, it seemed, the ban was lifted. She didn't enquire why, simply glad not to have to watch what she said.

Louise had envisaged, when during the last few days she had made herself picture this first meeting, that it would take place in the kitchen. She saw how centred round the idea of providing and cooking her fears had been, but there was barely time to think of that now. Here, without preparation it seemed, she was meeting the boys — a squirming, writhing, red-faced tangle on the floor of the barren little room, silted from wall to wall with an even more spectacular mess than before. They were struggling, choking with laughter, for possession of what looked like a draught excluder, with which they were striking feeble blows at each other.

'Hey, this is Louise!' Abby shouted above the racket, and they stilled for a second, turning shiny scarlet faces towards the door, chorused, 'Hello, Louise,' in an obedient sing-song and returned to battle.

And that was that. Louise was just another in a line of cooks who came and went. Another name to learn. They didn't even hope she would be better than Davina. Davina was history, to be remembered for throwing away the contents of the nursery bathroom, but even that had been shrugged off stoically. Roddie and Matt Erskine had refined survival tactics of their own, and living for the moment was the most useful of them.

Their acceptance of her, combined with a complete want of interest, effectively calmed Louise. The fence that had seemed so huge was taken, behind her, never to be faced again. These were two ordinary small boys, with their own place in the web of humanity, and there was little in this threshing snarl of limbs to remind her of her quiet daughters.

'You're in luck,' Abby commented as she opened the door of Louise's room, which had not been polished this time and which smelled overpoweringly of the kind of musky scent Louise most disliked. 'Maxine's in New York, and even old Hugh's taken off somewhere. Must have been a sudden change of plan, because he definitely said he'd be here for dinner. I got some steaks in so that it would be easy for you.'

'Or for you?' Louise suggested.

It was a relief that Hugh was away. Facing her private tests would be easier without those observant eyes upon her. She couldn't guess that at the last moment Hugh's own nerve had failed and, afraid that he had put too much pressure on her to come back, afraid that the solution he had convinced himself he had found would prove to be an empty fantasy of his own creation, he had removed himself from the scene.

'Me?' Abby mocked. 'Cook when you're here? You have to be joking.'

'Could you manage a pot of tea, do you think?'

'Well, if I must, but don't be long.'

Abby vanished, and Louise stood for a moment, absorbing what had happened. She had met the boys; the moment had come and gone. It was miraculous. Her fears had principally concerned them for she felt, and Hugh had indicated, that a thread of contact, however tenuous, had been established with Emily.

She was surprised to find Abby waiting at the foot of the stairs, her face full of anticipation.

'Look!' She threw open the kitchen door with a flourish, and Louise saw facing her a double oven and resplendent new cooker, at least twice the size of the old one.

'Did Davina kick up?' she asked, beginning to laugh, knowing the answer already.

'No, it's for you. Hugh said so. In fact, Davina went ape because it was installed one day when she was trying to cook something or other special.' Abby's lack of interest in the arcane business of cooking was total; that clever stuff was not for her.

'Pretty impressive.'

'I've hardly dared touch it, but I expect you'll know how to start it up.'

Louise felt her spirits lift with absurd pleasure that Hugh had thought of this and carried it out. Today had been like a gravity-defying ride, hurtling her into awful depths and spinning her back to giddy heights. Perhaps now she could return to some sane equilibrium.

The kitchen door was pushed jerkily open and Emily stood glowering on the threshold.

'*You* didn't have to come back. We don't need you. Dad's so pissed off about it he's taken off when he was supposed to be staying all this week, so it just shows, doesn't it?'

# Chapter Twenty-Eight

Though memories had been reawakened and could not be avoided, and there were many moments when Louise struggled with an anguish she could not share with anyone, there was one therapy which she had, incredibly it sometimes seemed, not taken into account. Apart from Abby's company, the beauty of Fallan which never failed to weave its spell, and being very busy, there was the pleasure of the children themselves. The exact opposite of what she had dreaded, she saw that perhaps all along this should have been the comfort she sought. Far as these turbulent casual boys, and even more the scornful Emily, were from her biddable daughters, they filled, in the most natural way, the gap that had yawned in her life.

After the initial truculence of Emily's greeting, which had given Louise such a shock of disappointment and dismay, she had reverted to her own brand of withering offhandedness, and though unapproachable had not been overtly combative.

Roddie and Matt were very different. Although — close in age and hard to tell apart — they could have been twins, their personalities were so strong, their way of existing at Fallan so much their own, that comparisons were impossible and soon forgotten.

They were a stocky, muscular pair, with square open faces and hair which, though lighter in colour, fell in the same heavy diagonal line as their father's. It was all Louise could see of him in them. They accepted her presence with a mixture of resignation at finding yet another stranger in the kitchen, and a kindly readiness to keep her straight — mainly about what they liked to eat. They were boisterously good-natured, letting little ruffle them, and as unlike Emily in temperament as they were in looks. Observing this, Louise would wonder about their mothers.

In theory Abby looked after the children's rooms and clothes, and a system had evolved which suited all parties. Emily she did not interfere with, on any level, and that was that. As to the boys, they would have worn the same T-shirts and jeans for the entire holidays if given the chance. They saw no reason for beds to be 'made' and Abby agreed with them, so Louise had to get used to passing their doors and seeing messy burrows dredged with earless, eyeless, napless teddies, an arsenal of weapons, uncapped felt pens and crumpled drawings, and far too many sweet and biscuit wrappers. She had to console herself on the question of hygiene by remembering that fighting, in no spirit of acrimony, wrenched these burrows apart on at least a daily basis, and that a couple of times a week Abby did round up everything she could lay hands on and sling it indiscriminately into the washing machine.

The point was, and this Louise took some trouble to bear in mind, that everything worked. Maybe not in the way she would have done it, but who was to say her way was better? The boys were obviously in storming health and showed no signs of the emotional damage which seemed to have scarred Emily. They lived, Louise was forced to accept, a very private life, rocketing out of the house as soon as they woke and only reappearing to be fed. They had mountain bikes, which Louise thought she wouldn't have given to children that age; certainly she wouldn't have let them go off on them unsupervised, but this prudence – this, to her, ordinary care – seemed vain at Fallan.

Emily also followed an agenda of her own, but whatever it was that she did with her time she looked perpetually furtive, rebellious and discontented.

'But where does she go?' Louise was driven to ask Abby, in spite of reminding herself a dozen times a day that this was not her concern. Abby was on hand a lot more these days, not only because of the children's presence but because with the recent announcement of Geordie's engagement she seemed to have lost her appetite for man-hunting. She had a listless, wing-dragging look about her which went to Louise's heart.

'Who knows?' Abby shrugged. 'And who would ask? Not me, that's for sure. She hangs out with the kids in the village, the ones that are always in trouble, of course.'

'But does her father know about it? Doesn't he care?'

'Who's going to tell him?' Abby asked again. 'He'd only be livid with me for letting her, and what can I do to stop her? I did try to talk to Maxine once, but she just tore into me about how useless I was, said she couldn't think why Hugh kept me on, and even told me I should brush my hair, as if that would help anything.'

When Emily was in the house there was an uneasy awareness of her presence, an uncertainty as to what she might be doing, a sense of imminent disaster.

'Don't leave any cash about,' Abby warned. 'She pinches everything. I wouldn't be surprised if that lot she runs about with is into dope.'

'In Glen Fallan? Surely not!' Louise exclaimed.

Abby laughed at her. 'What do you think they smoke on the school bus? Anyway, what's Emily going to get into here that she doesn't at school?'

It was all very well for Louise to tell herself that she was only here to cook. Hugh had seemed to want to check the slide his family was taking into dangerous neglect, and had hoped, she knew, that she would bring some cohesion to his household. He hadn't discussed how this might be achieved, however, which was one of the reasons she had been disconcerted to find he hadn't waited to see her on the day she arrived. How naïve to expect it. His passing involvement had been a mere flash of conscience, forgotten as any others must have been to produce the present state of affairs. He had got what he wanted; a cook who suited him. Anything else had been buried in his ruling absorption in his own affairs.

Louise had so much to do that the brief hope of

support, though not of concern, was soon overtaken by the pressures of everyday life, Fallan style. With Hugh and Maxine absent there was no timetable of any kind. After a few attempts to establish regular mealtimes Louise had to ask herself why she thought it mattered. Did she think that what she did with her time was more important than anyone else's activities? Or did she feel discipline was good for its own sake, that observing patterns was good training and instilled respect for other people's agenda?

It was a bit late, she told herself, working her way down a prolific row of spinach in the sunshine, to worry about any of that with the Erskines. Wasn't it an adequate arrangement for her to be out here, peaceful, unhurried and easily found? When the boys came down the garden, finding obstacles to negotiate all the way, and announcing loudly that they were starving, wasn't it simple enough to go up to the house under their circling escort and stick fried eggs in rolls as they wanted? Their ramping good health seemed to suggest that their chosen diet wasn't a matter for anxiety, but perhaps tempting improvements could be introduced without their noticing.

Emily was harder to deal with. She didn't so much eat as raid the kitchen in disdain, leaving a trail of waste and devastation behind her. When Louise asked her not to take things out of the freezer and then leave them, Emily stared at her coldly and said, 'You don't buy the stuff.' If Louise pointed out that time and effort had also been involved, the response was, 'You get paid, don't you?'

There seemed no way to appeal to Emily. When the boys were asked to put their plates in the dishwasher they complied without argument. When Emily was asked to do the same she stalked off with a gesture, vestigial as belated discretion made it, which Louise preferred not to see.

One afternoon, however, finding on the kitchen table a chocolate mousse which should have been setting in the fridge, a soup spoon sticking out of it which had been used to scoop out mouthfuls all over its surface, now pooled with cream and ice cream, the containers for which were also left out, Louise forgot requests and reason.

It was not hard to find Emily. Pop music was in full flow, pouring out of her room and along the nursery corridor. Louise, by good luck as the room was half dark, found the switch and turned off the torrent of sound.

'Hey, what are you doing?' Emily shouted in fury. 'You can't come in here!'

She was sitting cross-legged on her tangled bed, a wedge of Victoria sponge in her hand, the rest of the cake, at a tilt on the duvet which had caused its top layer to slide jammily sideways, in front of her.

Louise wasted no time on discussion. 'Emily, I am happy to cook whatever food you like but I am not prepared to cook food to be vandalised and thrown away. I take care and trouble over it, and I don't accept such behaviour from you. Do you understand me? I do not accept it.'

She didn't pause to wonder how Emily would react. It was irrelevant. But even in her anger she barely raised her voice, nor did she harangue Emily, she simply presented her point of view. This was something she was not prepared to tolerate.

This reluctantly impressed Emily, who though she flushed and looked defiant, mumbled, 'OK, OK.' What impressed her more was that Louise did not, like all other grown-ups of Emily's acquaintance, press home her advantage or use it to extract promises for the future. She only said, 'Good, then we understand each other,' and was gone, leaving Emily with her hunk of cake suspended.

Later, picking blackcurrants at the far end of the garden, for the abundance of fruit and vegetables normally left to rot was something Louise couldn't bear, she examined Emily's behaviour with more detachment, recognising the aggressive loneliness behind it. It was clear nothing could be done for Emily without basic problems being addressed, but what help was there in this house for a hurting thirteen-year-old, what company, what interests, what stimulus?

The first shooting guests, and Hugh, were expected in two days' time. Maxine was due to arrive tomorrow. Louise, expecting a rebuff, asked Emily if she would like to go down to Aberfyle with her to shop.

Emily pushed out her lips and turned away, but said grudgingly, 'Could do.'

Was she taking a risk, Louise wondered, checking a couple of items for her list. Would Emily use the opportunity for her own purposes? To do what? Run away? Where would she run to? Supply herself with harmful substances? This Louise had been unable to take seriously, seeing no signs that Emily did any more than flirt with the idea to gain attention. Not that Louise would know what to look for, she acknowledged, calling along the red corridor for Emily who had disappeared.

Louise didn't attempt to talk as they went down the glen. She remembered too vividly the trapped feeling she had known as a child when grown-ups used a car journey as a convenient opportunity to hammer away yet again about her faults and failings. In any case Emily sat screwed away from her, every inch of her warning, 'Keep off.'

Only as they hunted for a space in the inadequate carpark of the supermarket did Emily speak. 'You can sometimes find a place at the vet's out of surgery hours. They don't mind if they know you. It's behind here.'

'Great. Thanks, Emily.' There was a temptation to add, 'Local knowledge is always a help,' or, 'I had to park at the end of the High Street last time I came,' but the most normal of comments seemed gushing in the face of Emily's terseness, and Louise suppressed them.

'I expect you'll want to go off on your own,' she said, as she locked the car. 'Shall we arrange a time to meet?' She had taken it for granted that Emily would not want to be with her, but looking up she caught the strangest look on the set face, a look almost of hope dashed which she had never expected to see there. What was it Emily had wanted; where was she failing her?

'Unless you could bear to give me a hand first? I've got a list as long as my arm.'

Surely Emily was the last person to want to shove a trolley round a supermarket? But with an ungracious mumble of, 'I don't mind,' she led the way. Was it better to do anything, no matter how boring, than be left to her own devices once more? How sad that was.

Expecting her attention span to be brief, Louise was surprised at the way Emily applied herself to the job in hand. She was quick to spot things, and packed the trolley with an order few people would have bothered about. It wasn't the only surprise. Standing beside Louise in front of a range of pizzas she said disgustedly, 'Everything's so *red*. We get sick of all this *red* stuff.'

'Red meat, do you mean?' Louise asked. 'Do you prefer vegetarian food?'

'No, all this horrible tomatoey spicy stuff. We like proper food only no one cooks it for us.'

'Proper food? What do you like, then?'

'Oh, I don't know.' Emily looked ready to abandon the issue as too difficult and unlikely to produce results anyway. Then unexpectedly she rushed on, looking defensive, 'You know, stuff like mashed potatoes. With butter. And apple pie. And chicken, just by itself in the oven, not slobbered over with sauces.'

'With its skin crisp and golden?'

'Yes!' Emily sounded actually eager. 'With roast potatoes. And the boys like cottage pie, and bangers and mash, and dumplings. But you can't get anything like that now, can you?'

The resigned tone, like that of an eighty-year-old mourning the passing of seedcake or brains, almost betrayed Louise into a smile, but the moment was too precious to be risked.

'I can cook all those things,' she said. 'And anything else you like.'

Emily looked briefly hopeful, then cynicism returned. 'Oh, yeah, and then when all the boring people come to stay there's no time, is there? We're just in the way. Shove something in the mike for us. Yuk convenience stuff. Beefburgers. Chicken nuggets.'

Louise wanted to ask, Wouldn't it have been simpler to tell me this, instead of wrecking the kitchen? But the point didn't have to be made. 'Then let's get the things you like right now,' she said.

As they pushed the trolley to the car Louise asked, 'Are you all right for money for your own shopping?'

'What money?' Emily scoffed, her face instantly contemptuous.

'How is your pocket money paid to you?'

'Maxine. When she's here.'

Anger filled Louise. This arrangement, dependent on Maxine's presence or absence, was so callous in its indifference, placing Emily in the category of something unimportant and secondary. No wonder she stole.

'I can let you have some money.'

'How can you?' Emily still sounded scornful, but her eyes were alert.

'I can put my bill in for it, as I do for this.' Louise nodded at the bags they were packing into the car. 'Will this do?'

Emily looked at the notes then up at Louise with an

expression which, Louise thought, with a small ache in her throat, went far beyond gratitude for some spending power.

'Now, I've got to go to the butcher's,' she said, deliberately brisk. 'Not very entertaining for you, so you might like to spend some of that and then we can meet up in half an hour or so and treat ourselves to a cream cake, or whatever you prefer. What do you think?'

'Cool.'

Louise was careful to tone down her quick pleasure at the response. 'Thanks for helping with this lot.'

Emily, heading for the delights of W.H. Smith, didn't reply, but Louise, going her separate way to the butcher's, thought again of her competent help in the supermarket. Being needed? Doing something practical? Or merely the satisfaction of buying and getting? There was everything to discover about Emily.

Driving home the silence was less hostile, and Louise took the chance to enquire casually, 'Do you ever have friends of your own to stay at Fallan?'

'Not allowed to.' Emily stared out of the window.

Nevertheless, Louise thought it worth trying one more question. 'Why is that?'

Silence. She had decided there wasn't going to be an answer when Emily said abruptly, in an adult manner very unlike her usual monosyllabic dismissiveness, 'I suppose Abby couldn't be expected to look after us. I'm bad enough on my own. They can't bear to think what I'd get up to with someone else around.' Then, with a return to sullenness, 'Who'd want to come to Fallan anyway?'

Louise could see it through her eyes. If Emily was hankering for the pop scene, or whatever she perceived the culture of her peer group to be, then indeed, what was there to do at Fallan? Yet she seemed to have missed out on the ordinary pleasures of childhood there, and the fun of sharing them with someone of her own age.

'Do you ever go and stay with friends?'

'I'm too disruptive.' A glint of a grin.

'Ah, well, that I can believe.'

Emily gave a little spurt of a giggle, obviously against her better judgement.

She seemed to accept the situation, but Louise thought this, like so many other things swept carelessly under the carpet at Fallan, was capable of review. It was more than time that Hugh Erskine put in an appearance.

# Chapter Twenty-Nine

Louise's hopes of discussing any of these issues with Hugh turned out to be naïve indeed. He was never alone, available or, she decided with growing disenchantment, interested. The reality was that the house fell into two units, each functioning independently of the other. The doors closing off the kitchen and nursery corridors were more comprehensive barriers than she had ever realised when the house held only adults.

Now was added the world of the children, and Louise, whether she acknowledged it or not, became engaged in a struggle to win for it its rightful space and status. The clue provided by Emily gave her a starting point for making changes of her own, and in following it up she found other things falling into place.

If she was going to cook the sort of food the young Erskines were missing it was reasonable to expect them to be there when meals were ready. All three children saw the sense in this; in fact Louise guessed, watching their faces as a golden-topped pie or sizzling roast chicken was borne to the table, that such moments held a ceremonial quality they valued. Though probably not even Emily could have expressed it, they liked sitting round a properly laid table because they felt a reassuring rightness and stability about it. Someone had taken trouble for them, and that someone was also prepared to sit down and eat with them, without more urgent preoccupations taking precedence.

Louise was amused to find that Abby liked this as much as Emily and the boys did, and guessed that for her too there was an implicit security, a feeling of family which had been absent when she was growing up. Her presence added to the children's pleasure, for they felt for her the tolerant affection reserved for an adult clearly less adequately equipped to cope with the world than they were.

Though with the house busy breakfast had to be an *ad hoc* meal for kitchen dwellers, and at supper Louise was too busy to join them, she was there in the background, listening as she worked, and Abby was usually on hand to raid someone's chips or hoover up leftover puddings. But lunch could be made a gathering point, geared to the children's preferences, with nothing to distract or hurry Louise. Unconsciously the children responded with the appropriate behaviour, and the boys at least were happy to lay the table, clear away, be involved.

This would presumably be the norm when they were with their mother, but had probably been so at Fallan, too. Again it was Emily who provided the clue.

'We used to have chocolate upside-down pudding

before,' she said one day, watching with unconcealed delight the dark glory of the sauce slithering down. 'Angie used to make it for us.'

'Angie?' Doling out boy-sized portions, Louise failed to pin down the name immediately, vaguely supposing this to be some past cook.

'That's our mother,' Roddie explained. 'Emily calls her Angie, though.'

'She can make all the things you make,' Matt added. 'When we go there we have chocolate pudding.'

'She makes bread-and-butter pudding too,' Roddie said. 'With millions of currants.'

'Louise can make bread-and-butter pudding,' Emily flashed, and the comment, based on nothing, made Louise wince for the deprivation it revealed.

'Have you ever met the boys' mother?' she asked Abby later, as they ladled blackcurrant jam into jars.

'Once or twice. She's nice, sort of bubbly, laughs a lot like the boys. Old Hugh went to pieces completely when she bogged off.'

'You weren't here then, were you?'

'No, but that's what people say.'

Which people? Louise bit back that and other questions.

'Oh, no, look what I've done! Ow, that's hot!'

'Abby, why don't you use the funnel? And don't wipe the jar with that cloth, it's covered in jam already.'

'A bit different from Emily's mother, anyway.' Abby, sucking the finger she'd rashly used to catch the jam dribbles, was following her own train of thought. 'Um, this is good. Gabrielle she was called, and she was awful, according to Lennie, always flying off the handle about something, and she couldn't bear Emily.'

'Abby, that can't be true! In any case, it's not the sort of thing—'

'No, it's OK, everyone knows. She never wanted her. That's why she disappeared after Emily was born. Never been heard of again.'

'That's probably not true either.'

'Why shouldn't it be? She and Hugh used to have fearful rows. Half kill each other, so everyone says.'

'Who is this everyone?' Louise demanded. 'Though whoever it is we're just as bad, discussing other people's private lives.'

'God, you can be unrewarding,' Abby sighed, making cautious dabs with her tongue at the wooden spoon on which the jam was rapidly cooling.

'All right, then, I will ask one question. If Hugh and his father are at loggerheads, why does Hugh take his friends shooting on Fallan estate?'

'Your one question is totally boring,' Abby complained. 'I think it's to do with some agreement they made when Leo's will was altered.'

'Because of Gloria?'

'No, it was before Gloria turned up, when everybody was still chummy. It was when Hugh's elder brother died – he caught some potty bug out in the Gambia on holiday or something.'

'Hugh had an elder brother?'

'Yes, and he was going to inherit of course, so then it

had to be Hugh, but he was doing all his mining stuff by then and making a bomb and he didn't want to know, but Leo made him agree to take the shooting because he was too old to do it himself. It's bad for a place not to be shot, whatever that means. Sounds bizarre to me.'

It sounded bizarre to Louise too, part and parcel of the values which made her so impatient with Hugh Erskine. She had expected that as soon as he returned they would build on what they had discussed when he came to Bridge of Riach. Nothing of the kind. Hugh's days dovetailed without a chink, starting with an hour or so in the office before he had breakfast with the other guns, followed by a hectic period during which Cameron and a ghillie came in for the lunches, and not only Maxine and Hugh but everyone else phoned and faxed secretaries, stockbrokers or accountants, with a lot of frustration about their mobile phones. Then there was more chaos as they got themselves into boots, went back and forth to the gunroom, and poured out instructions to Louise about laundry, collecting pills for a dog with urinary difficulties, phoning the garage, and seeing that their post, invariably airmail or recorded delivery, went off safely. Louise would have thought most of this was Maxine's job, but Maxine liked to be at the centre of the action, wearing a knicker-bocker suit made in Paris.

After the crescendo of departure calm descended, but Hugh of course had gone too, and when he came back it was a dram with the ghillies, another office session crammed in before drinks before dinner, and once dinner began the evening was gone.

Louise, watching the pattern form, saw how completely side-lined the children were, and couldn't believe it had to be that way. If Hugh had wanted to include them they could have gone up the hill for a half day, could have gone to meet the guns coming down, could at the very least have been present at breakfast. Encouraging them to come to the drawing-room before dinner would have provided some contact, or if that was unacceptable then Hugh could have made time to sit with them for a while when they had supper. One of the things that made Louise angriest was hearing him go by along the kitchen corridor without so much as putting his head round the door to say hello. It was not the demands of his day which squeezed out the children, but his own inclination, she was increasingly convinced.

Hugh made it plain, however, that he expected Louise to live 'front of the house'. The assumption that she would be pleased to do so made her more indignant than ever. How did he imagine it would work on a practical level, for one thing? And he seemed once more to have conveniently forgotten Abby.

Hugh made the invitation specific on an evening when dining-room numbers were down to four.

'I should very much like you to join us for dinner if you would. Could you organise something Abby could serve perhaps, or that we could help ourselves to? We don't see nearly as much of you as we should like.'

He had been uncomfortably conscious not only of being caught up again in what seemed inescapable routine, but of having lost track somewhere of the warm image he had had of Louise drawing the disparate elements of Fallan together. He knew her calm even-handedness in looking after both groups, her unspoken determination that the children should not be turned into second-class citizens, was what, theoretically, he had hoped for. Yet he was dogged by an obscure resentment over it, which he knew was guilt. The very rapport she had established with the children brought his own inadequacies into sharp relief.

Louise, listening to this speech, turned over the word 'we' with disfavour. Hugh and Maxine? Or did the pronoun include the spoiled arrogant men who took it for granted that she would do their chores for them? She had assumed, why she couldn't imagine, that Hugh's shooting guests would be his friends, perhaps coming with their wives and families. It had been chilling to find they were colleagues, invited to kill a few grouse as a prestigious emollient to business relations.

'I'm sorry,' she said. 'I'm afraid I shan't be free this evening.'

'Not free?' Hugh was taken aback.

'No. I'm going down to the pub. As Abby does, you know.' The company of Fraser and other friends there seemed suddenly very attractive.

Hugh managed not to repeat, 'The *pub*?' This was not what he had expected of Louise. Of that giddy nympho Abby perhaps, and the other transients who frequented his kitchen. His face darkened, and Louise observed it with satisfaction. There was so much he would never understand unless he took the trouble to do so.

'I meet someone there,' she added, and escaped as the phone in the kitchen corridor, where Hugh had caught her on his way to the gunroom, rang at his elbow. How sad, she thought, that the only opportunity he had made to talk to her had been wasted on this.

Hugh used Maxine as his line of communication with kitchen and nursery, and Louise thought the system iniquitous. The children hated Maxine, with a mute helpless resistance which showed how complete her power was. In her mouth any message became an order, and she regarded the mildest protest as an attempt to undermine her personally.

Louise was also shocked to find that the children, in whatever terms they expressed it, or whatever the concept meant to them, believed that Maxine and their father were lovers. Repellent as the idea was, for Maxine looked a woman to whom sex would be part of a fitness programme or at best an appetite to be satisfied, Louise thought they were probably right. As for Hugh, it was hard to imagine tenderness for a woman, or loving emotion of any kind, from such a man, and nothing in his behaviour towards Maxine suggested that she elicited either.

How very disagreeable, Louise would think with a shudder, and the probability of a sexual relationship made her more protective of the children than ever.

It was a relief to take the chance of two days off before the next party of guests arrived, though Maxine created difficulties about it.

'Maxine, I'm due four days by this time,' Louise reminded her. 'I've waited till there are no guests, and I shall leave plenty of food ready.'

'You don't seem to realise this is the peak of the season. So much hinges on everything being successful, and naturally if you are expected to work over and above what you consider to be your proper hours then that will be reflected in your pay cheque.'

Louise let most of this pass. 'Not much can hinge on you and Abby and the family being alone here. If you find these dates a problem then we'd better revert to the arrangement in my contract, and I'll take two days off per week – shall we say Tuesday and Wednesday?'

Maxine flushed with annoyance. She disliked Louise intensely, for Hugh made no secret of his approbation. Also she had made the mistake of dismissing her as a cosy little blonde with no aspirations outside the kitchen, and it was infuriating to be outmanoeuvred.

Though the prospect of seeing Cass and Rick, sleeping in her little room in the barn again, and having a lazy time for two days was very alluring, Louise was surprised by a hint of reluctance as she went downstairs. The boys came scudding up on their bikes when she was putting her bag into the car.

'Are you coming back?' They had asked the question many times, but seemed unable to believe Louise's assurances that she was. It was as if they could not forget previous evidence and her words made no impact.

She smiled down at Matt's tense face, which had an anxious, vulnerable expression she hated to see. 'Go up to my room and look,' she told him. 'All my things are there, except what's in this small bag. The bed's ready for when I come back. Anyway, I promised to take you to the Games in Aberfyle, remember?' She realised as she said it that she could have saved her breath on this point. In Matt's experience promises of that sort were lightly made.

The more prosaic assurance had been successful, however. 'Can we go in your room and see?'

'Of course.'

'I'll tell Emily.'

He tore off across the grass, and Louise saw that Emily was hovering, scowling and not looking, by the arch which led to the garden.

Had Emily been the one asking the question? Louise hoped so, as she waved to them and drove away, reluctance deepening. It was a mixture of knowing she would miss them, and of being tugged at by trivia like hoping they would like the menus she had planned for them, and wondering if Abby would remember to turn off the stock pot or phone in the butcher's order. It was also, she discovered, a feeling of relinquishing something.

The days at Bridge of Riach were, in spite of this, great fun, with the unexpected bonus of Aidan turning up for a night on his way south from fishing in Sutherland. He booked into the Cluny Arms in Kirkton, and invited not only Louise to dinner but Cass and Rick and the friends they had staying with them. It was a resoundingly successful evening, with an instant welding of the group. Aidan was thrilled to be recognised by a holiday-maker in the bar, and by his exuberant friendliness (and lavishness in the matter of buying rounds) gathered in its entire population before the shutters came down at three in the morning.

Later that day, after their guests had left, as they walked by the hill track to a barbecue with the Mackenzies at Riach, Cass took the chance to ask Louise, 'How's Hugh Erskine behaving himself?'

Rick and Aidan (persuaded to stay for another night), two giants of men, were strolling ahead, the booming of Aidan's voice like a monologue with pauses, since Rick's quiet rejoinders could not be heard.

'Exactly as he's always behaved,' Louise replied. 'I often feel I'm at Fallan under false pretences.'

'But is it working out all right – for you?' This was what Cass wanted to ask. She had phoned once or twice, but had avoided potentially upsetting topics, feeling that unless Louise referred to them herself then a telephone conversation was not the best time to broach them.

'About the children, you mean?'

'Yes. I've often thought of you, and I know it must have been hard. Do you regret going?'

Louise paused, looking up towards the big house ahead, set squarely on a level stretch of ground that no one had attempted to turn into a garden, but seeing nothing. 'Regret going,' she repeated, turning the words over with care. 'No, I haven't regretted it.' It was good to state that unequivocally. 'I'd been wrong, you know, to avoid children. I find it's what I most needed.'

Moved by her courage, Cass took her arm and hugged it against her side for a moment, but said nothing. She could see a different problem looming. Knowing Louise's capacity for involvement with anyone she looked after, this time with children in the case, Cass was apprehensive about further hurt for her.

Walking on, talking about the Erskine family, laughing at stories of the boys' exploits, she almost wished Louise could be like some of her more casual employees who, though they might put less into a job, were able to walk away from it when it was over with a cheerful immunity from emotional entanglement.

# Chapter Thirty

The day was cloudy but sultry, the pavements thronged, the few serious shoppers struggling to get on with the business of ordinary life among the idling shoals of tourists. Louise didn't see the plastic carrier of the fat woman swaying along in front of her split; the first she knew of it was a tumble of oranges and tins of cat food round her ankles, and a crunch underfoot from what looked like minute ball bearings, which she recognised from long ago as those silver cake decorations which jarred one's teeth if bitten on unawares. They were beyond retrieve, but with one or two passers-by she pursued the other objects. When she straightened to hand back what she had salvaged she found herself looking into Gloria's damp, red, harassed face. Her first impression was that Gloria looked ready to collapse.

'Are you all right?' Louise put a hand under the podgy arm and found she was shaking. 'Come and stand here in the shade while I gather up what I can.'

'Let it go,' Gloria wheezed with an effort, flapping a fat hand in lieu of struggling with further words.

'I think most has survived,' Louise said, looking at her with concern. 'Why don't we go and find tea somewhere? You look exhausted and it might help to sit down for a few minutes.'

'You know I oughtn't to,' Gloria gasped, fumbling for a tiny handkerchief and fanning herself with it, though it was too flimsy to move the heavy air, merely releasing a wave of sickly scent which Louise thought could hardly improve Gloria's case.

'Don't worry about that now,' she said firmly. 'The Wheaten Loaf is round the corner. We'll go there.'

'No, I'll be fine, just give me a sec. Leo'd do his nut if I—' Gloria patted at the bags under her eyes with the absurd handkerchief, trying to take slow breaths.

'I'm not leaving you here.' Louise collected the shopping, hooked everything onto one hand and took a fat elbow with the other. 'Tea.'

'What a mercy you've got a mind of your own,' Gloria said with a faint chuckle, allowing herself to be steered to the nearby baker's shop with its adjoining restaurant. On such a warm day most people had opted to be outside, and Louise was able to find a cool dim corner free.

'You're a love,' Gloria said gratefully as the teapot arrived. 'I knew you were, first minute I set eyes on you. Oh my, that's good. Nothing like tea, is there?' She leaned her head against the wall, and even in the gloomy corner Louise could see the sheen of sweat on her fat cheeks.

'Are you sure you're all right?' she asked worriedly. 'This thundery heat is very tiring.'

'Right as rain,' Gloria assured her. 'The old ticker's been giving me the odd go lately, but nothing to write home about.'

'Are you here on your own? Then I think you should let me take you home,' Louise urged. 'Someone can fetch your car later.'

'Oh, yes, that'd be right.' Gloria's laughter turned into breathless coughing which did nothing to reassure Louise. 'No, give me a minute or two and I'll be fine. But thanks for the offer. They told me you were the looking-after sort and now I see what they mean.'

They? Abby's they? 'Who said so?' Louise asked with interest.

'Oh, Lord, me and my mouth. Don't give me away, love, but of course the kids said it.'

'The kids? The Erskine children?' Louise was thunder-struck.

'Come up to me every day, very near, the boys do any-way. If it's not the strawberries it's the kittens, or my doughnuts, more like. They told me about you making them toad-in-the-hole and jam roly-poly. Keep an eye on the clock these days, scared they'll miss something.' She laughed reedily to herself, adding water to the pot.

'They come up to the big house? But I thought—'

'Oh, well,' Gloria tapped her nose, 'what the eye don't see. Mind you, I don't let them in, and I keep clear of that Abby and the rest, and I'll never speak to their dad to my dying day after what he's done, but kids are different, aren't they? Poor little buggers have a pretty thin time of it, to my mind. I think Leo misses them, to tell you the honest truth, though he'd cut out his tongue sooner than say so. That's men for you, isn't it?'

Louise followed the Range Rover up the glen road, reflecting that the afternoon's events had not affected Gloria's driving. The big vehicle wove expertly through the clutter of traffic, reminding Louise of the gossip. A London cabbie? She wished there had been more time to talk, but Gloria, once tea and a slab of carrot cake had revived her, had been anxious to be on her way.

'Don't you think it would be sensible to let me take you home?' Louise had persisted.

'Lumme, some ructions there'd be. No, duck, I'll manage, but you come along behind me, just in case.'

Louise's natural reticence forbade her asking too many questions, but one thing she did want to know.

'Does Emily come up to see you too?'

'That one! Little madam.' Gloria's voice had held a mixture of disparagement and admiration. 'When she wants something, maybe. But I'll tell you this much, Emily's trouble. Want to watch her, you do. Runs about with all sorts in the village.'

Louise had found it hard to imagine there could be all sorts in a village the size of Fallan, but she had not said so.

'She'll get herself in trouble one of these days, you mark my words.' Gloria's lips had pursed into a disapproving button glossed with soft icing from the carrot cake. 'You won't be staying long, I suppose?'

'I'm just here for the holidays.'

'That's always the way of it,' Gloria had sighed, looking suddenly old and tired. 'Well, it's none of my business, but that Hugh Erskine has got plenty to answer for, if you ask me.'

Louise agreed, her disillusionment with him growing every day. This new evidence of the underground lives the children led, while their father used the house as a handy hotel, reminded her of how far they were from the changes he had talked about.

She decided the time had come to talk again, but it was almost impossible to find the chance. Hugh and his guests were dining at Gask and tomorrow he was inviting the Gask house-party in return, so Louise herself would have plenty to do. But after that a brief gap when no guests were expected should serve her purpose.

It looked as though she would be lucky, when on the day the guests were leaving she learned that Maxine was taking one of them to the airport. Perhaps for the first time there would be a family lunch, father and children sitting together round the kitchen table. Would Hugh do that, or would he expect them to join him in the dining-room? Whichever; Louise didn't mind. She would make something special . . .

But Hugh, via Maxine before she left, sent a message that he would be out for lunch.

Needing in her frustration to make a gesture of some sort, though if she was making it on behalf of the children it was wasted for they saw nothing unusual in their father's absence, Louise put together a picnic, included a frying pan, and went with Abby to find the boys who were fishing up the Fallan burn. Even Emily was drawn to follow, though in her own time.

It was too high here for anything but the smallest brown trout but the boys were thrilled to have the catch cooked. Cameron, seeing the smoke, came to investigate, and to Louise's surprise seemed to approve. In no hurry, as the moor was quiet today, he guddled for a much bigger trout than had fallen to Roddie and Matt's rods and then let them each have a try. Neither was successful, but they were full of enthusiasm for the new trick, and Louise and Abby left all three children flat on their faces by the burn when they started for home. It rekindled Louise's anger with Hugh. Why did it have to be Cameron who took the trouble to show them this?

Glancing out of the kitchen window as she and Abby unpacked the picnic, she saw the Daimler at the door. She tipped the unwanted fruit back into the bowl and said to Abby, 'I'm going to have a word with Hugh.'

Abby looked round in surprise. 'Sounds ominous. I think I'll go and get my head down. If you need help shout for Lennie.'

Louise didn't smile. She always found it hard to key herself up for confrontations, though any dialogue with Hugh seemed to result in little else. She reminded herself that this must be about the children, and only about the children.

Hugh was in the office, as she had expected, and it

struck her as sad that on a fine August afternoon in this beautiful place, with his children enjoying themselves out on the hill, this was the place to find him.

'Ah, Louise.' A curious expression crossed Hugh's face as he saw her — pleasure, guilt and defensiveness hardening into what looked like antagonism.

It did little to reassure Louise, but she was here to say things which she believed must be said.

'I apologise for interrupting your work,' she began, glancing at the desk. Some massive report was open in front of him, and she could imagine him settling down to it in anticipation of the first undisturbed stretch of time he had had for days.

'That's quite all right.' Perfunctory courtesy, followed by the sharper, 'What's happened?'

Louise reflected that his assumption that something serious must have occurred to bring her here was all part of why she had to talk to him.

'Nothing's happened. I wanted to talk to you about the children.'

Hugh glanced at his watch, and Louise felt the colour rise in her cheeks at what that gesture said. Irritating, boring, how long will it take?

'Is this an inconvenient time?' she asked, and there was an edge in her usually gentle voice which made Hugh say hastily, 'Not at all,' pushing the report away and turning his chair sideways.

If he steeples his fingers and puts on a listening face I shall walk out, Louise thought, then crushed down her resentment. This chance must not be squandered.

'There hasn't been much opportunity to talk since I arrived,' she began, careful not to make it an accusation, 'but I haven't forgotten what we discussed when you came to see me at Cass's. Do you remember?'

It really seemed to her that he might not, so inconsistent had his actions been since.

'Of course I remember.' The frown was in place, the straight brows down, the eyes intent and not friendly.

'Well, it seemed to me,' Louise was conscious of her voice sounding too light, too apologetic, and went on more firmly, 'that we haven't made much progress. I don't feel I've succeeded in doing what you wanted done.'

'It seems to me you're doing an excellent job,' Hugh objected. 'The house has been full for most of the time and your cooking has been praised by everyone.'

Louise stared at him in amazement, doubting for a moment that there was any point in going on. Hugh didn't meet her eyes, concentrating on a paperknife he had picked up and was flipping between his fingers.

How dared he reduce the conversation to such a level? 'You didn't come to Bridge of Riach to talk to me about cooking,' Louise said, coming to her feet with a movement that startled Hugh, who rose too, the knife held tip down on the desk. 'You said you wanted to do something about the children, you wanted this house to be a home and you wanted me here because you thought I could help to make it one. A home! It's more like a ship with first-class at one end and steerage at the other. You cut yourself off completely, pursue your own interests to the exclusion of everything else, and expect some stranger to make your children feel cared for. That wasn't what you said you wanted, and I believed it wasn't what you meant.'

'I really don't think you can come in here and harangue me like this,' Hugh began, but Louise's anger on behalf of the children had her in its grip now.

'Why not? Because you must never be disturbed? How can whatever you were doing when I came in be more important than Emily and Roddie and Matt? You asked me if anything had happened and I said no. Well, there's no immediate disaster to give me an excuse for breaking into your work, certainly, but there's the ongoing disaster of how your children live.'

'Louise, I don't think you have any right—'

The anger in his voice didn't daunt Louise, but it did make her alter her approach, recognising in time that accusations would get them nowhere. 'Don't you see,' she broke in, 'I want to help. I came here to try and help. I don't want to quarrel with you, only I've been getting more and more frustrated because there seemed no way of achieving what you hoped for. I can't do it on my own, you know that.'

The reasonable tone, and the concern she clearly showed, allowed Hugh to get hold of his temper. He tossed down the paperknife and turned to the window, standing there for a tense moment while Louise bit back the challenges she longed to hurl at him, making herself give him time.

'You're right, we should talk,' he said at last, and though his terse tone was not promising he did switch on the answerphone and put out an arm to usher Louise towards the door to the library, saying, 'Let's go in here. It's less business-orientated.'

'I hate quarrelling,' Louise said as she passed him, more to herself than to him, but the regretful tone reached him, and he was smiling as he gestured her to a chair.

'I'm sorry to have provoked you to it. Now, where do we start?' Hugh raised his eyebrows in brief amusement as they confronted each other, with suddenly nothing to say. Louise found that the anger which seethed so furiously against him when he was inaccessible, engrossed in his own affairs, was hard to formulate when he was present, for there was a helplessness about him, as of a man in a trap who saw no way out, which could touch her in spite of herself. That was absurd. She brushed the image away. Whatever problems he had they were of his own making.

'I'm worried about Emily,' she plunged. 'She spends half her time in the village, hanging round with the most disreputable characters she can find and—'

'Then don't let her,' Hugh said sharply. 'God knows, if I employ two people to look after three children I think I can expect—'

'Please stop there.' Sympathy in tatters, Louise faced him with renewed anger. 'How far you are from under-standing. Emily is beyond being ordered to do or not do things. She is desperately lonely, and feels desperately unwanted. Can't you see that? How can Abby or I, or any other employee, prevent her from looking for some kind of company or making some kind of statement about herself? And if we could stop her going to the village what do you expect her to do here?'

'Good God, there's plenty to do. Most youngsters would be delighted to spend the summer in such a—'

'Doing what, exactly?' Louise persisted.

'Well, as boys we used to find plenty—'

'What?'

'The usual things, I suppose,' Hugh disliked being put on the spot and showed it.

'What were they?' Louise supposed he meant enjoying the resources of the estate, like shooting and fishing, and didn't think she would tell him that Emily, when last seen, was busy guddling for trout. 'Were they activities likely to appeal to a thirteen-year-old girl?'

'Louise, for God's sake, what else can I provide? This place is paradise—'

'You know what I mean. We have to try and find something Emily can enjoy or be interested in. The boys are happy enough, in fact I can't imagine them being unhappy anywhere –' she was glad to see a smile light his face '– and it's easy to find ways of pleasing them.'

'I've been meaning to thank you for that,' he broke in swiftly. 'I haven't been entirely unobservant.'

'It's not enough,' she insisted, seeing her chance, but swept by compassion not only for the children but for this bitter man, so incapable of taking the first step to deal with what he knew was a serious problem. 'They need to be with you.'

'They haven't the faintest interest in being with me and you know it.'

'Because they're not used to you, that's all. There's no day-to-day dialogue. You don't know what's currently absorbing their attention or what they like and don't like. But it's easy to get to know. Now that the house is empty for a few days you could do things together, have meals with them for a start. And then, I've been thinking, they're madly keen about the Aberfyle Games. I've promised to take them, but they'd like it far better if you went. It would be a huge thrill and—'

'Louise, hang on a moment.' Hugh had been trying to break in but in her relief that they were talking positively at last she had rushed on. It was so simple after all.

Before Hugh could continue the door was flung open and Maxine stalked in, her hair newly cut and sleeker than ever, her eyes taking in the scene with hostility, angry to find Louise in her space, with the man she regarded as her property. In her hand was a long fax.

'Apparently this came in some time ago. I think Hellers wanted an answer right away.'

'Damn, I was waiting for that.' In an instant Hugh was sucked back into the world where he was safe, and as she watched him scan the fax bleakness filled Louise. What had she expected; what had she wasted effort and emotion on? Nothing would alter here. Hugh might flirt with the idea when his conscience stirred, but if he had really wanted to do something about his family he would have done it long ago.

She didn't think he'd notice if she went and with a nod to Maxine, which was not returned, she made for the door into the red corridor. She was surprised to hear Hugh call her.

'I'll be right there, Maxine,' he added crisply, and

Maxine, with a furious look, stalked into the office.

'I'm sorry we were interrupted,' Hugh said, following Louise. 'I do have to deal with this now. I appreciate the suggestions you've made, but I see you didn't realise – I shan't be here for the next couple of weeks. I shall be back during September when we have a couple of drives, and then there will be people here for the stalking.'

Louise stared at him blankly. Through the door to the office she could hear Maxine playing back a message on the answerphone and saw Hugh's attention caught by it. Without a word she turned and walked away.

# Chapter Thirty-One

The rest of August passed for Louise in a mood of quiet but rewarding defiance. It needed some persistence but she finally wheedled out of Emily the name of the friend she would most like to be with if she could. She then had a lengthy and frank telephone conversation with a Mrs Linklater who lived near Newtonmore.

'I can't promise there won't be storms, but if she does anything dreadful I shall come at once and bring her home,' she promised finally.

'Don't worry, I'm glad to help. It's a sad little family. A friend of mine knows the boys' mother quite well, so I'm familiar with the story and I've always thought Emily had a raw deal. We're a big crowd here, cousins galore at present, so there'll be plenty of people to keep an eye on her. There's no point in trying to send Dinah to you till the puppies have gone to their new homes. Such are her priorities, I'm afraid.'

Louise saw Dinah's point, on the day she drove Emily

to Newtonmore, with the boys along for the ride, and going into the entrance hall of an imposing turreted house up two miles of drive, found it had been fenced off to form a pen for a long-haired retriever bitch and her pups.

'Don't try to drag the children in,' called Perdita Linklater, coming to meet her from the main hall, dressed in red matador pants and a smocked shirt that looked like the remnants of a Victorian nightdress. 'Emily's here,' she shouted into the hinterland, and with a rush of feet and quick 'hello's to Louise, half a dozen children swept past.

'You mustn't pick them up like that. I'll choose one for you to hold,' a bossy voice rang out.

Perdita laughed. 'Dinah's in charge. They'll be all right. Come and have tea before you go back.'

The memory that stayed with Louise as she drove home, taking the boys to a Little Chef as a treat on the way, was of Emily's face as she held a round silken-coated puppy to her cheek. Never had Louise imagined the sharp features could look so soft, so rapturously happy. Rebellion – hers – seemed to bring results.

On the day before the Aberfyle Games Louise fetched Emily, and Dinah with her, and drove home in a trance of astonishment listening to the chatter and arguments and giggles, which turned temporarily to wails of grief as they described the brutal break-up of the family in the porch. It was as though Emily had learned a part in a new play. Louise hoped she'd stick to it but, remembering whose daughter she was, could hardly feel sanguine.

There had been a certain satisfaction in not telling Hugh, even via Maxine, that his daughter had been staying in someone else's house, or that Louise was letting her have a friend to stay in her own. She didn't seriously think he would object; she had just enjoyed arranging it on her own initiative.

The day of the Games was blustery and showery, with brief spells of hot sunshine which made everything steam, and produced a distinctive crowd scent of damp wool and tweed. Roddie and Matt joined in everything open to them, applying themselves to each challenge with red faces and bursting hearts, drawing amused applause.

Emily had less confidence, but with the enthusiastic and sporty Dinah to sweep her along forgot to despise everything. Louise was near enough to witness one worrying encounter, when Emily, briefly alone as Dinah had gone for ices, was suddenly surrounded by half a dozen jeering teenagers who started to push and jostle her. Louise was on her way to rescue her when she saw the incomparable Dinah, her already well-developed brown body exiguously clad in shorts and a T-shirt Louise thought she should probably have stopped her wearing, forge into their midst.

'Hey, what do you think you're doing?' she demanded. 'Don't be so pathetic.'

'Or you'll what?' jeered a lanky red-haired youth, but Dinah made a vigorous gesture with her ice-cream cone which seemed to convey something to him, for throwing a few more insults over his shoulder he slouched off with his mates, and Dinah unconcernedly set about her ice. Not for the first time Louise speculated about the expensive school the girls went to.

The day was momentous for one more incident. Geordie Macduff, taking his chance while Abby, long legs flashing, was mopping up the opposition in a mothers' race on behalf of the boys, appeared abruptly at Louise's side. He didn't speak, in his view that was up to her, but watched the race with grave interest, allowing himself the glimmer of a smile as Abby breasted the tape, slipped and sprawled headlong, then drew in her limbs like a jockey as the heavy and vengeful feet of the less fleet pounded over her.

'Hello, Geordie.'

Geordie nodded, still not turning his head. But he was there of set purpose, Louise was sure.

'Are you on your own?' she enquired.

'I am.'

Ah. Swept along on the heady current of action, Louise said on impulse, 'Abby misses you terribly.'

Geordie turned now, a tide of red flooding slowly up his neck and cheeks. He looked as though he was on the brink of asking if this was true, then with a movement of rejection said bitterly, 'Oh aye, I can believe that. With all yon rich toffs up at Fallan – and half the lads in the village besides.'

His pain could be felt. 'She really has missed you,' Louise said softly. It would shock him to his soul, she knew, if she put a hand on his arm.

'Ach, what would I do with a daft lump like that one?' Geordie muttered furiously, hunching his shoulder away as though she had attempted it.

Louise waited a moment. He made no move to go.

'She's been miserable,' she said at last. 'Truly.'

'Oh, aye.' Geordie still stood as though rooted, the conflict in him visible, then with a stifled exclamation flung away and pushed through the spectators.

Going to meet the boys, coming off the field gloriously happy after disaster on disaster at the greasy pole, Louise ran into Fraser, moving on a well-calculated converging course.

'I think I've just done something unforgivable,' she told him.

'Have you now? That I should like to hear.' He smiled down at her, taking in the fresh colours of her cotton top and skirt, the glint of sunlight on her hair. Worried she might for the moment be, but she was a different person from the haunted-looking girl of a few months ago.

'I've just told Geordie Abby's been missing him.'

'We'll no' be seeing much more of them today then,' was Fraser's calm comment.

'But what about Geordie's fiancée?'

'Ach, that was never going to work, now was it? They packed that in a week past. What do you think Geordie was telling you, seeking you out yon way?'

'I think subtlety can be overdone,' Louise retorted, beginning to laugh.

'Mind, he'll be taking on something there,' Fraser said meditatively, and Louise could only agree. 'I was on my way to find the wee lads,' he went on. 'Would Roddie like to do my running for me in the musical cars?'

'Oh, Fraser, he'd love it, and I didn't think I could face entering myself. I'm not even sure what happens.'

'No, no, we'll not have you trying it,' he said in pretended horror. 'It calls for a wee bit skill.'

'Thanks. But will Matt be able to go in the car too? He'd break his heart if he was left out.'

'Aye, he can come. I'll not be upsetting your little lads,' Fraser teased, then, about to stride off, turned back to add, 'I've never seen Emily looking bonnier than she does today. You're doing a grand job there.'

Although on the surface Dinah appeared a careless extrovert, interested in little beyond physical activity, she seemed to be taking in her stride the transition from childhood to adulthood, dipping into either world as it suited her. With her energy to sweep them along, all kinds of pursuits that had been dismissed as boring, futile, kids' stuff and pathetic, were suddenly acceptable. Louise hadn't known there was a games room in the barn, but now a whole rainy afternoon was taken up with a tabletennis tournament. Out came croquet set, badminton net, and the tennis ball on elastic which Dinah would thrash at for half an hour at a time. One evening they started a session of Monopoly which went on for days, delighting Roddie and Matt who hadn't known the game existed. Yet on another day Dinah and Emily disappeared to the village, vanishing upstairs when they came back (bearing no visible signs of battle, to Louise's relief) to experiment with make-up and hair colour, nail varnish and cheap jewellery.

The boys happily introduced Dinah to ploys they had

learned not to try to share with Emily, but now Emily came too, not prepared to be left out. Angry messages came down from the big house that they had been riding the garron after it had done a day's work on the hill, and from Gask that after an evening's happy tunnelling the sawdust heaps were scattered far and wide, followed by the more serious complaint that they had appeared suddenly out of a corrie, having set out to follow the Gask burn to its source, and ruined a long stalk in tricky conditions.

Louise fielded these and other grievances, for somehow responsibility for the children now seemed to be hers. Abby, as Fraser had predicted, was rarely to be seen. Louise wasn't sure if she was less use when pining for Geordie than when besottedly wrapped up in him. Her happiness was a delight, however, her look of vulnerable uncertainty replaced by a new confidence as she joyfully abandoned the promiscuous ways which had been no more than a yearning for affection and security.

Geordie developed a new authority, as Louise saw with amused approval. Not only was Abby to behave herself but serious saving was now the rule, evenings in the pub were rationed, and the nursery sitting-room at Fallan became a favoured retreat. Though the word engagement was not being uttered yet Louise thought the future looked fairly certain, and began to wonder whether Abby should tell her parents what was going on. Then she checked on the 'should'. Was there any duty here? Did Abby's parents care what happened to their unwanted and unsatisfactory fourth daughter? No doubt they would not be pleased if she married a sawmill worker and settled down in an estate cottage in a Highland glen, but did that displeasure, based on preoccupation with their own image, really matter?

Louise put the thought on hold; there would be time to think about it once Dinah's strenuous visit was over. On her last day they decided to make a fire by the burn again, above a pool now improved by a dam they had been working on all week.

After lunch Louise dragged herself away. So many things were ramping up in the garden that she could barely keep up, and she shouldn't put off any longer a session of blanching and freezing. Tipping the last bright green batch into the colander, her fingers brown after tackling a mound of broad beans, she was mildly annoyed when the phone rang before she had finished. Going into the corridor, drying her hands, she wondered if it was Perdita Linklater checking arrangements for tomorrow. A halfway picnic had been planned where Dinah was to be handed over. Would Emily then revert to her former sullenness? Louise so much hoped not, but the question was there.

It was Gloria on the phone. Matt had slipped in the burn and hit his head on a rock. The children had moved him as little as possible, Emily had run down for help, and Cameron was bringing him down.

'Is he badly hurt? Oh, poor little Matt. I'll get his bed ready—'

'Cameron is bringing him here, it's nearer.'

'Right.' Louise asked no more questions. The thought that it was strange for Matt to be taken to the big house never crossed her mind. Phone Hugh. Phone the doctor. No point in doing either until she knew how serious the accident was. And without pausing to analyse the conviction, she was somehow sure that Gloria would do all that should be done. Stopping only to check Hugh's schedule, finding he was in Johannesburg, she fled through the steading yard and up the steep path.

How small Matt looked. The boys were so independent, so full of a natural male competence about practical things, that it was easy to forget how young they were. Eight years old. He was very pale, the bluish lump on his temple grossly misshapen, and he looked lost in the old-fashioned bed with its dark towering headboard.

That, first and foremost, was what mattered to Louise. Matt himself, and how he was. There were no other bumps or lacerations but his eyes wouldn't focus and the doctor had been sent for. Then, perched on the bed with his small hand in hers, other considerations began to impinge. Louise couldn't remember anything about being taken up to this room, but now she wondered where the other children were and if they were all right. On being told that they were downstairs with their grandfather yet another set of reactions raised its head. Matt, she and the other children were in the big house, but Gloria was giving no hint that it was a problem, or even unusual. When Louise went down to check on the others she found them huddled by the fire in a small study, a miscellany of clothing wrapped round them, mugs of hot chocolate in their hands, being looked after by an old gentleman with wild white hair, a mouth like a gin-trap and tears on his cheeks.

Afterwards Louise was to marvel at the naturalness of it all. Feuding and aggression were wiped out; a child was hurt, one of the loved grandchildren from whom Leo had cut himself off in anger at his son, regretting it every day of his life while stubborn pride kept the rift open.

Moving Matt was not suggested. The doctor advised quiet and sleep and said he would come back in the morning. Only on the point of who should sit with Matt in case he woke did discussion arise.

Louise, racked with guilt, wanted to stay but Gloria dissuaded her. 'The others need you, don't forget.'

'Abby can stay with them. She's having a day off, but we'll find her.'

'I wouldn't put money on it. Anyway, it's you those kids want. I never do much sleeping at the best of times so I'll keep an eye on Matt, don't you worry.'

'But if he wakes and doesn't know where he is?'

'Well, you being there won't alter that, will it? He'll be happy enough seeing me, I reckon.'

Louise knew he would, but it was still hard to walk away from him. 'Perhaps I could come for an hour or so later on, if I can find Abby. I'd like to.'

'Fine by me, if it'll make you feel better.'

After the simplicity of this, the acceptance that Matt's condition took precedence over everything else, it jarred to be reminded of the different values of Hugh's world — or Maxine's. For it was Maxine who took Louise's call, saying Hugh was winding up an important meeting which was running late, and he couldn't be called away. The cliché, so pat, lit a flame of wrath in Louise, and she had to make an effort to remind herself that it could make little difference to Hugh, at such a distance, whether he heard now or in half an hour.

It seemed, however, that to Hugh, phoning the moment he heard the news, it did make a difference. His urgent questions gave no hint that anything else was competing for his attention. 'You should have told Maxine it was essential to talk to me. You must have known I'd want to hear exactly what happened and how he is.'

Only when Louise told him where Matt was being looked after did the mood change. 'At the big house? Good God, Louise, how could you let that happen? You know that's the last place where—'

Louise was not prepared to listen. 'Do you honestly think that matters now? You'd prefer Matt to have been carried twice the distance home after a blow on the head? Do you think your quarrels matter that much?' She was shaking, shock catching up with her.

'All right, I'm sorry, that was out of order. I know you've had everything to deal with. Louise?'

But she had nothing to say to him, tears of distress and anger ready to overtake her.

'Listen, I'm on my way back,' Hugh said urgently. 'Maxine's organising a flight—'

Louise put down the phone. The prospect didn't make her feel any less alone. Abby wasn't at Geordie's or at the pub, and there was no way of tracking her down. Though Louise did her best to cheer up the others, in the end it was they who comforted her.

'We'd look after Roddie, you know, if you want to go and see Matt,' Emily said shyly, following her into the larder as she was putting away untouched food after a late and subdued supper. 'We'd be all right.'

'Oh, Emily.' Louise looked at her with gratitude. The grown-up side was to the fore, reinforced by instilled standards of behaviour Emily normally shrugged off. 'That's good of you.'

'We wouldn't fool around.'

'I know you wouldn't.' Louise did know it. Emily and Dinah had both been eminently sensible in this crisis.

'We'll read to Roddie or something when he's in bed.'

'All right. Whatever you think best. Oh, and Emily, can I ask you one more thing?'

'What?' Emily sounded eager, and Louise thought how easy it was to forget that expecting things of people brought greater rewards than dishing out orders.

'Tomorrow, when Dinah leaves, would you mind very much if Lennie took you? I'll ask him to wait so that you don't miss the picnic. Only I want to be here – we don't quite know what will happen. Matt may come home or they may want him to stay where he is for a day or two.' Or take him into hospital. And Hugh might be back; Louise didn't feel sure enough of him to say so. 'I'm afraid it will mean keeping an eye on Roddie, though, which is a bore for you at a party.'

'I don't mind,' Emily said at once, and Louise, without

remembering to wonder whether she would hate it or not, turned and gave her a grateful hug. She felt Emily's body stiffen in surprise, then felt the awkwardness of her arms as she tentatively returned the embrace, but her heart lifted because the response had been there.

# Chapter Thirty-Two

The hotel dining-room was busy but Hugh, who often came here to entertain his guests in dire cook reigns, was given, as he asked, a late and secluded table, and private conversation was possible.

If he had known where to begin.

He had arrived home shortly after lunch and ever since had had the sensation of groping through a minefield. It seemed every reaction must be checked and examined, and in most cases discarded. In the first place there was no one to be angry with, and there was a lot of anger in him, form-less, irrational anger which filled him with frustration, but which he wasn't ready to analyse. It had boiled up when he discovered that although Matt had recovered from his slight concussion and had suffered no other consequences from his fall, he was still at the big house. It had shamed Hugh to the depths that his immediate response had been to demand why he hadn't been brought home, knowing the question had less to do with Matt's health and comfort than with his own bitter reluctance to enter his father's house. Or to ask if he could. Yes, that had been the worst part.

There had been a moment, and he winced to recall it, when he had thought that if Matt was all right there was no need for him to go to the big house at all. Then he had imagined facing Louise's incredulous eyes if he didn't, and angry shame had filled him. He had known he would have to walk once more into that gaunt, dark house with all its associations of conflict and misunderstandings – and, deeper buried, jealousy, failure and rejection – and he would have to speak to that dreadful woman, acknowledge her, thank her for her care of his son.

His overriding feeling, though, had been of isolation. In a startling way the little group he had left behind less than three weeks ago had become a unit, and though it was Matt's accident which had drawn his father and Gloria into it, he had the impression that the welding of the rest had taken place before that. It was impossible to define, but he had to accept that what he had hoped for in his own house, though he had not been able to put it adequately into words, had taken place, but taken place without him. He was on the outside, and he saw, bleakly, that without some effort or change on his part, he always would be. No arbitrary importing of a stranger, whatever her qualities of warmth and generosity, could draw him in. Nothing was that simple, and he could hardly believe he had ever hoped it could be.

There had been too, in the hours since he came home, an awareness of having no role. There was the blank feeling of being told before an operation to get into bed at eleven o'clock in the morning, feeling just as healthy as you were ten minutes ago but with all normal activity suspended. He had tried to shake the feeling off; his office was there, his lines of communication open, and there was considerable communicating to be done since he had abandoned a tight schedule so abruptly. But it had seemed unreal, as though the very room belonged to someone else. The image of Matt, tiny in the hideous Victorian bed, with his crooked grin and the kindly politeness he still managed to accord his father, hung between him and everything else. He had not known what to say to Matt, hadn't even known whether to hug him, and beneath the rationalisation that Matt was ill, that he'd had a nasty bump, a starker truth had lain – he didn't know whether a hug would be acceptable or expected.

It was almost as baffling to observe the new mood of the group formed by Louise and Abby, Emily and Roddie. Boredom and rebellion seemed somehow to have vanished. This afternoon, for example, Louise had proposed making a cake to welcome Matt home and though Emily could not be said to have helped she had wound herself into one of her convolutions on a kitchen chair, dipping her finger into the cake mix, pinching fruit, and chatting. Chatting! And at the back door Abby and Roddie had squatted companionably, cleaning Matt's bike, also deep in conversation.

It was this un-self-conscious flow of talk which had twisted the knife so painfully that Hugh had had to take action. He knew he couldn't break arbitrarily into this bonded circle, and didn't see how he could reach Louise, who had created it, without separating her from the rest. Yet when he asked her to come out for dinner he had seen at once that even that was to pursue his own need at the expense of others.

'Out to dinner?' Louise had looked at him blankly.

'I'd like to talk to you. If we have dinner here there will be so many—'

Claims. The phone, Maxine. No, be honest, what he wanted to take her away from was the claim his own children had on her and he could scarcely say that.

'I'm sorry, I'm rather tired,' Louise had begun.

'I'd be very glad if you would.' Hugh had known that yet again he was pushing for what he wanted in spite of someone else's wishes, but he felt he genuinely couldn't go on without some contact and help. 'We needn't be late. It might be good for you to have a break from Fallan for a couple of hours.'

What had his voice revealed? Louise had given him a quick look and said, 'Well, it's very kind of you. Perhaps if we're not too late . . .' and though he had known she was making an effort, and driving miles for dinner in a hotel was probably the last thing she wanted to do, he had seized the chance she had given him. If he didn't, if he let this time of heightened feeling after Matt's accident pass, the skin of habit would knit again, and he would be shut out for good.

Once he and Louise were facing each other across the table, however, in the conventional setting of shaded lamp, three flower heads in a tiny vase, gleaming silver and rigidly graded glasses, the things he had so desperately wanted to say seemed impossible to approach. He found himself wanting to protest, 'You can see I care about the children. I dropped everything and came, didn't I, the moment I heard Matt was hurt,' but he knew that to Louise this was so obviously the only thing to do that she would stare at him in astonishment. Of course he had come; did he want to be commended for it?

Hugh propped his head on his thumb and closing his eyes rubbed the first two fingers hard across his forehead, not even conscious that he was doing it.

'Do you have a headache?' Louise asked, and the unforced kindness in her voice at once distanced the scene around them, the voices, the movements of the waiters, even the cliché of the table with its curls of butter, the EPNS bowl of toothpicks, the icebucket, the ashtray of thick amber glass.

'Louise, I need so badly to talk to you.'

She looked at him for a moment and in spite of his tension he saw she was not surprised or disconcerted.

'I know,' she said, and tension dissipated in relief. 'You've had a lot to deal with. Seeing Matt—'

'This isn't just about Matt.' He didn't want to hide behind the legitimate cause for concern.

Louise nodded. 'I realise that. The problem of going up to your father's house was obvious, but I had the impression that you were — I don't know how to put it,' she finished on a different tone, leaning back in her chair away from him, conscious that she had come close to issues that had nothing to do with her. She glanced around her with conventional interest, and Hugh had a drowning sensation that the rope he had grasped was about to be plucked out of his hands.

'Louise, I want to talk. About all of it. I think I shall go mad if I don't. But I hardly know where to begin, or how to begin or even if it's fair to ask you to listen.'

'I'll listen,' she said quietly, leaning towards him again, restoring intimacy, sending him signals of comfort. 'There's just the two of us – you were right to want to be out of the house.'

Hugh reached out a hand and she put hers in it. He held it for a moment and then laid it on the table, giving it a pat of thanks as he released it. Then, exasperated by his own ineptness, he discovered that, having got this far, he couldn't find a starting point.

'It must have been hard to see your father and Gloria today,' Louise said, and this drew a harsh laugh from him, so perfectly did it smooth his path.

'Oh, girl, who brought you to my door?' he said, shaking his head. 'Yes, my father and Gloria. Where better to start? I hadn't imagined myself ever coming face to face with the woman, let alone thanking her.'

'She's kindness itself, and she was wonderful about Matt,' Louise said, not in defence of Gloria nor in accusation, but as though pursuing his own thought. 'I've never been so grateful for anyone's good sense.'

'I'd never thought of her as a person,' Hugh admitted, and Louise knew from his tone that he would talk now, and probably would not be talking to her, so she withdrew a little from the pool of light, and as he spoke she watched the lean brown hand pluck obliviously at a white chrysanthemum head, while water dripped from its bruised stem onto the cloth, and she caught the faint pungent scent, always later to be associated with this scene.

Hugh's elder brother, Roderick, had been the son his father related to. He had loved Fallan and its pursuits and pleasures and demands. From earliest boyhood it had been his consuming interest, and Hugh had been free to follow his own bent, engineering then mining, rapidly developing from relatively modest capital the world-wide interest he now controlled. When Roderick had died on that Gambian holiday, Leo, though stunned by grief, had never questioned Hugh's willingness to step into his brother's shoes. But behind the battle that now broke out lay the corrosive years of making Hugh feel second-best, unsatisfactory, uncooperative and self-seeking.

How extraordinary, Louise thought, that she, and Abby, had each in their own way been made to feel the same. Three of them under the same roof; how much they could have shared, yet how differently they had reacted. Hugh had resisted his father with a stubbornness that grew into violent resentment. He had decided at one point to leave Nether Fallan, much as he loved the house. 'It was so good to have somewhere where I could introduce comfort and colour — let the sun in,' he said, and with a sharp drop in sympathy Louise wondered why he had failed to introduce them into the quarters where his children lived. Had there been, after all, some inbred belief that what had been good enough for him would be good enough for them, or produce what he perceived as a satisfactory result? This was not the moment to challenge him.

'Why did you stay?' Louise asked instead, and was glad she had not been distracted by the side issue when he answered, his voice rough with pain, 'Because Angie wanted the boys to grow up at Fallan. She knew it would probably be Roddie's one day, even though my father always swore he'd rather raze it to the ground than let any son of mine have it, and I think she always hoped there would be a reconciliation.'

'Couldn't there have been?'

'Not when Father brought home that—'

That tart? Did he still cling to the prejudice which had given his resentment of his father new impetus?

'Tell me how they met.'

Hugh was embarking on the account when they were interrupted by being offered pudding. He was glad when Louise refused, and he ordered coffee for them both instead. Coffee, however, was not served at the table, but in the hall.

For a moment Louise thought Hugh was going to make an issue of it, whether consciously or not using the opportunity to vent some of his jangled feelings, but he abandoned the point with a gesture of irritation, an indication of how focused he was on his resolve to talk, and they went into the hall.

Here two or three groups were sitting, there was a buzz of talk, the lights were brighter and intimacy was destroyed.

Hugh turned to Louise with a disorientated look so unlike his usual incisive air of control that she was startled.

'Do you really want coffee?' he asked brusquely. 'Or would you mind if we – ?'

'No, let's go,' she said at once, and soon the big car was sweeping them smoothly up the empty road, a full moon riding with them above black cardboard hills. Louise was afraid the interruption might make it hard for Hugh to go on talking, but the outpouring of words about things so long bottled up could not be checked now. Almost at once he reverted, though in a cynical tone Louise didn't care for, to the subject of Gloria.

'She picked Dad up. As her fare initially, in her taxi. Took him to some appalling dives and went in with him. She saw him coming, in other words. She collected him on the next couple of evenings, then had the bloody nerve to follow him up here.'

There were so many assumptions in this that Louise felt bound to protest.

'Your father must have asked in the first place to go to the dives.' Sheltered as her life had been, even she knew that rich elderly men on the loose in London frequently sought out nocturnal entertainment that bore little relation to their normal lives. 'Why does it seem worse that Gloria went in too? Perhaps he wanted company.'

She felt Hugh's surprise as his head turned. Presumably no one questioned the version of the story which made him so angry. 'For God's sake, a London cabbie.'

'Well, at least a female one.'

He laughed reluctantly. 'Don't tell me she didn't recognise a good thing when she saw one.'

'Well, I haven't seen much of your father —' how she would have liked to tell Hugh about the tears she had seen on Leo's sagging cheeks, the tender clumsiness of his hands tucking Matt in, his unhesitating abandonment of his own quarrel in the face of a child's need, but this was not the moment to risk such precious images being rejected '— but I can't imagine anyone forcing him to do much that he doesn't want to do. And I certainly can't imagine him letting Gloria come here uninvited, or rewarding such cheek by marrying her. Can you?'

'He did it to spite me.' The childish mumble, torn out of him by a resentment too deep-buried to check, made Hugh cringe the moment it was out. 'God, I can't believe I said that.'

Louise was silent. She guessed that by involuntarily voicing that banality Hugh had freed himself of it. It wouldn't survive being spoken aloud.

'Do you mind if we stop?' he asked abruptly. Louise thought for a moment that he meant stop talking, but he swung the car onto a patch of turf, turning it to face the moon and the dark serrated outline of the hills. 'Is this all right with you?' he asked again, his hand on the ignition, the engine still running.

Louise had reached the stage of tiredness where another hour or two out of bed could make no difference. Anything that had to be done tomorrow was unreal and remote. 'I'd like to go on talking,' she said, and it was true. Had that been all, had they driven back now, parting at the foot of the stairs, she going through the door to her shabby room in the nursery wing, he turning the other way, there would have been great tracts of unsaid things between them, and the moment might never have come to touch upon them again.

# Chapter Thirty-Three

Hugh turned off the engine and let down the windows. The busy sound of the burn made itself heard, and the cool night air, fresh with the scents of dew on grass and bracken, and tinged with the faint smell of sheep, came flowing in.

'Not too cold for you?'

'No, it's lovely.'

Silence between them; the soft voice of the wind stirring the tips of a block of larches below them gradually becoming distinguishable above the bustling of the water; a tawny owl calling.

'I can feel the things you want to say,' Louise's voice was gentle, so much a part of the deserted moonlit scene that it exactly suited Hugh's mood and need.

'Yes, still milling,' he said. 'Perhaps a little more controllably now.'

'Choose one.'

How simple she made it.

'I've failed with the children.'

Although there was no room in his mind, in this un-imagined moment of being able to put it into words, for awareness of how they might touch her, he could have chosen no opening more calculated to arouse Louise's sympathy. Whatever she had thought of his behaviour till now, hearing those words she at once, in a quick move-ment of compassion, put her hand on his where it lay on the steering wheel. He brought his other hand across to hold hers there, then drew it down to his thigh where he could hold it comfortably.

'Go on,' she said softly.

He looked away from her across the wheel-scored turf, past the white litter bin glowing with an almost luminous brightness, a scuff of horrid objects around it, and his eyes followed the pale curves of the road reaching away up to Fallan. Go on? Open the floodgates on the regrets and guilt and doubt that swirled, dark and disturbing, below the ordered, polished surface of his life? He had a feel-ing that if once he let them loose he would be swept away, the control so essential to him snatched out of his grasp. Yet he passionately wanted to release some of this festering misery, and knew, had known since the first moment he saw her – or so it seemed to him now – that Louise was the only person to whom any of it could be expressed. He couldn't begin; a log-jam of words piled up.

'What was Emily like when she was small?' Louise asked.

Oh, blessed, blessed woman, offering a starting point

— had she guessed this? — which was rich with memories still bearable.

'Emily? Oh, she was a tough little thing, as you might imagine. Very bright and aware, and she moved like quicksilver. It was a nightmare trying to keep track of her, and she was permanently covered in bruises, looked like a candidate for a case of child abuse—'

Hugh broke off, having rushed into what he had thought safe and finding the image he had chosen uncomfortably apposite.

Louise waited. She could sense the pent-up feelings behind this and wondered if she wanted to hear any more, but knew she would never forgive herself if she deflected them now.

'It was a joke with everybody,' Hugh made himself go on. 'But she was a victim of abuse just the same — of neglect. Her mother, Gabrielle, was—' He broke off, not even aware that he had done so. 'Gabrielle,' he repeated, his voice harsh, and Louise guessed that he had been carried back to scenes and emotions which after thirteen years still had the power to hurt him. 'She hated Emily, and because of Emily she hated me. She hated the whole business of having a child. It seemed as though when Emily arrived, unplanned of course, she forced Gabrielle to recognise what marriage actually was, responsibilities, commitment, permanence, perhaps even being required to care about someone other than herself. And when she discovered how much she detested it all she was ready to throw everything away, Emily, Fallan, me, our whole way of life together. None of it had meant a thing to her, and

I'd never known, never even suspected. I know I deserved everything that happened, but it took a while to get over it just the same. Work was the easy panacea, of course. I was hardly ever here but all the time, wherever I was, whatever I was doing, I was haunted by the thought of Emily. I knew I was doing the worst thing by leaving her to the care of nannies — not even a permanent one, because not surprisingly they came and went. It's a remote place, and there was no stability for them, though to give him his due, my father did his best to keep an eye on things. I knew it was all wrong, but I just couldn't—'

He lifted his hand, still holding Louise's, though she thought he was unconscious of it, to the rim of the steering wheel, and briefly laid his forehead on this uncomfortable boss of knuckles.

'There seemed no way to break out of the situation. Gabrielle had gone, covering her tracks with great efficiency. I knew I was making a complete hash of bringing up Emily alone, but work was a powerful magnet. I could always pretend it was vital and that I had no real choices. It engaged the brain and shut out the things I knew were going wrong. I even thought of putting Emily up for adoption.'

He felt Louise's movement of shock and turned to her with a thin smile. 'How appalling that must seem to you, or to any normal parent. But often it did seem the only solution which would have answered Emily's needs.'

'But didn't you love her?' Louise could be silent no longer. 'When you were with her, holding her, playing with her?'

Hugh sat very still, staring ahead of him, then let out his breath in a little gust of ironic defeat. How could he make this girl, whose deepest instincts were loving and giving, comprehend the frozen emptiness in which he had functioned in those years?

'I could hardly bear to touch her,' he said. 'It was cowardice. I was terrified of the feelings she could arouse in me, of being forced to face up to my own inadequacies and examine the way I was living. I began to dread seeing her. I came home less and less. When I did there were terrible quarrels with my father. He couldn't understand why I wasn't here, taking over the estate, looking after my child. He was right, of course, but doling out orders about it didn't help.'

No, the arrogant Erskines didn't take kindly to being given orders, as Louise had already discovered. 'So when did you meet the boys' mother?' she asked, hoping this would not be another painful topic, but thinking that even if it were they had better get that out into the light too.

'Ah, Angie.' The altered tone caught at Louise, cynicism failing to cover feelings which the name could still rake raw. 'I suppose with Angie we come to my really serious failing in human relationships.'

The bitter self-mockery sent the hairs up on Louise's neck. This, she knew, brought them to the core of what had hurt this man. Did she want to hear more? Did she have the courage, or the right, to see these wounds laid open?

'Please don't tell me — I mean, this is very private and

unless you feel it will help to—' she said hurriedly, torn between the wish to give comfort if she could and a panicky dread of more pain for either of them.

Hugh's head turned and he studied her for a second. What right did he have to offload all this onto her? Was she bored, uncomfortable about what he was revealing? But she met his eyes with such open and anxious sympathy that he drew in his breath sharply, saying, more huskily than he had known his voice would sound, 'It does help. You can't imagine how much.'

Louise nodded, prompting him to go on. He was holding her hand with his fingers laced between hers, and she knew he had no idea how painfully he was crushing them.

'I'd known Angie vaguely for some years, as one does in Scotland. She was brought up near Melrose. Lovely house, looking towards the Eildon Hills. She was exactly right in all the ways Gabrielle, whom I'd met in Cape Town and who belonged to a rather rootless international set, was wrong. Right in the measurable, conventional ways, I mean. She loved the glen, knew all about the estate and the garden, got on tremendously well with my father – God, why am I talking about her like this, as though I despised her for it? She was, is, a marvellous person and I didn't deserve her, that's all there is to it. We were married three months after we met again and the boys came along quickly. Emily was four when Roddie was born, and she adored him. She was always more of a problem than the boys – with her mother who can blame her? – but she showed no signs of jealousy and it never occurred to me that we wouldn't knit into a normal, happy, loving family.'

His voice trailed away; he was very still. Louise knew he had forgotten she was there. She longed to free her hand and rub some life back into it but not for a second would she have let him guess. What had happened to Angie? She wasn't sure she wanted to know.

'We were extremely sociable in those days,' Hugh went on, again with that edge of self-mockery. 'Angie loved entertaining in the traditional style, solid comfort, country food, just what I'd grown up with when my mother was alive, and she drew back all sorts of friends I'd lost touch with, the people Gabrielle had dismissed out of hand. Among them was my closest friend, Freddie Charteris. School and Cambridge, and always some kind of contact, though I didn't see much of him when Gabrielle was around. She couldn't stand him; jealous probably. He's a great character, outgoing, generous, popular, all that sort of thing. In the nicest possible way. And agonising over hurting me, he and Angie fell in love. So there you go.'

The absurd phrase to end this painful story was inexpressibly bleak, flat with the chill acceptance of something Hugh could fully understand. Freddie and Angie, two wonderful people. What could be more fitting?

'Hugh.' Louise wrapped her free hand over their linked ones, and leaned towards him, her voice, her body language, full of horrified pity. She wanted to wrap him up, protect and save him from this pain. He felt it, and with an exclamation that was not far from a sob, he drew her head against his shoulder and pressed his cheek down upon it. It was awkward, clumsy, a gesture born of need and flayed emotions rather than tenderness or even mutual awareness, but it meant a lot to Hugh, who could feel his muscles relaxing from a rigidity he had not even been conscious of. Relief began to spread through him. He had never spoken of this to anyone; had not imagined it could help so much.

They talked for a long time. Louise suspected this mood might be hard for Hugh to recapture, and that by tomorrow he might regret having been so frank, but she was sure of its therapy tonight.

In time Hugh, with a feeling of emerging from some dark confined space where it was only possible to concentrate on his own situation, remembered with a stab of conscience that much of what he had revealed must have touched a nerve for Louise.

'You've been so good,' he said with gratitude. 'Letting me get rid of all this baggage I've been carting around for far too long. But I've been forgetting that you've had a lot to face yourself. I'm sorry.'

'It's quite all right,' Louise assured him quickly. Trails of cloud had drifted across the moon, half obscuring it, but their eyes had become accustomed to the faint light and Hugh saw the way her face tightened.

'I dragooned you into coming back, didn't I?' he asked gently. 'I knew it meant a challenge for you. Has it been very hard?'

'No, not at all.' A conventionally polite response very much at variance with the openness of their mood, and Hugh looked at her more closely.

'It has been hard, hasn't it? I don't think I really thought about how difficult it would be for you.'

'It wasn't that.' Leave it there; leave it.

Hugh was too aware of the healing that words had afforded him in the last hour or so to leave it there. And he hated, for its own sake, to see that shut warning look on her face. This girl had suffered too.

'Then what was it?' he asked.

Louise hesitated. But the level of tiredness she had reached, where ordinary constraints of time and reserve seemed unimportant, replaced by an almost light-headed recklessness, drove her on to speak.

'I was so disillusioned when I found nothing had changed at Fallan. I'd believed you when you said you intended to do something about it. I agreed to come back because I believed it. That's all.'

'I don't think so.' In spite of himself Hugh felt familiar defensiveness rise, and his tone was crisp.

'In any case, there's no point in talking about it.' It was Louise's own conviction and the cold note in his voice had reinforced it.

'I'd like to talk about it.' Stiff as the words were, they produced a response.

'All right then. When you speak of caring about the children, what is it that you really mean? You provide for them, they're clothed and fed and you pay people to look after them, but you don't *know* them, you don't spend time with them, you don't even go into the part of the house where they live. You wanted me to come back because you knew I wouldn't walk out, you knew I liked Fallan and got along with Abby and didn't upset Bella, you liked the sort of food I cooked and you thought Emily might not resent me too much. All tiny, unimportant things, but they meant you could remain free to pursue your own interests. You could put the children out of your mind; wash your hands of them till next holidays.'

'That wasn't what—' Hugh tried to protest, but now that the words were released they were unstoppable, and Louise herself scarcely knew where they came from.

'You didn't even talk to me about the children when you were last at home. You'd got what you wanted, and no further effort was necessary. But don't you see how outrageous it is that you don't even have meals with them, that you exclude them from everything you do? When you and your brother were growing up at Fallan didn't you do things with your father, learn from him? Oh, I know when you were older,' she swept on, so passionately that Hugh began to feel an astonished admiration for this unknown side of her, 'you decided it wasn't your scene, but I can't believe it wasn't a marvellous boyhood place, or that you don't have good memories of growing up here. Can't you let your own sons share in that? And can't you see how lonely Emily is, how uncaring it is to expect her to occupy herself in such an environment? I ought to tell you, I took her to stay with the Linklaters at Newtonmore, and brought Dinah Linklater back here. I suppose you'll disapprove, but I—'

'Louise, hold on, hold on!' Amusement overtaking his dislike of being attacked in such a thorough-going fashion, Hugh leant across and touched her cheek. 'I'm delighted that you did that. Why are you assuming I wouldn't be?'

Startled as much by his words, affectionate and teasing, as by the touch on her cheek, Louise checked. 'I suppose I feel that you're not interested in anything that pleases the children,' she said, examining the question fairly.

'My God.' The blank, desperately hurt tone dragged her out of her thoughts. Tiredness could lead to a dreadful honesty, she saw.

'Oh, Hugh, that was an awful thing to say,' she exclaimed with compunction.

'But you believe it?'

'Well, call it a two-in-the-morning distorted version of what I feel.'

'But don't you see,' he demanded, with a depth of feeling equal to hers but laced with a bitterness of which she could never be capable, 'I couldn't talk to you. I literally couldn't. I was so thankful to see you in the house again, and so full of hope, but then I was unable to see how my life could alter. I felt locked into it, with no choice available to me. The people who were up for the shooting were business associates, not friends, not part of a family scene. I had to go to Johannesburg for this conference, and I'm due in Chile next week. The arrangements for the children, the separate meals, the separate lives, have been in place for so long that I suppose we've come to accept them as the norm. And in a way, they work. Well, the boys seem content, at any rate. I don't know if I can explain this, but I feel actually shy about trying to move nearer to them. They're so damned polite, so tolerant of me, and so self-sufficient. Emily looks at me out of the tail of her eye with a contempt only Gabrielle could equal, and to be truthful I simply don't know where to begin.'

Louise's anger died at the stark honesty of this.

'I understand,' she said. 'I do understand. But we've talked now. It was ridiculous of me to expect changes overnight; it couldn't work like that. *This* is how it works – with problems being put into words and faced, and having the will to deal with them. Events bring their own changes too, like Matt being taken to the big house and you talking to Gloria and accepting her kindness. That's a good beginning.'

Hugh slipped an arm round her shoulders in a quick hug. 'You're a very positive person, aren't you?' he said, half teasing and half unbearably moved. 'You really think we've got something to work on?'

'I'm sure of it.'

He gave her shoulders another squeeze then started up the car, incapable of saying more.

# Chapter Thirty-Four

This strange night of talk seemed afterwards unrelated to anything which came before or after it, its memory as formless as the patterns of moonlight and shadow which had transformed the glen into a mysterious place as time lost all importance. The intimacy of their conversation, the naturalness of touch for reassurance and comfort, had receded by the next morning with the elusiveness of a dream. Yet though Louise felt she and Hugh had stepped for a while out of their normal roles in relation to each other, she also felt she knew him a hundred times better than before, and could understand at least something of what drove him to behave as he did.

Hugh went back to Johannesburg and when he and Maxine reappeared with the next batch of shooting guests the visit repeated the pattern of the previous one. Louise saw very little of him, except for one occasion when he sought her out. He wanted to make sure that she understood it was impracticable to change anything at this stage, since his guests were, as before, business associates, who had not come to Fallan with any wish to be involved in family life.

'And to be honest,' he added, 'I don't suppose Emily and the boys would find them much fun either.' He saw from Louise's expression that she thought this a convenient excuse and tried again. 'Don't forget, this has been organised for months. I don't think altering the plot at this stage would benefit anyone, but I promise you I won't be using Fallan in this way in future. I've done a lot of thinking about what we discussed –' she would never know how much '– and I realise changes have to be radical.'

Seeing she was still not convinced he persisted with a forcefulness she couldn't dismiss, 'I know I've said before that things were going to be different but then I hadn't made myself examine honestly what was wrong. Now I have.' He wanted to say, 'Thanks to you,' but a shyness he had rarely felt in his adult life constrained him, making it impossible to refer even obliquely to all that the conversation between them had uncovered. 'I want you to know I have definite plans, and they will come about. It's important to me that you believe that.'

Louise couldn't see why, but she did see, looking into his intent eyes, and wondering if he knew how formidable he was when he moved into her space like this with his ingrained habit of domination, that he needed reassurance, no matter from what source.

'All right, I believe you,' she said smiling, and was startled to see his face light up in a way she would not have thought it capable of, as he gripped her arm for a second in pleasure and relief.

The summer sped on with superficially little altered. Matt's accident, however, had had its effect on relations between the estranged houses of Fallan, for, without discussion or any apparent decision being made, freedom to come and go had been established, if not for Hugh then at least for the children and for Louise. She had liked Gloria from the outset, and had sympathised with the loneliness of an obviously gregarious person caught up in other people's quarrels, while respecting the loyalty which made Gloria support her husband. Leo was a hot-headed and irascible man, not endowed with the best of brains and not short on the arrogance which a lifetime of ruling a small roost had nurtured, but beneath his crusty veneer he was affectionate and soft-hearted. He was also inventive and dangerously addicted to eccentric enterprise.

He and Gloria provided an excellent supply of tales for the glen as they tackled all kinds of jobs together, felling trees, relining the water tank, tarring the drive, and running into almost daily disasters as they fell off roofs, bogged the tractor and tipped the hill buggy down ravines. It surprised Louise, having seen the cosy, cake-baking, housewifely side of Gloria, that she was prepared to share in these activities, but she seemed to relish them. Perhaps she recognised that in spite of her loving care, the dusting and polishing, the prettying-up with knick-knacks and dried flowers, the big house of Fallan, unwieldy and obdurate, would always resist such fripperies.

At Nether Fallan Abby was immersed in her own affairs, swanning about in a happy dream and leaving boring decisions to Geordie, who fortunately seemed eager for his new responsibilities. The assumption that they would be married progressed to talk of plans, and Louise, feeling this was too haphazard altogether, persuaded Abby to write to her parents and tell them what was happening. She wished she hadn't when they replied with a dismissiveness which cut Abby to the soul, saying it was time she gave up this absurd job and went out to join them, so that she could 'do something sensible'.

Louise was forced to recognise that she had pressured Abby into writing because of her own lingering hang-ups about parental approval, and she hoped, guiltily offering what comfort she could, that this had finally taught her to leave them behind.

Roddie and Matt went to their mother for the last week of the holidays, accepted practice since Abby was notoriously unreliable about such matters as lists and name-tapes, but it meant poor Emily was left behind once more. Did Angie, who seemed to have been a loving step-mother, never invite her too, or did Hugh refuse to let her go? Louise thought she would like to know the answer to that. She often thought of him, with far greater sympathy now that she knew the story of his two marriages, and wondered how he would manage to break out of the impasse he had allowed to develop. For the time being, however, she herself found a more than satisfactory recompense for Emily.

'Wow, Hugh isn't going to like this,' Emily prophesied, sounding as if she relished the prospect, hugging the squirming black and white bundle to her chest. 'We'll have to keep her hidden when he's here.'

'No, no hiding.' Louise intended to field any objections personally. 'The pup's yours, a present from me. Abby will look after her while you're at school.'

Emily looked doubtful. 'Abby's not specially bright about things like that. And what happens when she goes to Gask to live with Geordie?'

'They'll have the puppy there if necessary. It's all arranged.' It occurred to Louise that this was the first expression of concern she had heard about Abby leaving Fallan. Had anyone thought what it would mean?

She was caught unawares by the hollow feeling which filled her as she drove back from Newtonmore after handing Emily over to Perdita Linklater to be taken back to school. It was one of those still, bright days of early autumn when a new crispness in the air makes warm sweaters feel good, when the sun brings out the colours of bracken and turning leaves so vividly that the changing season cannot be ignored, when the roads are suddenly emptier and a sense of space and freedom returns.

Emily had sobbed when she said goodbye to the puppy, and Louise had felt first guilty to have been the cause of this misery, then on reflection glad Emily had something to love and a reason to look forward to coming home.

The house felt not only quiet and deserted, but seemed already to have withdrawn into a waiting mood, its sunny rooms blank and unresponsive. There was such a feeling of things ending, of nothing remaining to do, that she left as soon as she could, glad that this time she was not abandoning Abby to gloomy solitude.

It was good to come over the pass to Bridge of Riach and see the barn far below, solid and peaceful in the curve of the river, and to know that it was hers till the Allt Farr cottage, which the Munros were letting her rent for the winter, was available.

Rick and Cass both tried to persuade her, after a couple of frosty nights, to move into the house, but she insisted on staying where she was, enjoying her odd retreat for as long as she could.

She was wrested away from it before long, however, needed at short notice to go to Alford to help a young farmer's wife whose husband had had an accident. A cousin was due to come and take over, but for a week Louise looked after the house and two toddlers, and it was a special and private joy to realise that the barrier was down for good and there could be any number of future jobs with children. The time in Alford was an unmixed pleasure, and as she left she found herself wondering what it would be like back at Fallan without Emily and the boys there. Would there be any opportunities to talk to Hugh? Had he made progress with his 'definite plans'? She hoped so; she thought it would make him happier.

He had correctly booked her through Cass this time, presumably via Maxine, and she was due there next week, staying till the end of the stag stalking. After that she could move into the Allt Farr cottage, and was looking forward to having her own base for a few months in a place where she felt herself among friends. Before any of that, however, a treat was in prospect.

'He sees in you all he found in Angie. You realise that, don't you?'

Erica was propped against a rock, her purple skirt spread around her, patterned with dried mud, her eyes on the thronged silver waters of the Solway estuary, alive with migrating duck, geese and whooper swans under a pale October sky. The van was parked on the sea wall behind them.

Her invitation had been characteristic. 'My wheels need to roll. Come and roll with them. I can offer you a shelf to sleep on, a fascinating landscape of inter-digitating salt creeks and a million birds.'

Taken aback by Erica's remark, so casually dropped into their peaceful silence, Louise was speechless.

'You do know that, don't you?' Erica repeated, opening her eyes a slit to examine her with a mocking look. 'If you're going back next week, minus juvenile protection, isn't it time to be clear on that?'

'But it's complete nonsense,' Louise protested.

'Hum,' said Erica, raising her binoculars to watch the irresistible drama of the swans winging down from the element of air to become their other selves in the element of water.

'Hugh Erskine isn't aware of me as a female at all,' Louise said, casting about for some effectively repressive answer. As if anyone could repress Erica. 'He adored Angie, and if he does see me as some kind of substitute for her, which I don't believe, then it's as cook and home-maker. That's what he's looking for, poor man. He knows he needs help from someone. It doesn't have to be me, it could be anybody.'

Erica lowered the binoculars and turned to study her with interest. It was obvious that Louise believed what she said. She had no idea how men were drawn to her, and Erica's lips tightened sardonically as she recalled beating down Aidan's determination to join them here, and how often this summer she had had to endure his wails and moans because he wasn't twenty years younger.

'What sort of relationship did you and your hus-band have?' she asked, writhing her head against the rock to find a good spot for it. Though her eyes were closed she heard Louise's gasp, and her lips twitched again. 'It's probably time you talked about it,' she added calmly.

Louise, winded once more by this new attack from such a different quarter, did her best to sift out what was im-portant, something which being with Erica soon taught one. No point in enquiring why the topic had surfaced; no point in feeling defensive; certainly no point in offering an evasive answer. She needn't talk about it at all, come to that. Erica wouldn't press for a response. But if she did talk there was no merit in being less than honest. And, as so often happened in Erica's company, there came a sensa-tion of everything falling into place. She had buried thoughts of Owen for so long that by now they could be taken out like fleshless skeletons of themselves, their power to distress her leached away by time.

'You'd guessed that I'd stopped loving him?' To Erica such things could be said straightforwardly.

'Your grief was always for your little girls. Whenever you referred to the crash, to that day, to the time afterwards, the pain was for them. Tell me about your husband.'

'Therapy?'

'Therapy.' Tidying up, Erica added to herself. Preparing an empty room.

'In the end I just didn't like him.' Louise checked this statement with objective interest, and found it held good. 'I think it was mainly that he was so much under his mother's control,' she went on after a moment, and Erica could hear in her voice a faint surprise that she had never put this into words before. 'We were only happy – or the set-up only worked, I suppose would be more accurate – when we were living in his parents' house and Owen was working in his father's office. He wasn't a stayer. He had no self-motivation or ambition. Deep down he believed, I think, that someone somewhere would always provide for him. When he threw up his job and was talked into this vague, totally unrealistic enterprise—'

'Remind me.'

'Driftwood carving.'

'Ah, yes, driftwood carving.' Repeated in Erica's crisp voice it sounded more unlikely than ever. 'To support a wife and two children.'

'He was naïve.' Louise thought, looking back across the void of the years where Owen simply had not figured, that she could have added lazy, selfish and irresponsible. How tired she had grown of living in that miserable cottage, struggling to provide Charlotte and Gemma with basic needs, committed to long, cold hours among the dim, distressed furniture, the aching tedium broken only by the whispers of non-buyers prowling with pursed lips and stony eyes. When had communication, affection, laughter died? When had the daily battle to fight down impatience and resentment begun?

As they sat on in silence Louise, huddling her jacket around her against the sunless air, saw nothing of the activity on the inlet before them. She knew this acceptance of a truth she had refused to face was one more step away from the past and towards a future she was content to meet. Grasping the philosophy of the ganging foot had brought its rewards. Tomorrow, when she and Erica left the friend's garden where they parked the van at night, she would go to Kinnafoot to spend a couple of days with Aidan, and then return for a final night in the barn, going with Cass and Rick for dinner with the Mackenzies at Riach, before going back to Fallan.

On her way there a few days later she found her thoughts centring on Hugh Erskine. He often came into her mind, as the children did. By showing her his vulnerable side, by admitting his sense of failure and letting her see how it tormented him, he had become a candidate for her care and concern, just as they were. So much of his autocratic behaviour and apparent blindness could be forgiven him now that she understood more.

Then Erica's hints came back, ruffling her positive

mood. Was there anything to worry about in being seen as a surrogate Angie? Surely not, if all it meant, as she believed, was that Hugh was at last doing his best to make his house a comfortable place where his children were cared for and happy. And where he had yet to learn that a collie pup belonging to his daughter was accommodated. Unrepentant anticipation at the prospect of this discovery lightened Louise's worried expression.

Abby spilled out to meet her, the puppy, now christened Spice, at her heels. 'You'll never believe what's been going on. Don't bother going up to your room, nobody's touched it since you left, anyway. Come *on*.'

Louise, expecting to be deluged by details of Abby's own plans, blinked and reeled as Abby pushed open the swing door with a triumphant, 'Look!' The varnished tongue-and-groove, scarred with years of ill-use, was dazzling in fresh paint. Dragged past the kitchen, Louise saw that the dark and inconvenient larders were in the process of conversion into one store room with space for a big freezer, while next door a rational arrangement of washing-machine, drier and sink was already installed.

'What on earth is happening?' But she knew. Hard as Hugh found it to reach out to his children he meant to do so, and this was his way of making a start. Good for you, Louise thought warmly. Good for you!

'We're to look through these colour charts,' Abby announced, pulling her into the kitchen, which Louise was rather relieved to find hadn't been touched. Adorned by the boys' drawings and other favourite objects, it was a much brighter and friendlier place than it used to be.

'We've to choose. Your room, mine, the children's, bathroom, the lot. Old Hughie must have had a brainstorm, but who cares?'

Louise kept to herself the clue to this frenzy of renovation, but all evening it lay like a warm glow behind other thoughts. The evening was good, from taking Abby over to Gask and being shown the cottage she and Geordie had been promised, to a walk with Spice which included a call on Gloria, who made them both welcome.

Going early to bed with Spice – who had made it clear she did not spend her nights alone in large, dark, cold rooms downstairs – half in and half out of a tattered basket in the corner, Louise muzzily tried to decide how she would like her room redecorated. It amused her to find, as the last drifting thoughts fragmented, that, as with the kitchen, she was quite fond of it as it was.

# Chapter Thirty-Five

The two guns favoured with the last week of the stags on Fallan were very different men — a quiet Bostonian in the best-cut tweeds Louise had ever seen, and a hard-eyed South African who wanted as many good heads as he could get. Though Hugh always maintained that stalking bored him he was, according to Cameron, 'no' bad on the hill', and he took out the American, leaving Cameron to cope with the more demanding South African. Maxine, it seemed, did not figure in this pursuit, and had not appeared.

Hugh had been looking forward to this return to Fallan with an anticipation he hadn't felt for years but, though in his mind everything was already different, he found not everyone recognised the transformation. His thinking and planning, going far beyond a blitz on the nursery wing, had led him into the error of assuming that it would be clear a new era had dawned. He was angry and disconcerted to meet resistance, particularly from the quarter where he had secretly expected praise. Having believed divisions swept away, he was irritated to find that others (which meant Louise, for only her opinion mattered) saw them as still in place.

'I don't remember being invited to join you,' she said crisply, whisking on with deliberate busyness when Hugh came frowning into the kitchen after finding, as on a previous occasion, the dining-room table laid with fewer places than he had expected.

She was crisp because she was disappointed in him. After her initial pleasure at the improvements he was making, doubt had begun to creep in about how superficial his approach, after all, might be. For Abby had let slip that this was a weekend out for the boys but they were with their mother, adding that they always went to her if shooting people were staying. Taken with the pattern of Hugh's days, occupied with his guests who were once more business acquaintances rather than friends, it smacked too much of old habits for Louise's liking.

'I thought we'd got all this straight.' Hugh found it frustrating, having moved on so far himself, to be held back by reminders of an earlier regime.

'Not really,' said Louise. 'Anyway, though I like your Bostonian, I don't want to discuss mining, world markets or the future of the economy. I'm happier here, thank you.'

'But Abby's gone out. You'll be on your own. At least join us after dinner. Your presence might divert the conversation into more civilised topics.'

'I doubt it. No, I know you mean well, but it's not my situation that needs improving, remember.'

Anger flared in Hugh's face, but with a glance at his watch he controlled it. This wasn't the time. He mustn't neglect his duties as host.

The small piece of self-discipline did nothing to conciliate Louise. Apart from the work of refurbishment little had altered in the general lifestyle of Fallan. She knew that in his own way Hugh was doing his best, but she was saddened by the apparent absence of the children, the children as real and vital individuals, from the equation. In fact, she was so disillusioned that, after a celebratory dinner on the twentieth, she fully expected him to leave with his guests the following morning.

Instead Hugh appeared in the kitchen the moment the cars had rolled away, saying without preamble, 'Right, Louise, leave whatever you're doing. You and I need to talk.'

Abby, a left-over sausage in her hand, opened her eyes at Louise and then swivelled them towards the chewed trainer Spice had left by the cooker. Hugh had blazed with anger when he found a dog had been added to his household but had been too busy to deal with the matter at the time. In theory Spice was banned from the kitchen and at this moment was, luckily, asleep in the boiler room.

Louise raised her brows at Hugh's tone, but was not altogether surprised to be summoned. Apart from the matter of Spice, she had felt the anger and frustration building in him for days, and guessed that he felt he had come home full of good intentions which had met with nothing but obstruction.

She put down the scrambled-egg pan, thinking how

unlikely it was that Abby would have dealt with it by the time she came back, and knew she was looking for any glimmer of lightness to brace her. This in turn told her that she was more intimidated by Hugh's brusque tone than she had acknowledged.

He rounded on her as soon as the office door was closed behind them. 'I thought you wanted me to make changes. I thought you disapproved of the way things were done, yet when I try to alter them you resist me at every turn. I thought at least I could expect support from you.'

The way these accusations burst from him, raw and headlong, told Louise more than he imagined. This man was hurting, trapped and baffled. Sympathy instantly overtook every other feeling. 'I don't think I want to be roared at,' she said quietly, 'but I'm happy to talk.'

She saw him take a grip on his anger, relax his shoulders, assemble his words. 'You're right, I shouldn't have spoken like that. I just felt . . .' He made a gesture with his hand, abandoning the thought as too difficult, and turned to the window, moving with a heaviness in marked contrast to his usual energy.

'I didn't really mind,' Louise said truthfully. 'But shall we sit down if we're going to talk?'

'Of course.' Hugh came at once to turn a chair towards her, then stood looking down at her, his face tight. 'Didn't you understand what I've been trying to do? To remove the dividing lines as you wanted me to?'

'I know,' Louise said quietly, 'I do understand. But it's not about Abby and me joining you for dinner, or about cookers and freezers and new paint. It's supposed to be about the children. The boys could have been here at the weekend, for example.'

'But when stalking guests are here they always——' Hugh broke off. 'It never occurred to me,' he admitted flatly. It had all looked so promising. Louise said nothing as he searched for firmer footing. 'I do want to talk, however,' he said after a moment. 'There's a good deal to tell you. I know you find my approach crass but I haven't been wasting my time. Have a look at these.'

Energy fired up again at being able to seize on something tangible, he turned to the desk and spread a roll of plans across it. 'I've covered a lot of ground, as you see. These are for converting the steading. I think it can be made into an attractive house——'

'Hugh.' Louise put a hand over the drawings. 'Talk to me. Don't rush me into plans and blueprints. I don't know what on earth this is all about.'

He shook his head, exasperated with himself. 'God, you'd hardly think I address multinational conferences and actually make people understand what I'm saying. But you know,' he kept his head bent over the plans, not looking at her, 'I honestly don't know where to start. I'm so scared of getting this wrong.'

Louise found the humility of this admission immensely moving and, thinking it would help him most to stick to the practical, suggested gently, 'Start with a few whys and wherefores.'

Hugh let the plans fly back into their roll, then stood tapping it against his palm, still not looking at her. 'I want to operate in a different way,' he said at last. 'Use Fallan as my base and be here much more. I shall extend the office, probably taking in the library. And I shall need someone here permanently, otherwise I'll find that although I'm spending more time at home it's all taken up by work, which would defeat the object. So proper accommodation has to be provided, hence the plans.'

Maxine in her own house. Maxine here for good. Louise's heart sank. How the children would hate it. And this man sincerely meant to change things for the better. She nearly gave up on him there and then.

'Will Maxine want to be here full-time?' she asked, more as a last-ditch resistance than anything. 'Doesn't she despise this part of the world?'

'Maxine?' Hugh frowned. 'Maxine won't be here. That was all dealt with weeks ago. She has no place in the new scheme of things. The children can't bear her.' He began to unroll his precious plans again, then took another look at Louise's face. 'Hadn't I told you? I took your advice at once. I'd known for a long time I ought to make a change, and I can't tell you,' with a sudden relaxed grin, 'what a relief it was to get rid of her.'

Louise saw in that grin, with absolute certainty, that he and Maxine had never been lovers. 'So who's the house for?' In her relief she felt eager to know.

'A very useful Mexican. He's been here in the past and loves the place, and he assures me his wife will be happy here. I intend to consult her about the house, however, to give her every encouragement. Four children so far. That should help to keep the local school open for a few more years, and Roddie and Matt may like the company, in spite of being so used to operating as a pair.'

Louise laughed, but not unkindly. In a couple of sentences Hugh had revamped several lives.

He glanced at her, abashed. 'I know it's a major turn-around, but half measures are no use.'

'And you really intend to be here more yourself?'

This time he smiled. 'You don't trust me, do you? Well, time will tell. But yes, that's what I'm planning. Nowadays it's as easy to run an enterprise from one spot as another, though I'll still have to put in an appearance at my main offices from time to time. No,' he checked himself, and Louise understood that he was bent on being scrupulously honest, with himself as much as with her. 'I shall *want* to do that. I can't imagine spending my whole year here and I don't intend to. But I shall plan around the children's holidays, and stick to the plans. Not that I'm altogether certain they'll want me here.'

He looked rueful, self-mocking, but to Louise's eyes startlingly without defences. He deserved more than facile approval for what he was attempting.

'It will take time,' she agreed, 'but never forget, no matter how often you feel rebuffed, that more than any-thing in the world the children want you to be there for them. They don't know you very well, and they'll have to get used to you, but though the boys seem self-sufficient they love having people around. And the whole root of Emily's problem was loneliness. When she has company she's fine. Ah—'

She had seen in Hugh's face what was coming.

'Ah, indeed,' he said dryly. 'I had made it an absolute rule that there were to be no pets in the house, and I don't appreciate it being flouted in my absence, without any attempt to consult me.'

'I know I should have asked,' Louise had decided beforehand to be conciliatory about this, 'but I've—'

'It's not up for discussion,' Hugh cut in. 'I'm not letting Emily have a dog and that's the end of it.'

To his surprise Louise bounced up under his chin, pink with indignation. 'That's so like you! Rehash larders, convert barns, double the size of your office, but pause for one moment to consider what your daughter really wants, what she needs, what would give her pleasure – oh no, that's quite beyond you! What possible problem can there be in having one dog in a house this size, with someone here all the year round, no matter whether Emily is at school or not? Though as it happens, and you could have found out as much before slamming your foot down, I have made arrangements for the puppy which will take care of that.'

'Louise!' Hugh backed off with hands raised. 'Hold on. If you've made an arrangement which will work—'

'That's not the point, though, is it?' Louise rushed on. 'The point is what matters to Emily, and that should be your first consideration. Two minutes ago you were talking about getting to know your children, but I'm beginning to think that's just so much mealy-mouthed rubbish that doesn't mean a—'

'Stop, stop!' Hugh was laughing, irritation swept away by this vigorous attack. 'Forget the damned dog for a minute. Yes, all right, we'll sort something out. But first there's something more important we need to discuss. Will you smooth your feathers and hear me out?' His eyes were watchful again, and he could not conceal the fact that whatever was coming mattered to him.

Louise's wrath cooled at his serious tone, and she nodded.

'I gather Abby will be making a move soon,' Hugh began. 'Though she hasn't had the courtesy to tell me so herself,' he couldn't resist adding, and regretted it.

'I thought you wanted me to stop being cross,' Louise exclaimed. 'You certainly go the wrong way about it. Abby hasn't told you about her plans because in the first place it wouldn't occur to her you were interested, and in the second, since jobs are virtually non-existent in the glen, she hopes to go on working for you.'

'She can hardly combine a living-in job here with being married to a Gask employee,' Hugh objected.

'How heartless — and how final.'

'You think there could be some compromise?'

'Of course I do. They don't need to live on Gask. A flat in the nursery wing would be one possibility. There's hardly a shortage of space. In any case, they won't be married for ages. Geordie is the saving-up type, and wants everything done properly.'

'Good for him, but as to that, how promising is the overall plot? Wasn't Abby set on finding a rich playboy to carry her off into idle luxury? She's tried her hand on more than one of my guests to my certain knowledge.'

It occurred to Louise, not for the first time, that it had

been forbearing of Hugh not to have sent Abby packing long ago. Because the children liked her; that had to be a good mark.

'Um. I did remind her about that,' she said. 'Well, I talked to her a bit about the reality of marrying someone with Geordie's prospects. But she insists she wants nothing more than to live in a cottage in the glen and cook his mince and tatties, and actually I believe her. She has very mixed feelings, mostly negative, about the lifestyle of the grand and rich. All the talk about gold-digging was a sort of subconscious revenge, I think.'

'I see that you have fulfilled yet another of my neglected roles,' Hugh commented. 'Staff welfare.'

He didn't sound as though he particularly minded, but Louise said quickly, 'Only because I was on hand. All that will be easier for you when you're here more.'

Hugh regarded her with amusement and something else she couldn't define. 'You have to be one of the kindest people alive, do you know that? Which in a way brings me to what I really want to talk about.' A silence, for the first time tense, stretched between them. 'Perhaps it was misleading of me to seem annoyed because Abby hadn't told me about her plans,' he said awkwardly at last. 'In fact it might have proved appropriate timing if she had wanted to leave. Oh Lord, what's wrong with me? I'd better get to the point. Look, I was wondering if you would consider staying on, staying here permanently, I mean, taking charge of everything.'

'A long-term post?' Louise's thoughts scrambled as a dozen implications clamoured for attention.

'Well, yes, you could call it that. I mean, I'd like you to stay indefinitely. Be there for the children as they grow up. Be part of the new scene.' Hugh found the words hard to get out. For him so much lay behind them which he mustn't hint at yet. 'If Abby's still around, she could be fitted in. It might work very well.' Aware of a propitiatory note in his voice which he had not intended he broke off, watching Louise's face, not noticing that the plans in his hand were crushed and buckling.

'But would you need two people here in term-time?' Louise began, as thoughts of Cass, the Allt Farr cottage, Aidan and Erica at Kinnafoot, the pattern of jobs which had begun to form, revolved in her mind. Shot through these images were others, tempting her with a startling, vivid power – Matt, small and wan, dwarfed by the ponderous bed at the big house; Emily furiously scowling; Emily's face dazzled with joy as she picked up Spice for the first time; Roddie's anxious eyes the night Matt had been hurt; his gruff laugh which always produced smiles. She was arrested by a bright composite vision of the years stretching out, with the opportunity of giving these three the security of a familiar presence.

'But if you are to be based here, they will have you,' she said, deep in these thoughts.

'True, but they need more than I can offer them. They need a proper home created for them—'

'I'm not another Angie,' Louise said, Erica's words coming back to her.

'*What?*'

The whipcrack of the question jerked her attention

back to Hugh, and the tide of colour which rose in his face made her realise what an appalling thing she had said.

'I meant it can't ever be the same when you employ someone,' she explained hastily, horrified. 'I'm sorry if I hurt you by referring to—'

Hugh held up a hand to silence her, getting his own voice under control. 'It's not that,' he said after a second. 'I can't bear you to think it's that. Don't you realise that I want you here for your own sake? Marvellous as it would be for the children, that is not what matters to me at this moment. Don't you see that? Oh, Christ.' He shut his eyes and rubbed his hands harshly down his face. 'I was so clear about how this ought to be, how I had to wait, give you time. I knew you didn't have the faintest idea of how I feel. What you said about Angie just now rammed that home. But I thought if I could persuade you to stay with us, become part of the family, feel settled and happy, we could get to know each other better, and perhaps, just perhaps, you would begin to care about me. Even like me would do for a start! I was sure I could wait, I was determined to wait, and now look what I've done.' He gave a bark of laughter that held no amusement, turning away, unable to meet her eyes. 'I can only apologise. You will find this whole thing quite ludicrous.'

Louise, stunned, groped for some answer that would comfort him. His pain, his humiliation, were intolerable to her. Looking at his bent head and rigid shoulders, she knew that she had come to understand this difficult, arrogant man far better than she had realised. Clumsily, awkwardly, he was trying to straighten out all that had gone awry in his world. He was capable of seeing his failings and admitting them. He had already taken giant steps to bring about change. But principally she saw that his life was empty of love; that he neither received it nor knew any more how to give it, though it was there within him, frustrated and imprisoned.

Her throat hard, tears in her eyes, she moved to stand beside him. 'Hugh.' Tentatively she slipped her hand inside his elbow. At once his arm clamped it there, while he put up his other hand to cover his eyes.

Louise ached to realise he was fighting tears. Whatever the years brought, there was no place where she was needed more than here, or where she more longed to offer help. But she knew there must be no risk of misunderstanding, or of giving false hope which would cause this man more pain.

'Hugh, I truly didn't know you felt like that,' she said softly. 'Perhaps it's just—' But how could she tell him these feelings which were tearing him apart stemmed from loneliness and need? 'You know I care very much about what happens to you and your family. I could stay and try to look after you all, if that's what you want.'

'You'd do that?' His hand came down from his face and she saw the tears on his lashes.

'If you don't think it would be too difficult, having me here on that footing?'

'No, no, take no notice of this display. I'm just being a bloody fool. I knew it was all a delicious fantasy. Half the time you don't even like me.'

'Half?' She pretended to weigh that.

He laughed a little shakily. 'If we can joke about it we'll be all right. But you'll stay! I can't take it in yet. What we must agree on, though, is that we talk, openly, like this, if ever it gets too difficult. Will you promise me that?'

'You must promise too.' Louise saw the difficulties to be all on his side, and wondered again how rash the plan was. Then she remembered she was answerable to no one, had to justify her actions to no one. If she and Hugh went into this with honesty and understanding, if they were prepared to explore together the possibilities of a new way of living at Fallan, that decision was theirs and theirs alone.

Images of what it would be like to be here all the time rushed upon her. Making this house one, seeing the children grow up, the links strengthen with the big house as Fallan merged once more into the single entity it was meant to be, and maybe seeing this lonely man achieve some happiness. Erica could come and park her van here. It would be a new place for Aidan to escape from Alice's cooking. Cass and Bridge of Riach were a short drive away over the hill. There was a puppy to train.

'I want to be here,' she said positively. Then more quietly, seeing the realisation that it was going to happen dawn in Hugh's eyes, 'I want more than anything to help you.'

'I've never been home for half-term before,' Emily said, trying to hold her face out of reach of Spice's tongue as the car drew away from the station.

'I know.'

'Boring old Honor's.' Emily spoke as though she could hardly remember the reality of it.

'And the veggies.'

As Emily giggled and began to chatter about school, Louise thought how easy it was to be with her now that the points of reference were in place.

Would Hugh really come? He had genuinely seemed to mind that he couldn't meet Emily. 'Even if the flight's on time I doubt if I could make it. And I can't risk being late or not showing up, you must see that. Anyway, she'd much prefer you to go.'

But Louise had known this was thrown in to cover his own self-doubt and hadn't bothered to answer. She wanted to believe that he minded his trip coinciding with half-term, and yet, would the established pattern always have the power to draw him away? This was a first test. Would he keep his promise or would some unforeseen development or emergency delay him? What would his true priorities be? Or in Maxine-speak, how would he prioritise?

'Are you really going to stay?'

They were going to be hard to convince, these children who had long ago learned in self-protection to be distrustful. The assurance must be given in realistic terms. 'It's now a permanent job,' Louise said carefully, but from Emily's, 'That's cool,' mumbled into Spice's ear, she gathered this was good enough.

'And has the Maxi-Monster really gone for good?' Emily asked, as they passed through the village and she greeted one or two of her former acquaintances in a manner Louise chose to ignore.

Here too, the need for reassurance revealed a level of helpless resentment which Louise knew she hadn't fully appreciated. 'Truly, truly gone.'

'Old Hugh won't be there, though, will he? He always says he will, but then he gets "unavoidably detained", or some crap like that.'

'Well, he's not at Fallan at this very moment, that's true.'

'I told you.' Emily wrapped her arms so tightly round Spice that the puppy struggled energetically to get free.

'However, I can promise you with one hundred per cent certainty that he will be there very soon.'

'No, you can't. He—'

'Turn round,' Louise said smiling, looking again into her rear mirror where for the last half mile or so she had been watching the Daimler nosing quietly along behind her. Mind you, she admonished Hugh, trying to deal with a sudden soaring happiness, that may not be the best car for dogs and children.